Beyond the Cliffs of Kerry

Amanda Hughes

Copyright © 2014 Amanda Hughes
All rights reserved.
ISBN:10:146110734
ISBN-13:978-1461107330

DEDICATION

This book is dedicated to my mother. She taught me to love books and to love Ireland.

Chapter 1

Darcy burned her fingers on the kettle. She jumped back from the hearth, muttering an oath and then straightened up to examine the blisters on her hand. It was no surprise that the accident had happened. She was edgy and excited tonight. She had just received word that the contraband had rounded Rough Point and would demand her guidance ashore.

The weather was violent, and she could hear the waves smashing and tumbling against the rocks on the Kerry coastline. Wispy clouds sailed across the yellow moon, and the wind swept wildly across the cliffs and down through the valley.

The two-room cottage of Darcy McBride and her brother Liam was warm and quiet. The peat fire cast a warm glow across the tidy room and the clean whitewashed walls. A large kettle bubbled over the fire, filled with a hearty evening meal.

As Darcy bent down to shovel more coals onto the lid of the Dutch oven baking her soda bread, a gust of wind burst the cottage door open, startling her. She stopped to tuck her hair back in place. In Gaelic, Darcy means *dark,* and her hair was long, full and indeed dark as coal. It was in pleasing contrast to her fair skin, and although these characteristics were admirable, it was her intense green eyes which set her apart from other women. They were framed by long, dark lashes, and the color reflected the emerald hills of Kerry. Although her dress was shabby and her feet were bare, there was nothing lacking in this young woman's spirit.

Darcy was fiery and proud, her strength forged from years of deprivation. Darcy and her brother Liam had faced the famine of 1740. They watched their mother and five siblings wither away until their skin hung on their bones like dry parchment paper. Death found them in the end.

Darcy and Liam survived, emerging as strong and resolute young people, actively rebelling against the repressive system which caused the mass starvation. Times were hard in Ireland in 1755. To squash what was left of the Irish-Catholic, the British had imposed severe constraints on every facet of a Catholic's life. No Catholic could vote, buy land or worship openly. Existing clergy could remain, but new clergy was strictly prohibited. Each Irishman coped with it differently. Some of them accepted it while others rebelled. Some drank the hard times into oblivion but most existed with a surly resentment which boiled a country.

Liam and Darcy McBride chose illegal trade as their avenue to rebellion and survival. In their community smuggling was an old and well respected vocation. Liam accepted the job of *owling*, as the locals called it, with eagerness. Irish wool was traded for French brandy, and this enterprise provided food for the table and satisfied the desire to retaliate against the British oppressors.

Smuggling was a centuries-old tradition in southwestern Ireland. Absentee landlords demanded exorbitant rents for unyielding lands, and the British paid paltry sums for the Irishman's wool. The government allowed the Irish to trade with no other country but Great Britain, so the residents struck a bargain with France to trade Irish wool for French brandy. The agreement fed the community but at a high cost. The penalty for smuggling was death, and even if a smuggler enjoyed a life undetected by the authorities, he ran the risk of drowning in the treacherous waters off the coast of Kerry.

These dangers though were not what caused Darcy's anxiety tonight. Liam told her that the current shipment not only included brandy but a more unusual cargo a dangerous and more valuable commodity than any wine.

The suspense sent a thrill of anticipation through Darcy. The danger was exhilarating, but she also felt guilty. Wishing for an atmosphere of peril seemed reckless, so she pulled a pewter cross out of her bodice, wrapped her fingers around it and asked for forgiveness. She took great comfort in this necklace from her mother. The Celtic cross was a sacred symbol in Ireland. Huge stone crosses dotted the landscape everywhere, reminding the faithful that a shred of Catholicism remained.

Darcy dreaded the thought of going out tonight. She knew the wind would snap her apron and twist her hair into knots, blinding her as she traveled up the bluff to hold her lantern high.

"Where could he be?" she asked irritably, as she paced up and down the dirt floor of the cottage. Darcy waited anxiously for her brother and news of the ship's arrival.

In spite of years of starvation, the young woman was tall and her bones were straight. Knowing the benefits of flaxseed tea, Darcy's mother had insisted her children drink the foul-tasting beverage, and it resulted in healthy, white teeth for Darcy and Liam as well.

Suddenly, a large man sprang into the room, bringing the wild wind inside with him.

"It's here, Darcy! You must gather your things quickly!" barked Liam McBride. Darcy's heart began to thump in her chest.

"Don't just stand there, find your lamp!" he roared.

Liam took three large steps over to the hearth and quickly ladled out a bowl of stirabout. At first glance, one would not guess that Liam and Darcy were siblings. As much as Darcy's looks were dramatic and beautiful, Liam's were coarse and unrefined. He was raw boned and hunchbacked and his brown hair was dirty and tangled. He seldom looked directly at anyone and always emitted a surly unsettled presence. His one desire in life was to outmaneuver the British, and he channeled every fiber of his being into hating the existing order.

In spite of his sour attitude, Liam had never been cruel to Darcy. The two had a bond rooted in blood and survival, and Liam loved his sister dearly.

"Don't let that candle go out, and hold it high! We must make no mistakes tonight," he demanded.

"Don't you accuse me of mistakes, Liam McBride. I've always done right by you," she snapped back.

Liam realized his tone had been sharp, and he softened. "You're right, girl. You've been here with me all along."

Tonight's endeavor had made them both edgy. From the start, Liam had been against the group's decision to obtain this cargo, and he resented the extra danger and risk that it posed. "Go now and remain at the abbey until I arrive with the others," he said.

Darcy turned and unlatched the door. When she stepped out, the wind spun her apron around her body and sent her hair flying madly about her face.

She picked up her lantern and walked briskly towards the abbey bluff. She was worried about the candle resting precariously inside her lantern. If it blew out, it would mean precious moments lost running back and relighting it. Her lantern was the beacon for the French vessel, and if she wasn't there the ship would miss the rendezvous. Down below the cliffs in a narrow inlet, Liam went to wait with the others. The men had packed their curraghs with wool for the French. They in turn would provide the Irish with brandy. The curragh was the only small craft navigable in these treacherous waters. The small boats were constructed of tarred canvas stretched over a wicker frame.

Darcy's heart was racing. She ran wildly uphill blinded by gusts of wind. Steadily upward she pulled herself until at last she saw the ruins of the ancient Cistercian abbey. The skeleton of what had once been a seat of enlightenment and devoutness was now reduced to decay. There was no roof and the black fingers of the abbey walls reached to the heavens in ruined desperation.

Darcy did not like coming here. Even though she was not superstitious, she always felt the presence of something restless and unsettled within the abandoned walls. It was as if the dead Druids and monks resented being driven away and continued to haunt the environs of the abbey.

Although Darcy did not like being in the abbey at night, she realized that it was the highest and most visible point along the coastline, and it was her responsibility to be there as a beacon for the French vessel. Halfway up the bluff, she stopped to catch her breath. The ascent was steep, her walk had been brisk, and she bent over double, panting.

When she stood up straight and brushed her tangled hair from her eyes, a cloud moved off the moon, shedding light on an ashen sail moving along the coastline. Panicked, she raced up the hill to hail the vessel with her lantern. She ran through the abbey to a vaulted opening facing the sea. She thrust her lantern high, stretching her body to its full height. *Oh please let them see it. They must see it!*

She moved the beacon from side to side, but the ship continued past the abbey. Her stomach sank, and just as she was about to give up she thought of crawling on top of the old stone cross in the churchyard.

Out she dashed to the Celtic sculpture, looked up at the sky and whispered, "Forgive me," and quickly scrambled to the top of the stone cross holding the handle of the lantern in her teeth. She stood upon the crossbar and thrust the lantern high into the night sky, swinging it back and forth desperately. She stretched high on her tiptoes. The vessel seemed to have stopped. When she spied three wickerwork curraghs cross the cove toward the ship, she was jubilant.

* * *

The men worked swiftly in the moonlight, exchanged their goods and then with silent speed they slid back to shore. All was done in a matter of minutes, and the owler's mission was complete.

Darcy waited for Liam sitting on the cold, stone floor of the abbey. She was at her ease now, leaning on a wall with her knees drawn up, watching the moonbeams sparkle on the waves. The jagged walls of the abbey surrounded her, sheltering her from the wild wind. She sighed and stretched like a cat. Her dark hair lay scattered across her shoulders, and she put her head back, closing her eyes.

Pleased with herself for hailing the ship, Darcy knew she could rest now. Soon Liam and the others would come to bury the casks of brandy in the abbey churchyard.

All of Kilkerry knew Liam as the local grave digger and on any day one could see him winding his way up to the abbey churchyard bearing some soul to his final resting place, but what many of the townspeople did not know was that Liam buried residents by day and brandy by night. Many a deceased resident of Kilkerry slept next to their favorite beverage, and the owlers thought it was a grand honor bestowed upon those who passed.

Darcy reflected on what sort of cargo it was that they were to bury tonight in addition to the brandy. What could be so dangerous that she could not know the identity of it until the last minute? She speculated on a number of options. *Was it guns? Surely Liam was not transporting guns. An insurrection would be suicide. Perhaps jewels?*

Darcy dismissed that possibility as well. Shrugging her shoulders, she gave up guessing and yawned. Suddenly, she heard something which sounded like a footstep. *It is too early for Liam to be up on the bluff with the cargo, and superstitious villagers fear the restless monks, so what could it be?* She rose, straining her eyes in the darkness, as cold fear washed over her. Finally, Darcy shook her head and chuckled, attributing everything to an overactive imagination. She turned to step out of the abbey and came face to face with a tall figure in a dark, hooded robe. A bolt of terror shot through her, and she stood frozen, unable to move or to speak.

Every tale of phantoms and apparitions at the abbey raced through her mind, and the specter moved silently toward her with a white hand outstretched. She stepped back and gasped.

Suddenly Liam stepped out of the shadows and hissed, "Don't be a fool, girl. It's not what ya think."

The figure in black reached up and lowered his hood. There in the moonlight stood a tall man with a pleasant face. "I am pleased to meet you," he said in a gentle voice. "I am Father Etienne, your new parish priest."

Chapter 2

Darcy stood in the moonlight, thunderstruck. The wind had died down and the black cassock of the priest hung motionless. She was still panting as she turned to Liam and gasped, "A priest! Liam, have you lost your mind? Priests are forbidden. They will hang us all."

Liam turned toward her, his eyebrows drawn into a scowl and growled, "You keep your mouth shut! This is none of your affair!"

Still agitated, Darcy turned to apologize. "I'm very sorry, Father. My name is Darcy McBride. I was so startled a minute ago, I forgot my manners."

The priest was a man in his middle years with short, curly, brown hair and a close-cropped beard. He gave the appearance of someone who was confident but not impressed with himself. He did not at all resemble a sinister figure. In fact, he had a playful twinkle in his eye. He said with a smile, "You mistook me for one of the devout Cistercians that once inhabited this abbey, but I am a mere mortal here to minister to your village."

"I hear an accent, Father," said Darcy.

"Yes, I was born in the American Colonies."

Liam jumped in. "There will be time for talk later. Darcy, take him back to the house immediately. I must help the others bring up the rest of the shipment."

Liam vanished into the darkness, leaving Darcy alone in the abbey with the priest. She looked around furtively and stepped into the moonlight with Father Etienne behind her.

They walked down the bluff quickly, neither saying a word. Darcy was uneasy with this dark, silent figure and tried not to look at him as he followed her down the hill.

She caught sight of the thatched roof of her cottage and quickened her pace. It was essential that they go undetected tonight. The owlers would choose the appropriate time to inform the village that a Catholic priest had come to minister to them.

Darcy ushered Father Etienne into her modest home and began to resurrect the peat fire. He watched her as his eyes adjusted to the dim light. The cottage was small but immaculately kept. On one side of the fireplace rose a short set of stone steps, probably leading to a loft. The chimney of the fireplace was painted red to break the monotony of the four white walls. A wicker basket holding peat bricks sat near the hearth, and recessed into one wall was a neatly made bed with a faded quilt. Father Etienne would learn later that a bed in Kilkerry was a rare commodity. On the dirt floor, near the bed, rested a worn out trunk and a little braided rug lay nearby.

Darcy pulled a chair over in front of the fire and offered Father Etienne a seat. The priest sat down and leaned forward to warm himself, as Darcy wiped her hands on her apron. "Would you like some tea, Father? You look very cold and you must be tired."

Father Etienne guessed that tea was dear in this part of Ireland, and being sensitive to their needs, he asked instead, "No tea, thank you, but would you have anything stronger?"

Darcy laughed and said, "Aye, Father, we have plenty of that." She turned to a stone crock, drew some brandy into an earthenware mug and handed it to him.

"Surely you'll join me, Miss McBride? You too have had quite a night."

It seemed ungracious to refuse, so she poured herself a mug, raised it and said, "A toast to your courage, Father. Thank you for coming to help us."

Father Etienne smiled as Darcy took a sip and sat down, resting back into the chair. She hadn't realized it until now, but she was tired. The brandy felt warm as it went down, and she felt the tensions of the day start to dissolve. Suddenly she realized that she had nothing to say to this stranger. She hadn't the vaguest idea what to say to a priest. Should she discuss the Lord? Dare she ask questions about his life before he was a priest?

Sensing her uneasiness, Father Etienne started the conversation. "Is it just you and your brother living here, Miss McBride?"

"Aye, my brother is unmarried and so am I. Please, Father, call me Darcy. I am more comfortable with that."

Darcy was growing weary of the tension, and she believed it would be best if she was candid so she blurted, "Forgive me, Father Etienne if I seem awkward. You are the first priest that I have met, and I don't know how to talk with one. Please tell me. Do we talk about The Blessed Virgin or Jesus or--"

Smiling he said, "Please, don't feel uncomfortable with me, Darcy. I am a person like you, and we may talk about anything we choose. The Almighty is everywhere. Thus, when we speak of everyday matters, we speak of Him."

Darcy sighed and sat back, relieved. Her religious training had been limited to memorizing only a few prayers, and she felt inadequate on the subject. She thought this priest seemed very kind indeed, not pious and stuffy as she had imagined, and she was delighted to see that when he smiled, he had dimples.

Father Etienne was flabbergasted. In a land so devout, it seemed impossible that there would be Catholics who had not met clergy, but his placement here had been impromptu, and he had little chance to study the plight of these people. This is only one young woman unschooled in the faith. He wondered how many sacraments must be given. *How many were in need of spiritual guidance?* Nevertheless, he was unshaken. Seventeen years of preparation in France for his vocation gave him unswerving resolve. He had many challenging missions prior to this assignment, and compared to the tortures his Jesuit brothers endured converting the Indians in New France, this was nothing.

"When was the last time this village had benefit of clergy?" he inquired.

Darcy paused to think a moment, "Well, I was baptized by Father Fitzgerald shortly after I was born," said Darcy as she tried to count the years, "and when he died, we weren't allowed to replace him so it has been years since anyone has been to a Mass or given a confession."

"Have many given up their faith?"

Darcy shook her head. "Very few. They may deny us churches and clergy, but they will never break our spirits as Catholics. There was talk that in some parts of Ireland during the famine, they bribed Catholics with food in exchange for their faith. They chose starvation."

Father Etienne leaned forward, listening with great interest. He longed to ask Darcy about the famine but dismissed the idea. He sensed there was a whole side to this young woman which was closed and private. There were volumes of silent suffering that she had never shared.

Although she was clothed in a threadbare skirt and blouse, the dignity beneath the peasant dress was apparent. He saw a proud and graceful young woman with a strong sensuality, which stirred him. He quickly moved the conversation along to distract himself. Any trace of desire must be crushed.

Father Etienne moved to Darcy's mind where he could open as many doors as he pleased. "Darcy, what about you, do you have any education?"

"My father died when we were all quite young, so my mother, God rest her soul, only had time to teach us a few prayers. To be honest, we thought more about food in those days than our souls."

Father Etienne shook his head and set his empty mug on the table. "What I meant was has anyone ever tried to teach you or your brother to read?"

She looked astonished and said, "No, of course not, Father. The only person that can read in all of Kilkerry is Squire Scot, our landlord in Granager."

Her eyes widened. "Can you read?"

He nodded his head, not telling her that he was fluent in French, Greek, and Latin as well. He read the wistful longing on her face and asked, "Would you be interested in learning to read, Darcy?

"Oh, how wonderful that would be. Ever since I was a little girl, I've longed to read, to go beyond these-" Suddenly, Darcy realized Father Etienne was smiling. She jumped up abruptly and smoothed her apron, wishing her face had not turned crimson.

"No thank you, Father. No reading for me. I must keep house for my brother."

Father Etienne jumped to his feet and grabbed her hand. He eased Darcy back down into the chair. "I am not making sport of you. Thirst for knowledge is so pleasing that I laughed from delight. So many people think that reading is a waste of time. I am overjoyed when someone like you comes along. I understand your desire to learn, Darcy, I have it too, and it's wrong to deny it. You would be refusing God."

Darcy nodded her head, but the conversation was over. She showed Father Etienne the small bedroom upstairs. She placed clean linens on the bed for him and a quilt on the floor for Liam. After a hasty good night, she went downstairs to bank the fire. She cursed herself for revealing so much to this stranger. From the time she was a small child, she knew that she aspired to a different future than her young friends. They had dreams of family and a plot of land in Kilkerry, but Darcy longed for much more. She surrounded herself with a host of imaginary friends, dreaming of make-believe lands where she embarked on daring adventures. As an adult she would stand on the cliffs of Kerry looking out to sea, dreaming of what was beyond the shores.

Most of the time, Darcy preferred to be alone with her thoughts and dreams, but sometimes her loneliness became unbearable, and she would risk sharing her thoughts with others. She was usually met with mockery. Darcy sensed that even her mother found her odd, so she drove her secrets deep, feeling ashamed, vowing never to tell anyone what was in her soul.

"So where is the priest, girl? Upstairs?" asked Liam as he came in the door.

Darcy blinked and nodded. "Is everything buried now?"

Liam nodded and sat down heavily, stretching his legs out. "Damn but I'm tired. Be a good girl and fetch me a brandy."

"Where will he go?" asked Darcy, as she poured her brother a drink. "What about when the soldiers are in residence? It will be dangerous."

Liam put his arms up and stretched. "Michael's already considered everything. He is the leader of the owlers, not you, Darcy. Mind your own business. He'll live in our caves by the sea and do his work after dark."

"Liam," Darcy said. "Those caves are too damp. Sure as I'm standing here, he'll get consumption."

"Those caves were good enough for us during The Hunger. They will be good enough for him," he barked. Liam rubbed his forehead wearily and added, trying to be patient, "We'll just have to see how it goes. I know that you're scared."

Darcy made no reply. She knew that arguing with Liam would do no good. He would only out-shout her, and he had been increasingly irritable lately.

"We will move him to the caves in the morning. O'Malley is circulating a story that an old man from Granager died and wants to be buried at the abbey, but the man lying in the shroud will be this priest. Wake him shortly before dawn, put a shroud on the donkey cart and sew him into it, and then I will take him over the bluff to the caves on the other side."

"Why can't you wait until tomorrow night and move him under darkness?"

"We cannot wait a day."

Darcy wanted to say, "Why don't you move him tonight," but remembered men resented advice from a woman.

Liam climbed the stairs to bed and then returned with a confused look on his face.

"Where did you tell him to sleep?" he asked.

"In your bed," Darcy replied.

"Well, he's on the floor," said Liam.

Darcy said, "That doesn't surprise me."

* * *

Father Etienne rose the next morning prior to dawn. The sound of the ocean awakened him, and although he was born near the sea, it had been many years since he had slept near its rhythmic beat. The room was dark, but he could see from the rumpled quilt on the bed that Liam had left already.

After morning prayers, Father Etienne lit a candle, poured water into a basin and washed up. He inspected his face in a mirror which hung over a wooden commode. Out of a small traveling bag, he took a pair of manicure scissors and began to trim his beard and mustache. His soft brown eyes moved quickly over his face, and although he was not given to vanity, he held personal neatness in high regard.

Etienne was an attractive man with curly brown hair and the dark complexion of his French-Moorish ancestors. He had a mole on his lower right cheek, which added interest to his pleasant face, along with a perpetual twinkle in his eye, a mischievous twinkle which seemed inconsistent with the severe garment of the Jesuit.

As Father Etienne came down the steps of the cottage, he expected to see Darcy bending over the fire making breakfast. A fire was glowing in the hearth, but the room was empty. As he reached the bottom of the stairs, the door opened, and Darcy stepped into the room.

"Good morning, Father. Your breakfast will be ready in a moment."

She stepped to the hearth to prepare some oatmeal. She did not look at Father Etienne, and he knew that she was anxious about something.

After a moment, she scolded, "Now why did you go and sleep on the floor last night? Surely you knew that the bed was for you."

"I am much more comfortable sleeping on a hard surface. Your brother needed the bed more than me," he replied.

She pulled the pan off the spider trivet where some potatoes had been frying and scooped some oatmeal into his bowl. "I am sorry to hurry you, but we must be ready to go before sunup. Liam told me last night that we must move you to the caves first thing this morning. I wish there was some way we could keep you here. The caves are not very comfortable."

"Please don't apologize. I would never want to put you or your brother in any danger."

After eating he wiped his mouth on the coarse homespun towel, gave thanks to God once more for the meal, and then disappeared upstairs, returning with his bag and a few books under his arm.

"Darcy, I was wondering if I might ask a favor of you. Caves are not very friendly to books. The moisture puts a rot into them that one can never remedy. When Liam brings my crate of volumes, may I store them here?

"Of course, we will put them upstairs." Darcy swallowed hard, and then said, "Father, this may be unpleasant for you, but I'm going to have to sew you into a funeral shroud before you make your journey up the bluff."

His jaw dropped, and then he laughed. "This sounds exciting!"

"Are ya daft?" she gasped. "Oh, begging your pardon, Father."

He chuckled and touched her arm. "Please, you must realize that I am not stuffy. I believe life is a grand adventure, and Jesus smiles on those who laugh and enjoy it."

Darcy smiled. "You are a most unusual man, Father Etienne."

She picked up her sewing kit and lantern and walked out the door where Liam's donkey was hitched to a cart. Except for a dim light in the east, it remained dark.

Darcy raised the light above the bed of the cart illuminating a shroud. The priest put his foot on the wheel and hoisted himself upon the shroud and stretched out. Darcy folded up one side, and then the other asking, "Are you going to be all right?"

He winked as she put the cloth over his face. It was a curious sensation being sewn into the bag. The linen lay heavily on his face, and he was concerned that his breathing may move the cloth. Darcy snipped open several stitches by his nose and mouth and whispered, "I was afraid you couldn't breathe. Liam is here now. I will come to the cave later. Are you still having a good time?" He could see her smiling in the lantern light.

Father Etienne felt the cart jostle to the side as Liam climbed aboard. He snapped the reins, and they were off with a jolt. Liam settled into his usual hunched-over position, and to the village, it was just another day in the life of a gravedigger.

Streaks of sun steamed across the sky as Darcy watched the cart make its slow ascent to the abbey. She shuddered. The feeling of being trapped inside a shroud struggling for air was not her idea of a "grand adventure".

She turned and walked to her plot of potatoes and

began pulling weeds. Even her most diligent efforts yielded small inferior potatoes, and every year brought renewed worries about the crops. Everyone lived in constant fear of another poor harvest and anxiously studied the growth.

Darcy stepped inside the cottage, returning with peelings for their two pigs. They pushed and snorted excitedly as she arrived. Once more she looked up at the bluff. The cart continued its tedious progress up the hill, and she sighed. Darcy rehearsed the story Liam had fabricated about who had died. She had survived repeated questionings by the British soldiers, regarding everything from smuggling to worship, and it taught Darcy that bearing false witness was the least of her worries on earth.

Returning again to the cottage, she gathered the dirty breakfast dishes and grabbed a pottery jug for water. She stepped out into the yellow morning sunlight and started for the town well. Every woman in Kilkerry appeared there in the morning and Darcy knew, if she hurried, she might miss their interrogation about the identity of the deceased.

The McBride cottage was on the edge of town, where the abbey bluff began. The village was small and most of the mud cottages clustered around a narrow slope down to the sea. Few of the homes had windows and many of the residents resided with their pigs and chickens.

Darcy stole a glance over her shoulder and saw that Liam had reached the crest and was passing through the churchyard. She waved to her neighbor, Paid Lillis as she passed by his cottage. He looked up briefly from his weeding to return her wave. It was a relief that he did not invite conversation.

Darcy spied the large cross rising above the well. No one was there. Quickening her pace she arrived at the well, pushing the hair from her face and looking around.

She lowered the bucket, her heart pounding, and then looked up at the abbey one last time. The churchyard was empty, Liam was gone. They had made it to the other side safely. Darcy sighed and pulled the water bucket up. The caves, which had sheltered her and offered her asylum during the famine, were once again giving refuge to someone who needed a home.

A gravelly voice behind her barked, "Who died, McBride?"

Startled, she turned to see Edna O'Malley, the town busybody. Her fat, pinched face reminded Darcy of a prize pig.

"Who died?" echoed Darcy.

Edna impatiently motioned toward the abbey, shaking the fat on her arm. "Who did Liam take up?"

"Oh, just an old man from Granager, none of us knew him."

"Oh," replied Edna, disappointed. She wanted to be the first to bear news of a noteworthy death. This old man did not qualify.

Darcy despised Edna. When the solders had been in residence in Kilkerry several years ago, everyone suspected Edna of being on the payroll. She was shallow and self- serving and few loyal Irishmen were overweight these days. She would not have the benefit of clergy once Father Etienne's presence was shared with the town.

"Any word from Bran?" pried Edna as she put her face close to Darcy.

"Considering he can't read, Edna, he probably

wouldn't write to me," Darcy said, turning on her heel.

Edna O'Malley was not deterred. Walking alongside Darcy, she continued her line of questioning. "Darcy McBride, you certainly must love that man. You've waited for him to return from the American Colonies for seven years now. You better be careful. You're approaching the end of your bloom, girl."

Darcy opened her mouth and then reconsidered as Edna grabbed her arm. "How do you know that he's even alive?"

Darcy said nothing. She wrenched her arm free and headed for home. As she walked back swinging her water jug, she thought about Bran. She knew that there was a good chance that he was dead. Life as an indentured servant in the American Colonies was severe, but she remained hopeful, looking for him every day. She looked up at the soft dark mountains of Kerry and then at the cliffs leading out to the sea. She knew in her heart Bran would return. If he were still alive, he would be drawn back to the land of his fathers.

Darcy reached home, and after several chores, she began dinner. Her life seemed an endless cycle of making and cleaning up after a meal. She knew that marriage to Bran would make that fate permanent, but like every other Irish woman of the day, Darcy had few choices. In fact, marriage to Bran was quite an appealing future. He was handsome, capable and an experienced lover.

Ever since she was a child, the village had paired the two of them together. During the famine, Liam and Bran had taken care of her, and the three of them had lived for many years in the cave, eating what little they could forage from the surrounding area and the sea.

Darcy had been wild about Bran in those days, and

right up until the time he was transported to the American Colonies for resisting arrest she had considered herself his future wife. Darcy knew that his seven year period for servitude was over, and he would return any day, but she worried. He may have been lost at sea or succumbed to disease. Anything was possible.

Nevertheless, she continued to snub overtures from the young men of Kilkerry. Bran alone held her heart.

She remembered how strongly he had held her when they had made love, and she was grateful that she did not breed. In fact, there had been so many moments of passion with Bran that she wondered if maybe the lack of food in her early years had left her barren.

Darcy wished they had wed before his arrest, but he insisted on having a few more years pass before he settled down. Bran was a wild, rambunctious youth, keeping late hours drinking and carousing with his mates.

Darcy awoke from her reverie when the stew began to boil. She swung the crane out into the warming position and set a place for Liam. After that, she ladled some stew in a crock for Father Etienne. She would feed him well today, but after that, she would have to ease him into a diet consisting of less meat and more potatoes. She placed the stout, soda bread, and stew into a wicker basket and covered it snugly with a woolen cloth.

Darcy stepped out into the sunlight marveling at the glorious weather. In a land of drizzle and gray skies, sunny days are not taken for granted. She felt the warm earth under her bare feet. Even the abbey didn't look threatening today. Its jagged remains seemed innocuous as she climbed the hill and crossed the churchyard to the cliff walk. She followed the coastline along the cliffs until she saw an opening with some uneven moss-covered steps.

She remembered the day she had discovered those steps with her sister Mary Kathleen and their delight as they entered their own secret cave. Darcy stopped and looked out to sea thinking back.

The Hunger claimed Mary Kathleen's life first and then the rest of the family followed, leaving Liam and Darcy alone. The soldiers told Liam and Darcy to leave their cottage and find lodging elsewhere. If you couldn't pay the rent, you had to leave, so the two set out looking for a home. They sought refuge in this cave, and after several weeks, Bran Moynahan joined them.

Darcy couldn't believe that she was back here again, and slinging the basket over her arm she climbed down the rugged steps knowing instinctively where to place each foot. The descent was perilous and one slip could mean death on the rocks below. As children, these dangers never occurred to them, and even today Darcy had little concern for her safety. She hopped onto the ledge of the cave and encountered Father Etienne putting linens on an old bed which Liam and Bran had constructed years ago. It was in poor condition, but it kept him off the damp floor of the cave.

"Why, Darcy. You are my first guest," he said with a smile.

"I brought you something to eat," she said looking around. "They have done a fine job of making it a home here."

Next to the bed, was a nightstand brought by the owlers, a large cask turned up on end for a kitchen table, a wooden chair, and even a braided rug. Darcy was glad to see that Father Etienne's lodgings weren't too Spartan.

She took a step and felt something crunch under her foot. When she looked down, she saw the broken remains of hundreds of snail shells, littering the floor of the cave. Darcy stared for a moment and then slowly her memory returned. The days of deprivation came back to her. All of a sudden, the air seemed stuffy, and she felt like she was going to retch.

Father Etienne watched Darcy turn as white as the bleached shells underfoot and tried to divert her attention. "Is there something for me in that basket?" he asked. "Something tells me, that you are a good cook," and he touched her on the elbow. Father Etienne's gesture steadied her as she walked over to the table.

Darcy's reaction to the cave was entirely different from her brother's response. Liam had shown no feeling whatsoever when he brought furniture into the cave, grumbling the entire time. He could see the hard times had left Liam a bitter, empty shell in contrast to his sister who was so alive and vibrant.

Father Etienne had little knowledge of the Irish famine of 1740, and although the Jesuits offered prayers at the time, they had no idea of the extent of the suffering. What finally brought Ireland to their attention was the suppression of the Catholic faith.

Fearing political ramifications, the British government took great care to hide the abuses from the Catholic nations of Europe, and most had no idea of the abuses. When Bishop Keen of County Mayo sought asylum with their order, the Jesuits finally became aware of the misery and tribulation afflicting Ireland, and now Father Etienne had first-hand knowledge. He had no idea how crippling the repression had been for the Irish Catholic.

Feeling more grounded, Darcy took her gaily colored woolen tablecloth off the top of the basket and spread it over Father Etienne's table.

She had picked some blooms of the yellow gorse on her way, and she arranged the flowers in a small brown crock. The priest was touched by her thoughtfulness, and he helped Darcy remove the food from the basket.

A seagull landed on the ledge of the cave and looked in cocking his head at the two of them. This gave Father Etienne the idea to move the table out into the sunshine and fresh air. He believed Darcy would be more comfortable in the open. They dragged the cask and two chairs onto the ledge and sat down to dine by the sea.

The view was breathtaking. In the past, Darcy had been too young and hungry to appreciate the view. The panorama was spectacular. The ledge hung over the coastline where the tide crashed onto the rocks, and the wide blue sky opened up above their heads. They could look down the broad expanse of coastline and admire the cliffs of Kerry rising up majestically.

"Oh, but this is beautiful," marveled Father Etienne, as he gazed out at the vast ocean with the gulls circling. "You have no idea how comforting it is for me to hear the sea again. It reminds me of home."

"You said last night that you were born in the American Colonies. Do you still have family there?" asked Darcy, as she took a bite of soda bread. Her stomach had settled enough for her to eat.

"Yes, my mother and brother are over there. You would find life to be quite different in the New World,

Darcy. The wilderness is so vast and boundless. Many have lost their way, never to return."

He shook his head and looked across the ocean as if he were trying to see home, "No European knows how deep or how wide it expands, and few venture to the interior. My brother is one of the few white people who dare to explore its mysteries. For all of its perils, it's a wildly beautiful land and surviving every day there is a privilege."

Darcy's attention was riveted to Father Etienne. This was the kind of story that spoke to her, and until today, her knowledge of the world had been bounded by the Atlantic coast and the mountains of Kerry. Father Etienne's speech confirmed her suspicions that the world was full of wondrous sights and grand adventures. She was enthralled, but she would not shower him with questions right now. Instead, she asked politely, "How many years has it been since you've been home?"

Father Etienne wiped his mouth and sat back to contemplate. "Well, I suppose it's been nearly twenty-two or twenty-three years." He stared past Darcy in disbelief, gazing out to sea. "I miss it. Yet my travels and work distract me from homesickness. I had no idea Ireland was so beautiful, yet I can tell living is hard here, so little food, so little freedom. You are a very strong young woman to endure these hardships, Darcy."

A light breeze loosened a few strands of her dark hair, and they danced lightly across her pale skin. When she looked up at the priest, her eyes were laughing, and they shimmered a brilliant green as she said, "I don't know any other way to live, but the Irish way."

"Excuse me if I seem bold," Father Etienne said suddenly. "But why is such a lovely young woman unspoken for?"

"But I am spoken for," she replied. "A lad from the village named Bran Moynahan is my betrothed. He was transported to your homeland eight years ago. I look for him every day. His bondage time is up."

"Why was he transported? Was he in some sort of trouble?"

"Aye," replied Darcy, nodding her head. "My Bran was always in some sort of trouble, but the last time when the soldiers picked him up for drinking too much, he caused a ruckus. Bran is a large lad and almost killed one of the king's soldiers. He was sent away to be sold as an indentured servant. I've not seen him since."

Father Etienne could see Darcy had her doubts that her young man would return, and he said gently, "I do hope he comes home to you soon."

Darcy turned her head and looked into the cave. "Do you know we used to live here when I was a young girl, Father?"

"Liam mentioned it."

"Out here on the ledge in the fresh air with food in my belly, it doesn't seem real. You won't hear many of us talk about it. We prefer to forget The Hunger, but it lives with us every day in our misshapen bodies and minds."

"I will not ask you to talk about it, Darcy. I realize that it is far too private and painful."

"No, Father, if you are to help us, you must know about it and the scars it left behind."

A visible change swept over her. Her face clouded, and her eyes lost their luster. She took a breath and closed her eyes. "If you were lucky, the fever killed you," she said slowly as she opened her eyes again. "It claimed the lives of my sisters right away. Disease was quick and kind. Eventually, there was no food, and our bodies started to feed on themselves. I'll never forget the look on my mother's face as she watched her babies wither away and die. She was torn between surviving for her remaining children or giving up her meager portion of the food to feed them. Eventually, she chose starvation. My mother's story is the story of all Irish mothers, Father Etienne. You'll see few women her age alive in Kilkerry today."

Father Etienne sat motionless, his brown eyes resting on Darcy.

"I've never been able to figure out why Liam and I survived. One by one my remaining brothers and sisters went beyond. They could fight no longer." Darcy stopped and swallowed hard. She turned and gazed out across the ocean, her hair blowing away from her face. "My most vivid memory is that it was so quiet. No one had the strength to speak and sometimes, even today, when I smell a peat fire I remember the stench of the corpses as they burned by night. It was hard to find Jesus in Ireland in those days."

As Darcy spoke, it became clear to Father Etienne what his mission was here in Ireland. These people needed hope, and more than anything, faith. They had lost everything, even their God.

"Eventually, the soldiers turned us out," Darcy continued. "Oh, not just Liam and me. Everyone was evicted for not paying rent. Many dug holes and lived in them with their families, but Liam, Bran and I were lucky. We knew of this cave."

"Could you fish these waters?"

"No, you cannot. It is far too dangerous, but the tide would recede and leave us mussels, snails and lots of kelp, so the three of us survived. My story has a happy ending, Father Etienne. Most do not."

"Thank you for telling me, Darcy. I feel honored to be living in your sanctuary."

She smiled, and he saw her sparkle return, "It is your sanctuary now, Father."

Chapter 3

Kilkerry awoke to a more typical landscape of drizzle and darkness. The clouds dangled in long fingers over the mountains and jagged coastline. Kerry had few trees, and the sky seemed vast. Clouds seemed closer, storms stronger, and even the stars seemed more numerous.

The villagers continued their chores in the rain, but there was gladness in their hearts. They would receive the Eucharist from the hands of a Catholic priest once more, and they were grateful to God for sending a man of the cloth to minister to them at long last. The villagers were nervous and privately rehearsed their introductions and greetings to Father Etienne. Not everyone in Kilkerry was told of the priest's arrival. King George offered substantial reward money for information about clergy smuggled into the country, and the owlers used discretion spreading the news.

After much discussion, Mass was set for one hour after sundown. Not everyone was allowed to attend the first night. A large crowd would attract attention, and the villagers must set out at different times to avoid detection. They would be armed with credible excuses in case they encountered an informant, and they had instructions to dress in everyday clothing.

Some thrilled at the sense of danger while others were more anxious. In other settings, a secret of this magnitude would be hard to keep, but the bond among the residents of Kilkerry was impenetrable. The villagers were united forever by mutual miseries, past and present, and that was why the owlers were confident that Father Etienne could do his work here unmolested.

Dusk was hard to identify on such a dreary day, but as the sky darkened, one could spy an occasional wayfarer step out into the elements, pull up a shawl or collar and head up the hill. A mother with several children, an old woman, and three young lads--there was no typical parishioner attending this Mass. They brought with them a zeal and devotion known only to those who have been deprived of the right to worship freely, and they made their way joyfully over the bluff to the caves beyond the abbey where the sacrament would be held.

The rugged cliffs sloped down gradually after Father Etienne's cave, offering access to a huge cave which had been inhabited by the O'Hearn family during the famine. It had a tall ceiling of Gothic proportions and was perfectly suited for holding a large number of people.

Father Etienne stood outside his make-shift chapel and greeted villagers as they entered for Mass. Some hugged him, others cried but most, especially the young, stood back in awe. He was particularly sensitive to those who feared him, and he took great pains to put everyone at their ease.

Inside the chamber, an altar table had been brought in with several candles illuminating the area where Father Etienne would say Mass. One of the men helped him dig a hole in the sand floor of the cave for the tall tabernacle candle. It was a brilliant crimson illumination next to the altar, and several torches had been placed around the chamber. Miraculously everything that was needed for Mass was produced. When the village church had been destroyed many years ago, many of the sacramentals had been saved by the villagers and placed in hiding, waiting for this very day.

Father Etienne installed two youngsters as altar boys and their proud parents, more nervous than their offspring, fussed and straightened the boys' clothes over and over.

Darcy arrived at the last minute. She slipped into the cave and stood off to one side, ready to witness her first Mass. She had never been in an enclosed area with so many people at one time, and she found it stifling. The high ceiling of the cave shot echoes around the chamber and every cough or cry of a child seemed magnified a hundred times. The heavy sweet smell of incense, mixed with the unwashed bodies of the parishioners, turned her stomach.

Once Mass began, she caught glimpses of Father Etienne gliding around the altar, genuflecting and saying words she could not understand. Her mother told her once that Mass was said in another language, but she had long since forgotten its name.

Darcy looked around at the villagers in attendance. Many of the older residents were crying, and others bowed their heads in prayer, but many seemed bewildered and self-conscious.

Since Darcy was unable to see over the heads of those in front of her, her mind wandered. She recalled a story her mother had told her of the early Christians and how they too had to hide their Masses for fear of persecution and worship in caves.

Their plight was much the same, thought Darcy but then, as she looked around the cavern at friends and villagers she had known all her life, she chuckled. There were no saints or martyrs here.

Suddenly, old Mrs. Casey burned a look into Darcy, which said, *"There will be no nonsense in church. Pay attention!"* Darcy lowered her eyes, kneeling down with everyone else. After Communion was distributed, Father Etienne gave the final blessing, and everyone made their way to the door.

Darcy wondered why she didn't feel any different after Mass. She overheard many saying they felt uplifted, and Darcy felt cheated. Walking along the ocean or sitting peacefully watching the sheep graze filled her with more feeling than standing in a room filled with incense and smoke. She made her way home, feeling disappointed and alone.

For many weeks Father Etienne was busy performing baptisms, hearing confessions and generally ministering to a parish which was spiritually starved. It was essential these duties be performed after dark in great secrecy, and it was almost a month before he had a chance to speak with Darcy. One Sunday afternoon after Mass, Father Etienne excused himself from the throng of parishioners that surrounded him and caught up with Darcy, grabbing her arm as she started for home. The surf breaking on the rocks made it necessary for him to shout, "Darcy, I must talk with you!"

He pulled her back toward the mouth of the cave where it was quieter. "I'm sorry I have neglected you, but I have been very busy. It's one of my vows as a Jesuit to educate, and we must start our reading lessons."

Suddenly, Darcy felt petrified. She reminded herself that reading was for the upper classes, a privilege reserved for people of high birth.

"Father, Liam is right. Leave education to the uppity ruling classes. It has no place here among us commoners. Thank you anyway."

Darcy turned to go, but Father Etienne stopped her

and said, "You're afraid, aren't you?"

"I am not afraid!" Darcy snapped, yanking her arm away. "I'm simply not interested. Now please attend to your own business, Father."

She turned away, and he said sharply, "Don't you ever address me in that tone again!"

Darcy's jaw dropped and then she lowered her eyes, murmuring, "Forgive me."

"The sin of pride is yours, Darcy McBride. I strongly suggest you correct it. Now I try to meet each spiritual need as I see it. Some find God in the Church, some find Him in doing good works, and still others find Him in working the earth. I believe you will find Him in words."

She continued to look at the ground, afraid if she looked up, she would give away her feelings.

"By denying yourself the written word, you deny God an avenue to your heart."

She stood motionless, holding the clasp on her black, woolen cloak. Her palms began to perspire; she swallowed hard and said, "When do we start?"

"Meet me tomorrow at the abbey at four o'clock."

When Darcy, at last, had the courage to look up she saw that Father Etienne's eyes were twinkling. As he walked back to the parishioners, he smiled to himself. Darcy would be a challenge, but he admired her spirit.

Father Etienne settled into a comfortable routine in Kilkerry. After sundown, he would visit the sick or dying, perform baptisms or hear confessions and return before sunup.

He was always thoroughly exhausted but fulfilled. The Jesuit order aspired to see the love of Jesus in everything, and this came easily to one of such good nature and strong faith. He would say prayers and fall into bed, sleeping heavily for several hours and then spend his remaining daylight hours studying or meditating. He was truly growing to love the people of Kilkerry. His mission was demanding but extremely satisfying.

It was just before dawn when Father Etienne made his careful descent to the cave to get some sleep. It was tricky lowering himself down the rock face onto the ledge, especially in the dark and in his cumbersome robes. At first, he thought that it was strange that Liam would put him in a cave with such a challenging entrance, but when he witnessed how accessible the other caves were, he realized no soldier or informant would discover him.

His last duty this night had been to administer Last Rites to an old woman. She had died peacefully, and he was grateful to God that she did not suffer. After lighting a candle, he sat down at the table, took up a quill and began to compose a letter to his brother in America. Father Etienne didn't have much time to correspond, but sharing his thoughts with another person, no matter how far away, helped to fight the loneliness.

He stared at the bright candle which was perched on top of the cask and listened to the ocean breaking on the rocks. The priest missed the company of other learned men, and he longed to share ideas and compare thoughts on literature, philosophy or theology. Letter writing met only one side of the conversation, but for now, it would have to suffice.

After thoughtfully composing the letter, he set it aside for Liam to give to the next French vessel. Father Etienne stretched. It was late, and he knew that he should get some rest. He hated this time of night when he had to blow out the candle. He thought of the flame as his own little companion, flickering and dancing merrily, banishing the darkness.

He laughed out loud and blew out the candle. *How absurd, a candle as one's companion. Etienne, what a pathetic creature you have become.* He shook his head crawling into bed. Pangs of loneliness nagged at the pit of his stomach, and he turned over impatiently. Gradually the day's labors pulled him into sleep, banishing his shame and despair.

* * *

Darcy arrived the following afternoon, wearing a look of nonchalance. He suspected from the dark shadows under her eyes that she had not slept a wink because of anxious anticipation. It amused him to see the bored facade she presented to him.

Father Etienne was excited too, and they walked from the abbey to the cliffs for their lesson. They came upon a cluster of boulders and climbed on top of them, settling themselves on one large, smooth stone. The gray clouds were thick and heavy, but it was not raining. He liked it up here. He was far enough from town to avoid the dangers of discovery, and the scenery was beautiful. He looked at the mountains and the stone fences, the dark green turf, and the lavender heather. He noticed how Darcy's multi-colored shawl stood out in stark contrast to the gray sky above her.

Reaching down into the canvas bag, he produced a flat board with figures written on it, which was called a *hornbook.* Father Etienne told Darcy that this was his book when was a small boy. It pleased him to see her handle it with reverence.

Darcy was thrilled. Even though the shapes on the board were alien to her, they awoke an excitement that she could barely contain. Next, Father Etienne wrote figures on a flat black rock he called a slate and told Darcy that this was the alphabet. They worked together for hours, writing and then erasing, passing the chalkboard back and forth.

Father Etienne looked up at the darkening sky and said, "I think we should end here for today."

Darcy looked up in protest and said, "But I can't read yet, Father!"

"Oh no, Darcy," he chuckled. "It will take many more lessons, but you will read soon. I can see that you have a quick mind."

Gathering their things, they agreed to meet tomorrow, but before leaving Darcy said, "I don't have any money, Father, but I wish to pay you something."

Father Etienne started to protest, but remembering Darcy's pride and said, "It is the custom in England and the Colonies that young women make a needlework sampler of the alphabet. It gives them practice on their letters and their needlework. Sometimes they add a quotation from Scripture as well. The only payment I ask is to have your sampler when it is complete, to adorn my home."

Darcy agreed instantly. As she turned to go, Father Etienne asked, "Do you still think I should mind my own business?"

She raised an eyebrow and then turned abruptly for home. He watched her walk briskly down the bluff thinking how he had underestimated her intelligence. He knew that she had a hungry mind, but he had no idea how quickly she would grasp academics.

Father Etienne chuckled when he remembered what she had said earlier in the day. "Father, I must tell you the truth about something. Several nights ago I opened your crate of books, and I have been reading them at night. Not really reading them, but I take them out, look at the covers and then make up the story."

He remembered the look in her eyes when he told her the titles of those books--*Plato's Republic, Dante's Divine Comedy, and The Canterbury Tales*--and said to her, "I think you would enjoy some plays by an Englishman named, William Shakespeare. He wrote some wonderful plays which speak to all of us."

For all the benefits Darcy would receive from an education, it occurred to Father Etienne that maybe it was a disservice to her. A woman's choices were few, and she would have no peers. In a land where food is rare, books are unheard of, and he worried that maybe he'd opened up Pandora's Box.

Father Etienne sighed and rubbed his brow. He was tired, and the entire night lay before him. He had many confessions to hear and several sick villagers to comfort, so he turned to look one last time at Darcy as she descended the bluff, but Pandora had vanished from his sight.

Chapter 4

The owlers were expecting another shipment from France soon, and in the eight months following the arrival of Father Etienne many shipments of brandy had been delivered safely to the shores of Kilkerry. The routine was always the same, Darcy would hail the vessel, and the men would exchange wool for brandy and then bury their cargo in the churchyard. Several nights later Liam and Michael O'Hearn would retrieve the casks, load them onto donkey carts, and by the light of the moon travel ten miles to the inn at Granagar Village. At the inn, they would receive payment and obtain wool for the next rendezvous with the French. This endless rotation of wool for brandy was conducted without interruption because no British troops were posted in Kilkerry at that time. The owlers had enjoyed this freedom for almost seven years now.

Although when the troops were in residence, things changed. Every precaution had to be taken. The donkeys were shaved and greased so they could make a slippery get-away if stopped by the British. The animals were also taught their commands in reverse, so if an owler was told by a soldier to stop, the owler would shout, "Whoa!" and the donkey would burst into a full run, making a quick get-away. Tricks and safeguards had been passed on through several generations of the O'Hearn family, who were the most highly skilled owlers in all of County Kerry. They had been smuggling goods since the Battle of the Boyne, and Michael O'Hearn was proud of his family heritage. When The Hunger claimed the family patriarch, Michael shouldered the responsibility of running the operation by himself with no regrets. It was agonizing waiting for the sheep population to rise after the famine, but eventually, enough wool was being produced again to sustain a trade.

Although Michael was younger than Liam, he directed the smuggling operation with efficiency and prudence. He allowed Liam to swagger and boast that he was a partner, but the village knew that Michael quietly shouldered all the responsibility. He was a good-hearted person in all matters, but he was no fool. He knew how to set limits when necessary, especially when the business was involved.

The famine had not been kind to Michael. Rickets had deformed his legs, and he walked with much pain and difficulty. Had his family moved to the ocean like the McBrides and existed on kelp and snails, he would never have been afflicted. Like so many Irish Catholics, his home had been destroyed by the British troops, and having nowhere to go, the family of nine moved into a scalp, a large hole roofed with sticks and turf. It offered little shelter from the elements and pneumonia killed his father and six of the children. When the crops returned, Michael, his mother and the remaining children moved into a vacant cottage that faced the town square and resurrected the owling.

It was another rainy night, and Michael and Liam pulled up their collars as they returned from a meeting. They entered the McBride cottage, and Liam fully expected to see Darcy standing in front of the hearth preparing his evening meal, but instead he found the home cold and empty.

"Damn her hide!" he snarled and quickly looked out the window.

"I'd bet my life that she's with that empty-headed sister of mine going on and on with their silly prattle," said Michael, as he limped over and began to build a fire.

Liam was in a surly mood, and he slumped down at the table, grumbling, "She knows that I expect my supper to be ready for me when I get home. I can tell by the looks of things that she hasn't been here for hours."

"I don't know how my brother-in-law can stand it," chuckled Michael. "Their brainless notions and secrets would drive me to drink. Say there, now that I mention it, I am a bit dry."

Liam rose from his chair and walked to the cupboard, pouring them both a drink and said, "Sometimes I wonder if she's bedding one of the lads in town. She acts funny lately like she's hiding something."

Liam was right. A change had come over Darcy these past months, but it wasn't because of a man. Ever since she had learned to read, she forgot to attend to the most basic of her chores. When she wasn't reading, she was thinking about reading. She became so absentminded that frequently she would overstay her lessons with Father Etienne and forget Liam's supper entirely.

Her brother viewed academics and education as a symbol of the landed gentry, and it was Darcy's greatest fear that he would find out and ruin her opportunity to learn. Liam believed that Irishmen needed only food, a cottage, and freedom. Anything beyond that was a waste of time.

Liam was furious. Although forgetting her chores was unforgivable, what really angered him was the fact that she was acting like some damned independent female. She would use words that he didn't understand, and she knew what he thought before he said it. "Stupid wench," he thought. "Imagine *her* thinking she's smarter than me."

"Well, Liam," said Michael rising up from the fire with a sheepish grin on his face, "I don't know a thing about Darcy's love affairs, but I do know about my own, and I've asked Bridget McGill to marry me. Father Etienne has agreed to perform the ceremony right in town, in my own cottage."

Although Michael had grown up with Bridget McGill, he had never really noticed her until about a year ago when she was fetching water for her mother one sunny afternoon. She was not a pretty girl and rather big-boned, but Michael saw a quality of beauty in her that the other young men in the village had missed. Their courtship had been quiet and Michael shared his private affairs with few, so Liam had no idea that he was interested in a young woman.

Michael was ecstatic when Bridget accepted his proposal, and he assumed Liam would feel the same way. Instead, Liam stared at him and then exploded into hearty laughter saying, "You fool! What do you want to marry that wench for? Why she has the face of a horse's ass!"

Michael was thunderstruck. He blinked and asked, "What did you say?"

Liam took a long pull on his brandy and sneered, "You're a damn fool. That's what I'm saying, O'Hearn. Granted you are a gimp, but you must be pretty desperate to want to bed that creature."

Michael couldn't believe his ears. Liam had always been coarse and abrupt, but he had never been cruel.

Rage boiled inside him as he started for the door. He turned and said, "Liam McBride, I don't know what's come over you lately. I should smash your face, but *you're* looking for an excuse to pummel me or anyone."

Michael slammed the door behind him as Liam sat staring straight ahead. He had been drinking more lately and boiling with hatred and resentment. The only person he cared about was pulling away from him and whether he admitted it or not, Darcy was important to him. She was not there to greet him at the end of the day, and he resented that she no longer catered exclusively to him. He felt as if he was being left behind, so when Michael had news of his marriage, Liam felt a burning jealousy begrudging their happiness. Liam had little desire to find a wife, and even if a woman were attracted to his coarse appearance, his courting skills were nonexistent.

He sat at the table brooding for some time when he heard footsteps. The door opened and Darcy burst into the cottage announcing that she was home, tossing her shawl over the chair. Her cheeks were apple red from the cold, and she was in a good mood.

"You're late! Where have you been?" demanded Liam.

"I'm late? Oh, Liam, I am sorry. I had no idea."

"Where have you been?"

"With Teila, we spent the day carding wool," Darcy lied. She grabbed some potatoes from a bag in the corner, hoping Liam would press her no further. She hated having to lie to him about her lessons with Father Etienne, but if he knew the truth, the lessons would end.

"You liar!" he snarled. "I want you home here every night with my supper ready, and that's an order!"

Darcy's eyes flashed as she looked up from her cooking, but she decided to say nothing.

"Tell me. Who's the bastard giving it to you when you should be home cooking?"

Darcy took a breath ready to counter and then decided to use his words to her advantage. "Liam, please don't be angry with me. Yes, I have been seeing someone, but please don't ask me who it is."

He grabbed her chin and yanked her face upward, examining her eyes and then let go. Liam did not want to know, so he pressed her no further, but Darcy knew eventually he would learn the truth and squash her dreams forever.

Chapter 5

For the first time in her life, Darcy was happy. Her days with Father Etienne had exacted a profound change on her. It seemed, at first that the reading lessons were not progressing fast enough, but eventually she began reading simple stories Father Etienne wrote for her. She then moved quickly from elementary compositions to great literature.

The first book he had her read was *The Arabian Nights*. She marveled at the cleverness of *Scheherazade*, thrilled at the adventures of *Sinbad* and was filled with wonder at Aladdin and his Genie. The priest thoroughly enjoyed watching her explore his boyhood favorites, and he vicariously relived those first precious moments of discovering good books.

In nine months, Darcy went from learning the alphabet to discussing Shakespeare and The Bible with Father Etienne. Her vocabulary changed too, and she found herself making a deliberate effort to hide her improved speech from Liam and the other villagers.

She matured from a one-dimensional female with few choices to a woman with new insights ready to expand her horizons. Until now her mental boundaries had been the green mountains of Kerry and the rugged coastline of the Atlantic, but now books carried her to the far reaches of the Orient or across the Seven Seas on a search deep within herself. Every moment she could find, she would steal upstairs to open the crate of books, drowning herself in other worlds. She realized there was a multitude of ways to look at life and a multitude of ways to live it.

Father Etienne felt transformed during this time as well. Darcy helped eliminate his intellectual isolation. He was not only fulfilling the Jesuit's supreme goal, to educate but for the first time in his life, he was close to a woman. There had been sexual encounters prior to taking vows, but he had never had a friendship with a woman. He delighted in the fresh perspectives a female brought to topics which he had discussed previously with men. They would debate for hours, delighting in the unique views each had to offer.

Their personal relationship changed as well, and they became best friends and confidants. Darcy no longer put Father Etienne on a pedestal. He, in turn, treated her as an equal, laying aside his professional distance, opening himself up.

In spite of the new friendship, Father Etienne still had misgivings regarding Darcy's education. He was afraid that after he had carefully designed and sculpted an intellectual equal, she would have no peer in Kilkerry. She adamantly wanted to stay in Ireland, but only the gentry had an education. *Where in the village will she find someone with whom to share her new interests?* He felt that he had been selfish and imprudent, yet he could never have neglected her hungry mind. *Once a mind has been awakened, how do you tell it to go back to sleep?*

He watched Darcy pull herself up the hill for another lesson. Today they were meeting at the abbey. It was a warm and peaceful day, and the priest sat partially concealed behind a wall observing the pastoral landscape which opened up below him. Cottages with thatched roofs were scattered across the landscape.

Each homeowner put his or her own personal touch to his or her cottage, a red window sill and a container of flowers or a white fence. One quality all the homes had in common was their neatness. Father Etienne watched a small boy and his donkey carrying peat bricks in baskets, and then an old man leaning on a wall smoking a pipe.

He realized that he had grown to love these simple people and their land of green fields and stone fences. He found beauty in the simplicity of their lives and the enormity of their faith. He ignored the fact that someday he would have to leave this village, or be expelled from it.

Darcy approached, and Father Etienne jumped to his feet. In the past months, she had grown more poised and self-confident, and although her outward appearance remained unchanged, he knew the emotional transformation was profound. He knew that some might be intimidated by her, especially Liam.

"There is a cool wind up here," she said smoothing her hair as they settled onto the stone floor of the abbey. She leaned over and looked at him. "Is your hair wet? Shame on you! You have been bathing in Glinnish Stream again." Darcy shook her finger at him. "You will catch your death of cold and die. Where would we find a priest to give you Last Rites?"

"I stand a better chance of dying if I *don't* bathe, and you should too, Darcy. I'm surprised at you. You behave like a primitive. Most of the great civilizations bathed regularly and built elaborate bath houses. It's only now that people think it's unhealthy."

She pursed her lips and looked at him skeptically. "I'll consider it, but I'm far from convinced."

Darcy turned to a basket covered with a woolen cloth and produced several books. "Look, I have a surprise for you. Your new shipment of books arrived with the last French vessel, and I brought a few up for you. See, here are some plays by Shakespeare and a work by Chaucer."

Father Etienne was pleased, and he began to thumb through the books. He handed her one of the volumes and said, "This is *Don Quixote* by Cervantes. I think it will amuse you. Now you can go from *Arabian Nights* to Spanish windmills."

They sat together chattering back and forth, thumbing through the books engrossed in conversation. The waves crashed on the rocks below, and the wind howled, but they did not notice.

"Have you ever heard of a lending library, Darcy?"

She shook her head.

"There are libraries all over the world, but in the Colonies, a man by the name of Franklin has established a somewhat different way of distributing knowledge. Every member of his library pays dues and with these dues he buys more books and allows the members to borrow these books whenever they choose. Imagine all that knowledge, right there at your fingertips. He's quite an amazing man. There are many men like him in America, men with new ideas and insights."

"Tell me again about your childhood, Father. I shall always remember your story of the dark wilderness and how you and your brother felt eyes watching you from within the forest."

"Oh yes," he said, leaning back against the abbey wall, looking wistfully out to sea. "It is beautiful and thrilling, but I am increasingly afraid for my family. War is escalating, and I fear for their lives."

"War with the Indians?" questioned Darcy.

"Well, they are involved, but it is the English and the French who are starting the hostilities. They are struggling for domination of the vast resources on the continent. It is a very precarious position for my mother and my brother since they bear French surnames and live in the English Colonies."

"So your father was French?" asked Darcy.

"Yes, a French Catholic, which is not very popular in the English colonies, but my mother is of English birth."

A look of worry passed over Father Etienne's face. "What concerns me are the Indian raiding parties sent by the French. I fear that there will be surprise attacks on the homesteads along the English frontier. They are a brutal and a bloody thing to witness, Darcy."

"You have seen these raids?"

Father Etienne made no reply. He reached down and picked up a book out of the basket. "My mother taught me how to read. She came from a highly educated family and chose to leave her privileged lifestyle behind and follow my father into the frontier. She's an amazing woman."

Darcy smiled. "I can tell that you miss her."

"It's been twenty-three years. I can still see her vividly, standing on the docks of Boston, waving goodbye to me as I left for France. She was a much younger woman then, I imagine she looks quite different now," and suddenly he laughed. "Of course, *I* have not changed!"

It was getting late, and Darcy was the first to stand up. She smoothed her apron, picked up her basket and said, "Do you know what a *thin place* is, Father?"

"A thin place? What do you mean?"

"The ancient Celts believed certain spots on Earth have thin boundaries between the natural and the supernatural world. I believe the monks felt that transparent quality here and for that reason chose this site for a monastery."

"What a beautiful idea. I've never heard of such a thing."

"Some think it's romantic superstition. I prefer to think of it as evidence of eternity," and turning with a sigh she said, "I'd better not be late with Liam's supper tonight. A bit of the devil's been into him lately."

He looked up at the abbey ruins. "I fancy sometimes that the ghosts of the monks listen to us here. I think it would appeal to them knowing that learning is still going on within these walls," and he looked into Darcy's eyes. "Thank you for being my friend. I believe I was lonely before you came along."

She smiled. "I too was lonely. It all fell into place when you said one can find God in many places, so you see I must thank you too."

Darcy extended her hand, and he pressed it between his own hands. Carrying the new book in her basket, she hiked down the hill toward home. As she approached her cottage, she spied a figure waving. It was Teila Mullin, Darcy's best friend, and she felt a pang of guilt for neglecting her lately. She prepared herself with a hundred excuses.

Teila was breathless when she met Darcy. An uphill walk was difficult because of her twisted left foot. She suffered from rickets like her brother, Michael O'Hearn. Teila was a slight wispy young woman now in the bloom of pregnancy. She had fine strawberry-blond hair and a light-hearted attitude. They embraced, and Teila said, "I just saw Liam. He looked confused and angry when I said I had seen you near the abbey with Father Etienne."

"You saw us?" asked Darcy.

"Yes, that's one of the reasons I came to see you. Father Etienne must be more careful. I could have been an informant."

Teila saw the troubled look on Darcy's face and asked, "Why have you been seeing Father Etienne? Are you in some sort of trouble?"

"No."

Teila looked searchingly at her friend. "I know you, Darcy, and I can tell when something is amiss. What is it? Are you ill? Are you going to have a baby?"

"What? No!" laughed Darcy. "But you're certainly showing *your* baby, Teila," said Darcy, patting her friend's belly.

Teila looked down and smiled. "I feel better with this baby than any of the others."

They turned and started down the hill. Darcy decided to tell Teila the truth. She took her friend's thin wrist and said, "I have something to tell you, but no one else must know, especially Liam." She swallowed hard and said, "Father Etienne is teaching me to read."

Teila's eyes grew wide. "To read? Why?"

Darcy laughed and said, "So I can learn."

"Why, that sounds just like you, Darcy McBride. You've always wanted something different than the rest of us. I can't say that I understand you, but if it's what you want, then I'm happy for you."

"Oh, it is wonderful. Let me teach you to read, Teila."

"No. Now, what use would I have for books? They can't tend sheep or feed my babies. I'll leave that to you."

They chattered all the way down to the McBride cottage, excited to be in each other's company once more. When they arrived at the cottage, Teila said, "You have spent no time with me lately. Keenan and the wee ones are up in the pastures today. Come home with me. You can help with my baking, and we can talk."

Darcy opened her mouth to protest and Teila said, "There is no excuse. I have even prepared Liam's supper for you," and she handed Darcy the basket she carried. "Throw that in your stew pot, and he'll never know the difference."

Darcy laughed. The offer sounded tempting, but she hesitated by the door of the cottage. She had been away from home so much lately, and she felt guilty. "You're right, Teila. He shouldn't expect more. After all, I'm not his wife."

Darcy disappeared inside the cottage to put the stew into her pot. She brought up the fire to warm it and grabbed a shawl. Thunder rumbled, and they pulled their shawls up onto their heads walking briskly to the Mullin home. All evening the storm came in great waves off the ocean, but the Mullin cottage was warm and cozy as the two women baked bread and shared news.

Keenan and the children returned to find the house filled with the aroma of bread and puddings being prepared. It felt good to be part of a family, thought Darcy. Teila and Darcy were as close as sisters, and for years, they had shared almost everything. Teila knew there was a side to Darcy that she would never understand, but she accepted it and asked nothing more from Darcy than what she could give.

"Well, if it isn't Miss McBride!" bellowed Keenan, as he hung up his jacket. "It's been far too quiet lately. We need some giggling and silly prattle from you two."

"Oh, go on with you and wash your hands," ordered Teila.

Keenan winked at Darcy as the children ran to hug her. They were fresh, rosy-cheeked little ones ranging in age from two to ten. Never experiencing a famine, they were strong, healthy and filled with life. Teila's husband, Keenan also appeared in robust good health. His energy and vitality were reflected in his good-nature. Even though his rumpled brown hair and pug nose made him look like a troll, his booming voice and generous nature endeared him to all. He was perpetually smoking a pipe, and the sweet smell of tobacco surrounded him.

He was grateful to Darcy because she made Teila happy, and he sat contentedly smoking his pipe while they discussed village news and prepared his supper. Keenan eased back in his chair and took a long draw, watching Darcy. She was different from Teila or any of the other women in town, and although he couldn't identify what was so extraordinary about her, the distinction became more apparent each year. He had known Darcy all his life, and she had never quite fit in with the others. Many of Kilkerry's young men found her mystery alluring, but Keenan was merely amused by it.

After dinner, Rowena, their ten-year-old daughter, played a tune on her tin whistle as Keenan carried the children to bed. Darcy clapped enthusiastically when the child was done and then made her farewells for the night. She hugged Teila and said, "I didn't realize how much I missed you."

"May God go with you, my girl," Teila replied. "Now, quickly run between the raindrops!"

When Darcy arrived home, the front door was open, swinging back and forth in the wind. She hesitated a moment and then entered the dark room lighting a candle. Nothing seemed disturbed, a few embers remained in the fireplace, but when she bent down to resurrect the fire, she saw the charred remains of Father Etienne's copy of *Don Quixote*. She groaned and pulled it gingerly from the coals.

Suddenly, the door crashed open, and there stood Liam, his large frame weaving back and forth in the shadows. He stumbled into the room and leaned heavily on the table, glaring at her. His greasy hair was plastered to his head, and his breath smelled of stale alcohol.

She stood up holding the charred book in her hand and said, "Are you responsible for this blasphemy? Don't you ever burn a book!"

Liam's attention went from the book to Darcy's face. His eyes narrowed, and he met her challenge with a snarl. "No, Darlin', there won't be any more burning 'cause there will be no more reading!"

She tossed her head and said, "If you want to waste your mind, Liam, that's your choice, but I'll not join you on the road to stupidity."

Quick as lightning he smashed her across the face with the back of his hand, and she reeled onto the table sending the candlestick flying. Putting her hand to her face, Darcy looked at Liam in shock. There was a vacant, lifeless expression in his eyes which struck terror into her heart. She knew he equated education with the aristocracy, and tonight she represented the ruling classes. Lunging for the door, Liam caught her waist. She felt the iron grip of his huge hands as he slammed her against the plaster wall.

As she slid down the wall dazed, Liam grabbed the back of her blouse. As he pulled her up, he snarled,

"You think you're better than me, don't you?" and he vaulted her into the fireplace. She hit the mantel squarely across her shoulders, her legs crumpling beneath her. Darcy's head hit the hearthstones like a melon. Liam rolled her over planting his knee on her chest. The last thing Darcy saw was his huge fist rising to smash her face. As the room moved farther and farther away, Darcy struggled to remember the prayer "Hail Mary, full of grace--"

Chapter 6

It felt like fingers were tapping all over Darcy's body. Her mind moved in a thick fog until she realized rain was pelting her as she lay in the mud. The earth felt cool on her burning face. Suddenly, a wave of nausea washed over her, and she rose to her hands and knees retching. A flash of lightning illuminated the McBride cottage as she fell back down into the mud.

Darcy couldn't understand why she was outside, and she tried to rise again but the intense pain would not allow it. Her wet hair lay in long, muddy tangles, and her clothes were filthy and plastered to her skin. Gradually the details returned to her, and she shuddered to think of someone finding her out here disgraced and humiliated. She remembered all the justifications for the thrashing of a woman such as, "I think she likes it," or "She must have done something to deserve it." She couldn't bear the thought of anyone blaming her for Liam's shameful behavior.

She pulled herself up onto her hands and knees, shaking from pain and weakness and crawled like a hurt animal to the door of the cottage. Leaning heavily on a small bench, she gathered all her strength and hauled herself into a standing position. On wobbly legs, she entered the cottage, supporting herself on the walls and furniture until she struggled to the bed where she threw herself down. She slept for hours until sharp pains roused her, and she opened her eyes.

Pushing herself up, she looked down at her blouse. "Oh sweet Jesus!" she exclaimed. It was covered with blood, vomit, and mud. The bed sheets too.

She rose from the bed, managed to light a candle, searching for Liam. With every ounce of strength she could muster, she pulled herself up the stairs to check his bed.

The room was vacant, and she heaved a sigh of relief backing down the stairs. Darcy limped over to a small, cracked mirror and gazed into the glass. She gasped. She didn't recognize the monster with purple, swollen eyes. Caked blood had hardened around the cuts on her face, and her lips were swollen to double their ordinary size. Moaning, she fell back onto the bed.

Darcy was too exhausted to move, trying hard to ignore the throbbing in every part of her body. She turned her head and noticed that streaks of light were breaking across the dark sky. She knew that she needed to clean her wounds, but there was not enough water in the house. The town well would be surrounded by women at this time of day, so Darcy lay helplessly in bed trying to think of what to do. Suddenly, it occurred to her that Father Etienne bathed in Glinnish stream. The spot was secluded and offered lots of fresh running water.

She moved to the cupboard, removed a crock of soft soap, and then turned to her linen chest gathering a towel, clean clothes, and rags for bandages. Clamping the top down tightly on the crock of soap, she rolled all the articles into a bundle and sat down to rest before starting her strenuous hike up the hill.

She cracked the cottage door to search for villagers, but many still slumbered in the half-light of dawn. As Darcy stepped out the door into the fresh air, another wave of nausea overtook her, and she fell to her knees, retching once more. Pushing the hair out of her eyes, she turned toward the bluff and began her painful ascent. She hobbled and stumbled her way up the incline, hunched over with the pack under her arm, and when she, at last, reached the summit, Darcy turned toward a cluster of trees behind the abbey where Glinnish Stream was concealed.

She could hear the brook bubbling as she plunged into the brush and was grateful to be under the cover of darkness once more.

She spied a small clearing where the stream broadened out between the rocks into a deep pool and began to peel off her soiled clothing. Her skirt dropped easily to the ground, but her blouse was painful to remove. The blood had dried the material to her wounds, and she clenched her teeth pulling the garment from her skin. At last, Darcy stood naked by the water, her body covered with purple bruises and open wounds.

Setting her soap and wash rag on a rock, she eased herself down into the running water. At any other time, this stream would have felt icy, but her body was so inflamed with injuries that the cold water was a pain killer.

Darcy felt it rush over her skin, floating her black tresses around her head, as she lay almost completely submerged. The stream gurgled in her ears, and she listened to the comforting rush as hot tears welled into her eyes. Feeling frightened and betrayed, Darcy knew that she would never trust Liam again. It was apparent that her worth did not extend beyond that of housekeeper, and she realized that all her years of loyalty had been misguided.

She sat up and reached for the soap. She washed her hair and her body, dabbing gingerly at her wounds, and lying back squeezed water from her rag onto her face, soaking the dirt out of the wounds.

As Darcy climbed up on the bank, the cold air hit her wet skin and she quickly toweled herself off, getting dressed. After she had covered her wounds with bandages, she gathered up her things and stepped out into the open meadow.

As quickly as she could, Darcy limped back down the bluff breathing a sigh of relief when she ducked inside the cottage at last. She was relieved that she did not run into Father Etienne returning from his nightly rounds. He would corner her and insist on answers. This was a minor problem, but what terrified her was that Liam would return and renew his assault.

For days Darcy stayed in her bed, growing ever weaker and more delirious from fever, eating nothing and sleeping fitfully, tossing and turning. She couldn't tell if she had been there for minutes or days, and her dreams turned to bizarre nightmares as she sank deeply into delirium. She dreamt that she was walking in the freezing sunshine. Next, she was standing naked and humiliated in front of the villagers about to be beaten by monks in the Abbey.

Darcy's head was pounding from fever. It became so intense it sounded as if someone was drumming on her head. In reality, someone was banging on the door. There was a rush of air, muffled voices and then she had the sensation of being lifted. Someone ran icy cloths up and down her arms, and she wished they would stop, but people returned choking her with foul tasting drinks and more wet compresses. When Darcy finally awakened, her eyes focused on a glowing peat fire. People nearby were talking in hushed tones.

Suddenly a child screeched, "That's mine!"

"Shhh!" and the room fell silent once more.

Darcy stared at the fire and after some time realized someone was watching her. With difficulty she rolled over and spied a toddler standing at the end of the bed, sucking her thumb, staring at her.

"Ashling?" she murmured.

Hearing Darcy's voice, Teila and the others came running to the bed. Her friend dropped to her knees, crossing herself by the bed saying, "The saints be praised. I thought you were going to die." She put her hand on Darcy's forehead and announced to the children that the fever had broken.

"How long have I been here?" Darcy whispered.

"Over a week, I can't tell you how happy I am. There is something I must do, before we talk, Darcy. Rowena will take care of you. I'll be back in a few minutes," and Teila dashed out the door.

Teila's daughter gave Darcy some broth. It was the first bit of sustenance she had taken in days, and she felt it revive her with a warm glow.

"Well, this is an improvement indeed! We've been very worried," said Father Etienne walking in the room, followed by Teila.

He patted Darcy's hand, as she asked in a raspy voice, "How did I get here?"

"I found you at the cottage. I knew something must be wrong when you missed your lesson, and after banging on the door repeatedly, I found you drenched in sweat and fever. Keenan came and helped me move you to their cottage."

Suddenly his expression turned serious, and he said, "Who did this to you?"

Darcy said nothing. Fear of retaliation kept her mute. She could not risk another beating.

"I found the burned volume of *Don Quixote* on the floor of your cottage, Darcy. It was Liam, wasn't it?" When there was still no reply from Darcy, he continued. "I wanted to wait until you were awake to be sure that I didn't unjustly accuse him, but now my suspicions are confirmed. Darcy, it is your moral obligation to tell me now if Liam is innocent."

Father Etienne paused, waiting for an answer, and Darcy still said nothing, staring down at the quilt.

"So be it," he said and left the cottage.

The priest walked briskly down the road toward the outskirts of town. The rain soaked his black cassock and ran down into his eyes. He wiped his face impatiently. He heard raucous laughter as he approached a small rundown cottage. He banged several times on the door with a heavy fist until a large man with a bright shock of red hair answered the door.

Father Etienne was not acquainted with Joseph Tierney. Like Liam, he stayed away from the priest, never attending Mass preferring the company of a bottle. He curled his lip as he regarded Father Etienne. Blue smoke and the smell of stale beer rolled out from the door. The priest demanded, "I want to talk to McBride!"

Tierney stuffed a piece of meat into his mouth, wiped his greasy hands on his shirt and shouted with his mouth full, "McBride, get out here!"

Father Etienne could hear laughing, and Liam thrust his head out the door saying, "I got no business with you!"

"But I have with you!" said Father Etienne. He reached in, grabbed Liam's shirt and pulled him out into the rain, slamming the cottage door shut with his foot.

The men stood face to face in the downpour. Although the priest was a head shorter than Liam, he looked him squarely in the eye and said, "I'm here to save your pathetic soul, McBride. Give me your confession, now!"

"I'm not sorry for beating that uppity bitch. I was doing her a favor. I knocked some sense into her!" snarled Liam.

"What was her crime? Trying to learn?" demanded Father Etienne.

Liam poked his finger in the priest's face and said, "Thinking she was better than us," he said, spraying spittle in Father Etienne's face. "That was her crime. Get something straight, you girlie-faced meddler. You breeze in here to preach to us ignorant bastards, and the whole time you think you're better than us. We don't need your books *or* your God."

Liam turned and staggered back toward the Tierney cottage, but stopped when he heard Father Etienne say, "You'll not beat her again, McBride."

"I'll beat her whenever I want," he said.

As Liam put his hand on the latch of the door, Father Etienne warned, "Touch her again and I'll tell your friends about the young man you meet at the abbey at night."

Liam turned with his mouth open. Father Etienne added, "I assure you, it won't be *me* they'll be calling girlie."

Chapter 7

Over the next few days, Darcy spent most of her time sleeping. She was too weak to rise from bed for almost a week. Fighting the fever sapped her strength, and she lost a great deal of weight. There was little she could do for herself, and it was hard to allow the Mullins to wait on her, but the children loved the responsibility, and Teila enjoyed the company. She would bustle around the kitchen talking to her best friend about everything.

This atmosphere of warmth and love did more for Darcy's healing than any medicine. When Teila tended the sheep, Darcy helped by entertaining the children. She told stories of the glorious days of Brian Boru and the High Kings of Tara. They would listen intently as she told of the ancient adventures and daring deeds.

Darcy healed physically, but emotionally the cure took longer. For a long time, she feared Liam's retaliation, but gradually as her strength returned so did her resolve. She had survived more difficult ordeals, and no brute force was going to beat her into submission. With renewed determination she pursued her love of learning and devoured the books that Father Etienne left for her on the nightstand.

It took more than a month for Darcy to completely recover, and she spent hours with Teila speaking of many things. On countless occasions, Teila saw Darcy staring out to the sea as if she were bewitched, or during a conversation, Darcy's eyes would drift out the window as if some secret lover was beckoning. All of this saddened Teila. She knew that she would never truly know her best friend.

Darcy's strength grew quickly, and her wounds healed. Her complexion returned to its smooth texture, and except for a small scar above her left eyebrow, the effects of the beating were no longer apparent. She worked hard in the cottage and out in the pastures. She ate heartily and returned her figure to its appealing curves.

Teila was filling out as well, entering the final months of her pregnancy, and she needed Darcy's help more than ever. One summer evening after a meal of potato leek soup, there was a sharp knock at the door. It was Father Etienne standing in the bright sunshine.

"What are you doing," Darcy scolded, pulling him inside. "Someone will see you."

He said to Teila, "I'm sorry, Mrs. Mullin. The good woman who was to attend to my supper tonight forgot about me. Might I find a bite to eat with you this evening?"

"But, of course! You are welcome here anytime," she said. "Darcy, take Father Etienne to the fire for a brandy while I get his supper."

Darcy ushered Father Etienne to a chair and after handing him a drink, took a seat beside him. She knew something was wrong as she watched him raise the mug to his lips, his movements wooden.

He said nothing, staring into the fire.

"Do you have a busy evening ahead?" Darcy asked.

He made no reply. She saw dark circles under his eyes as he emptied his mug without stopping.

"Twas a grand day today, wasn't it, Father?" said Teila handing him a bowl of soup.

"Indeed, it was, Mrs. Mullin," he returned flatly.

Darcy saw tears began to roll down his face. Startled, she told Teila that they were going out to enjoy the summer evening, and Darcy directed him behind the cottage where she pulled him down on a stone bench.

The evening was fair, and the setting sun cast a golden hue on them. Darcy touched Father Etienne's arm. He closed his eyes took a deep breath and said, "The ship brought a letter last night. My mother was massacred in an Abenaki raid."

Darcy gasped and clutched her bodice.

"My brother would give no details, but every time I try to sleep, Darcy, I see her running. She's terrified, and at last, they catch her, and I see her struggling." He looked at Darcy. "Did they take her long, beautiful hair? Did they rip it savagely from her head while she still lived?"

"Don't do this!" Darcy gasped. "You don't know what happened. It is between God and your mother."

He sat with his head in his hands for a long time. At last, he rubbed his brow and said, "If only I could get some sleep, I think I could open myself to the comfort of the Holy Spirit, but it seems now when I need it the most, I cannot feel the light."

"Come," said Darcy. "We shall walk the cliffs tonight, and I promise you will sleep,"

"No, I cannot, Darcy," he said, shaking his head. "I must make my rounds."

"Do you have anyone, in particular, expecting you?"

"No, but--"

"Then no one will miss you," said Darcy taking charge. She disappeared into the house giving a hasty explanation to Teila, who handed Darcy a basket of buns, saying, "Give this to the poor darlin'."

The full moon flooded the coastline with a pale light which guided their footsteps along the steep bluffs. They walked in silence for an hour, and at last Darcy said breathlessly, "Please, I must rest for a short while."

Father Etienne said with a start, "Oh, Darcy, you are still recovering. I have been so self-absorbed that I didn't think of your fatigue."

Darcy shook her head. "Being up here is the best medicine in the world for me. You, of all people, should know that. The air is so much sweeter here, and it makes me strong."

They sat on the rocks, watching the moonbeams glisten on the breaking water. Father Etienne looked out to sea and said, "This reminds me of my mother's favorite poem."

"What is it?" asked Darcy, as she hugged her knees.

He paused a moment, sorting through the words and said, "There, now I have it." He closed his eyes and began,

'To see a World in a Grain of Sand
And a Heaven in a Wild Flower,
Hold Infinity in the palm of your hand
And Eternity in an hour.' "

He smiled wistfully. "How she loved that little piece. I don't know how I ever remembered it. It was like she was here whispering it in my ear."

After a while, he continued, "I never realized it until now, but I didn't lose my mother three months ago to a raiding party. I lost my mother the day I left for Europe. I knew in my heart I would never see her again, and now with no ocean to part us, she is closer to me than ever."

Father Etienne rose to his feet and pulled Darcy up. "Let's go home," he said. "I know that I can sleep now."

"I am glad," she replied.

At the descent to the cave, he took Darcy's hand and said, "One day I will leave Kilkerry and have to find my way alone. As much as that saddens me, I know that I will carry *you* in my heart forever as well."

* * *

It was Michael O'Hearn's wedding day. Darcy rose before the sun, crawling out of the loft where she slept with the children and walked up to Glinnish Stream. Father Etienne had at last convinced her to bathe regularly. After scrubbing her body and scalp until it tingled, she stepped lightly out of the water and dried herself. Looking up, she could see the day was going to be mild and cloudless.

For over a week, Darcy had been collecting petals from the roses which grew wild in the meadow, and she rubbed them onto her skin, capturing their scent. After scrubbing her teeth with a small frayed sapling branch, she combed through her long, dark hair and pinned up the tresses. Darcy slipped a red gown over her head, and although it fit tightly over her round breasts, it fell all the way to her ankles and molded to her figure gracefully. Although threadbare, the gown had been her mother's best dress, and she ran her hands over the fabric lovingly. To complete her ensemble, she put on her only pair of shoes, well-worn black slippers which had also belonged to her mother.

Darcy gathered her things and returned to the Mullin cottage. Teila would need plenty of help cooking and getting the children ready before the wedding. There was an air of excitement when Darcy walked through the door, and she could see everyone busy with preparations. Teila was frantically packing food in crocks while Keenan struggled with his buttons in front of the mirror. "I can't do this!" he burst out, still holding his pipe between his teeth.

Two of the children wrestled on the floor while the toddler was climbing onto the cupboard looking for food. It was chaos, but it was good-natured excitement. It had been a long time since Kilkerry had anything to celebrate, and a wedding on a sunny afternoon made spirits high.

Keenan bellowed, "Why, Darcy McBride! You're a sight for sore eyes. I'm betting that you'll be married yourself before the day is over."

Teila looked up, and said, "You look beautiful today, Darcy. It seems like only yesterday your mother was wearing that dress."

Keenan grabbed Teila around the waist and roared, "Speaking of beauties, just look at my bride!"

He gave Teila a squeeze, and she snapped a towel at him laughing, "Settle down, you old fool. That sort of attitude is why I'm the size of a cow today!"

Teila was dressed in a saffron-colored gown, which draped loosely over her generous belly, and her light hair was gathered into a knot at the back of her head with a ribbon.

Darcy opened a basket and double-checked the number of bowls. Everyone attending the wedding was expected to provide their own eating utensils as well as food to share. There was no one wealthy enough in these parts to provide a feast for an entire village, so it was expected that everyone bring enough food to feed the number of family members they brought to the celebration.

Darcy packed several stews, puddings, and bread into baskets, as Teila finished dressing the last child. In a flurry, they set out for the wedding on the village green. The ceremony would be performed at the O'Hearn family cottage by Father Etienne and then the feasting and celebration would begin.

Those who were aware of the priest's presence in Kilkerry knew of this arrangement, but those who could not be trusted were told the bride and groom had taken their vows earlier in the week by an existing priest in Granager.

The green was alive with activity when they arrived. Tables were being arranged and carts were beginning to pull up, filled with excited guests. Everyone commented on the beautiful sunshine, and spirits were high.

The interior of the O'Hearn home resembled most cottages, but today it had a look of celebration. It had been recently scrubbed and whitewashed, and it sparkled with the nervous excitement of its inhabitants. Michael and Bridget stood by the fireplace, anxiously watching Father Etienne place an altar cloth over the kitchen table.

Michael was dressed in a newly woven white smock with dark breeches. Everyone marveled at his black boots, which he had borrowed from Casey

Mulligan. Many a bridegroom in Kilkerry had borrowed these boots from Casey, but they still inspired awe when they were worn publicly.

Bridget stood quietly by Michael, looking down at the dirt floor of the cottage. She was painfully shy, and all this attention was unbearable for her. She longed to be home alone with Michael away from all the prying eyes. Bridget was a tall, big-boned girl with broad hips and a freckled face. Her brown hair was tucked neatly under a white mob cap lined with fine lace she had woven by candlelight. Michael linked arms with her, patted her hand and nodded to Father Etienne that they were ready.

Outside on the green, pony carts continued to pull up, unloading guests, eager to spend the warm, sunny day dining and dancing. Women scurried about, carrying pots filled with their best suppers, and tables were moved out into the open air to hold food. They were arranged in long lines with homespun tablecloths which snapped in the breeze. The men gathered in groups around the square, starting on the stout and the brandy earlier than usual, ribbing each other about who would win the races and games. Their voices would occasionally grow louder and frequently end in hearty laughter as the children ran back and forth across the green, turning somersaults and playing tag.

The green was filled with guests when the bride and groom stepped out of the cottage into the sunshine. The crowd let out a hearty cheer. A group of fiddlers struck up a jig as guests swarmed the couple offering best wishes and congratulations.

Long lines formed to consume the stews, puddings and mutton pies which graced the tables. Potatoes and cabbages, ordinarily so mundane, had been dressed in special ways for today's festivities. Everyone donated their best recipes, and the aromas were delectable.

At the end of the line, there was a table reserved for fresh bread and dainties. This was considered extravagant fare, reserved for special occasions only, and it was here that the hungry villagers found flummeries and tarts. The rich, deep colors of the berries alongside the generous creams were a feast for the eyes, and one guest donated a trifle. To post-famine Kilkerry, such excess seemed sacrilegious, but the guilt was fleeting. Plates filled up quicker than consciences, and everyone made merry.

Many spread tablecloths and blankets on the ground or simply sat directly on the grass. Many of the men, preferred to indulge in spirits before clearing their heads with food, and several games of chance sprang up, including the shell game.

The bride and groom received guests at their table, between bites of food. During the festivities, Father Etienne found it prudent to remain in the O'Hearn cottage, and he was chatting with old Mrs. Mallory as Darcy stepped inside to see him. John Kinsale, one of the young men in town, was watching the door to be sure no informants entered the O'Hearn cottage. Father Etienne noticed the look he gave Darcy, as she swept past him. The priest was glad that he did not have the game of courtship to distract and confuse him.

As Darcy approached, Mrs. Mallory rose and said, "You take my chair, dear. My bones need warming in the sun."

Darcy sat down, handing Father Etienne a mug of stout and said, "I wish you didn't have to hide in here like a prisoner."

He shrugged. "It doesn't bother me. I feel like a king holding court as they drift in and out paying homage to me."

"Oh, is that what I'm doing?"

"No, *you* have never been impressed with me."

Darcy grew serious and asked, "Have you been sleeping at night?"

"Most nights I sleep, but there are times when the slightest memory triggers it all again."

There was little time to visit. The cottage was filling with people wishing to greet Father Etienne. They were chattering and laughing, and one of the young men handed him a plate of food saying, "If you can't come to the celebration, it will come to you. One of the fiddlers stepped into the cottage and started to play a tune.

Michael grabbed Bridget and swung her into a dance inside the cottage while others kept time clapping. It had been a long time since Father Etienne had felt this light-hearted. He marveled at how good life could feel.

The afternoon grew warmer, and after filling their bellies, some people dozed in the warm sunshine. Some of the more ambitious male villagers organized footraces and wrestling matches in the meadow as the women watched.

Darcy and Teila walked over to snicker at them as they heatedly tried to outdo each another.

They watched for a long time laughing and cheering when Teila said suddenly, "Darcy, there will never be a husband for you in Kilkerry."

Darcy looked at Teila surprised. "You are wrong. He is coming home from the Americas any day now."

Teila shook her head. "When are you going to give up? He's not coming back, Darcy. Have you ever thought of leaving Kilkerry?"

"What!" said Darcy, stiffening her back. "What are you saying? You want me to leave?"

"I would keep you here with me forever if you would be happy, but you need something that we don't have here."

Darcy jerked her chin and said, "I will decide what is best for me."

The women were silent for a moment, pretending to watch the wrestlers. Suddenly, Darcy grabbed Teila's hand and pulled her toward the green. "Look! The sun is setting and the dance will start soon."

Several torches were set up and five musicians stationed themselves in front of the town well under the large stone cross. There were three fiddlers and two tin whistlers. Once the music started, Keenan swept Teila into a jig, and John Kinsale dashed over and held out his hands to Darcy. She flashed him a smile and accepted. Everyone cheered, and clapped after the first song and then scattered back to the edges of the square to catch their breath. By the time the sun set everyone was gathered on the green or crowded around the casks of brandy. The musicians started a new song, a contra dance called the *Childgrove*. This was different from the jig, and Darcy was anxious to give it a try. As she turned to join the line of dancers, Liam stepped in her path and startled her. He was drunk again and smelled foul. He was covered with grime and sweat.

Darcy stepped back and asked, "What do you want?"

"I have a surprise for you, little sister," he said thickly.

Darcy's throat tightened, and her heart began to pound. A man stood behind Liam, and when he stepped forward, the light from a torch flooded his face. He was large and raw-boned, his blond hair falling loosely around his shoulders. Bran Moynahan was living proof that the Norsemen had once inhabited their land.

"You don't know who I am, do you?" Bran asked with a crooked smile.

Darcy was stunned. "Bran, I--"

Liam pushed the two of them together and slurred, "Why don't you kiss or something?"

Darcy stepped back, and Bran chuckled. "I expect she'll be giving kisses free enough before long."

He looked her up and down lustily, and Darcy's heart raced. She couldn't believe it. Bran was back. She blushed and dropped her eyes.

Bran said to Liam, "Go and find something to do. I have a lot of catching up to do with your sister."

Bran took Darcy's elbow and escorted her toward the brandy. "You look like you could use a drink."

The men eyed Bran suspiciously and fell back, allowing him to make his way to the cask, intimidated by his size. She said when he returned with her drink, "They don't recognize you. You left a boy and returned a man."

"I don't recognize most of them. A lot has changed," admitted Bran as he took her arm.

They found a bench in the shadows of an oak tree where Darcy sat down. Bran preferred to stand, placing one foot on the bench alongside Darcy. He leaned close and said, "Did you miss me?"

She didn't answer and instead tried to calm herself by taking a gulp of brandy. Her heart was pounding, and her face was burning. "Were you in America all this time?"

He ran his eyes over her face and shoulders, lingering on her breasts until Darcy said, "Bran, I asked you a question."

"Begging your pardon, Miss.". Reluctantly, he dragged his eyes up to her face with a smirk. "I've been in the Colonies the whole time," he said taking a pull of his drink. "They sold me to the East India Company. I worked with a shipwright in the Massachusetts Colony. They liked me. When I return to the Colonies, I will have a paying job with them."

"So you're leaving? You just got back."

"Do you want me to stay, Darcy?" he asked, grinning. He yanked her into his arms and murmured, "Or do you love another?"

"My heart belongs to no one," she said wriggling away.

Agitated, she started to walk away, but he caught up to her. They walked through the village, Darcy keeping the conversation light. She learned that Bran had arrived in Cork last week and planned on staying in Kilkerry only a few months. He would return to the American Colonies, and although he didn't tell her why he had come back, she suspected that he was here to claim her as his bride.

Darcy told him all the village news and informed him of the new tenant in their cave, Father Etienne. Bran was surprised and interested in the new priest. As they approached the Mullin cottage, he remarked, "You don't live with your brother anymore?"

"He has changed, Bran. He has grown hard and callous, loving nothing better than the drink. He is so consumed by bitterness and hatred for the British that nothing remains of the boy you once knew."

He pulled her close. Darcy's legs grew weak in the warmth of his arms. She felt small, as he enveloped her. "You have changed too. You have filled out into a woman."

Darcy was breathless. He pulled her chin up and placed his lips firmly onto hers. Abandoning her reserve, Darcy began returning his kisses passionately. Sensing her desire, he slipped his hand inside her bodice. His hand felt warm, as it cupped her breast. "No more," she said pushing him away, both of them breathing heavily. "I'll do no more tonight."

Anger flashed across his face, but he quickly turned it to a suggestive smile, "So, you will tease me. No matter," he shrugged. "It will make the conquest that much sweeter." Bran kissed her on the cheek and strode off.

Chapter 8

Bran returned to the dance and found an eager conquest in Mary Kerrigan. She sated him physically until his next encounter with Darcy. Darcy was an extremely desirable woman, and he would not rest until he could have her.

Half the night, Darcy tossed restlessly in bed, and in the early hours, she tiptoed out of the Mullin cottage, taking her shawl. The moon cast long shadows on the rolling moor as she approached the cliff walk. Finding a rock, she sat down and hugged her knees.

She marveled at how quickly things changed and how in one evening her life had taken a different course. Bran had given her a new path, and at last, she would be able to have a home and family. He was everything that she had hoped for--handsome, virile-- and even if they had little in common, he was the finest Kilkerry had to offer. Darcy noticed the other young women looking at him, and she was proud to be on his arm. At last, she would be safe and have someone to take care of her. It was very comforting.

Father Etienne did not sleep that night either. He returned to the cave around three in the morning after the dance and lit a candle. He picked up his quill to compose a letter to his brother. He knew that he would be grieving for his mother as well and that any word from family would be welcome.

News of this small hamlet would be an interesting diversion for his brother, and almost like characters in a novel, he presented the villagers of Kilkerry to him. He knew that he would enjoy the escape from the world of turmoil and war in the Colonies and that he would take pleasure in the pastoral setting of rural Ireland. Tonight he would describe the wedding including the long-awaited reunion of Darcy and Bran.

He sat back a moment and mused. The reunion was an answer to a prayer, and he was happy that this handsome young man had returned to Darcy, but he sensed something was wrong.

The candle had burned low before Father Etienne finished composing his letter, and sealing it with drippings, he set it aside for the next French vessel.

The morning after the wedding, heavy clouds moved in and perched themselves over the coast, drizzling throughout the day and into the evening. Reluctantly, everyone returned to the mundane routines of tending sheep, weeding the plots of praties and cooking suppers.

There was a meeting scheduled that night for the owlers at the O'Hearn cottage, and Michael was being very mysterious about the agenda. Darcy's instincts told her that the news was not good. When she entered the room, smoke and the smell of spirits choked her. Yesterday's gaiety had vanished. It had been replaced by serious faces pinched tight with tension, and Darcy swallowed hard, sitting down in the corner.

She counted eight men present, and sitting by the fireplace was Michael's new bride, Bridget. The girl did not look up, giving all her attention to her sewing.

Suddenly, the door opened and Liam and Bran entered the room. It was obvious most of the men did not recognize Bran, but they said nothing. After Michael had looked around the room, he said, "Fine, then we are all here."

He rubbed his brow and said with a sigh, "As you know, there is a shipment arriving. But special precautions must be taken starting tonight. I have news that we are scheduled for an encampment."

There was silence in the room. Michael continued. "It's likely ten or fifteen soldiers will be posted in our homes. I have been informed that they will be coming tomorrow."

A collective groan went through the room. Jerry Joyce, a man of later years who had worked under Michael's father, asked, "Ya think they know of us?"

Michael shook his head. "From what I've gathered, they know nothing of us, but it is common knowledge that smuggling exists on this coastline. The point of my meeting is this," said Michael, as his bride watched him nervously. "We must be on the alert. As of tonight, we return to the old ways and use all the old precautions, and there is one more thing we must take into account. We must limit interactions with Father Etienne. Meetings with him must be for the sacraments only." He looked at Darcy. "He has been told that a red candle burning in a window is a summons to him. There must be no mistakes. We cannot endanger him."

In conclusion, Michael stood up and pulled Bran to his feet saying cheerfully, "Some of you may remember Bran Moynihan."

There were exclamations of surprise and recognition. "Well, he is back now from his transportation, and we welcome him into our operation." Several of the men applauded, as others slapped him on the back.

Michael signaled that it was time for them to go to their posts. When Darcy moved toward the door to get her lantern, she felt someone catch her wrist. "Will you be at the abbey tonight?" Bran whispered.

Darcy nodded, feeling intoxicated at being so close to him again. She smiled and then reluctantly pulled away to retrieve her lantern. She watched Bran go down the road to grease the donkeys and hitch them to the carts. His presence warmed her blood.

Returning to the cottage, Darcy walked over to the fireplace to light the candle for her lantern. Bridget was still sitting by the hearth sewing.

"You must be very happy, Bridget," said Darcy.

The girl tried to smile, but her eyes filled with tears instead. Darcy was astounded and slid onto a chair beside her.

Dabbing her eyes with her apron, Bridget said, "There's so much I didn't understand about marriage."

Darcy knew Bridget was referring to her wedding night, and she patted her hand. "Men certainly take great stock in it, don't they?" said Darcy. "I thought the whole thing sounded disgusting when I first heard about it."

Bridget snickered. Darcy continued, "If you love him, it will someday be an expression of affection for you."

"It was all such a surprise, and I just had to tell someone," said Bridget, heaving a sigh.

Darcy jumped up suddenly, lighting her lantern. "I must not wait any longer. The ship will be here soon. Teila is a wonderful person to talk to about these things, Bridget. Please come and see us."

The drizzle made Darcy's skirt heavy as she pulled herself up the bluff. It was curious, but the abbey didn't look ominous to her anymore. The walls once again served as a seat of enlightenment, at least for her. But then she remembered there would be no more visits with Father Etienne. No lesson was worth endangering his life. She would have to wait until the encampment moved on.

She entered the abbey and stood in a spot where she was visible to the French vessel. She lifted her lantern into the air, stretching to her full height. The rain made it impossible for her to see a ship off the coast tonight, so pacing back and forth, she swung the lantern in front of her. Her arms ached, but still she continued her march.

Just as she turned around, she crashed into Bran. His hand shot up to stifle her cry and whispered, "I'm sorry I scared you, but the ship has dropped anchor. You can rest now."

"Where are the others?" she asked, catching her breath.

"They're still unloading. I'm a wee bit early 'cause I was hoping to find you here alone," he said with a grin.

He took her hand and led her to the shelter of an ancient oak tree. He took her by the waist and swung her around pinning her against the trunk. "I won't be taking 'no' for an answer tonight, girl."

Darcy struggled. "No, Bran. Not here--" but Bran's lips bore down on her own as she felt a wave of passion wash over her. He pressed her against the tree and ran his hands up and down her body. Her blood began to run hot, as he lifted her skirt. Before Darcy could move, he was taking her. He moved quickly and mechanically, moaning in her ear and slobbering on her neck. An impatient lover, he was eager to satisfy his lust as quickly as it had surged. In moments, Bran was finished.

He stepped away from her, wiping his brow and said, "You'll be enjoying that from me the rest of your life, my girl."

Darcy nodded her head and said nothing. He pulled her back into his arms and demanded, "I want to hear you say that you love me."

Darcy took a breath and wiped his saliva from her lips and neck. The whirlwind lovemaking had left her breathless.

"Say it," Bran repeated. "That you love me."

"Give me a moment, Bran," she said, feeling irritable. She stepped back and straightened her skirt, pushing the hair from her face. "You know that I've waited for you all these years," Darcy said. "Would someone do that if they weren't in love?"

Bran scowled. He was not satisfied with her answer. He thought his skills as a lover would thaw her icy demeanor, but she held herself back, giving nothing. *Maybe Liam was right--she had become an uppity bitch.*

In the eight years he had been gone, Bran learned that he must take what he wanted in life. Darcy was the best-looking woman he had ever seen, and he was entitled to possess the finest. He knew that he was handsome and to have anything less would be unthinkable. *Darcy could not help but submit to his charms soon.*

* * *

As predicted, the soldiers arrived in Kilkerry and life became severely restricted. Women did not gather at the well, children did not run through the streets, and everyone stayed inside fearing an encounter with the troops. The town, which had finally recovered from disease and starvation, slid back down into depression and despondency.

Major Russell had been in Kilkerry for six months. He set up headquarters in one of the O'Hearn cottages and requisitioned several other homes for his regulars. When in residence, the British soldiers reigned supreme, and they viewed the Irish Catholic as subhuman.

They dismissed the famine as a blessing on the ignorant peasants and saw it as a way to reduce their pitiful numbers. It enabled the British to make more room for the large plantations they were populating with Scots. They saw the Irish Catholics as a belligerent and troublesome lot clinging fanatically to their pagan relics and saints. They boldly took the housing and food supply, requisitioning whatever they chose, including the women. Any disturbance from a villager would mean transportation or death, so fear and trepidation walked among all.

Darcy was concerned about Father Etienne. He boldly passed through the village at night, disobeying the curfew and ministered to the spiritually hungry. He believed more than ever his flock needed him, and single-mindedly he ignored his own welfare to meet their needs. Father Etienne did take one precaution, though. He dressed in lay clothes. It had been many years since he had worn secular garments, and in truth, he found it amusing.

He appeared at the door of the Mullin's cottage one night, as Darcy sat at the spinning wheel. There was a sharp knock on the door and everyone jumped. A hush fell over the room as Keenan opened the door.

There stood Father Etienne dressed in a linen shirt and breeches. Casey Mulligan insisted that the priest wear his famous wedding boots so Father Etienne even had the look of a gentleman. At first, no one recognized him. He shut the door, as they all stared at him trying to put a name to the face. With wide eyes, Darcy finally said, "Oh, Heaven and Earth! It's Father Etienne!"

Collectively they gasped, and then everyone laughed. Keenan shook the priest's hand and ushered him to a chair saying, "We heard that you were no longer dressing in robes, Father. Still we did not recognize you. You look very different."

"It has been many years since I have dressed in lay clothes. It's rather novel," he confessed.

"If you are caught being out after curfew, you must not say a word, Father Etienne," Teila warned. "If they hear your accent, they will take you."

Darcy sat at the spinning wheel, still in shock, as she studied her friend's transformation. She began to realize Father Etienne had been at one time simply, Etienne a man like any other, laughing, perhaps drinking in a tavern with other men. It occurred to her that she didn't even know his full name.

He could feel her eyes burning into him. "Surprised to see that I am a man, Darcy?"

She knew that he had guessed her thoughts, and to cover her embarrassment she said, "I think it's disgraceful."

Stifling a smile, he said, "It has been a long time since I have heard confessions here. Who would like to go first? You perhaps, Darcy?"

Father Etienne may have taken the vow of chastity, but he was not naive, and he guessed that in the six months since Bran had returned, Darcy had done more than hold hands. Wedding plans must be discussed, and he suspected that her terse attitude toward him tonight may have something to do with a guilty conscience.

He heard confessions from the Mullins and then signaled to Darcy to come over to the fireside corner where he had pushed two chairs off privately to one side. Darcy froze. She could not tell Father Etienne the sins she had been committing with Bran.

"Darcy," he said firmly, "It has been months since I have heard your confession. You must relieve your mind and your soul."

Reluctantly, she walked over to him and sitting on the edge of the chair, said quietly, "I cannot."

"Why are you uncomfortable telling me your sins?"

"Because I refuse to 'go and sin no more.' "

Father Etienne nodded. "It is for this reason, Darcy, that I think we should discuss wedding plans for you and Bran."

Father Etienne read the panic in her face. She took a breath and nodded. "I am in agreement, Father. Bran told me that there must be a wedding soon because we will be leaving on the next vessel for France. I suppose a wedding would be in order."

His eyebrows shot up in surprise. "Not exactly spoken like an eager, blushing bride."

"How would you have me act? Like some lovesick girl?" she said sharply. Realizing her tone had been harsh, she shifted in her seat and softened her voice. "I am well aware that true love is not remotely similar to the silly musings of the poets or the lyrics of the troubadours."

Father Etienne raised an eyebrow and sat back. It had never occurred to him that maybe she was not in love with Bran, and he suspected that maybe she had not admitted it to herself yet.

"If there is ever anything, Darcy, anything at all, just put a red candle in the window, and I shall come."

He rose from his chair to leave. After saying good night to the Mullins, he looked at Darcy one last time. She had not moved. She was still sitting on the edge of the chair staring straight ahead.

Chapter 9

Major Jeffrey Russell sat up in bed and stretched. After pulling on his breeches and boots, he pulled the covers back, and with a resounding crack, slapped the bare buttocks of the plump redhead sleeping next to him. She yelped and jumped up, looking at him with surprise and then started to laugh. She pressed her breast against his arm and said, "Come back to bed. It's too early."

The sun was beginning to lighten the room, and Maggie O'Rourke could see the officer's handsome profile in the dim light of morning. She felt his indecision and pressed closer to him. He jerked his arm away and snapped, "Get away from me. I need to think."

"Think about what? The days drag on and on and the nights are an endless rotation of drinking and whoring. All one has to look forward to in Kilkerry, Ireland, is a headache the next day."

"Damn it! I wish those orders would come for us to quit this god-forsaken place," he grumbled.

Maggie kept quiet. She liked this young, ambitious major, and she hoped that when the troops left, he would take her with him.

Women found Major Russell attractive. At twenty-five, he was in the prime of his life. He was tall with broad shoulders and sandy blond hair which he kept tied back in a club. He had a fine, aristocratic face and a keen mind, but there was a quality of cold steel in his character which prevented him from being likable. Surprisingly, it was this ruthlessness that enticed Maggie O'Rourke. His dangerous nature appealed to her.

Major Russell was the commanding officer of the encampment in Kilkerry, and from the beginning, he resented being buried in this backward Irish community. He longed for a commission in which he could exploit his power and provide sustenance for his overblown pride. Hoping that a challenge might improve his character, Major Russell's wealthy parents refused to buy him a more prestigious military commission. He hated his rank and was consumed with vindictiveness and smothered rage. The young officer was looking for an opportunity to gain attention and a name for himself. He believed if lives were lost in the process, it was of no consequence.

Major Russell looked out the window at a mother and her four children walking to the well. Stupid people, he thought, reproducing so fast that they will starve again.

He felt warm skin make contact with his back and realized that Maggie was pressing her body against him. Feeling desire mount, he turned and said, "Damn it all, there's nothing else to do."

* * *

It had been several nights since Darcy had seen Father Etienne at the Mullin cottage, and she still rankled when she thought about their last conversation. Maybe she wasn't an enthusiastic bride, but she was no longer a child filled with unrealistic dreams either. Marriage is a convenience, and it is folly to believe it is anything more. He had no business making observations about anyone's love affairs, having no first-hand experience himself.

Darcy continued to accept her role as Bran's fiancé, but she could not give him her heart. This aloofness fueled Bran's desire. Lusting for the unattainable, he thrilled in the chase. Eight years ago, he had left an eager girl standing on the road waving goodbye, and when he returned he found a beautiful woman holding him at arm's length.

To the casual observer, Darcy appeared devoted and affectionate. The town saw a handsome, happy couple, and many thought their courtship was idyllic, but the undercurrents of dissatisfaction flowed in them both, distressing one and exciting the other.

They took great care to conceal their trysting spot near Glinnish Stream. It was a lovely little secluded area of green shrubbery bordered by wild fuchsias. When in bloom, the deep splashes of pink enveloped their bed of moss, drowning them in brilliant color. The spot was quiet with only the murmuring of the stream in the distance. They met there every day just before sunset. The curfew imposed by the soldiers limited them to these few moments together, and Darcy would arrive a few minutes early to drink in the surroundings. Bran would arrive, overcome with desire and be so engrossed in his own passion that he would forget Darcy. He would drive forward in a hot, selfish rush until he was completely sated.

The scenario was always the same, and Darcy believed that this was all that love had to offer. She found Bran's lovemaking occasionally satisfying but usually far too hasty and rough. She became resigned to the fact that sex was simply something to endure. Once it was over, she would put it from her mind and turn back to her books.

Darcy continued to receive reading material from Father Etienne, but she missed their talks together. Meeting him was far too dangerous, and she began to feel restless and irritable. On every front, she felt confined.

She returned to her walks along the coast, gazing across the water as if it held the answer. It was here where she could truly forget everything and allow her mind to drift and transport her to places offering freedom and a chance to set her own course. She chided herself for not being satisfied, but she could no longer deny the longing.

On her return from the cliffs one sunny afternoon, she encountered Bran climbing the abbey hill. He had been working hard, and sweat soaked his shirt. Darcy felt a pang of desire when she saw the outline of his broad chest under the wet material. His masculinity and rugged appeal usually helped Darcy build passion, but today he was frowning, and he was devoid of appeal.

He strode up to her and grabbed her roughly by the arms. "What are doing, girl? You can't be up here alone."

"I'm all right," she said frowning and jerking away from him. "I must come up here every now and then."

"Why? To do what?" he asked suspiciously.

"To walk and to be alone with my thoughts."

"What thoughts? I don't understand you," he growled.

"Don't try," she replied and began to walk down the bluff.

He watched her with his jaw clenched. She could be raped up here. The thought of another man defiling his property enraged him. Bran decided he must marry Darcy immediately. She was far too strong-willed, and he could hold her no other way.

That evening Father Etienne stepped out of the home of Seamus Donnelly and looked around cautiously. He pulled up the hood on his woolen brat and started down the road, searching for red candles burning in windows. His visit to the Donnelly's' home had been to give Last Rites to a seriously ill child. When an older member of his flock joined Jesus, Father Etienne felt peace, but the death of a youngster always disturbed him. Even without the famine, life continued to be hard for the villagers. The added strain of having the soldiers in residence brought the villagers to the breaking point.

He heard some raucous laughter on the road and spied some British soldiers, obviously drunk, making their way home. Father Etienne silently stepped into the shadow of the high cross on the town well and observed them as they stumbled past. The king's soldiers were becoming bored with this sleepy hamlet, and he knew that trouble was brewing.

Once the merrymakers were safe inside, Father Etienne resumed his rounds. There was a red candle burning in the cottage of Casey Kennedy. Several families resided there because their homes had been requisitioned by the British. Christmas Eve was the last time he had seen a candle in that home.

He remembered seeing Darcy at the Christmas party. She wore her mother's red dress, so dramatic against her white skin and dark hair. Bran was there too and others and he nodded his head in greeting to Father Etienne when she came in.

Darcy said, "Happy Christmas, Father Etienne! Do come in."

Mrs. Kennedy came to greet him with a huge smile. It was an honor to entertain a priest on Christmas Eve. He ran his eyes over the platters of sausage and loaves of soda bread, potatoes, and root vegetables but what dominated the board was a lovely, round cake on a footed plate decorated with a sprig of holly.

Darcy picked up a plate and cut a piece of the cake for him.

"This is no ordinary cake. It is filled with small charms, and each charm predicts the future. It is fun to see what everyone gets." She handed him some cake. "Now eat your cake and see if you get a charm."

He took a bite and said, "I must take care not to break a tooth."

"Aye, that is something I forgot to warn you about," she chuckled.

After the second bite, he spit something into his hand saying, "This is a most undignified tradition, Darcy."

Leaning over, she peeked into his hand and saw a small pewter bell and cried, "Oh, a bell for betrothal!"

Surprised, he said, "I think not!"

They laughed, and then it was Darcy's turn. On the first bite, she discovered a small thimble. "The thimble is a very good charm. It brings hope for the year."

"Our charms were mixed up, Darcy. You have the betrothal charm. I'll take the thimble. I need every bit of hope that I can get right now."

The smile dropped from her face. Laughter distracted them, and they looked at the men who were having brandy and telling jokes.

"Bran's stories of the American Colonies may be amusing for you," Darcy offered.

"I don't believe he is comfortable with me."

"He doesn't know what to say to you. I too was uncertain of what to talk about with a priest."

"We eventually found common ground. Didn't we?" he said. "Have you told him yet that you read?"

"No, but he will allow it as long as I don't neglect his needs."

Darcy appeared to be on the defensive. "I have known Bran all my life. He and Liam kept me alive during The Hunger, and there is an impenetrable bond that forms between people that have endured suffering together. I believe that our love is rooted in that bond, and no one can break it."

He knew she was looking for a fight, and he wasn't going to give one to her. Now more than ever, he believed Darcy was marrying Bran out of obligation.

The flame from the red candle flickered in the window, bringing Father Etienne back to the present. He stepped forward to knock on the Kennedy's door. He knew before long a red candle would appear in Darcy's window too.

Chapter 10

When Father Etienne entered the Kennedy cottage, he was greeted by a tiny, middle-aged woman. Her hair was tied back in a tight bun, and she darted a look out the door saying quietly, "Do come in, Father. We've been expecting you. Bran placed the candle in the window for you, but he is not back yet."

Father Etienne hung his cloak on a peg and said, "Why don't I hear some confessions in the meantime?"

Wiping her hands on her apron, Molly Kennedy nodded and called upstairs for her boys. She reminded him of a little bird darting nervously around the cottage, picking up dishes and straightening up the room. She turned to him and said with a proud smile, "I've news, Father. We will have a new one for you to baptize in about seven months."

"That *is* good news. I'm very happy for you, Mrs. Kennedy. Are the men at the meeting tonight?"

"Aye, they'll be back soon. Ever since the troops set down here, I can't sleep nights, worrying about my Paddy. I don't know what I'd do if anything happened to him and now with another babe on the way."

At that moment, three boys tumbled down the stairs, pushing and shoving and roaring with laughter. Molly gasped and flew at them saying, "What are you knuckleheads thinking? There's a priest sitting here in our cottage, and you're acting like good-for-nothing ruffians. Stand up straight and address Father Etienne properly."

They snapped to attention, straightening their clothes and greeting him cordially. Molly nodded her head with approval. To break the ice before confessions, he told the boys a joke about the British soldiers, and they dissolved into hearty laughter.

Shortly after confession, four men burst into the cottage, slamming the door behind them. They were wearing long black cloaks with hoods. They blew out the candles and Paddy darted to the window, peeking out. "Do you think they saw us?

"Don't be stupid," said Bran. "If they'd seen us, they would be searching the house right now."

Paddy turned to Father Etienne, "You see, we are not only breaking curfew, but there are four of us which is unlawful assembly."

Bran moved over to Father Etienne and said quietly, "I would like to talk to you privately."

Father Etienne nodded and followed Bran to the back of the cottage near a badly decaying barn. Three walls of the rickety structure remained, and several chickens scattered about clucking and scolding. The wind howled through the structure, snapping their cloaks, and Father Etienne looked up apprehensively at the walls.

Bran looked up for a moment too and then said abruptly, "I want you to marry Darcy and me right away."

Father Etienne frowned and sat down on the stone foundation. "What's the hurry?"

"I love her," Bran said, gruffly, pushing his hair away from his face. "I want her to be my wife, of course."

"Of course, of course," the priest echoed. "Darcy has consented?"

"Why wouldn't she?" asked Bran defensively.

Father Etienne studied this large raw-boned man. He had rugged good looks and sharp blue eyes, but he lacked polish and intellect. "You know, Bran," he said smiling and crossing his arms. "We've never really had a chance to get to know one another. I was born in the American Colonies. Tell me about your experience there."

"What is it you want to know?" asked Bran, shifting impatiently from one foot to the other.

"Oh, I don't know," said Father Etienne, as he paused to think. "Who held your indentured service?"

"I was sold," Bran said sharply, "if that's what you mean, to the East India Company. They have a contract with the king to buy prisoners for labor in the New World."

Father Etienne saw the man's fists clench. He continued, "What sort of labor did you do?"

"Shipbuilding, they treated us like dogs, working us twenty hours a day and fed us less food than what I had during The Hunger. They used whips if we didn't move fast enough. Sometimes they locked us in a hole, but I was smart I learned ways to avoid it."

Father Etienne stroked his beard and nodded. "I see. They hated you at first, but then they learned to respect you."

Bran's eyes narrowed and he said, "I vowed when my servitude was up, I would never be enslaved again, and the only way to be assured of that is to have money and power."

"You'll not get rich in Kilkerry," said Father Etienne.

"You'd be surprised. If you have brains and a plan, anything is possible. I have what it takes."

Father Etienne could see that Bran was impressed with himself. He decided to stoke the fire.

"From the first time we met, Bran, I knew that there was something different about you."

A proud smile flickered around Bran's lips. "Of course, I'm different. I have plans. This village is filled with fools. I know that I am different and so is Darcy. That's exactly why Darcy is the only suitable mate for me in this pathetic--" Bran stopped, and his nostrils flared when he realized the priest was baiting him. "You son of a bitch," he snarled. "Don't think you can stop me."

Father Etienne's eyebrows shot up. "Ah, blind ambition."

"Call it what you want. No one will stand in my way, not even a priest."

Father Etienne chuckled and stood up. "You have never met a Jesuit."

* * *

Major Russell examined his playing cards and let out a puff of smoke. His black, polished boots rested carelessly on the top of the table, and his jacket was slung over the back of his chair. Several other officers were playing cards with him in front of a fire in the O'Hearn cottage. A regular stood guard outside the door.

The cottage no longer resembled a home. It had the cold, bare look of headquarters. It was the epitome of British military efficiency. Sitting across from the fireplace was a highly polished mahogany desk with papers stacked neatly, a few barrels and crates and some muskets propped in a corner.

Major Russell yawned and threw a card down. He was bored and so were his men. Even the drinking and whoring began to bore them. A few instances of rape had been brought to his attention, but this did not disturb him. He understood the men were trying to entertain themselves.

He had no knowledge of the smuggling operation. As far as he was concerned, the town of Kilkerry was completely law abiding. He speculated that there may be a few Catholic rituals in practice, but for the most part, he had not witnessed any outbursts or unlawful assembly. He believed that the people were too stupid to be capable of any conspiracy.

Suddenly, the door swung open and the guard informed Major Russell that there was a villager to see him. He looked at his officers, and they shrugged their shoulders.

Bran Moynahan stepped into the room. Several of the officers jumped to their feet, intimidated by the man's size, but Major Russell did not move a muscle. His boots remained on the table as he scrutinized Bran. "What do you want?"

Bran removed his cloak, hanging it on a peg. Completely astonished with this gesture of audacity, Russell removed his boots from the table and looked Bran up and down. "Please make yourself at home. May we offer you some tea?" he said sarcastically.

The men snickered and Bran said, "If you want your promotion, you will treat me with respect, Russell. I have information."

Major Russell's eyes narrowed and he looked at the officers. "Get out," he ordered. The soldiers picked up their jackets and muskets and left the cottage. Turning to Bran, he demanded, "Who are you?"

"My name's Moynahan. I've just returned from the Colonies where I was bound to the East India Company.

When my seven years were up, I agreed for a price, to return to County Kerry and expose a smuggling operation for the East India Company. It's an agreement with the Crown."

The major's eyes narrowed and he leaned forward. "Prove it."

Bran produced signed papers from Russell's commanding officer ordering him to cooperate fully with Moynahan. Russell looked up from the paper and ran his eyes over Bran.

Bran sniffed and lifted his chin. He felt a surge of power. "The Crown needs wool to clothe their troops during the war in America. The French are stealing this wool for *their* troops, right here in British waters."

"Here on the shores of Kilkerry?"

"Aye."

"How often?"

"Every few months."

It took a moment for Russell to absorb the news. Then he stood up and put his jacket on. "When is the next shipment?"

"In a few nights."

"You will take me to their meeting place," he demanded.

"I will," said Bran, mentally counting his money.

Chapter 11

It was a warm, cloudless morning as Darcy returned from the pastures to discuss spring shearing with Keenan. Around the clock she worked on the farm, picking up extra chores and doing her best to attend to Teila and the children. Ever since she delivered her baby, Teila could not get out of bed, and she had grown frail. She had developed a persistent cough, which sapped every bit of strength from her frail body. Although her skin had always been pale, it now looked transparent.

"I don't think that we should delay the shearing any longer," Keenan said. "I know Teila wanted to help, but she is not strong enough. "The furrows on Keenan's face had grown deeper lately. Darcy and Bridget O'Hearn worked constantly, nursing Teila, helping in the fields and tending the children.

Today, Teila sat by the open door while Bridget made their midday meal. She watched Darcy and Keenan discuss shearing, and she was pleased to see how strong Darcy had become. Liam had beaten Darcy physically, but he hadn't touched her spirit, and she emerged from the ordeal even stronger.

For hours on end, Darcy labored in the fields, and the springtime sun turned her skin a golden brown. She rose before the sun and went to bed long after it had set. In addition to her generous help, Teila suspected that Darcy was trying to avoid the iron grip of Bran.

There was no doubt in Teila's mind that he was determined to own Darcy and display her as a prize trophy. She had approached Darcy about it several times, only to be shut out with a curt reply. She had been irritable lately, and Teila guessed that her independent spirit was starting to rebel.

She knew that one day, with or without Bran, Darcy would leave Kilkerry and find her way in the world. Although she would be heartbroken, she knew Darcy must go.

Teila was content with the fact that she herself, would not go beyond the abbey churchyard. She sighed and sat back, closing her eyes. She could see the green hills bathed in sunlight and the ever present abbey. When she opened her eyes once more, she saw Bran striding up the road. Teila noted his broad shoulders and thick blonde hair. He had animal magnetism, but he seemed to lack character, and she certainly did not trust him.

Darcy started down the road to meet him. He reached Darcy and put her face in his hands, kissing her possessively.

"Why are you here at this time of the day, Bran?" Darcy asked.

"Michael told me yesterday that the French vessel will be here soon."

Darcy's stomach jumped. She realized now that the courtship had drawn to a close and marriage was about to occur. The sunshine, which had seemed so warm and comforting a moment ago, now felt stifling and hot. She licked her dry lips and said, "When will it be here?"

"Tomorrow night, darlin', " said Bran as he kissed her forehead. He was pleased with himself. Everything was going as planned, and soon he would have money, power, and a beautiful wife on his arm.

From Darcy's standpoint, it was her chance to escape Kilkerry and travel the world. Bran was back, promising her a new life, yet she could not understand why she felt so empty.

"I've spoken with Father Etienne already," Bran stated. "He has agreed to marry us, but he insists that you speak with him tonight. Then he will marry us in the morning." He pulled her chin up, kissed her and murmured, "The whole world will know tomorrow that you belong to me."

Darcy packed for the journey that evening all the time wrestling with her doubts. Everyone was quiet around the dinner table, feeling Darcy's anxiety. Even the small children sensed that there was something wrong. Darcy picked at her food and almost fell off her chair when there was a knock on the door. She stopped, took a breath, and opened it. It was Father Etienne. "I'd rather not talk here," Darcy said. "Let's go outside."

They walked to the back of the cottage and seated themselves on a stone wall in the moonlight. Father Etienne was the first to speak. "I wanted to see you for several reasons tonight. First of all, I want to offer my best wishes. Bran's return was an answer to my prayers, Darcy."

"It was?" she said, surprised.

He nodded. "It was always my secret torment that I had awakened your mind only to leave you alone and isolated in a world devoid of books and education. Now you can escape. Bran can take you to Paris or Philadelphia, places where you can continue your learning. He can take charge of everything in your life while you only have to worry about enriching your mind."

Darcy tried to make sense of this sudden turn of events, and she said suspiciously, "I thought that you were going to talk me out of marrying him."

"No, I would never do that. You know your own mind. Since the ship departs tomorrow night, I shall marry you in the morning."

She started to say something, and he put his hands up, "I'm sorry, Darcy I have many engagements tonight. I must be going."

Darcy's eyes grew large. She was furious. She was about to embark on the greatest journey of her life, and he was too busy to talk.

"Aren't you going to ask me if I love him?" she asked indignantly.

"Why should I?" he said. Pulling his hood up, he squeezed her hand and said, "Good night."

When Darcy returned to the cottage, her green eyes were flashing, and she marched straight up to bed. She tossed and turned all night, and when she finally fell asleep, she had dreams of Bran holding her so tightly that she suffocated.

The next morning, she was stiff and tired. After dressing, she fed the children and changed the linens on Teila's bed. Teila felt the tension but said nothing.

That afternoon, when Darcy was weeding the garden, Bran stole up quietly behind her and grabbed her waist. Startled, she stood up, and he yanked her into his arms kissing her lustily. His blonde hair fell in tangles about his face and his tan chest was visible through his open shirt.

"Come. I want to make love to my bride," he murmured.

"No, Bran! Not now. We can wait."

He kissed her neck and said, "You need to get used to me being in charge."

Taking her hand, he led her up the hill to Glinnish Stream. At the entrance to their trysting place, he picked Darcy up and carried her in, setting her down on a bed of moss. Bran made love to her in his usual hasty manner and in a rush of passion he was done. Darcy was glad it was over. She sat up and began to dress while Bran dozed.

She looked down at him as she tied her gown, and suddenly she remembered all the years he had taken care of her when she was a child. He had fed her and kept her safe in those days. Together they had survived, and in all the years she had known him, he had never once been cruel to her.

A wave of affection washed over her, and Darcy brushed the hair from his face. "Bran?" she said.

"Hmm?"

"Did Liam ever tell you that I know how to read?"

"What?" he said drowsily.

"Do you know that I can read, Bran?"

"Darlin'," he said, raising himself up onto one elbow. "You don't have to make things up. Everyone knows that you landed Bran Moynahan on your good looks, not your brains." He gave her nipple a playful pinch and lay back down closing his eyes again.

Darcy stared at him thunderstruck. His words burned a scar into her more damaging than any punch. Her heart started to pound, and she said, "You're right, Bran, I have no brains. I was stupid enough to think that you were worthy of me." She stood up, pushing the branches aside and stepped out of the bower. She could hear Bran calling her, but she did not respond. A rush of fresh air filled her lungs, and she realized how stifling it had been back there in the darkness alone with him.

Chapter 12

Darcy looked over her shoulder as she walked along the bluff toward the abbey. She knew that Bran might follow her, so she quickened her pace. Then she began to run. She could not allow him to catch up with her and try to change her mind.

When she reached the ruins, she was breathless but feeling free. For the first time in her life she felt completely independent, and even though she would not be on that ship, she no longer felt as if she were a prisoner in Kilkerry. She would now make her own choices and be in charge of her own future. The thought of Bran dictating to her was unthinkable, and she was surprised that it took her this long to realize it. *I will be in charge, in charge of my own mind and my own body.*

She stopped and leaned against the abbey wall, thinking back to her last conversation with Father Etienne. He was responsible for planting the doubt in her mind about Bran. He knew how dearly she held her independence, and he cleverly orchestrated her epiphany.

Darcy looked in the direction of his cave and then scanned the meadow. Bran was nowhere in sight, and she decided to pay Father Etienne a visit. This day belonged to her, and she would do with it exactly as she pleased.

The wind was refreshing as she walked along the cliffs, and it combed through her hair leaving the fresh smell of sea air in her tresses. Grabbing her skirt, she climbed down the rock face to the mouth of the cave, and as she landed on the flat stone ledge, she called, "Good morning!"

Father Etienne looked up from his reading with a wide smile and said, "Well, good morning to you!"

Darcy noticed two chairs and a table on the ledge. A small crock held yellow gorse. "Are you expecting company, Father?" she asked.

"Yes, I've been expecting *you,* Darcy."

A slow smile of recognition came over her face, and she began to laugh, shaking her finger at him. "You are very sure of yourself."

He smiled and then held a chair for her. Darcy took a deep breath of the fresh air and sat down. With the ocean below her and the wide sky above her, it was like sitting on a cloud. She remembered the first day she and Father Etienne had dined here almost two years ago. It had been a day like this--warm, sunny and filled with hope.

Father Etienne placed some bread and cheese on her plate, and as a special surprise, he produced a handful of wild strawberries. When Darcy saw the plump fruit, she clapped her hands marveling at how this day had been filled with unexpected treasures. The priest took his seat and said, "You were just thinking about our first meal here together, weren't you?'

"That I was," she said nodding her head. "You had only just arrived. We hardly knew one another."

"A lot has happened since that day."

"Yes it has, but I must know something, Father. Did you really pray for Bran's return?"

He wiped his mouth and nodded. "Everything I said to you is true. I did pray for his return, but when he arrived, I could see that you had moved far beyond what he could offer you."

"Then why did you encourage the marriage?"

"If you think back, I never said anything to encourage it. I allowed you to make all the decisions yourself, Darcy. I was well aware of your independent spirit and stubborn nature, and any hint of disapproval from me would have sent you directly into marriage just to spite me."

"You know me too well," she said smiling and shaking her head. Darcy picked up a strawberry and studied its beauty. "Bran could never understand me. He would think it folly that I could see this strawberry as something more than a piece of fruit," and she popped the juicy morsel into her mouth.

Father Etienne frowned. "Beware, Darcy. Do not underestimate his resolve. I believe that he is incapable of love and will stop at nothing to satisfy his own ambitions."

Darcy shrugged, as the wind lifted her dark tresses, "Well, he needn't include me in his master plan any longer." It didn't seem right to worry about anything dark and threatening that day, and they watched the seagulls circling off the coast, gliding up and down on the breeze.

"Have you been happy here, Etienne?"

He looked up at her, aware that she had dropped his title. Turning his attention to the rugged cliffs and the brilliant green hills beyond, he mused, "I've never been happier anywhere. Your strange and beautiful land has entwined my heart like a vine, and I will never be free of it."

"I'm glad," Darcy said smiling.

"I have the feeling that I may never leave Ireland," he mused.

"Oh, that would be wonderful! We all need you."

"You will be the one to leave, Darcy. You must leave. Your destination is beyond these cliffs."

She dragged her eyes away from the bluffs and gazed across the ocean feeling the flow of the tides, "Perhaps, but today we are here dining on beautiful red strawberries by the sea, you and me, together, on top of a cloud."

* * *

Bran returned to the village searching for Darcy. He was not particularly concerned. He knew Darcy had a hot temper and could never resist his charms for long.

He went to the Mullins' house first, awakening Teila, rudely demanding information from her and Bridget. He boldly searched the loft, paying little heed to their assertions that she was nowhere in the cottage.

Next, he ventured into the pastures to question Keenan. As the day progressed, Bran became increasingly agitated. He believed that Darcy was weak and that she would eventually succumb to his will, but he could not persuade her if he could not find her. If he could find her before sundown, he would have time to marry her and board the French vessel tonight.

He went repeatedly from the abbey to the cliff walk and back to town again.

After demanding her whereabouts from almost everyone, he encountered Liam trudging down the road carrying a sack of potatoes on his back. He thought it unlikely that she would seek refuge with him, but he must exhaust every possibility.

"Where is Darcy? Have you seen her today?"

"No, but I'd bet that she's with that meddlesome priest," growled Liam.

Bran clenched his fists and growled. *Why didn't I think of that?* With his heart pounding, he turned toward the bluff.

Liam shouted after him, "Don't be surprised if you find them abed, Moynahan!"

Daylight was fading fast, and when he reached the abbey, it held nothing more than the wind. He dashed along the cliff walk and climbed down the rock face to the Father Etienne's cave. That too was empty. Enraged, he turned over the table. Standing there panting, he remembered that this had been his home a long time ago. He swallowed hard and looked around with a growing tightness in his chest.

Shrugging off the memories, he climbed back up to the cliff top to resume his search. A thick fog crept in along the coast as Bran ran back to town. He had one last hope of finding Darcy at the Kennedy cottage where a meeting was scheduled tonight. As he entered the house, his eyes scanned the room for Darcy. He found her sitting by the window, her hair pulled back in a knot, wearing a black, woolen cape suitable for traveling. Her eyes rested on him with a look of icy indifference.

It was crowded and stuffy in the cottage, and the meeting was about to begin. All the necessary precautions were reviewed by Michael, including a warning about the fog. He turned to Darcy and said, "It will be very difficult for the ship to see your beacon tonight.

You must light several lanterns and try to get at least one up as high as possible."

"So," thought Bran, "she thinks that she will be the beacon tonight. Before the hour is up, she will be boarding the ship with me."

Bran had no feelings of remorse, as he watched his comrades file out of the cottage to get ready for tonight's shipment. Within a few short hours, every one of them would be at the mercy of the British soldiers. That was not of interest to him. What he wanted was a thick wad of British notes in his pocket and Darcy on the vessel heading for Paris.

Darcy saw Bran approaching as she was bending down to light her candles. "Darlin', I'm willing to forget about this afternoon. I know that you are just overexcited about the wedding, but you must put these silly worries to rest."

Darcy said nothing until she finished lighting her last lantern. She stood up and said, "I'm sorry, Bran, but you no longer figure into *my* plan."

He threw back his blonde head and let out a hearty guffaw. "Damn it, woman, you have spunk, and I love you for it."

Grabbing her waist, he pulled her close placing his wet lips on her neck. Darcy pushed away, picked up her lanterns and walked out the door. It suddenly occurred to Bran that allowing her to proceed as the beacon tonight meant that she would lose her freedom, maybe even her life.

"Darcy, stop! There is something--"

He took three large steps over to her and grabbed her wrist. When she looked at him, he saw the contempt in her eyes. He had seen that look a thousand times in the eyes of his jailers. It was something he could not abide.

"What?" she questioned, impatiently.

Bran hesitated, and then he said, "Uh, nothing, nothing. It's the fog. The fog is dangerous tonight."

Darcy turned on her heel and left Bran standing in the open doorway. "Go to your death," he murmured, as the mist swallowed her up.

He knew that he must hurry if he were to catch the ship tonight. He hastened to the Kennedy home to gather his belongings. Bran found the cottage empty and bounded up the steps, throwing a few belongings into a bundle and tying it tightly. Getting down on his knees, he ripped some stitches from his mattress and reached inside, pulling out a fistful of notes. He stuffed them deep within his pockets. *This is all I really need to get the respect I deserve, and I will certainly never be hungry again.*

He stopped a moment and did not move. Usually, Bran refused to think of the famine, but after seeing the cave yesterday, the memories suddenly flooded him. He could see little Liam bending over gathering kelp and Darcy's frail little body climbing up the rocks to the mouth of the cave. Suddenly, his eyes widened, and his heart beat furiously. The drumming grew louder and louder. Visions of his childhood friends flashed before his eyes, and he whispered, "Oh my god, oh my god, what have I done!"

He walked to the wash basin and retched. He splashed water on his face to steady himself, but the drumming intensified. He stumbled down the stairs and tripped over a chair, sprawling onto the dirt floor. He could not see or hear anything beyond the infernal roaring in his ears. He pulled himself to his feet running blindly into the night fog. He could think of nothing but ridding himself of the roaring in his ears. He staggered through the mist, crying out in fear and pain. He spied a red candle on a windowsill, and his heart leaped.

Redemption! He stumbled over to the cottage and released three heavy blows against the door.

A woman answered, her jaw dropping. Frowning, she turned into the house and cried, "Father, come quickly."

Bran saw it was the black robe of the priest, and his only thought was to unburden himself. He grabbed Father Etienne and roared, "I am going to burn!"

"What are you talking about?" Father Etienne said.

"Liam, Darcy, the others--soldiers--for money," confessed Bran. He slid down Father Etienne's body, landing on his knees, sobbing uncontrollably.

The priest's eyes widened as he realized that Bran had turned informant, and he gasped, "What have you done, man?"

Hoping that it wasn't too late, Father Etienne broke away from Bran and dashed into the fog, praying that there was still time to warn the smugglers of the ambush.

Bran was sprawled out on the ground, tearing at the sod beneath him and wailing. After a while, the roaring in his ears slowed and then stopped entirely. He pulled himself to his feet and wiped his nose on his sleeve. His face was streaked with tears, and he was covered with mud, but he felt better. In fact, he felt much better, and he reached down for the money in his pants. It was still there. He realized it was too late to catch the French vessel but with money to spend, anything was possible. With a light heart and heavy pockets, he stood up and left Kilkerry forever.

Chapter 13

The density of the fog alarmed Darcy. Using her memory to find her way to the abbey was the only way through the blinding mist. The fog was less upon the bluff, and she had renewed hopes that the ship may see her lanterns after all. She climbed onto a crumbling stone wall in one corner of the abbey and placed one lantern down. Using great care, she walked to the cliff's edge and placed another lantern on top of a large boulder. The last lantern she would take to the top of the high cross in the monastery churchyard.

Darcy strained her eyes and looked out to sea. Nothing was visible, and all she could do was hope that the candlelight would penetrate the mist and signal the French vessel. She could have been on that ship tonight heading for France, maybe even Paris, but she had no regrets.

The high cross of the churchyard was barely visible, and the mist swirled around the sculpture as if it were a phantom. She loved the Celtic design adorning it, and similar to the small cross on her neck, the high cross was covered with lovely, flowing patterns and a circle on the crossbar representing the circle of life and immortality of the soul.

As Darcy stood staring at the cross, a sense of uneasiness crept over her. She reached down to clutch her little pewter cross. Deciding that she must focus on her work and not allow her mind to wander, Darcy asked the Almighty's pardon and pulled herself up to the top of the cross. The stone was slippery, and she struggled to the top, stretching tall, thrusting her lantern into the air.

Suddenly, a hand yanked her ankle. She clawed at the air and came tumbling down, hitting her hip on the hard stone of the crossbar, and then the ground. The impact of the fall knocked her breathless.

Two soldiers jerked her to her feet and began dragging her toward the abbey. She stumbled along blindly with a sharp pain in her hip, choking and gasping for air as they pushed her.

"Hurry up, you ignorant bitch!"

As they swept her along, she tripped sprawling to the ground, and the men lost their grip. Seizing the opportunity, Darcy dashed toward the cliff walk, terror driving her to run faster than she ever had in her life. She could hear them shouting and swearing behind her. Darcy's knowledge of the terrain allowed her to run full speed in the blinding fog, even though she was bruised and shaken. On and on she ran until she could go no farther. She doubled over, panting and struggled to listen. The only sound she heard were the waves breaking. She realized now that her comrades were walking into an ambush.

Suddenly, the pounding of hooves sent her bolting toward Glinnish Grove. Darcy was no match for men on horseback. The thunder of the horse's hooves behind her roared in her ears, and one of the soldiers grabbed her hair, pulling her up off her feet. Darcy struggled madly trying to free herself. The horses slowed their pace, and the men jumped down, pushing her to the ground. She felt a sharp pain as one of them dug a knee into her back and bound her hands tightly. She thought her lungs would explode. Lifting her like a sack of meal, they threw her over the back of one of the horses and carried her to the abbey.

"Put her here, Cooper," ordered a fat, wheezy sergeant. "We must tie her to something before we help catch the others."

It was exactly as she had feared, the owlers were being ambushed. Cooper, a skinny, pimply-faced regular, dragged Darcy inside the abbey, not far from the lantern she had placed there earlier. The mist crawled across the floor like a poisonous vapor. Darcy had never seen the abbey look more hideous. Terrified and desperate, she called for the monks, asking them to intercede as guardians giving her sanctuary from these violent men.

"Get over there, and I don't want you looking!" shouted the fat sergeant to Cooper, as he unbuttoned his pants.

The young man moved away. Sergeant Beardsley pushed Darcy down onto her back and snarled, "I'm going to give you a pounding that you'll never forget," and he pulled up her skirt.

"No!" she screamed through her teeth, writhing on the floor.

Without the use of her hands, Darcy was helpless. As the man bore down upon her, he violated something deep within her. The hatred he unleashed on her was terrifying and the act humiliating.

After pounding her violently, Darcy heard him grunt, and the full weight of his huge body fell upon her. Initially, it knocked the air out of her lungs, but when her breathing returned, she could smell the greasy closeness of his hair and his foul breath. Filled with hatred, she lashed out the only way possible. She turned and tore his ear with her teeth. Beardsley roared and jumped to his feet, clutching his head.

As hard as he could, he kicked her in the ribs. "I should kill you, you filthy whore!"

He lunged at her once more, but Cooper grabbed him before he could touch her. "Not so fast," said Cooper. "I want a piece of her too."

Panting with rage, the sergeant yanked his arm away and walked over by the lantern to nurse his wound. Every fiber of Darcy's being was on alert. Her instincts said this younger soldier was even more dangerous than his predecessor.

He mumbled, "You'll not get the better of me."

He removed his belt and rolled Darcy face down, strapping it tightly around her neck. As he raped her, he tightened the belt slightly. She choked and sputtered, gasping for air and trying to cry out. Gradually he drew the belt tighter and tighter until Darcy lost consciousness. When he was finished, he tied her battered body to a headstone in the churchyard where she slumped over, unconscious.

Beardsley and Cooper mounted their horses and rode along the cliff walk to the precipice just above the smugglers. They knew that Major Russell and his men were waiting in the shadows below, watching the owlers while they made final preparations to meet the ship.

Oblivious to the danger, Michael O'Hearn supervised the loading of the curraghs. When everything was done, he shouted, "Jerry! Is your craft ready?"

"Aye, she's ready!" said Jerry Joyce, as he secured the last bundle of wool.

Other curraghs were being tied off, and the group was ready to row out and make the exchange with the French ship. Michael limped up and down the shore, looking for Bran. Stopping at the last craft, he pushed the damp hair off his forehead and said, "Liam is Moynahan with you?"

"No, I haven't seen him all night."

Michael shook his head and then climbed into the boat with Jerry Joyce. He shared his curragh with Jerry just as his father had done thirty years before him. Jerry was growing old, but he was a trustworthy and a faithful owler.

"Let's shove off!" shouted Michael, and the five narrow boats pushed into the sea. The fog was thick, but these men had operated many times under bad conditions. With their intimate knowledge of these waters, they could navigate blindfolded.

They pulled their crafts out a short distance, and suddenly like a specter, the ship loomed up before them.

They approached the hull and exchanged their goods while Michael coordinated the next rendezvous with the French. In no time they were rowing back to shore--another mission successfully completed.

Michael and Jerry rode up and down on the huge waves, guiding their craft smoothly toward shore. It took great skill to maneuver these narrow boats especially when they were loaded to capacity. They could easily topple, given any mishandling.

Michael felt better tonight than he could ever remember. Although the soldier's presence in the village had a sobering effect, he believed they would be leaving soon. He thought of Bridget. He was wildly in love with her. Everything was going well. She was in her sixth month carrying his child, the crops were good, and it appeared as if the village would prosper once more. To Michael O'Hearn life was at last worth living.

Liam and Paddy Kennedy were the first to return to shore. The owlers had chosen a small sandy cove surrounded by large rocks with a narrow access for the donkeys. It was a natural shelter from the strong winds and very secluded. But tonight behind those rocks, Major Russell waited with his men ready to strike. Every soldier present was eager to show these ignorant Irishmen what the British regular was made of, and at last, they could retaliate against these surly villagers.

The next three crafts were pulled onto shore, the men chattering back and forth. Next, they began to load the donkey carts with brandy.

Suddenly, Major Russell stood up and ordered, "In the name of His Majesty, King George the Second, you are under arrest."

The regulars sprang out of hiding and pointed their muskets at the stunned owlers. Complete silence fell as the group looked around helplessly.

Beardsley and Cooper stumbled down the hill to stand by Liam, who remained motionless by his cart. Kennedy was nearby, and the other men were scattered around the cove completely surrounded.

Cooper couldn't resist the temptation to taunt someone who was at his mercy, and under his breath, he said to Liam, "Irish fuckin' scum."

In a flash, Liam knocked Cooper's musket barrel into the air, discharging a round. Stunned, Cooper jumped back, but he was too late, Liam gathered him into his arms. "No, don't!" whined Cooper. "Don't! Please don't!"

Without a second thought, Liam pushed Cooper's head back, and with a resounding snap, broke his neck. He threw the twitching body to the ground and began to scramble up the hill, but he was stopped by a bullet in the shoulder from Major Russell's musket and one in his leg from a regular.

The scene dissolved into chaos. More shots were fired, and several men engaged in hand to hand combat while others fell to the ground, soaking the sand with their blood. One soldier, who attempted to restrain Kennedy, was smashed by an owler in the face with the blunt end of a heavy walking stick. Blood gushed from his nose, as he fell to his knees, spitting out teeth.

Taking full advantage of the limited visibility, Kennedy and two of the other smugglers bolted up the rocks and disappeared into the mist.

Major Russell was enraged. He had underestimated their determination. He noticed Liam lying face down in the sand and ground his boot heel on the bullet wound in his shoulder. Getting no reaction, he kicked him and ordered his men to gather their prisoners.

"My god, Michael, what's happening on shore?" asked Jerry at the sounds of gunfire.

"It's an ambush! The soldiers are on shore!" shouted Michael.

Upon hearing those words, Jerry panicked and began to turn the curragh back out to sea.

"No, Jerry! You'll swamp her!" exclaimed Michael, but Jerry didn't hear. In his terror, he continued to turn the craft. Everything seemed to Michael as if it were in slow motion; the shouts of the men on shore, the panic-stricken face of the old man and the slow overturning of the curragh. He saw Jerry tumble into the sea, and then he too hit the icy waters of the Atlantic.

The shock of the cold was so great that Michael involuntarily sucked in volumes of water. It roared in his ears, bubbling and swirling around him. He grabbed frantically for anything to hold onto, splashing on the surface, and then he saw a barrel. *"Salvation!"* But when he struggled to move his frail legs he found them paralyzed with cold, rendering him helpless in the icy water. He slid under once more and was churned about until he was unclear which way was up to the surface. Soon the waters felt warmer and the waves less turbulent. He thought maybe he would be swept to shore, riding this peaceful current, but then he realized his foolishness.

There was no such wave--he was drowning.

Again the panic and fear consumed him. He would never see his unborn babe, never kiss his sweet wife's lips again, and never work the fields in the warm sunlight.

No! I'm not ready to die! How can the God I've loved all my life be so cruel?

Then he heard someone whispering to him, and it was growing clearer, more insistent. He raged, "I will not go with you! Not yet!"

The whispering continued, and finally, Michael listened. A gentle voice reassured him that it would be all right and that it was time to come home. Again Michael refused, but it urged him on. Then, as if someone dropped a veil over him, he was at peace. Michael went home.

Chapter 14

The fog lifted, and pale moonlight washed over Darcy as she regained consciousness. The cool breeze, which swept away the mist, now swept away the cobwebs of her mind, and she opened her eyes. She saw the moonbeams glistening on the waves, and she blinked several times to clear the blur of delirium.

Her body was lashed to a tombstone, and when she tried to move, the pain was excruciating. All of the night's horrors revisited her, and with a pounding heart, she listened for the soldiers.

Darcy looked down at her bruised and battered body, and even in the dim light, she could see that her skirt was drenched with blood. She had no idea how long she had been lashed here, but judging from the position of the moon, it had been a long time.

Suddenly, she heard the thunder of hooves and dropped her head, pretending to be unconscious. Two soldiers rode up and dismounted.

"Is she dead?" asked one.

"No, she's alive," stated the other indifferently after he placed his hand on Darcy's forehead, checking for body heat.

Her head throbbed with pain, as they carried her down the bluff on the back of a donkey to headquarters. The soldiers led the donkey around to the back of the cottage and pulled open the door of a shed. They dropped Darcy onto some hay in the corner and locked it from the outside.

Moonlight streamed through the slats of the shed, illuminating the shack. The rays shining over her body reminded Darcy of the bars of a jail cell.

All night long she fought sleep, but her feverish mind played tricks on her, terrifying her with ghoulish nightmares and chase scenes.

The following day brought no visitors and no news. The soldiers did not provide food, water or any opportunity to use an outhouse, and she had to relieve herself in the corner. As the day progressed, Darcy grew weak and despondent.

News of the assault spread through town, leaving everyone stricken with grief and despair. Two of the men had drowned, three had escaped and seven were to be executed in the morning. Liam continued to fight for his life, but either way, he would be hanged in the morning.

Molly Kennedy's husband had escaped. This would not be the case for Michael O'Hearn. His body and that of Jerry Joyce had washed ashore that morning.

Bridget was on a bed of hay in the loft of her sister's home staring at the ceiling, stricken with grief. Over and over, she speculated about the terror of Michael's final moments and the agony he must have endured in the cold ocean water.

There was a soft knock on the door downstairs, and she heard her sister, Gweneth speaking in muffled tones. She called up the stairs. "Bridget? Are you awake? There's someone here to see you!"

Bridget pretended to be asleep. She couldn't bear anyone's pity. She wanted to be left alone with her memories of Michael.

"Bridget, it's Teila," she urged.

Bridget stirred. Teila was Michael's sister, and she could not turn her away. She too was in mourning.

I'll be right there," Bridget said in a hoarse voice. Pushing her hair back, she dried her eyes and came down the ladder.

As Gweneth slipped out of the cottage, Teila and Bridget embraced affectionately. They held each other for a long time as if to gather strength.

"Teila, you are not well enough to be up and about. You shouldn't be here."

Teila was thin, and her face was pale, but she shook her head. "We must not talk of my feelings. I bring terrible news. Major Russell intends to hang Darcy in the morning."

Bridget's eyes grew wide, as Teila continued, "I believe that he wants to set an example. I have been walking the floor trying to think of what we can do."

When the shock of what she had heard finally wore off, Bridget said, "What does Father Etienne think?"

"No one has seen him. Has he come to see you?"

Bridget shook her head.

Teila swallowed hard and said, "I have an idea, it but I need your help."

"Of course, I'll help. What must I do?"

She leaned forward and lowered her voice. "Here's my plan. You are to go and see Major Russell to make a plea for Darcy's life on the grounds that she is with child. Keenan and I will go to Granager to find the midwife, Annie Ryan. I'd bet my life that Russell will send for the old woman to verify that Darcy is full."

"But she'll testify that Darcy is not with child," protested Bridget.

"Aye, that she would, but it will not be Annie Ryan testifying. It will be me. I have heard that she loves the drink and can be bought so none other than Teila Mullin will answer Annie's door when the soldiers come looking for a midwife."

"But can you stand the journey, Teila? You aren't well."

"Keenan will help me. I have no choice," was her answer. Teila embraced her sister-in-law and said, "May God protect us both."

Wrapping their shawls around their shoulders, the two women set out to save Darcy's life.

* * *

Late in the afternoon, Darcy was awakened by scraping of the shed door. A flood of light blinded her, and she sat up, squinting. A gruff voice said, "Get up. The major wants to see you!"

He yanked her to her feet and Darcy staggered in front of the soldier toward headquarters to meet with Major Russell. She was filthy, and her hair was tangled and littered with bits of hay. She stumbled into the cottage, and Major Russell looked up from his desk. He had dark rings under his eyes, and his face appeared drawn. With a look of distaste, he said, "So you're the ship's beacon. What's your name?"

Darcy said nothing, looking at her floor. The guard gave her a push, and she mumbled, "Darcy McBride."

Russell wrote her name down and asked, "You're related to this Liam McBride?"

"He is my brother."

Darcy's head felt thick and her eyes would not focus.

The major looked in the corner of the room and said, "There's someone here to plead your belly. Is it true?"

Darcy didn't understand why the officer was asking her such a question. He hadn't even given her food or water. She wondered why he had this sudden interest in her well-being.

"Well? Do you carry a brat or not?" he asked impatiently.

Slowly her eyes adjusted, and she could see Bridget O'Hearn standing in the corner. There was no expression on her face, but Darcy saw her, ever so slightly, nod her head. Darcy said, "Yes, I am with child."

Slamming his hands on the desk, Major Russell barked, "Goddamn it! Now I have to address this."

He stood up and paced the room. Looking at the guard, he ordered, "Dispatch a rider to the next town. What is the closest town anyway?"

"Granager," Bridget replied swiftly.

"Yes, Granager, dispatch a rider to obtain a midwife who can verify this pregnancy. Don't stand there! Do it now, and get these women out of my sight. Their stench disgusts me."

Just as Darcy and Bridget were about to step out the door, Major Russell remembered something and stopped them. He demanded, "What do you two know of a priest here in Kilkerry?"

The women remained silent, looking at the floor.

"So, you will tell me nothing. No matter. My men found his body near the smuggler's cove this morning. It appears that he lost his footing on the cliffs and fell to his death on the rocks below."

Darcy and Bridget looked at Major Russell in disbelief.

"It was a ghastly mess. We had no choice but to put him out to sea." There was the hint of a smile on his mouth, and he said, "It seems you people had all sorts of activities going on behind my back, and now you'll all be punished."

With a nod, he dismissed the women. Darcy stumbled back to the shed, dazed and blinded with denial. It was a trick. Father Etienne was not dead. It was only yesterday that she had dined with him on the ledge in the warm sunshine. He would be back. That was someone else they found.

Darcy stopped walking, and the guard gave her a push snarling, "Get going, you filthy pig."

The guard's words echoed in her ears, and suddenly she turned and threw herself on him like an animal. Darcy tore at him, kicking and biting until he grabbed her by the hair and flung her to the ground. Another soldier rushed up to help, and the two of them threw Darcy into the shed with so much force that she hit the back wall with a smack and fell to the ground.

They have won again. They would always win, thought Darcy as she lay on the hay feeling broken. She was tired of fighting. She had been fighting all her life, and she didn't have the strength to continue.

As night fell, Darcy dropped into a deep apathy, caring for nothing but death which held a tranquil appeal. She refused to think of Father Etienne. She could not accept the fact that she would never see him again. She lay motionless, staring at the ceiling until the middle of the night when she heard the door open and the guard say, "Do your examination and be quick about it."

He slammed the door, leaving Darcy alone in the shed with someone holding a lantern. She closed her eyes and rolled over facing the wall.

"Darcy! It's Teila. Look at me!"

"Leave me," mumbled Darcy. "You'll get yourself in trouble."

Teila grabbed Darcy by the arm and rolled her over, "I am posing as a midwife to testify that you are teeming. The Crown will not hang a woman carrying a child. All you have to do is say that my name is Annie Ryan and that I examined you tonight."

Darcy pulled herself up and leaned against the wall. "Go home. You have a husband and children. I care not what happens to me."

Teila's eyes sparked, and she squared her thin shoulders giving Darcy a resounding slap across the face. "How dare you speak indifferently of your life, when we risk our lives for you! Father Etienne gave his life trying to save you and the others, and now you repay him with this blasphemy!"

Darcy was thunderstruck. Her lips moved but no words came. Finally, she murmured, "What are you talking about?"

Teila took a deep breath to regain her composure and said, "Father Etienne learned of the ambush and was on his way to warn you, but the fog was thick, and he slipped off the bluff."

"Oh my god, oh my god!" moaned Darcy, putting her hands over her face.

"Bran confessed before he ran off. He was an informant for the Crown, Darcy. He was last seen in front of Paid Lillis' cottage, his pockets bulging with notes."

Darcy covered her ears rocking back and forth. "No, No! It's not true!"

Teila grabbed Darcy's hands and pulled them down. "Listen to me, Darcy. I haven't much time. Don't let Father Etienne die in vain. He couldn't save the others, but you have a chance to live. Don't throw that away."

Beyond the Cliffs of Kerry

Teila reached quickly inside her cloak and put a small bundle into Darcy's hand and said, "Here is some bread and something of Father Etienne's. They destroyed everything else. I found it on the floor."

Teila wrapped her arms around Darcy. She held her close and rocked her, reciting the Irish saying, "There's hope from the ocean, Darcy but none from the grave." She stood up, brushed the straw from her skirt and gave the door three smart knocks. Teila turned and looked at Darcy one last time, and then she was gone. The bar fell heavily across the door once more.

Darcy opened the cloth and saw a small trinket. She recognized the charm that she had given Father Etienne from the pudding last Christmas. She remembered telling him that the thimble was a sign of hope, and now when she needed it the most, he had delivered it to her. Closing her hand around the thimble, she reached deep within her soul and found a glimmer of hope to carry on.

* * *

Darcy finally slept but not for long. She felt a sharp kick in her side and heard someone tell her to get up. She pulled herself to her feet, trying to clear her mind. Her long hair was tangled and matted, falling around her face wildly, and her clothes were filthy. She resembled a woman from a madhouse as she climbed aboard a cart, where she was bound to the base of the driver's seat.

The sky was dark and heavy with rain clouds, and thunder rolled in the distance. As the cart bumped along, Darcy wanted to look up and take in the fresh air, but she did not have the strength to raise her head.

Suddenly, the cart came to an abrupt halt, and she felt a large hand grip her hair and yank her head up.

Darcy could see Major Russell at the end of the cart, and she believed that he was talking to her, but the words sounded far away. He shook his head in disgust, came around to the side of the cart and yelled, "I don't want to have to say this again, you stupid slut, so listen! You have been sentenced to death by hanging for your crime of treason, but you have been spared this punishment because you carry a brat inside you. Instead, you will be transported to the American Colonies where you will be sold into servitude for a period of seven years. You will leave directly after the hanging."

Darcy looked at him blankly not fully comprehending the meaning of his words. Everyone seemed so far away, and their voices seemed so muffled. When the guard let go of her hair, she rested her head on the back of the cart and through swollen eyes began to look around.

In spite of the thunder, the village green was filled with people. Darcy could see the British regulars forcing villagers out of their homes at gunpoint. She strained to recognize their faces, but they melted into distorted figures.

Slowly she rolled her head away from the crowd and over to the high stone cross where someone had constructed a wooden platform with a cross beam. Dangling from the beam were several looped ropes, and standing nearby was a soldier banging out a steady rhythm on a drum.

The drum, along with the rolling thunder grew in intensity, but Darcy could hold her eyes open no longer. Her mind drifted back to peaceful times--days spent playing in the sunshine with her sister, Mary Kathleen, sharing secrets with Teila and reading lessons with

Father Etienne. She remembered his words, "I have the feeling that I may never leave Ireland," and now it had been fulfilled. He was at sea between his beloved home in America and his cherished land of Ireland.

A peal of thunder roused her, and she opened her eyes in time to see a soldier place a noose around Liam's neck. She was lucid enough to know that he was weak and near death. It must have taken every ounce of his massive strength to hold himself up--with the assistance of a chair.

All seven owlers were lined up, each with a noose around his neck. Some mumbled prayers, others wept, only Liam was expressionless. She could hear a voice reading a list of crimes against the Crown including resisting arrest, smuggling, and treason.

Darcy watched, but she could not comprehend what was happening. She drifted off until the drum stopped, and she heard a dull thud. Opening her eyes, she saw seven men gasping for their last breath. They all danced and twitched grotesquely on the ropes, except Liam. He did not move. It seemed that the first blow was enough.

Darcy looked at her brother's face. She remembered he used to smile when they were children, but after the famine, he never smiled again. The Hunger never ended for Liam. It had eaten him alive.

The cart jerked abruptly, and she realized that she was leaving Kilkerry. It rumbled roughly through town, and she saw several men remove their hats as she passed. The town grew steadily smaller, as she moved out into the countryside until all that remained in her sight was the abbey on the bluff. Darcy stared at it as the cart jostled along. She knew that the abbey would remain standing long after she was gone from the earth. She would miss being under its protection but would carry its memory with her always.

Suddenly, she had the strange notion that she could see the shadow of Father Etienne inside the walls. He was dressed in his long, black cassock. She told herself that it was fancy, but when she raised her hand in farewell, the shadowy figure did the same.

Chapter 15

The journey to Cork took several days, and Darcy began to feel her strength return. She was grateful for the indifferent attitude of the soldier that escorted her to the seaport town. He seemed to be enjoying his brief escape from Kilkerry. He did not bother with small talk and allowed Darcy enough food and lots of fresh water.

They arrived at Cork late in the afternoon, and the town was bustling with activity. Cork was one of the largest ports in Ireland, and it was here that Major Russell booked passage for Darcy to the American Colonies. She drew the attention of the townspeople as she was escorted down the bumpy lanes to the British Port Authority. Many stopped to stare and some spat at her, either way, she made no eye contact.

The soldier parked the cart in front of an old building which had at one time been a custom house but now served as the Port Authority. As he jumped off the cart and headed inside, Darcy noticed him pull some papers out of his breast pocket which she assumed to be orders regarding her transportation. After a brief time, he climbed back onto the cart. He pulled around to the stable in the back and began to untie her. "You're very lucky," he said. "Your ship for America embarks in the morning, and you will not have to go to that stinking jail built over the city gate. You'll sleep here tonight instead."

He took her to an empty stall toward the back of the stable and tied her hands to a ring for tethering horses. He was considerate enough to allow her ample rope so she could lie down if she desired and left her with bread and cheese and some water.

The horses rolled their eyes suspiciously at Darcy as she settled in for the night. Raucous laughter and bawdy shouts came from people passing on the street. She was glad to be tucked to the back of the stable, hidden from the sight of the city dwellers, and she slid back into the shadows.

She had never gone beyond the limited boundaries of Kilkerry, and it was very overwhelming to be in a city of this size. It appeared so loud and dangerous, dizzying to the senses. After eating, she felt unbearably tired and slept. The stable grew dark, and occasionally a visitor would rouse her, but they were oblivious to her.

Darcy had been allowed to bring no possessions. She had only the clothes on her back, the pewter cross and thimble of hope close to her heart. Together they gave her the strength she needed to carry on.

Darcy was awakened early by snorts from the horses, as several British officers came in to saddle up. She sat up, rubbed her eyes and stretched. Today she would leave for America, and she was terrified. Darcy had longed for adventure and excitement, but being sold into indentured service was not what she had planned. They set off for the docks shortly after sunrise. The air smelled thick from stale fish and vomit. As they passed an old town house, which had fallen into disrepair, an old woman in an upper story threw the contents of a chamber pot out a window, splashing all over the cart. The sights and the smells of this town sickened her. Many people were covered with pock marks and pustules, and the old men leered at her through yellow, watery eyes.

They started down a wide street, and when Darcy turned around, she saw tall masts and ship rigging. The quay was a loud and busy place every day, but this morning a ship was departing for the New World, so it was completely in chaos.

Large, burly-looking men rolled barrels up ramps while others mended sails and carpenters swung hammers making last-minute repairs. Vendors called out to customers, enticing them with fresh fish or local produce, and seagulls circled, screeching and diving at food.

The soldier stopped the cart at a large desk at the base of the ship's gangplank. He handed some papers to a prosperous-looking gentleman who had been scratching figures into a log. He had a shock of snow-white hair and a kind face. The two men briefly discussed the terms of transportation, and the guard came over and untied her. A large man with curly, dark hair and a long black mustache was summoned to take Darcy on board. He grabbed the rope tying her hands and led her up the plank. She felt her stomach lurch as her eyes ran along the coastline of cliffs and green hills rolling into the distance.

The man said, "Better look good. You'll not see her again for a long time."

Darcy looked at the leathery face of her jailer. Something in his voice sounded familiar. After clearing her throat, she licked her lips and said hoarsely, "You are from the Colonies?"

His eyebrows shot up. He had not expected this dirty, disheveled woman to have spoken in a manner so direct. When she looked at him, her eyes were as brilliant as the green hills behind her. "Yes, I am from the Colonies. It's been four years since I've been there to see my wife and six little poppets." He studied Darcy a moment and then said, "Come now, girl. I've got to get you to the hold."

They crossed the deck and went down several sets of stairs between decks into the dark belly of the ship.

As they descended the companion ladder, the stench of unwashed bodies sent Darcy into a fit of coughing. The jailer laughed and said, "Get used to it. None o' you smells like primroses."

Her eyes needed to adjust to the darkness, and although she could not see the other prisoners, she could hear them.

"Get a corner with some straw and call it your own but be prepared to fight for it," he said.

"Crackstone! Get up here! There's a slave to bring down."

Jonah Crackstone pulled his heavy body up the ladder, leaving Darcy standing alone in the middle of the hold. Gradually, her eyes adjusted, and she could make out the figures of several people sitting on straw. Two of them were in chains and eight or nine were unrestrained. Barrels were stacked everywhere, and there was straw scattered all over the floor. Darcy noticed necessary buckets in several corners and in the ceiling were two round tubes which let light in from above.

Darcy took a seat in one corner. An old crone began to cough, and it became so violent that Darcy thought that poor woman would expire on the spot.

Crackstone brought the slave down into the hold, and Darcy was stunned when she saw the woman. She had the darkest skin Darcy had ever seen, and instantly she thought of *Othello.*

Crackstone told the woman to find a spot to sleep and that they would be embarking soon. The slave chose a bed of straw directly across from Darcy and sat down cross-legged. She turned her cat-like eyes on each prisoner in the hold, warning them, without words, to keep their distance.

Not wishing to challenge her, Darcy looked away, but she could not help stealing glances in her direction. She was beautiful with long legs and a willowy body. Her coarse hair was long and full, and she had cool blue eyes. She wore a colorful skirt with a clean white blouse, and although she was a slave, she was cleaner than the rest of them. From the way she wrinkled her nose, Darcy knew she found their stench disgusting.

Suddenly, the walls began to creak, and she heard shouts and footsteps above her head. The entire ship started to groan as if it was breaking apart. Darcy's heart jumped, and she looked frantically at the others to see if they too were frightened, but there was no reaction from any of them. As the vessel lurched out over the ocean waves, Darcy had the sensation of falling, but she hid her fear.

For the first few days of the journey, Darcy was ill. Despair and seasickness flooded her, and she spent most of her time stretched out on the straw, staring at the narrow light in the ceiling. Her sleep was fitful, and on more than one occasion, she was awakened by a rat crawling over her leg. The hold was teeming with the creatures and the putrid smell of human feces. It was a hellish nightmare.

The two men in chains appeared to be very weak, and Darcy doubted if they would survive the voyage. At first glance, they appeared to be along in years, but upon closer inspection she could see that their long hair and grizzly appearance aged them. The rest were women. Aside from the old lady who had consumption, the others looked like street whores from Cork.

The prisoners were served two meals a day of salt herring and hardtack. The water was warm and had a foul taste to it, but Darcy forced herself to drink it. The hours passed slowly, and the prisoners who were healthy enough amused themselves playing dice or telling stories.

Darcy never spoke to anyone, but occasionally she would watch the slave woman rock back and forth, mumbling. She never let go of an elegant oak traveling case in her lap. Sometimes in the morning, when she opened it, Darcy would catch a glimpse of the contents. It was lined with red velvet and filled with bottles of salts, elixirs, and vials. The containers were made of beautifully cut crystal, and the woman clutched the case as if it were of great value. Darcy noticed when the slave appeared ill, she would drink from a bottle of green tonic kept in her case. The medicine appeared to cure her, but the following day she needed the medicine again.

One morning, she saw Darcy watching her, and her eyes narrowed into slits as she hissed threats at her in French. The woman spent the rest of the day guarding her traveling chest and stealing suspicious glances at Darcy.

The winds picked up that night. The groaning of the ship was deafening. Everyone in the hold was tossed about, and it concerned Darcy that one of the large barrels stacked near her bed would break free and crush her. She slept fitfully for a few hours and was awakened suddenly by moaning coming from the slave woman's corner. She looked up and saw two men climbing up the companion ladder, and they shut the hatch quietly behind them.

The following day Darcy watched the slave woman but seeing nothing out of the ordinary dismissed the incident. The following night she was again awakened by the sound of struggling in the corner.

Her heart pounding, she strained to see in the darkness and saw a man on top of the woman. Darcy remembered the rapes she had endured, and she jumped to her feet. With all her strength, she grabbed the man's hair, snapping his head back. Spewing oaths he rose to his knees. The slave saw her opportunity and lunged forward sinking her teeth into his neck. The man roared and jumped back, just as Darcy dragged her nails across his face. He elbowed Darcy, sending her sprawling across the floor. He scrambled up the ladder, slamming the hatch.

Aside from a bloody lip, Darcy was unhurt. She pulled herself to her bed of straw, trying to catch her breath. Seeing movement again, Darcy jumped to defend herself, startling the woman. Holding a cloth and a bottle of medicine, she signaled for Darcy to clean her lip. Darcy soaked the rag with the tincture and dabbed it on her swollen mouth.

"*Oui, sur la levre,*"

The woman asked Darcy something in French, and Darcy shook her head to say she didn't understand. The woman leaned forward and examined Darcy's lip and then put the stopper back on the bottle. She touched her chest and said, "*Je m'appelle, Dominique.*"

This time, Darcy understood and touched *her* chest. "Darcy."

Dominique looked up at the hatch, saying something about the incident. Darcy knew that she was thanking her. "*Bonne nuit,*" said Dominique and retired to her corner.

* * *

Another week passed and the boredom became unbearable. Darcy's muscles ached for exercise, and she thought that she would lose her mind for want of fresh air. The old woman's cough turned to a steady wheeze until she was unable to sit up. The two men in chains fared no better. One had a fever, and his moans of delirium could be heard around the clock while the other lay weak and listless.

One morning, Darcy noticed that the hold was unusually quiet, and she wondered if the old woman had died. She went to her bedside, and as she had expected, her lifeless body was on the hay. Darcy had seen death a thousand times during the famine, and she was indifferent to it. She climbed the companion ladder and with her fist struck the locked door of the hold above her head.

After some time, there was a crack of light, and Crackstone shouted down, "What is it?"

"The old woman's dead," stated Darcy.

Crackstone pulled the trap open and followed Darcy down into the dark hold. "Here help me," he said.

Although it was disgusting to move the cold, rigid corpse, Darcy knew that this was her only opportunity to breathe fresh air and feel the warm sun again.

They pulled it up several sets of steps into the bright sunshine on deck. Instantly, Darcy was blinded by the light. It was as if she were staring into white lightning. They carried the corpse to the railing and pitched it into the drink.

Her eyes began to adjust, and Darcy took a deep breath of the fresh sea air. Without warning, her head began to spin. She rushed to the side of the ship vomiting what little breakfast she had consumed.

Crackstone guffawed, as she wiped her mouth with the back of her hand. "Ha! That air wasn't as delicious as you thought it would be."

Feeling better, Darcy looked around the deck, drinking in every detail. The rich oak deck was polished to a high shine, the tall timbers that soared above her head were dressed with clean white sails, and the brilliant blue sky stretched out above the sea.

"What did you do back in Ireland?" Jonah Crackstone asked.

As if waking from a dream, Darcy blinked several times and then said, "I tended sheep, raised potatoes."

"No, no. I mean what was your crime?"

"Smuggling."

"Smuggling what?"

"We traded goods with France."

"During wartime?" Crackstone whistled, and said, "Them British don't take kindly to that."

"You're from the Colonies. You're British."

Crackstone's eyebrows shot up, and he said, "If you are going to America, you had better get something straight right now. Not all of us think of ourselves as British. They like to think of us as little loyal subjects, but were a group of ragtag adventurers who answer to no one."

Darcy understood his resentment. She too was considered a British subject even though she swore allegiance only to Ireland.

She started to walk around on deck. She touched the polished brass fittings, ran her hands up and down the ropes, while Crackstone followed her. He felt there was something intriguing about this dirty wild-looking Irishwoman, in spite of the disheveled hair and rags.

Darcy looked up on the poop deck and saw the distinguished gentleman who had discussed her terms of transportation at the beginning of the voyage. She asked, "Is that the Captain?"

"Yes, that's Captain Bingley. He's not a bad sort."

Darcy watched a sailor coil some rope. Under the mainmast, she looked up at the huge sail bulging in the wind. She was fascinated with everything. The breeze blew her hair back, and for the first time, Crackstone got a good look at Darcy. He was amazed to see the exceptional woman hiding behind the filthy facade. He admired her fine bone structure and intelligent face.

"What character is the figurehead on the ship, Mr. Crackstone?"

"What?"

Darcy gestured toward the bowsprit. "The figurehead on the ship, is it a mermaid?"

"No," he said pulling on his mustache. "No, no It's a man. I think I heard someone say that he is the god of the wind."

"Aeolus? That's nice."

Crackstone's eyebrows shot up.

Passengers pulled their children away, as Darcy passed by, turning up their noses at the filthy convict. She was oblivious to their sneers. Crackstone followed her and said, "How would you like to work on deck occasionally?"

Darcy swung around and her face lit up.

"Oh, could I? I could mend sails or scrub the deck. I'm not afraid of hard work."

"We'll give ya a try, but there will be no loafing!" he warned. "Now get back down to the hold. You've been up here long enough."

Darcy started toward the companionway, but before she went down the stairs, she said, "Some of the crew members have been looking for free entertainment. Tell them, if you would, Mr. Crackstone that we will leave marks on them which will be difficult to explain to the captain."

Crackstone's face darkened. He looked at several of the crew members busy with their duties, and his eyes rested on one man whose face was badly scratched and bruised. "Captain Bingley frowns on this sort of entertainment. You have my word. It won't happen again."

* * *

One afternoon Dominique beckoned to Darcy. "Darcee, Darcee."

Darcy slid over and sat cross-legged facing her. The woman smiled and started to talk rapidly in French. Darcy put her hands up and said, "Stop, Dominique. My French is poor."

Dominique sighed. "You, Darcee, I teach *Français*."

Instantly Darcy lit up. "*Oui?*"

They smiled at one another. The thought of conversing together excited them. The lessons gave them a much-needed occupation to fill the long hours in the dark hold of the ship. Dominique taught Darcy French, and Darcy taught Dominique English. She considered schooling her new friend in Gaelic but realized that in the Colonies, Dominique would benefit more from English.

Days passed quickly and the women went from acquaintances to confidantes. Darcy learned that Dominique was the property of Mr. Charles Villiers, who was also on the ship, but inhabiting quarters on deck. Dominique said that she was not badly treated by this

Monsieur Villiers, but she could never accept the fact that she was owned by him. She very candidly told Darcy that she was his paramour. She prided herself on her sensuality and prowess at giving him pleasure.

"Is he attractive?" Darcy asked.

"Oui, it is not difficult to give pleasure to a man with a nice face."

"Where did he find you, Dominique?"

"In New Orleans, that is where I was born. My mother was a paramour, and she taught me to be a paramour. One day I will teach my daughter the art of giving pleasure to a man. Do you have a beau, Darcee?"

"No."

Dominique looked Darcy up and down and commented, "Darcee, you will be owned soon by a man. You must improve your looks to profit. I will show you."

"No," protested Darcy shaking her head. Until now she had assumed she would labor in the fields as an indentured servant.

"Oh? The princess is too good?" said Dominique sarcastically.

She grabbed Darcy's arms and looked into her eyes. "Listen to me. Do you want to be abed with a rich man or a poor man? Either way, they will take you there. You are their property. This is the way it is done."

Darcy yanked out of her grasp. She was angry and frightened at the possibility and retreated to her corner. The harsh reality Dominique presented to her was terrifying. It had never occurred to her that being an indentured servant might include sexual favors.

Although it disgusted and humiliated her, Darcy gradually accepted the cold realities of ownership and allowed Dominique to school her in grooming. Out of her wondrous box of herbs and medicines, Dominique produced almond and honey creams for the skin, containers of berry red stain for the lips and perfumes for the hair. She taught Darcy how to turn her eyelids a soft green with sage, highlighting her dramatic color and how to grind charcoal with honey for simple toothpaste.

Dominique had convinced her at last, to present herself in the best possible light to obtain the best possible position when they arrived in the New World. Toward the end of her schooling, Dominique insisted that Darcy listen to her instructions in matters of pleasure and sensuality. She endured the tutorial, but with an attitude of distaste. Darcy may have to please a man someday, but she refused to enjoy it.

On the last day of tutoring, Darcy dropped down on the straw, feeling fatigued and weak. A headache had been plaguing her all day, and she closed her eyes. She tossed and turned all night, with repeated nightmares. In the morning she awoke with a nosebleed and slid over to Dominique, awakening her. "Do you have something for my bloody nose?"

Looking groggy, Dominique sat up, drew her knees to her chest and with trembling hands pulled out the familiar crystal bottle filled with green liquid.

Darcy asked, "Dominique, what is that medicine for? What illness plagues you?"

Dominique's eyes narrowed, and she hissed, "It is called *absinthe*, and if you take any, I will kill you!"

Darcy frowned and moved back to her bed. She had not liked the look in Dominique's eyes, and she believed now that there was a side to her friend that she did not care to understand. She put her head back, to slow the flow of blood from her nose. Her head continued to pound relentlessly.

The hatch opened suddenly, spilling light down into the hold. Several of the prisoners moaned and turned away. Crackstone called, "The Irish wench named, McBride can come up and work."

Darcy stood up stiffly. As sick as she was feeling, she did not want to miss the opportunity to go on deck. As she passed the prisoners in chains, she noticed one was motionless on the straw with his mouth open.

"We have another dead one, Crackstone!" she called, weakly.

The ladder groaned as Crackstone's heavy body descended. Dominique came over next to Darcy. The dead man was bathed in the light from the open hatch, and Crackstone squatted down to inspect the body more closely.

The prisoner's shirt was open, and his skin was covered with a bright red rash. "May the Lord protect us all!" he gasped.

Dominique nodded her head gravely.

"What? What is it?" asked Darcy.

Crackstone swallowed hard and murmured, "Typhoid."

Chapter 16

After disposing of the body, Crackstone said to Darcy up on deck, "Say nothing of this sickness to the others. I'll not have a panic on the ship."

Crackstone had seen how swiftly typhoid spread on these voyages, sometimes killing over half the population. He knew that he must report the information immediately to Captain Bingley. Darcy studied his weathered face and then bent down to scrub the half-deck.

When Crackstone returned, he sat down on a barrel and watched Darcy run her scrub brush back and forth. He crossed his huge arms over his chest and took a draw off his pipe demanding, "Look up here, McBride."

Darcy rested back on her heels, looking up at Crackstone.

"Push your hair back from your face."

With both hands, she pulled back her dirty, tangled hair and looked at him expectantly.

"Now take the soap and wash up," he ordered.

Darcy lathered her hands and scrubbed her face, rinsing in the clean water he had brought for laundry. Crackstone pulled her chin up, and observed, "You're a handsome woman, McBride. I'd take an interest in you myself, but my wife would tan my hide." He turned to the rail and gazed out at the broad ocean. "She's a good woman, my wife. Not particularly fair, but she's the only one for me. To think she put up with my wanderings all these years."

Darcy smiled. She liked Jonah Crackstone. In spite of his rough ways and straight talk, he was kind. He had been generous to her, expecting nothing in return, and Darcy was grateful to him.

Suddenly, they heard someone demand, "Bring up my slave from the hold."

Crackstone stood up and came face to face with an arrogant-looking man dressed in an expensive suit of clothes. He wore deep-green knee breeches and the most luxurious leather boots Darcy had ever seen. Fashionably placed at the corner of his mouth was a small black patch.

"Be sure that she has had a bath before she is presented to me and be quick about it," he said, sniffing the air. The gentleman turned on his heel and walked off. Darcy could smell the scent of his violet toilet water. She had read about colognes in books, but she had never met anyone with enough money to spend on such a frivolity.

"Who was that?" she asked.

"Why, that's the fine and dandy Mr. Charles Villiers. He never worked a day in his life. His family owns sugar plantations in the Indies, but he lives in Charlestown right now."

"What was he doing in Ireland?"

"Buying horses, they say you Irish breed the best horses of anyone."

"Is he the man who owns Dominique?"

"The slave wench? Yes. I've got to get her cleaned up. You can help me."

It was unsuitable for a slave to bathe in her master's quarters so Crackstone chose a secluded spot just under the poop deck. Several crew members brought up a small tub and filled it part way with water.

Crackstone turned to Darcy and said, "The damned fool doesn't know how precious fresh water is on a voyage, and even if he did know, he wouldn't care."

He sent Darcy for Dominique, and when they returned several of the crew had gathered to watch. Darcy looked over her shoulder at them and held up a large blanket to conceal her friend. Draped over a barrel were the clothes that Villiers wanted Dominique to wear, and Darcy marveled at the luxurious fabric. How she envied Dominique's opportunity to clean up. She recalled the warm summer afternoons she had spent bathing in Glinnish Stream, and a pang of homesickness shot through her. Try as she might, she could not completely recall the little cove. It seemed lately that Kilkerry was nothing more than a fuzzy memory.

Darcy felt dreadfully tired, and the sea breeze seemed icy. "Please hurry, Dominique. My arms are tired," and she began to tremble.

"I am almost dressed," Dominique called back.

Darcy lowered the blanket and gasped. Dominique took her breath away. She was dressed in a black taffeta gown with a stomacher of gold lace. Darcy guessed the dress to be the latest fashion of the day. Her clean hair was pinned up high, revealing her long neck. Every inch of her was supremely elegant.

"Dominique, you look beautiful."

Dominique smiled and gracefully draped a lace shawl over her shoulders. She was accustomed to fine things, and she handled them as if she were of high birth. She reached out and touched Darcy's hand. "I am sorry if I was harsh with you this morning. I would never hurt you, Darcy. I owe you my life."

"Down to the hold with you now!" barked Crackstone.

Darcy was glad to retreat to her bed of hay. All through the night, she trembled uncontrollably, tossing back and forth restlessly, and by morning, she was unable to rise. For days she shivered on the straw, falling in and out of delirium. Unable to distinguish fantasy from reality. She believed that she was back in Kilkerry being nursed by Teila and Keenan and that she was still recovering from Liam's beating. They seemed to hover over her, sponging her with cold cloths. She could not tell if she had been on the straw for days or even weeks. Eventually, she sank into a dreamless stupor, not caring if she lived or died.

One night she heard a familiar voice calling to her, and when she opened her eyes, she saw her mother. It was not her famine-ravaged face but the smooth ivory-skinned countenance which Darcy remembered as a child.

Mrs. McBride said, "I am here now, Darcy. Everything will be all right." She began to hum an Irish lullaby and stroke her hair lovingly. Darcy struggled to stay awake, but sleep overcame her, and when she opened her eyes again, Dominique was leaning over her.

"*Oui,* the fever has broken. You will recover now. Go back to sleep."

Darcy fell back to sleep. Gradually she recovered from the typhoid and became aware of her surroundings once more. Dominique had never left her side, diligently sponging her with wet rags for days trying to reduce the fever.

When she finally could speak, Darcy asked, "How long have I been sick?"

"Maybe two weeks," replied Dominique as she opened her medicine chest. She removed a small bottle filled with an amber colored elixir and pulled the stopper.

"Oh no, Dominique, no more of that brew!" protested Darcy turning her head.

"That medicine helped save your life," Dominique said.

"Thank you for saving my life," she murmured.

Dominique pushed a spoonful of medicine into her mouth, and she gagged. A thick smoke coiled up from a brass bowl and curled around Darcy's head. "What is that, Dominique?"

"Incense."

"Don't they use that in church?"

"*Oui,* frankincense for spirituality, but this is juniper. It purifies the air of disease. My mother taught the stillroom to me. I can cure many things, but the heart is the best medicine. You are strong in here, Darcy," she said pointing to her chest, "This why you survive the fever. She reached for some hardtack and said, "Come, you must eat, Darcee. You must have your strength back before we reach Providence."

Darcy struggled to sit up on her elbows and looked around the hold. Aside from two women sitting in their corners, the room was empty. "Where is everyone?" she asked.

"Dead," Dominique replied.

Darcy's eyes grew wide. The chains were empty, and most of the straw was unoccupied.

"The sickness took them fast. Many on the upper decks are dead also."

"Crackstone?"

"Crackstone lives, but Monsieur Villiers is ill."

"If he dies, Dominique, will you be free?"

Dominique shook her head, picked up her things and went back to her corner. When they had first become friends, Dominique told Darcy, "When you are a slave, you must learn to hide your feelings." Darcy knew that Dominique was hiding her terror. An uncertain future plagued them both.

The next few days Darcy spent getting her strength back. One afternoon the hatch opened and Crackstone called her up on deck.

"You're skin and bones!" he bellowed, as she stumbled onto the deck. "God knows with everybody dead, we have more than enough food now. Weatherby!" he roared, "Get me a plate of food from the galley." Turning back to Darcy, he said, "Captain Bingley gave me orders to fatten you up so you bring a good price."

"Ugh, I sound like a prize cow," Darcy said, frowning.

"It's Bingley's responsibility to strike a bargain with someone in Providence who may be shopping for an indentured servant. I told him that you could bring a fair price. He gets a percentage of the profit," explained Crackstone.

Weatherby handed Darcy a bowl, and she sat down on the steps of the companionway eating the fish stew. Crackstone disappeared down the companionway and reappeared some minutes later with Dominique. He directed a crew member to take her to the stern to gather her clothing, Darcy asked, "Is Villiers dead?"

Crackstone nodded.

"What will happen to her?"

"She's now the property of the family. I suppose they will return her to Charlestown or sell her."

Darcy frowned, afraid for Dominique.

* * *

Over the next few days, as she gained in strength, Dominique weakened. She ate little and spent many hours rocking back and forth in her corner, refusing to speak. Only a few days were left before the ship would drop anchor in the New World. As each day passed, Darcy became more alarmed about Dominique's health and appearance. She noticed her tremors were increasing. Dominique would take sips out of the absinthe bottle, but the contents were low, and one morning when Darcy awakened, she found Dominique curled up on the straw, shaking uncontrollably.

"Let me get you your medicine, Dominique. I'm worried about you."

"Go away. There is no more medicine," mumbled Dominique.

There were dark circles under her eyes and tremors shook her body. Darcy reached out and brushed the hair from her friend's face pleading, "What is your illness? Tell me and maybe I can help."

Dominique sat up and screamed in French, "Are you stupid! The absinthe is my illness. I need it to feel normal. Now get away from me!"

Darcy retreated to her corner. She suspected that Charles Villiers supplied Dominique with the absinthe, and when he succumbed to typhoid fever, she lost her access to the drink forever. She was not optimistic about Dominique's future. The very advice she had given Darcy about presenting herself in the best light, she could not put into practice herself. Her prospects were grim. On several occasions, Darcy attempted to help Dominique while she was groaning in pain, but she was always met with a violent outburst.

One afternoon the hatch opened, and Crackstone called for Darcy to go above to clean herself up. He placed a tub of water in Villiers' empty cabin along with some fresh clothing and towels, telling her that she could use all the water she wanted because they were at destination's end.

Darcy entered the cabin and bolted the door behind her. She wondered if it was her imagination or did Charles Villiers' *Eau de toilet* still linger in the air? She looked around at the luxurious room, running her hands over the plum-and-gold furnishings. In the middle of the room sat four mahogany chairs and a table with a tray attached to the top. Four crystal goblets and a decanter fit snugly onto the tray. Darcy longed to taste wine from the delicate glasses. She touched the velvet curtains at the bay window and marveled at the built-in bed covered with a plum-colored spread and Turkish pillows.

She took her filthy rags off, letting them drop to the floor and eased herself into the water. Darcy washed briskly, scrubbing her scalp until it stung. To rid herself of bugs, she applied a tonic to her hair, which Dominique had given her some time ago, and after rinsing it out stepped out of the tub. She toweled herself off, opened the window and tossed her filthy rags into the sea.

After pulling a white shift over her head, Darcy stepped into the gown Crackstone had left for her and went to the mirror. She was delighted with what she saw. It was a modest gown, everyday attire for women in the New World, but to Darcy, it was the most exquisite dress she had ever worn. The gown was cream-colored with pink, vertical stripes and blue embroidered cornflowers. The collar and cuffs of the white shift peeked out smartly under the muslin, and the large open sleeves displayed her shapely arms. Darcy ran her hands back and forth over the material, marveling at the workmanship. At last, she understood what Dominique had been trying to tell her. She must use every asset to her advantage. Her brains and her good looks must be exploited to their fullest if she was to survive alone in the world. Darcy was a long way from the sheltered life of Kilkerry. She must now rely on her wits and appeal. Every resource must be used to thrive in the New World, and she was determined to chisel out a satisfying life for herself.

Feeling elated with her new self-confidence, she combed her long hair and tied it up into a loose knot. She pulled a few wisps down to frame her face and put on a pair of soft leather slippers. Except for special occasions, Darcy had gone barefoot, and it was a curious sensation wearing leather around her feet. Footwear would take some adjustment.

She opened the cabin door and walked onto the deck. Passengers lined the railing looking toward the bow of the ship, and she heard one of them say that they had entered the Narragansett Bay and were approaching the city of Providence. They stared at Darcy, clearly wondering why they hadn't noticed this woman on board before. The very people, who recoiled from her this morning, admired her this afternoon.

She leaned over the railing and her heart jumped. There it was! There was America! How pleased Father Etienne would be if he knew that she was about to set foot on the soil of his homeland.

There was much commotion, and people were chattering with excitement as the ship drew near Providence. Darcy was amazed to see the size of the city. Her only glimpse of America had been through the eyes of Father Etienne. He had lived on the frontier, but this was a busy, bustling seaport city.

"P--Pardon, Ma'am, but Mr. Crackstone is looking for you," stuttered Weatherby.

When Crackstone saw her, his jaw dropped. He whistled and said, "I knew you was a diamond in the rough! I can't believe my eyes, girl. You will bring a fancy price indeed. Now understand, you are not to leave the foc's'l without me. Go over there and sit down."

Crackstone went about his work but continued to steal looks at her shaking his head in disbelief. It gave her the confidence she needed to face the uncertain future.

The ship dropped anchor, and Darcy watched the frenzied passengers make preparations to disembark. It was heaven to see green trees again, smell the soil and see homes once more. She saw a black slave on the docks, and panic shot through her. Where was Dominique? She strained her eyes amid the throngs of people flooding the deck. The confusion of passengers and crew was overwhelming, and then Dominique stumbled out of the companionway onto the deck. She was in chains, bound to other prisoners being led off the vessel by a crew member.

"Dominique! Dominique!" called Darcy, but amid the shouting and commotion, she could not hear her. The prisoners moved toward the gangplank. Darcy bolted down the steps. She threw her arms around Dominique and cried, "You will be all right, Dominique! You will survive because you have the same healing medicine within you that I have."

Beyond the Cliffs of Kerry

Tears welled up in Dominique's eyes, but she could not speak.

Suddenly, someone grabbed the back of Darcy's gown, yanking her away from Dominique.

"You are coming with me," said Jonah Crackstone firmly. "It will be my ass, McBride if you get away."

Tears rolling down her face, Darcy watched Dominique walk down the gang plank and into the throngs of Providence. The crowds swallowed her up, and she was gone.

"I beg your pardon, Madame," said a male voice.

Wiping her eyes, Darcy turned and faced a tall, dignified man of later years, in a British officer's uniform. Darcy guessed that he held high rank. His hair was almost completely gray, and he had a vigorous build, which was unusual for a man of his years.

Before she could reply, the Captain stepped up and said, "I am Captain Bingley. May I be of service to you, sir?"

"Yes, Captain, I am Colonel Nathan Lawrence, and I have an appointment with Mr. Charles Villiers."

Bingley's polite smile dropped, and he said, "Oh, I do have sad news. We had an outbreak of illness on the voyage, and Mr. Villiers succumbed."

The Colonel looked sympathetic, but far from grief-stricken. "That *is* sad news although I must confess, I never met the gentleman. We had some business to discuss, but beyond that, I knew him not."

Colonel Lawrence turned to Darcy and said, "I wish to apologize for not introducing myself, madam."

The Captain jumped in and said, "May I present Miss McBride. She arrived today from Ireland."

"I too have recently arrived from the British Isles, Miss McBride. If I can be of any assistance," and he bowed slightly.

"Forgive me, Colonel," said Captain Bingley. "But are you completely settled here?"

"I have not even unpacked my trunk," he said with a chuckle. "My dear wife attends to my housekeeping, but she will not be joining me here for some months."

Captain Bingley saw his opportunity and suggested, "Might you be in need of a housekeeper? This lovely young woman has an obligation of indentured service to complete, and all the papers are in order if you are interested."

The Colonel's eyebrows shot up, and he said, "You are an indentured servant? You certainly do not look the part."

Darcy smiled and stared into his eyes boldly. She found this gentleman most appealing, and she knew that even though he represented everything she hated, he might be her best opportunity for placement in the New World. She remembered what he had said about his wife not joining him for several months.

Continuing to stare at Darcy, he said to Captain Bingley, "May I speak further with her Captain, perhaps over some dinner?"

"Of course, of course," said Bingley eagerly, "Take as long as you want."

The Colonel offered Darcy his arm, and they started down the stairs toward the gangplank. Darcy saw Crackstone with a duffel bag on his back coming up onto deck. She excused herself for a moment and approached him with her hand outstretched.

"Mr. Crackstone, I wanted to say good-bye and thank you for all of your kindnesses."

"Best of luck to you, McBride," he said with a broad smile, "I want you to know that I've decided to pay an extended visit to Mrs. Crackstone and the little ones."

"I think that Mrs. Crackstone is a very lucky woman," she said smiling.

She returned to Colonel Lawrence's side. When they stepped off the ship, Darcy's head began to spin, and her knees buckled. Colonel Lawrence steadied her and laughed. "You must get your land legs back."

He guided her through the noisy streets of Providence, and Darcy's senses were bombarded with the hustle and bustle of the thriving port town. The streets were crowded with merchants and sailors. Men were loading huge barrels of rum and molasses onto carts, and putting timber onto ships bound for England. Shops lined the streets and vendors hawked their wares. They passed a platform where a crowd gathered and Lawrence told Darcy a slave auction was about to begin. He said that Providence was one of the largest slave ports in the Colonies. Darcy's stomach churned to think Dominique may be sold here. She searched the crowds for her but without success.

The fresh air and sunshine gradually renewed Darcy's strength. It was hard to believe that only a few hours ago she was in the filthy hold of the ship, and now she walked through the streets of Providence on the arm of a gentleman. *Yes, he is a British officer, but this is the New World, not Ireland.*

As they approached a two-story tavern, Darcy looked up at the sign swinging overhead and said deliberately, "Welles' Oyster House."

Colonel Lawrence looked startled. "You read?"

Darcy said with a shrug, "And write."

The tavern was dark and filled with smoke. There was a bar lined with fresh oysters and clams where a bartender in a white apron dished up delicacies. Darcy had never seen so many fine clothes. The establishment was filled with people drinking and laughing, and Colonel Lawrence took her to a table in the back where it was quieter. Darcy had never dined in a tavern before, and she watched him closely, mimicking his manners. The Colonel did not seem to notice. He was too busy studying her physical attributes. His eyes traveled from her dark hair, over her face and shoulders and down to her round breasts.

The owner fussed over their table like a mother hen, disappointed when Darcy declined the oysters. Even with the coaxing of Colonel Lawrence, she refused the stuffed quahogs. They reminded her too much of the old days scouring the beaches of Kerry for food. She decided that the mutton pie was a better choice instead. Pushing a mug of ale over to her, Colonel Lawrence started the conversation. "Now to business. Is the indentured service to pay for ship's passage?" he asked.

"No, I'm a convict," she said, jerking her chin in the air.

His eyes narrowed. He wasn't sure he liked this new information. "A convict, what was your crime?"

"Smuggling goods to the French," she replied.

He raised his eyebrows in surprise. "It seems a light sentence for such a crime. You are very lucky."

"Oh, I'm *very* lucky," she said sarcastically.

He shook his head. "I have heard of this occurring on the west coast of Ireland. Was that your home?"

"It was."

He sat back and crossed his arms over his chest. "The West Coast is exceedingly poor. How, then, did you learn to read?"

"We smuggled a Jesuit priest into our town. He taught me to read and write."

The Colonel chuckled and took a pull off of his ale. In spite of her rebellious nature, he found Darcy extremely engaging. He did not want to be saddled with a professional courtesan or an adventuress, though, so he asked, "Have you been a housekeeper for a gentleman before?"

Darcy knew what he meant. "I may be a convict, Colonel Lawrence, but I'm not a whore," she stated.

Lawrence smiled slowly. He was satisfied, and as the evening passed, he found his interests in her heighten. They discussed many things over dinner. He found her intelligent as well as physically desirable. He told her that he would be in Providence only a short time before taking command of a fort in upper Massachusetts Colony.

"Should I purchase your service, you would be venturing into a very dangerous area. It is unsettled and extremely rugged. I don't need a woman who will be a burden to me."

Darcy lifted her pewter mug, took a drink of ale and said, "Colonel Lawrence, I assure you I have survived more privation than you can ever know, and you'll find that I am far from a shrinking violet although I guard my independence jealously."

"I would not call being an indentured servant, *independence*." he argued.

"True, I do not have my physical independence, but there is no man who will ever own me."

Colonel Lawrence raised his eyebrows at her cheeky response. He enjoyed her saucy attitude, and he decided that he must have her. He stood up, took her hand from the table and lifted her from her seat saying, "Come, we have papers to sign."

They returned to the ship, and a most delighted Captain Bingley produced the papers for Colonel Lawrence to inspect. Darcy was curious about the terms of the servitude, and she leaned over Lawrence's back to read the document. She scanned it and was about to look away when she saw the day's date inscribed on the bottom of the page. The line read, "The city of Providence, April 20th, 1757."

She shook her head and chuckled. This was indeed the final insult. Today was her birthday.

.

Chapter 17

Darcy stretched on her luxurious bed in the temporary quarters of Colonel Nathan Lawrence. She was not expected downstairs until nine, and she had plenty of time to drink in her new surroundings. Modest quarters had been provided for Colonel Lawrence on Benefit Street in Providence, but to Darcy they were Versailles. She ran her hand over the cream-colored duvet that covered her bed and reached up to touch the curtains which hung in thick folds at all four posters. The highly polished hardwood floor felt cool to her bare feet as she stood up to look out the second-story window.

She watched as people passed by and marveled at how richly they seemed to be dressed. Men wore topcoats with knee breeches, crisp tricorne hats and their hair pulled back in a single pigtail. The women too looked elegant in gowns rich in detail, and Darcy saw one woman with powdered hair piled high on her head, riding in a sedan chair.

She marveled at the homes lining Benefit Street. They were all very straight, proper and neatly presented. Each two-story home had more windows than Darcy had ever seen, and even though the shuttered facades were flat, they were attractive. All the structures were constructed of wood and painted in light, cheerful colors. Providence was a very modern place indeed.

She hoped that her arrangement with Colonel Lawrence would go well. Darcy did not relish the thought of having to give herself to a man, but at least, she found him appealing and wealthy. She opened a small oak writing desk and found several sheets of paper and a quill. The thought occurred to her that a home such as this must have many books. She heard the rich chimes of a clock downstairs and knew that it must be time to meet Colonel Lawrence.

"Do you have any clothing beyond what you are wearing now?" he asked, as she entered the drawing room.

"I have nothing more."

"We shall have you fitted for several gowns immediately, Miss McBride," and he rose from his desk, walked to a china cabinet and poured two glasses of claret. He handed her a glass and smiled. Colonel Lawrence was a man used to being in charge, and Darcy would be no exception. He showed her to a richly patterned wing back chair by the fire and stood by the mantel, sipping his claret, looking at her.

"Our arrangement will be as follows," he instructed. "You will have your complete freedom here. I do not have the time or the inclination to be your jailer. The penalty for jumping your servitude is severe, and believe me, you would be found. Your good looks work against you in that regard."

Darcy listened, but she was not intimidated. She had no intention of running away.

Colonel Lawrence continued. "I enjoy dining out, so there will be few nights when the cook is here. Keep the house clean, my uniform in order, and if all goes well, we will journey to the Upper Massachusetts Colony where your duties will be even fewer." He paused and said, "I will ask you to my room when the mood suits me. You will always be compliant and accommodating. Is that clear?"

Darcy raised an eyebrow and said, "I understand fully."

His look softened, and reaching down, he pulled her out of the chair putting his arms around her. "You are an incredibly inviting woman," he murmured.

Darcy could feel her body respond immediately to his embrace. He was not only handsome, but he had the appeal of a man who is sure of himself, and he moved down, kissing her neck. Suddenly, she felt him sweep her up and carry her into his room across the hall. Sliding her on the feather bed, he said, "From now on you belong to me," and he reached up and unfastened each of the four brocade bed curtains, enveloping them for the rest of the night.

* * *

Nathan Lawrence was as good as his word. The following morning Darcy was fitted for several gowns, which were suitable for everyday wear, and he instructed the dressmaker to sew only one evening gown, no more. Lawrence knew Providence society would tolerate a mistress, but they could not abide an Irish mistress. He thought it was a shame to have to hide her beauty, so he decided to escort her to more casual functions.

The two sincerely enjoyed keeping company. Every evening about nine, they ventured out to dine and stroll through the streets of Providence. They would stop and listen to street musicians or watch jugglers, and it was here that Darcy enjoyed her first Punch-and-Judy show. The evenings were slow and leisurely, always ending the same way, on Nathan's feather bed.

Most days Lawrence conducted business away from the home, so after Darcy had completed her housekeeping, she was free to explore the library.

Ironically, this was the most freedom she had ever possessed. In Ireland, she had to answer to Liam and for a brief time Bran, but Colonel Lawrence demanded little of her.

Darcy found him to be an experienced and competent lover. She believed that his age enhanced his proficiency, and she marveled at the vigorous physique he possessed for a man of his years. He introduced her to new avenues of lovemaking and seemed to enjoy awakening new sensations in her. Darcy was an eager and willing student, but as she was gaining skills in passion, she was losing her innocence.

Slowly the role of being exploited as property took its toll on her. Her outlook began to change, and she walled off places where she might be weak and vulnerable, especially her heart. She became cynical about men and believed that they wanted two things out of women: sex and work. She came to scoff at those who sought true love.

"Men don't love women, Nathan. They need them," she said to him one night as they dined at Chilton's Tavern.

"You really believe that, Darcy?" he asked, shaking his head. "Then you have met all the wrong men."

"I agree with you there," she said taking a bite of ham.

Nathan studied Darcy closely that night over dinner. Not only was she lovely to look at, but her company was incredibly stimulating. She was intelligent and quick and always a surprise. He was pleased that his wife would not be joining him for months; he could explore every inch of his new paramour.

Days turned to weeks, and they fell into a pleasant routine. They sat for hours, dining and laughing, discussing everything but their pasts. All Darcy knew of Nathan's life was that he was of a good Devonshire family and that he bought a commission in the military at a young age after marrying a woman by the name of Lydia Collins. Together they had produced three children, who were now fully grown. His wife would not be arriving for months, and they never discussed where Darcy would go when that time arrived.

Nathan asked no questions about Darcy's past, and even if he had, she would not share anything with him about Ireland. She felt it would be a violation of her privacy, and she was already giving enough of herself to him.

She seldom allowed herself thoughts of home. She fought the memories and ghosts by throwing herself headlong into her new life, refusing to look back. On one occasion, she ventured to the oceanfront for comfort and vowed never to return. This was not the same ocean. It couldn't be. There was no crashing surf to console her, no green hills to soothe her, only a noisy, dirty harbor on the Narragansett Bay.

One afternoon Nathan arrived with news that he must ready himself for the journey to the northern regions of Massachusetts. He stood in the doorway of her room with a concerned look on his face and said, "Darcy, I must be honest with you about something."

She turned around in her desk chair and looked at him. He looked very handsome standing in his red officer's uniform, but his face was weary. For the first time since she met him, Darcy thought that he looked his age.

"The northern frontier is very dangerous, and as you know, we are at war. It is not uncommon for bands of Abenaki to swoop down over settlements killing everyone. There is little protection afforded to those who venture into hostile country. The French are also saturating the area, escalating everything. I cannot endanger your life. I have changed my mind, you cannot come with me. I must sell your indentured service. I'm very sorry."

Darcy was stunned. Life had recently taken a turn for the better, and she would not allow him to ruin their perfect arrangement with this sudden attack of conscience.

"I have no qualms about venturing up north, Nathan," she said without hesitation.

"You don't know enough to be afraid," he argued.

Darcy's temper flared, and she said sarcastically, "I didn't realize that women weren't allowed on the frontier, or are they simply stronger than I am?"

"I will be busy supervising this new fort, and I will not have time to take care of you."

"When have I ever asked you to take care of me? In fact, I find the idea of anyone fawning over me repulsive."

Nathan chuckled. It was his turn to be sarcastic. "I've always loved your vulnerability, Darcy."

He was not willing to argue with her any longer. In fact, he was secretly pleased that she wanted to stay by his side. Nathan shook his head and sighed, "I hope the French are easier to conquer than you. Pack your things, Darcy McBride. We leave tomorrow at dawn."

* * *

Darcy and Nathan traveled by carriage to Boston, where they were joined by a company of the 50th Infantry. It was here where they made final preparations for their journey. Darcy and Colonel

Lawrence would be the only ones riding, and he warned her that the days would be long and arduous.

The first day of their journey, when Nathan's back was turned, the men in ranks gave Darcy indecent looks. She hated their lewd whispers and obscene gestures. She avoided eye contact, remaining cool and aloof. Gradually they viewed her as arrogant and left her alone.

North of Boston they encountered tidy homes with farmers working in the fields, their entire families bending their backs assisting with the spring planting. Gradually the road became a path, and the tall conifers joined overhead forming a huge, dark umbrella. The further north they rode the denser the vegetation became, and Darcy marveled at the abundant wildlife. Ireland had been depleted of its game long ago, and she was in awe at the number of deer, beaver, and rabbit she had seen on the first day.

Nathan regularly consulted with a weather-beaten old man who was their guide. To Darcy, he was the epitome of the backwoodsman. He was a little man, thin and dirty and wore a loose, buckskin hunting shirt and breeches. A tomahawk dangled from his belt, with a sheath for his hunting knife, and across his chest was a strap holding a powder horn and shot pouch.

She was fascinated by his tall moccasins, which traveled all the way up to his knees, where they were secured by rawhide thongs. He wore no hat, and his thin gray hair lay in tangles all over his head. The feature which attracted the most attention was his completely white left eye, but it did not seem to deter his capabilities as a scout. Nathan appeared to have every confidence in this man. He fascinated Darcy, and she was determined to become acquainted with him before the journey was over.

As sunset approached, they found a clearing, and the regulars broke camp. A good-sized tent was pitched for Colonel Lawrence and Darcy while the men slept in smaller two-man shelters. Cots for Nathan and Darcy were included on the pack horses, so the two of them were able to sleep comfortably off the ground.

Darcy could smell dinner being prepared over the open fire, as she stood and stretched inside the tent. She was not used to riding, and she would have to hide her stiff back and legs from Nathan. Darcy was determined not to show him any weakness on the journey.

After the evening meal of salt pork and hard tack, everyone prepared for bed knowing that tomorrow's journey would be taxing. After posting several guards, Nathan joined her in the tent. He sat down by her on the cot and said, "Now listen carefully to me. If there is a raid tonight or at any time stay close to the guide. His name is Moses Tinker. He will take good care of you. I will be too busy with my command."

"I thought we were in the land of the Iroquois, our allies."

"True, but we must always be on our guard. Farther north, above Fort Pepperell and the Piscataqua River, we may run into the Abenaki. They have been conducting raids on the settlers there for years. We have plantations there now, but the Abenaki are undeterred."

The word *plantation* gave Darcy an unsettled feeling. She had heard this word used in Ireland in reference to the British and Scot settlements on Irish land, particularly in Ulster. She could understand the

Abenaki being outraged. Her home, too, had been raped and confiscated by the British.

"Is there a settlement where we are going?"

"Only a few cabins, we have erected Fort Lawrence mainly as a deterrent to the French. Quebec is not far off, and they could easily come down to New England through the back door. Already we have news of French settlers just to the north, and the area is simply crawling with those damn Jesuits."

Darcy's eyes sparked. "I'll have you know, Nathan, that a *damned Jesuit* was the best friend I ever had. I suggest you keep your opinions to yourself about Catholics."

A look of shock turned to anger on Nathan Lawrence's face, and he said firmly, "Might I remind you that you are my indentured servant and that I am the commanding officer here? You will always show me respect. Is that clear?"

"Yes sir!" snapped Darcy.

Nathan's temper cooled, and he laughed putting his arms around Darcy. "Come now, my little colleen. Let's not quarrel. I'm as weary tonight as you are. Let us end the day giving each other sweet pleasure," He brushed the hair away from her face and said, "I see the envious looks on the faces of the men, and I know that I am very lucky to be holding such a desirable woman."

Darcy softened and looked into his eyes. He pulled her down onto a sheepskin rug on the floor of the tent and removed the shoulder of her shift, running his lips over her skin. Darcy could not remain angry with Nathan for long, and she returned his caresses affectionately.

As she fell asleep that night, she listened to the crickets and the wind moving through the trees. It became apparent to her why Father Etienne loved this vast and wonderful place. She too felt honored to be a part of it.

Chapter 18

The journey into the frontier continued for days. The pace was grueling, and the anxiety of the party heightened as they ventured farther north. Darcy had to keep herself from thinking about the ocean of trees surrounding her. Father Etienne had told her that no white man had ever found his way across the vast terrain to the Pacific coast beyond and that many settlers had lost their way in that confusing maze of trees, never returning home again. For this reason, Darcy stayed close to the group; she did not want to join the ranks of those unfortunate wandering souls.

In spite of all the peril and uncertainty, Darcy had never felt so alive. The thrill of adventure burned within her and the possibility of danger ignited every fiber of her being. Gone was the dull apathy born of long-suffering and disappointment; she was alive again.

As sunset approached each evening, Moses Tinker would go ahead of the party to find a suitable spot to break camp and look for signs of Indian parties in the area. They had seen no evidence thus far, but Nathan was not about to grow complaisant, and he drove the group on at a feverish pace. The thrill of adventure quickly turned to fatigue.

Darcy assumed that they would stop and rest at Fort Pepperell, but when they crossed the Piscataqua River, she rode up alongside Nathan and asked, "I thought Fort Pepperell was on this river?"

"It is, but farther to the southeast."

"I thought we were going to rest there."
"No, we must keep on. Are you tired?"
"No, I'm just curious. That's all," she lied.

Darcy was indeed tired and anxious to rest. She was exhausted and sick of being surrounded by men, longing to be away from their prying eyes. She missed the company of a woman, and she reminisced about her conversations with Dominique, wishing for her friend.

She could see the journey wearing on Nathan as well. Conversation did not come easily with him, and his brow was furrowed. They had traveled in a steady rain since sunrise, and it showed no signs of stopping. Darcy's clothing clung to her body, and her hair was plastered to her skin. The trail was becoming soupy, and the horses kicked mud onto the soldiers behind her. When she dropped to the rear of the line to be courteous, Nathan signaled her back--the position was far too dangerous.

The rain ended by evening, and everyone was busy drying out bedding and supplies at the campsite when Darcy spotted Moses Tinker mending his moccasins by the fire. She sat down next to him, and he looked up at her in surprise. He looked around for signs of Colonel Lawrence. To put him at his ease, she said, "You don't have to be concerned, Mr. Tinker. I may talk to whomever I choose."

He continued to work on his moccasins, keeping his eyes down.

"Were you born in these parts?" she asked.
"Not born, but raised."
"Where?"
"I was raised up by Windsor River, ma'am."

Darcy noticed the funny way his gray beard jumped up and down as he spoke, and she watched his hands move the needle deftly through the leather as he repaired his moccasin.

She suspected that beneath that dirty and disheveled exterior, Moses Tinker had a keen mind.

"Windsor River, that's where Fort Lawrence is built," she said, "You must be going home."

"Home for the last time, I'm done scoutin'. I'm going to build a little place near the fort and stay there for good. I'm too old for this. "

Even a seasoned guide can get road weary, Darcy thought.

"How do you know these lands so well? It is so vast, and every turn looks like the last one."

"There's nothing special about it. You probably know your home just as well." He stopped sewing and looked at her. "Say, you're Irish, ain't you? My pappy was Irish. Listenin' to you talk is like having him alive again. You people have a way of sounding like you're singin' a song when you talk."

"So your father was Irish?"

"He was. He came over here after that big battle in Ireland. What was it called again?"

"The Battle of the Boyne?"

"Yes, that's it," and he nodded. When he smiled, Darcy noticed he had few teeth.

"My, my," she said. "It's a proud thing to say that your ancestors fought at the Boyne, Mr. Tinker."

"He lost one of his legs in that fight, but he said it was worth it."

"Was your mother Irish too?

"Naw, my mother was Nipmuc Indian. We moved to the Windsor after she died of the pox. The English took her home away too, just like they did in your land." He looked over in the direction of the soldiers and shook his head, "They sure have a way of coming in and just helping themselves. I can't understand how you could--" He abruptly broke off, returning to his mending. The fire popped and snapped during Tinker's silence.

Darcy replied, "Yes, Mr. Tinker, I am sleeping with the enemy, and right now, it is how I survive. Might I remind you, that you too are on His Majesty's payroll?"

He snickered and said, "Well, I guess we've all gotta dance with the devil, don't we? But someday we'll be rid of 'em. Mark my words."

As they were going to bed that night, Nathan told Darcy that they were less than a day away from Fort Lawrence. Relief washed over her, and she sighed deeply. At her first opportunity, she would find a stream to bathe. The dust and mud covered her skirt, and it was speckled everywhere with small seeds, which refused to dislodge themselves. She began to see the practicality of buckskin.

Darcy slid her weary body under the blankets, and Nathan rolled over on his cot, instantly asleep. They had been too dirty and road weary to be amorous for many nights now, and Darcy was grateful to Nathan for leaving her alone.

The next morning brought sunshine and renewed hopes. Everyone was eager to arrive at their destination, and the pace quickened. About midday, Nathan said that Fort Lawrence was just over the hill, and when they reached the clearing at the summit, Darcy stopped her horse. The panorama was breathtaking.

Directly below her in a lush valley was the Windsor River, winding its way past the star-shaped timber fort as it rested on a hill in the center of the valley. The cliffs on either side were topped with dark green pines, in striking contrast to the aquamarine of the river. The hills of Kerry were a bright emerald color, but the dark rich green of the New World was equally beautiful.

Darcy realized that she was holding up the party. She moved on, her horse picking its way carefully down the hill. They passed a grove of maples, which had several wooden spouts protruding from the bark. Darcy recalled someone telling her once that sweet syrup could be derived from the sap of these trees, and she wondered if this was the case here. She would make a point to ask Nathan about it later.

Realizing that the fort was still several miles off, Nathan ordered the company to stop in the clearing and eat their midday meal. The soldiers sat down on overturned logs or sprawled out directly onto the ground, eating their rations. Darcy dismounted to stretch her legs. She walked around the small clearing and spotted an overturned bucket in the underbrush. She wondered if settlers had tapped maple trees here too, and she picked up her skirts and walked through the brush to have a better look.

A crow was eating bugs off a log by the bucket, and he flew up into a tree to watch from a safer distance. As she waded through the brush, she saw the badly decaying corpse of a human being. Maggots crawled everywhere over the remains, and although the man's face remained intact, the skin from his skull had been ripped savagely from his body. Darcy could not move or even scream. Her eyes were locked on the expression of agony forever frozen on the face of the dead man. When she saw the crow sitting in the tree waiting to resume his meal, bile rose in her throat.

Moses Tinker stepped up behind her. He took Darcy by the arm and urged, "Come along quickly, Miss. It's dangerous."

After Moses had informed Colonel Lawrence of the scalping, the company left immediately. Darcy now understood what Nathan feared. She recalled Father Etienne talking about the death of his mother, and after seeing the brutality of the act, Darcy understood why he was so distraught.

They arrived safely at the fort in the afternoon. Everyone was relieved. There was already a garrison posted there, commanded by Major Joseph Howell, but when Colonel Lawrence arrived, he would return to Boston.

Darcy was shown to her room located near Nathan's quarters. It was a small room with a rustic table and chairs and a bed covered with a well-worn patchwork quilt. Darcy sat down on the bed and began to unpin her hair. She was determined to wash the mud off her body before the day's end and change into some clean clothes.

There was a knock on the door, and an attractive young woman stood in front of her. "I'll tighten the ropes on the bed for you, Miss McBride, and I'm boiling some water to wash out that old quilt too."

"I don't expect to be waited on," protested Darcy. "I'll bring out my own laundry and do the wash myself. You must have hundreds of other things to do."

"Oh, there's not so much. This is a small fort compared to those to the south, Miss."

Darcy could hear the unmistakable Scottish brogue in this woman's voice, and she asked, "Are you from Scotland?"

"No, I am from Ireland," the woman said.

The smile dropped from Darcy's face. She raised an eyebrow and said, "Let me guess, Ulster Plantation."

With Darcy's icy attitude, the cheerful expression faded from the young woman's face. She said nothing more and left the room.

Darcy detested the people who moved onto the plantations the British had organized in Ireland. She considered them outsiders and usurpers.

Without a second thought, she washed her hair, pinned it up and ventured into the large courtyard the colonists called a *parade ground*. It was busy with British regulars trying to situate the new arrivals, and she saw few women.

Cabins stood against the inside walls of the fort upon which sentries were stationed. Darcy remembered hearing their footsteps above her head when she was in her room. She noticed that the chimneys of these buildings faced the interior courtyard, and she guessed that this was to prevent the timbered walls of the fort from catching fire. Several cannons stood on the battlements and a powder magazine was erected in the center of the parade ground.

Holding her laundry, she headed over toward three women building a fire under a large crucible. "Is this where I wash my clothing?"

"Yes right here. You are welcome to join us," they replied. They were cordial and helped her find everything she needed, but when the Scotch-Irish woman handed her a crock of laundry soap, Darcy's back stiffened, and her smile faded. She pushed her clothes down into the pot with a stick, saying nothing.

With her arms crossed over her chest, the woman watched Darcy. Finally, she said, "Why do you hate me?"

"I have nothing against you *personally*," Darcy said, without looking up. "Just your kind."

"How dare you come to my home and treat me like I'm not good enough," the woman said.

"Well now, how does it feel?" replied Darcy. "The only difference is I will let you keep your home and your religion. That's more than you did for us in Ireland."

Darcy bent over, and the cross she wore inside her bodice slipped out.

The woman said, "You seem to be forgetting the meaning of that cross you wear around your neck."

Darcy straightened up, burned a look into her and then walked away.

After finishing her laundry, she returned to her room where there was a tub of warm water waiting for her. She removed her filthy clothes and stepped into the small tub. The water felt heavenly as she scrubbed off the grime of the trip.

Darcy removed the cross and charm from her neck and then remembered what the woman had said to her earlier. A pang of guilt shot through her. She had been self-righteous and judgmental, and as much as she hated to apologize she knew she must do it.

As Darcy was putting on a white shift and pulling a clean gown over her head, there was a knock on the door. A guard said, "Colonel Lawrence wants to see you in his office."

Nathan was busy with Major Howell when Darcy was admitted. He had cleaned up as well. He was dressed in a clean uniform but wore no jacket. He was in his shirt sleeves, vest and breeches. Someone had polished his boots, and he looked very dashing, sitting behind his desk.

When Major Howell left, he said, "Darcy, there is something that I would like you to do. I have the identity of the man scalped in the maple grove. It seems that he has been missing for some time. He was a settler living not too far from the fort. His wife and children are living here now waiting for his return. I think that the news should come from a woman. I would like you to be the one to tell her."

Darcy gasped, "You want me to tell her that her husband is dead?"

"Yes."

"Oh, Nathan, what a thing to ask."

"I know, Darcy, but I know none of the women here, and you were the one to find him."

Darcy sighed and reluctantly gave her consent. Nathan thanked her and told her the woman's name was Adrianna McDermott. She stepped out into the sunshine and straightened her back. This was going to be difficult, and she did not relish the thought of bringing misery to anyone.

After asking a small girl to direct her to Mrs. McDermott's quarters, she took a deep breath and knocked on the door. She heard footsteps, the door opened and there stood the Scotch-Irish woman. Darcy's heart jumped into her throat and with a shaky voice she asked reluctantly, "Is Adrianna McDermott here?"

"I am Adrianna McDermott," the woman said with her eyes narrowing. "What do *you* want?"

Darcy's eyes widened, she swallowed hard and said, "I have come to speak with you for two reasons, Mrs. McDermott." She took a breath and said, "My resentment and bitterness was wrong, and I must apologize for my behavior earlier. I am sorry to have judged you."

The woman studied Darcy's eyes and then offered, "Please come in, Miss McBride."

Darcy stepped into the quarters. It was a large room shared by several women and children. Adrianna showed her around and explained, "These are the laundress quarters, and that door leads to the surgery. The women work in these areas of the fort."

As they walked, Darcy took a good look at Mrs. McDermott for the first time. She was a woman of medium height with blonde hair and freckles sprinkled lightly across the bridge of her nose. She reminded Darcy of Teila, but she was taller and more robust.

Darcy's palms began to sweat, and she stuttered, "Um, Mrs. McDermott. Thank you for the tour, but Colonel Lawrence has sent me here with news."

"News of what, my husband?" she asked, her eyes growing large.

"They have found your husband, Mrs. McDermott. In fact, *I* found your husband," she said in a shaky voice, "I am sorry. He is dead, an Indian attack."

The woman let out a cry of despair, and as if she were a rag doll, she slumped to her knees, sobbing into her apron. Adrianna was inconsolable. Women rushed over enveloping her as Darcy stepped back, covering her face with her hands.

Darcy hated herself. She walked outside, filled with shame for bringing misery to the life of this woman. She leaned on a timber support and stared into space. As distraught as she was, Darcy did not cry, could not cry. How long had it been since she had cried? She thought back. Had she ever shed a tear for Father Etienne or for Dominique? *No, never.* Darcy realized that in her quest for survival she had become callous and hard. She bit her lip, squared her shoulders and headed back to her quarters to wait for Nathan.

Chapter 19

Spring turned to summer at Fort Lawrence. For the first month, Darcy stayed within the confines of the fort. Initially life at the fort held her interest, but as time went on she found herself longing to walk in the woods or bathe in a stream. Most of the women were content, if not afraid, to venture beyond the timber walls, but Darcy was restless and needed diversion and new surroundings.

Frequently, she thought of Moses Tinker and wondered if he was building his new cabin. One evening she asked Nathan what had happened to the guide, and he replied, "I believe someone said that he is building a cabin not too far down the river."

"Has anyone checked on him lately?"

"Why?" he laughed. "That old man can take care of himself better than anyone I know."

"I want to go out and see him tomorrow," said Darcy as she popped a piece of maple candy into her mouth.

"Don't be foolish, Darcy. It's dangerous out there."

"Oh pooh, women have been living on the frontier for years, Nathan," she said, sitting down in his lap. "I will go mad if I have to stay behind these four walls any longer."

"Now, Darcy, you are outside every day working in the garden and helping with the crops."

"That's right next to the fort. I want to see the countryside and walk the river," she argued.

Nathan put his arms around her, shaking his head. "I haven't the strength to argue with you, Darcy. You would try the patience of Job so I'll agree to it, on one condition that you venture no more than one mile from the fort *and* that you have a dog."

"A dog!" she said, with delight.

"The settlers have been using them for years to warn of Indians. Let's see," Nathan said, stroking his clean-shaven chin. "I think Cavenaugh's bitch had a litter. He may have a dog for you. I'll check into it tomorrow."

"Oh, thank you, Nathan! I can't wait!" she said hugging him.

The following day, Darcy was presented with a tall retriever named Shenanigan. She hoped that he didn't live up to his name, but after several days of training, the dog appeared to be intelligent and loyal. They became inseparable friends.

She felt confident that the dog was ready to accompany her outside the walls of the fort, and after spending most of the day dipping candles with one of the women, Darcy needed to clear her head and walk along the river. She grabbed some cheese and a large portion of Sally Lunn cake and set out with Shenanigan for Moses Tinker's cabin. The dog seemed happy to be out of the confines of the fort as well, and they stepped out of the gate feeling exhilarated.

They passed the hills of the three sisters--corn, beans, and squash--and headed south towards Tinker's cabin. They left the sunshine and entered the dark silence of the woods as Shenanigan dashed in and out of the brush, flushing birds and rabbits.

Darcy followed the deer path, which ran parallel to the Windsor River, and when she crossed a small stream, she spotted another trail leading to the west. She was tempted to follow it but decided to stick to her original plan.

As she drew close to Tinker's homestead, she heard an ax hitting a tree. She smiled knowing he was nearby. She stepped out into the clearing, and there he stood saddle notching a log for his new home.

"Good day to you, Mr. Tinker!" shouted Darcy.

He looked up from his work, surprised. He wiped his brow, put down his ax and walked over to her.

"Good day to you, Ma'am," he said somewhat suspiciously.

"I see you are almost done. It's going to be a fine home."

Moses relaxed. He was proud of his cabin and happy to show it off.

"How are you going to get those logs up on the top part of your walls?" asked Darcy.

"There are ways," he replied.

She walked around the cabin admiring his workmanship and stopped at last at a stump and took the cloth off the basket she carried. "I brought you something to eat."

Moses stared at Darcy as she unpacked the food, looking confused. No one had ever taken an interest in him, especially such a lovely young woman, and he was taken aback. They sat on some stumps, and Darcy watched as Moses gobbled the food ravenously. She guessed that most days he was too tired at the end of the day to cook for himself, so he ate poorly.

"That dog's a good idea," he said gesturing toward Shenanigan. You should get a musket too. You can't be too careful out here," he warned.

Darcy saw his new flintlock rifle. It was considered superior to the cumbersome musket, and she wondered if he might be willing to sell his previous firearm. She took a sip of cider and asked, "Moses, would you happen to have a gun for sale?"

"Might."

"I have something to propose. If you give me a gun and teach me how to shoot, I'll help you finish your cabin and do some cooking for you."

He looked at her and took a bite of cheese. "Maybe."

"I make a very good steak-and-kidney pie," she urged.

"Not a bad Sally Lunn either," he agreed, taking another bite. He tilted his head back, looked at her out of his good eye and said, "Consider it done."

"Good! I'll be back tomorrow at the same time," and she hopped up, shaking his hand. "Good day, Mr. Tinker."

"Call me Moses, Ma'am," he shouted after her, as she waved good-bye.

Over the next several months, Darcy completed her chores at the fort as quickly as possible and raced down to help Moses with the cabin and barn every day. He spent the morning getting the logs notched, and when she arrived in the afternoon, they worked on the upper half of the cabin.

Darcy climbed to the top of the cabin and steadied the log while Moses pulled up the other end, resting it in the notch of the log underneath it. They repeated this process until the cabin was the desired height. After that, they started the roof. Their routine never varied. They worked on the cabin all afternoon, made an evening meal, and then Moses worked with Darcy on her target practice until dusk.

Darcy was becoming a fair shot, and Moses was impressed with her keen eye. The biggest challenge was keeping the musket steady. It was a heavy firearm, and after lifting logs all afternoon, it was hard to hold the gun upright, but once her strength improved so did her prowess. Darcy liked target practice, and it gave her peace of mind knowing that she could defend herself if necessary.

"I'm done washing up the bowls. I'll be going back now," Darcy called to Moses.

He was busy mortaring a row of glass bottles into the cabin wall, substituting them for windows. They would let much-needed light into the cabin and were a less-expensive alternative to glass, which was unheard of on the frontier.

He did not look up from his work and simply raised his hand as a goodbye. The two had grown comfortable with one another, and Darcy began to look upon Moses as a sort of father. The old man's lifestyle had never been conducive to a home and children, so the friendship with Darcy provided him with a chance to have a daughter, an opportunity which he thought was lost forever.

Darcy whistled for Shenanigan, picked up her musket and began loading it. It was a time-consuming activity, and Darcy knew that she would not have time to load before an attack, so she completed the task now.

She measured a charge from her powder horn, funneling it with her hands into the muzzle of the gun. Next, she placed a patch with a bullet on it over the muzzle and shoved them both down into the bore with a ramrod. She primed the lock, closed the pan and was ready to go.

This procedure she had repeatedly practiced until it took her less than one minute to load, and even then Darcy was not satisfied. She did not want the stress of an attack to ever confuse her memory.

The sun was sinking low as Darcy and Shenanigan made their way back to the fort. As they passed the stream, Shenanigan suddenly stopped in his tracks, growing stiff-legged listening to something. Every fiber of Darcy's being went on alert, and her heart raced.

She looked into the silent woods and listened too. Her ears picked up a low moaning sound as if someone was hurt. *Was this a trick or was someone in need?* She could not live with herself if she left someone alone to die in the forest, so she started down the path which ran along the banks of the stream.

Like lightning, Shenanigan shot past her to be the first to encounter danger. Her musket slung over her shoulder, Darcy ran behind the dog. As she came around a huge oak, she found Shenanigan standing cautiously in front of a little girl.

The child was sitting on the ground oblivious to both of them. She rocked back and forth, shaking her hands and moaning. Darcy looked around for a parent, but the girl seemed to be alone. She was a white child who looked to be about six or seven years of age, and Darcy asked gently, "Are you hurt?"

She reached out and put her hand on the girl's shoulder, and the child recoiled from her.

"Are you all right? Where is your Mother?"

She never looked at Darcy and there was still no response. Darcy recalled several of the residents of Kilkerry, who had emerged from the famine with feeble minds due to poor nutrition or difficult births, and she wondered if this little girl was afflicted with a similar problem. Judging by her clean dress and well-combed hair, someone cared for her. Shenanigan began to sniff her hair and face. Instantly the child giggled and reached out to touch him. The dog jumped back, and the child stood up, laughing and reaching out to stroke his coat. He looked at Darcy, confused.

She saw her opportunity to lure the child to a place of safety, so she whistled for Shenanigan to follow her. The nearest home was that of Adrianna McDermott, and Darcy set off in that direction. She must move quickly; night was falling fast.

The child followed Shenanigan into the clearing of the McDermott homestead. A boy of about twelve years of age was the first to spot them walking down the hill toward the log cabin. He started yelling for his mother to come quickly.

Instantly children of all shapes and sizes emerged from the woods and ran up to the little girl, hugging her and showering her with kisses. Adrianna burst out of the brush too and ran across the clearing, scooping the child into her arms, kissing her and crying.

"Oh Nan, where have you been?"

Even with all this attention, Nan's expression did not change.

"How can I ever thank you, Miss McBride. You have brought my baby back to me," said Adrianna, her eyes full of tears. "It was so close to nightfall, I would have lost my mind wondering if she was alive."

"I was returning from Moses Tinker's cabin, and I heard her moaning. She was sitting by the stream, rocking back and forth. I couldn't get her to move, but she liked the dog and was willing to follow him," explained Darcy.

"Ma, maybe we should get a dog for Nan. He could lead her back home if she was lost," said one of the boys.

Adrianna nodded her head and said, "This has happened before. Next time we may not be so lucky. Thank you. Please come in and break bread with us tonight."

"I dare not, Mrs. McDermott. The sun is too low. I must head back to the fort right away."

"Well, then please come and have supper with us on any night you choose. You will always be welcome in our home."

Feeling self-conscious, Darcy shrugged and said, "I am glad to bring you good news at last."

Adrianna and the children watched Darcy as she disappeared into the dark woods with Shenanigan. Adrianna thought she was a curious woman. No female in her right mind would venture out into the woods at night, and she couldn't understand what she saw in that crazy old scout. But more than anything, Adrianna could not understand how Darcy could be the mistress of a British officer. There were even rumors that she had been educated by a Catholic priest. The woman's beauty was apparent, but her lifestyle was mysterious. She was just the sort of person Adrianna would like to get to know.

* * *

The following morning Darcy stretched lazily, enjoying having the bed to herself. Nathan had dressed and gone out to his office early.

He received word that Governor Shirley wanted another fort erected, this time on the Kensington River to the north. Nathan was expecting some men to help him make plans for the site and do a survey for the construction.

Darcy dressed and pinned up her hair. She stepped to the mirror and examined herself. She was dressed in a curious blend of feminine apparel and frontier accessories. Over her soft gown, she had a brown leather belt, buckled around her waist to be used for hiking up her skirts in the event that she must run, and across her chest was a strap for her shot pouch and powder horn. A musket over her shoulder finished off the odd ensemble. She shook her head chuckling. She wondered what Nathan saw in her.

Darcy continued to find Nathan attractive, but lately, she felt dissatisfied. More and more she longed for intimacy of the heart, something which Nathan could never provide and Darcy did not want from him. She knew she could never love him, but the question nagged her; was she capable of loving anyone?

Shaking off the feeling of loneliness, she grabbed her musket and set off for Moses' cabin. She was granted a brief escape from her duties at the fort today to help him put the roof on his barn. The day was hot, and the sun-drenched them in perspiration as they toiled on the roof. Relief came at last when the sun dropped below the horizon at the end of the day. Their work completed, Darcy climbed down to prepare a fire outside since it was too hot to cook in the cabin.

Moses sat on a stump, wiping his face with a rag. He declared, "I've got to make some chairs. At the end of a hard day, a man wants to sit on a chair, not a stump."

"It will all get done in good time," reassured Darcy. "Why, look at how far we have come today."

The cabin was done. He needed a few household articles, but the structure was complete at last. Moses was in the process of erecting a rope bed, and Darcy was tying a quilt for him as a surprise.

He watched her fry up some venison chops in an iron pan, which she placed over the campfire on a three-legged spider trivet. He caught the rich aroma of gingerbread baking in the Dutch oven also.

Moses was feeling better now that the sun had dropped and dinner was almost ready. There would be no target practice tonight. They were both too tired, and after dinner, when Darcy stood up to collect the dishes, Moses said, "You go back now. It's late and I can take care of these few things."

Too tired to protest, Darcy loaded her musket and whistled to the Shenanigan. She bent down and kissed the old man on the cheek. "You're good to me, Moses Tinker."

He said gruffly, "Go on! Get out of here, you and your silly notions."

Darcy smiled. She could see Moses was pleased. It had been a long time since anyone had been kind to him, and he didn't know how to react. She looked over her shoulder, and he was shaking his head and chuckling.

As Darcy entered the forest tonight, something felt different. She was unsure what it was, but Shenanigan felt it too. They went as far as the stream, and nothing appeared out of the ordinary, but Darcy's intuition told her something was wrong.

They continued walking, and suddenly Shenanigan's legs stiffened, a low gurgling sound rolled in his throat. She saw his lips curl into a snarl, and she scanned the forest for danger. Her hands were shaking, but she managed to hike her skirt up into her belt so she could run. At first, she walked briskly. Then when Shenanigan started to snarl again, she ran. Suddenly, someone jumped out of the brush behind her, chasing her. Shenanigan was barking and snapping, but she dare not look back.

At a frenzied pace, Darcy raced down the path towards the fort, jumping wildly over rocks and logs, not caring if branches slashed her or tore at her skin. If only she could reach the clearing in front of the fort, the sentry would see her and sound the alarm. Darcy knew the clearing was just ahead, but the dog's snarling had moved closer, and she knew that her pursuer was gaining ground.

She rounded the last stretch of the trail and broke into the clearing at full stride. Feeling as if her lungs would explode, she looked up, and to her horror, saw the sentry leaning on a post, sleeping. The yelp of the Indian behind her struck terror into her heart. Darcy reached deep within herself to find the speed she needed to save her life. She stretched her legs out before her, hurtling herself at lightning speed. The Abenaki was gaining rapidly and just as he reached out to grab her hair, her gun accidentally discharged with a blast. The sleeping sentry awakened with a start and scrambled to his feet. He lowered his rifle, aimed and put a bullet into the Indian's forehead. The force kicked the assailant back onto the ground, as Shenanigan tore at him savagely.

Darcy did not stop to look back. She continued to hurtle herself toward the fort, not slowing down until she was well inside the stockade. Panting, she staggered to a post for support while people came running. Shenanigan bounded into the fort, blood on his jowls.

Collecting herself, Darcy reported to Nathan's office to give a full account. He was relieved to find her unharmed, but he did not seem overly concerned about the threat of an attack. "I am not convinced that this Indian was part of a war party. It is likely he is a renegade acting alone, but I will take precautions."

Darcy retired to her room to bathe and steady her nerves. The cool water relaxed her body, but she could not quell her fears regarding the safety of Moses and the McDermott family.

After dining alone in her room, Darcy changed into her green muslin gown and strapped on her shot pouch and powder horn in case there was an attack. The parade ground was alive with activity as preparations were being made for an influx of settlers seeking shelter at the fort. Darcy looked for familiar faces in the crowd.

The sun had set, and many torches were lit, casting a golden hue over everything. Militiamen and regulars alike cleaned their muskets and joked about the possibility of an attack. No one seemed to think it was likely, most of all Colonel Lawrence.

Darcy was filling buckets with water to quench fires in case there was an attack. She was glad to be busy. It kept her mind from reliving the terrifying events of the afternoon.

Nathan had been consulting with three men all day regarding the construction of the new fort. He was forced to cut their meeting short to assemble the militia. The men emerged from his office and sat down at a table in front of the officers' quarters to have a drink. They were served pints of ale per Nathan's request, and they settled in to observe the activity on the parade ground.

They were men in the prime of their lives, two in officers' uniforms, one in civilian attire, and they lounged in chairs making casual conversation.

"So what did Lawrence do with the stupid bastard anyway?" asked one of the officers.

"I hear he threw him in chains. The guard may have been a crack shot, but if the woman's gun hadn't discharged, waking him up, her hair would be swinging from the top of an Abenaki stick tonight."

The man in civilian clothes seemed disinterested in the conversation, and sat back in his chair with his boots on the table, drinking his pint and observing the frantic settlers pouring into the fort. He had dark hair tied back in a leather thong and a clean-shaven face. Although he was dressed in a coarse linen shirt, his breeding and education were apparent. His complexion was dark, and he had sharp blue eyes.

He was drawn into the conversation by Lieutenant Brewster, who said, "That wench must be fast to be able to outrun a savage. Do you know which one she is, Jean-Michel?"

"Hmm?"

"Which one is the woman who was attacked this afternoon?"

"I've not seen her," he replied.

"I think I know which one she is. I'll try to point her out," said Major English. "She's one I wouldn't mind tumbling."

He looked around and then jerked his head, "There. She's walking by us in the green dress."

Jean-Michel Lupé was bored. He sighed and turned to look at Darcy as she walked by. Suddenly, his eyes widened, and he sat forward on his chair removing his boots from the table.

Tom English laughed, and said, "I told you she was good looking."

English went on talking, but Jean-Michel did not hear him. His attention was riveted on Darcy. She had taken his breath away. Never in his life had any woman moved him so quickly and so profoundly. English waved his hand in front of Jean-Michel's face, trying to get his attention.

"What is it, Tom?" Lupé asked irritably.

"I'm trying to tell you she's not available. She's the colonel's whore."

"That can change," and Jean-Michel grinned slowly. The men broke into laughter, as Jean-Michel sat back. Darcy disappeared behind the surgery.

"It's bad enough she's Irish, but they say she's an arrogant bitch too, so don't say I didn't warn you, Lupé," said Brewster.

"Your concern for my well-being has been noted," said Jean-Michel, sarcastically.

The officers moved on to other matters, but Jean-Michel was preoccupied with Darcy, and he continually scanned the crowd for another glimpse of her. Suddenly, she returned from behind the surgery and headed past their table again. The officers did not notice her, but Jean-Michel burned a look into her that she could feel.

Darcy slowed her pace a little and looked around. She had the sensation that she was being watched, but no one seemed to be staring, so she dismissed the feeling continuing her pace. When she reached the table where the men were sitting, her eyes rested on Jean-Michel, and she took a second look. He was leaning forward in his chair, staring directly at her with his forearms resting on his knees.

Darcy's eyebrows shot up, and then she jerked her chin in the air and turned away. It was as if this man looked into her soul, and suddenly she felt vulnerable. No one had ever looked at her with such intensity, and she looked over her shoulder to be sure that this bold stranger was not gazing at someone else. He was watching *her*. She continued walking, but she was unable to control her curiosity and looked over her shoulder one last time. The stranger was sitting back now, but he still had the audacity to be watching her. Tossing her head, she turned around and entered Colonel Lawrence's quarters for the night.

Chapter 20

The sun was beginning to come up over the horizon when Darcy rose from Nathan's bed. He was still asleep after a hard day organizing the militia and dealing with frantic settlers. Darcy could not stay in bed any longer. She was too worried about Moses and Adrianna McDermott. Hoping that they might have come in during the night, she dressed and went out to the parade ground. She stepped out the door and stretched.

Large red clouds were hanging in the sky, and the morning air felt cool and refreshing after a night of stifling heat. Aside from those on sentry duty, the fort was deserted. As she passed the officers' quarters, she spied the man who had been staring at her last evening, and she quickened her pace. He was bending over a wash basin, splashing water on his face and chest, and Darcy thought if she hurried, he might not notice her. He straightened up to dry himself and caught sight of her. Jean-Michel reached for a towel and said with a suggestive smile, "Well, good morning!"

Darcy did not reply and kept walking. He grabbed his shirt and ran after her. "You must not have heard me. I said good morning!"

"I heard you," Darcy said, looking straight ahead.

He was presumptuous to be naked to the waist and walking by her side, and she resented his disrespect. He made no attempt to put his shirt on and merely flung it carelessly over his shoulder.

"I hear you had a close call with an Abenaki yesterday. They say you outran him. There are few white people that can outrun an Indian. In fact, you even walk fast," he said, chuckling and picking up his pace.

Darcy made no attempt to encourage conversation, as she walked on briskly, looking straight ahead.

"So you're from Ireland? What do you think of the Colonies?" continued Jean-Michel, not yet discouraged.

Darcy stopped, faced him squarely and said, "Who are you, and why are you bothering me?"

Her abrupt manner surprised Jean-Michel. He was not used to being rebuffed by women, and his attitude changed from friendly to sharp.

"All right, have it your way. My name is Jean-Michel Lupé, and I will tell you exactly what I want. I am very interested in you, and I was wondering if you would consider taking on another customer."

Darcy's eyes narrowed. Certain that pride would be his Achilles' heel, Darcy looked him up and down and said, "I don't keep company with riff-raff."

Jean-Michel frowned, and Darcy knew that she had hit the mark. His hot temper got the better of him, and he snarled, "Those are mighty high airs for an Irish whore!"

Just as she was about to slap him, there was a loud crack, and one of the sentries fell off the wall landing with a thud on the ground near them. Darcy froze, staring at the body. When she realized what had happened, she ran one direction as Lupé ran the other. Darcy pulled the bell rope alerting the fort, as Jean-Michel dashed back to the wash basin, grabbing his rifle. He scrambled up to the south battery looking out over the river, but he could see nothing unusual.

He pulled his shirt over his head, as the garrison made frenzied attempts to get organized. Suddenly, shots rang from a wooded area.

Darcy looked up at the handful of guards on the walls and realized they needed every musket immediately. She climbed up by Lupé and began loading her own musket. "Get down, you fool!" he barked. "You're in the way."

Darcy loaded and sat down with her back against the wall to wait for the assault. She cursed Nathan for not taking the threat seriously and failing to post more guards.

Suddenly, the French and Abenaki started up the hill, running furiously toward the fort. They planned to scale the walls before the garrison had time to even get out of bed. Jean-Michel was firing continually and reloading. Darcy knew it would be most effective for her to fire as he was loading, so after watching him take a shot, she took a deep breath swung around and fired. She only grazed the Indian's arm. He was stunned for a moment and then continued to dash up the hill.

Darcy loaded again and swung around to take another shot when the Abenaki's chest exploded with blood. She realized that Jean-Michel shot him.

The attackers were drawing nearer, and in a frenzy the regulars loaded the cannons. Darcy looked down and saw a grizzly Frenchman in a fur cap beginning to scale the wall below her, and her heart jumped to her throat. Jean-Michel was reloading, so it was up to her to kill the man without hesitation. She brought the musket up, aimed--and nothing happened. She froze. Terrified, she let the barrel drop. She couldn't do it. Raising her eyes, she looked once more into the man's face. She recognized the expression in his eyes; she had seen it on the faces of the soldiers who raped her at the abbey. All compassion drained from her, and she brought the musket up putting a bullet into his forehead.

Jean-Michel was stunned. After killing a man he fully expected her to dissolve into hysterics, but there she sat, loading her next volley. He shook his head, swung around and took a shot.

After several more rounds, Darcy was replaced by one of the regulars and went below to assist with carrying wounded to the surgery. There was smoke everywhere, and it choked and blinded her as she stumbled across the parade ground. People ran throughout the fort, putting out fires or tending to the wounded. In spite of the panic she felt inside, she knew that she must get to work, people were dying.

Darcy pushed up her sleeves and reached down to attend to a man with a bullet in his knee. Most of the wounded had taken shots to their arms or legs, but a few had their bowels or chests open. She knew if the trauma did not kill them fever would. She cleaned their wounds with witch hazel and applied dressings, but many of the men died within minutes, some of them crying out in agony, others with quiet resignation.

As evening fell, the gunfire slowed down and the air began to clear of smoke. The attack appeared to be over until dawn when the French and the Abenaki would try again to take the fort. Darcy washed up, changed her blood-soaked clothes and went to get something to eat. She did not feel hungry, but she knew she must put something in her belly.

As she crossed the parade ground, she looked for Moses and Adrianna McDermott. They were nowhere to be found, so she requested to see Nathan. He was examining maps with Lupé when she was escorted into the room. He looked up at her and said impatiently, "What is it, Darcy? I'm busy."

"Adrianna McDermott and her eight children are not in the fort."

Nathan ignored her and resumed talking with Jean-Michel, pointing at the map. She repeated her statement again, this time, louder. Nathan looked up and said, "Who is Adrianna McDermott?"

"The woman whose husband was scalped last spring. She and her eight children didn't make it to the fort before the siege began, and now they are trapped out there."

He sighed. "What do you expect me to do about it? It was their responsibility to get up here before the siege. I cannot go after them now."

"There are eight children out there! How can you dismiss that so easily? If you'll do nothing, then I will. I want permission to leave the fort and bring them back to safety," she demanded.

Nathan rolled his eyes, and Jean-Michel smirked. Nathan said firmly, "You'll do no such thing. This discussion is over." Turning to the guard, he said, "Please show Miss McBride out."

Jerking her arm free from the guard, Darcy cried, "Wait a minute, Nathan, I'm not through."

Nathan slammed his fist on the table and barked, "You are most certainly through! Don't you ever forget you are my property, and I have supreme authority regarding your whereabouts. You will *not* leave this fort, *and* you will *not* remain in my office! Is that clear?"

Darcy blanched. To be reminded that she was nothing more than a piece of property in front of this arrogant newcomer was more than she could bear. She would never forgive Nathan for demeaning her publicly. Jean-Michel saw her jaw tighten before she turned on her heel and left the room. He thought Darcy was impudent, but he also thought Lawrence had been hard on her.

Darcy stood outside Nathan's office clenching her fists. She had to clear her mind of this rage and come up with a plan as quickly as possible. Lives were at stake. All of a sudden, the office door opened, and she found herself face to face with Jean-Michel. With an exasperated sigh, she turned her back on him and walked on the parade ground.

He called after her. "You're going out there anyway, aren't you?"

Darcy kept walking. He caught up with her and said, "I'll take you to that woman's cabin."

She laughed and said, "Oh, no."

Jean-Michel watched her walk away and desire stirred inside him. *What am I doing? This can mean only trouble*. Something drove him on. He ran after her again. "I mean it. I will take you."

Darcy scowled. "What's in it for you? You could get into a lot of trouble helping me. Colonel Lawrence has a lot of authority."

"Do you see me in a uniform?' he said grabbing his lapels, and grinning. "I answer to no one. If I choose to walk out there and commit suicide with you, that is my business."

Darcy looked at him closely for the first time. She noticed his eyes were an indigo blue and his skin dusky. She looked away feeling uneasy. He was certainly a capable escort and a good shot, but she did not trust him.

"Thank you, but I'd rather go alone," she answered.

Jean-Michel couldn't believe what he was hearing. He had offered to escort her on a perilous journey, and she said that she would rather go alone. Then the reason occurred to him.

"Are you afraid of me?" he said, raising one eyebrow.

"What?" asked Darcy, feigning ignorance.

"That's it, isn't it? You're afraid of me."

"Ridiculous."

"That can be the only reason that you would decline a capable escort." he said, jumping in front of her and walking backward so he could face her.

"Believe me, you don't intimidate me, Mr. Lupé," laughed Darcy, stepping around him.

"Then let me take you out to rescue those children. Refusing my help may cost them their lives. Do you want that on your conscience?"

This argument gave Darcy pause. She rubbed her forehead and said, "All right, but we leave tonight. I can only hope that they're still alive."

"Meet me at the gate in fifteen minutes," he said.

Jean-Michel thought he must have lost his mind. *What was he doing going out onto the frontier tonight? His impetuous offer might cost him his life, all because this damned woman was clouding his judgment.*

Clad in a dark dress with her musket in hand, Darcy met Jean-Michel at the gate. She noticed that he had changed into a buckskin shirt and leggings. He had a shot pouch and powder horn strapped across his chest and a hunting knife in his belt.

"Where are your orders?" barked the guard as they approached the gate.

"Why would we need orders to go *out*?" asked Jean-Michel as if the guard was stupid. "You'd do better to worry about those who want to get in."

This logic confused the sentry long enough for him to open the gate and let them slip out. They agreed

Darcy would lead since she knew the way to the cabin.

To the right was the enemy encampment, on the left a path to the McDermott cabin. It was a warm, humid night, and the crickets were loud. The moon was hidden behind a thick blanket of clouds, and a roll of thunder in the distance heralded a storm.

Darcy felt vulnerable standing outside the fort. She hadn't realized how much comfort the walls had given her, and when she looked at Jean-Michel, he signaled to her that it was time to go. Taking a deep breath, she bolted down across the clearing as fast as her legs would carry her. If they could make it to the trees undetected, they would be passed their first and most dangerous hurdle.

Darcy crossed successfully and threw herself into the underbrush of the woods waiting for Lupé. Jean-Michel was soon beside her, and he yanked her to her feet roughly. They raced down the deer path as another peal of thunder rolled in the distance. He was grateful for the upcoming storm. The thunder and rain would drown out the sounds of their footsteps.

Just as they rounded the oak tree where Darcy found Nan, Jean-Michel heard voices. He reached out and grabbed Darcy's belt. He yanked her up next to him and whispered, "It's the French. Where would it be safe for us to wait?"

Darcy thought of Moses' cabin. It was off the path of the soldiers and not well-cleared. They returned the way they had come but this time turned downriver to Moses' cabin. Darcy was relieved to see that it was still standing, but when they entered it was empty. Moses had obviously learned of the siege and fled.

Darcy lit a candle. Keeping their weapons handy, they sat down at the table to wait until the French had passed through the area.

The thunder was coming regularly now, but there was no rain yet. Jean-Michel looked around the cabin and asked, "Is the person who lives here up at the fort?"

"No, Moses wouldn't go to the fort," returned Darcy.

"Moses. Moses Tinker?" asked Jean-Michel.

Darcy nodded.

He said with a chuckle, "So old Moses finally settled down. He talked about it for years, but I never thought he'd do it." Jean-Michel looked around at the cabin, smiling.

"You know him?" she asked.

"I've known Moses ever since I was a boy. He used to trap with my father up around Quebec. It was on one of their expeditions down south that my father met my mother. How do you know him?"

"He was our guide coming here. I helped him build this cabin in exchange for a musket and shooting lessons."

"You're a fair shot. He didn't do a bad job. Knowing Moses, there's some rum around here. I could stand a drink."

He looked in the cupboard and found a bottle and two mugs, which he set on the table. The candlelight illuminated the two of them as they sat at the table, throwing everything else into the shadows. Jean-Michel couldn't help but notice how the flame illuminated Darcy's green eyes. After pouring them each a drink, he sat down, crossed his arms over his chest and scrutinized her.

He had looked at her that same way on the parade ground last night. Darcy shifted uncomfortably in her seat and asked, "Why have you been meeting with

Colonel Lawrence?"

Mention of his name was a sobering reminder that Darcy was unavailable, and he answered, "Governor Shirley has ordered a fort to be built up north, and I am here to survey the area and present my findings to Lawrence. I was finalizing plans with him when the attack happened."

"You do not wear the King's uniform. Why is that?" asked Darcy.

"I have no love for King George and his Parliament. I believe them to be selfish and opportunistic, and we would be better off governing ourselves."

"You sound like all Irishmen," laughed Darcy. "I find it hard to believe that the British trust you in military matters with your French name."

"I find it hard to believe as well," he said, shrugging. "But they are desperate for surveyors, and they know that my mother was English."

"How did your father fare living in the British Colonies?"

"He didn't live here. My mother raised my brother and me by herself near the Piscataqua Plantation, just south of here. It was very difficult for her because of the bad blood between France and England. My father came to see us maybe twice a year. He owned a successful trading post near Quebec."

"Why didn't she go there to live?" asked Darcy.

"It was too dangerous, and there were no white women. My mother would have died of loneliness up there. Staying in the Piscataqua Valley was lonely enough. She loved my father very much and missed him terribly."

"Has it been difficult for you to live in English settlements with a French name? Wouldn't it be easier to go by John Michael instead of Jean-Michel?"

He shook his head. "I'm proud of my French heritage, and I would never deny the name my father gave me. I have been caught between the two worlds all my life, and I am accustomed to it."

It was Darcy's turn to study Jean-Michel. He seemed well educated, but he was living on the frontier, well-bred but dressed in coarse linen. She was unable to put this man into any category, but one thing was certain; whenever he was around, a strange, unsettled feeling came over her.

The French background helped explain his dark complexion and fine features. He was tall with broad shoulders but not big boned, and under the buckskin shirt, Darcy could see that his body was taut and firm. Although his face was clean shaven, it had the hint of a heavy beard.

Suddenly she realized that he was laughing at her, and he asked suggestively, "Do you like what you see?"

Darcy took a sip of rum and shifted in her chair. She looked up at him, and she saw he was smirking. She tried to hide a smile. Darcy admitted that she was attracted to this man, but she was not about to be lured into a tawdry liaison.

There was a crack of thunder, and the rain began to hammer the roof of the cabin. Jean-Michel leaned forward and with a look of distaste asked, "Why did you allow yourself to be bought by Lawrence?"

Darcy sighed and sat up straight. "I had no choice. I did not choose to be his indentured servant or anyone's slave. I am a convict."

"You go to him unwillingly?" he asked with surprise.

"I told you I am a convict serving my sentence, not

an Irish whore."

Jean-Michel recalled his words from the morning. "It seems I spoke out of turn earlier today, my apologies."

Darcy shrugged and continued, "For the most part, Nathan has been fair with me, and I am better off than my comrades who were hanged for the same crime.

"Which was?"

"Trading with the French during the war. We weren't getting rich, just trying to feed ourselves and our families. They punished us most severely."

"Did your husband hang too?"

"No, I have no husband. I will never marry."

"Why in heaven's name would you never marry?" he asked with astonishment.

"Because men don't love women. They only need them. They need them to take care of the home and children and to satisfy their pleasures."

Seeing his frown, she added, "Nathan didn't like my point of view either."

"It's very cynical," he answered.

"It is how I see it. Where is your wife?" she asked in return.

"My wife is dead. She died in childbirth over thirteen years ago."

"Did you love her?" Darcy asked bluntly.

Jean-Michel's jaw tightened. He swallowed hard and said, "I am afraid I did not."

"You see? You are a perfect example of what I was talking about," she gloated.

"In this case, I suppose you are right," he agreed.

Jean-Michel's eyes dropped to the floor for a moment, and then he continued, "We met when I was studying to be a surveyor at the College of William and

Mary in Virginia. She was very pretty, yet she was very fragile. I suppose as a young man I was attracted to that. I thought I could take care of her. I killed her when I brought her to the frontier. She was meant for drawing rooms, not the one room cabins in the wilderness. When she was with child, that first winter, she grew very thin and pale. I tried to keep her healthy and her spirits up, but after five months she died giving birth to a still-born."

Darcy was horrified. *How could I have gloated over this man's misfortunes?* She rubbed her forehead and then said, "Now it's my turn to apologize."

He chuckled. "Now why did I tell you that story?"

He stood up suddenly and announced, "We have been here long enough. I think it's safe to go."

As he stepped out into the pouring rain, Jean-Michel had to regain his composure. He was not sure he liked the feelings that were churning inside him. This McBride woman had the ability to reach into his soul and open doors he thought were closed forever. She ignited a desire in him that was beyond anything he had ever imagined.

Confused and overwhelmed, he blamed it on long months without carnal pleasures, and pushing it from his mind; he started down the path for the McDermott homestead.

Chapter 21

The wind tossed the trees wildly, and the cracking of the thunder reminded Darcy of cannon fire. Her skirts were heavy with mud, and her soaked hair clung to her face and shoulders. She stumbled clumsily down the path, unable to see the roots and rocks in the darkness of the forest. Jean-Michel walked behind her, trying to quell his fears about the effectiveness of gunpowder in the rain.

A yellow light flickered through the trees as they approached the McDermott homestead. Darcy thought it was a campfire, and then suddenly she realized the cabin was in flames.

"Oh, Good Lord!" she cried. She bolted down the path with only one thought--to save the family burning in the cabin. Blindly she dashed, jumping over rocks and pushing branches aside when suddenly a root caught her foot, and she tumbled to the ground. Fast as lightning she jumped to her feet running directly into the clearing. In an instant, Jean-Michel was upon her. He grabbed her arm and yanked her back swinging her around to his chest and clapped his hand over her mouth. Darcy struggled to break free, but his arm around her waist felt like steel. She kicked and squirmed, but he tightened his grip.

He dragged her back into the cover of the trees, as she watched the cabin engulfed in flames. The blaze shot high into the night sky, illuminating everything in the clearing, and Darcy closed her eyes. Jean-Michel felt her body relax, and he loosened his grip. He scanned the clearing for danger. All was quiet.

Jean-Michel could feel Darcy's heart pounding and

her soft breasts against his chest. He dropped his arms, and she stepped away still watching the blaze. He whispered, "I believe the danger is passed, but we must approach with caution."

Holding their muskets in front of them, they walked down the hill to look for survivors. The heat from the fire was intense, and it shed enough light for them to see that there were no dead bodies in the clearing. The family had either been taken prisoner or burned in the fire. Darcy stepped over debris and scanned the woods. The fire threw long shadows across everything, and more than once Darcy mistook them for assailants. She saw Jean-Michel straining to listen, and when Darcy stood motionless she heard it too--a low, moaning sound coming from the direction of the well. Instantly, she recognized the wailing of Nan and picked up some burning debris as a torch running to the well. Holding the flame overhead, she looked down expecting to see only Nan, but instead, she saw Adrianna and the children. Jean-Michel ran over as well.

"Is this everyone?" he asked. When Darcy nodded, he stated, "Then we must get them into the woods quickly."

One by one he pulled Adrianna and the children from their hiding place. As fast as he could pull them out, Darcy would race them to the shelter of the trees. The older children tried to walk, but the water had numbed their legs, and it was difficult to stand. The last child to go into the woods was Nan, and when Jean-Michel bent to pick her up, she let out a blood-curdling scream. He jumped back and looked at Adrianna with surprise. She picked up Nan and dashed for the woods with the child struggling and screaming in her arms.

"Is everyone here, Adrianna?" asked Darcy.

She nodded. "When we heard the cannon fire this morning, we knew what was happening and went directly to the well. When the French and Abenaki arrived, they assumed we had fled to the fort, so they did not search for us. They moved on to burning the house."

"Didn't a rider come by to warn you of the attack?" asked Darcy.

"We saw no one."

"I am not surprised," said Darcy frowning. "Nathan would only alert the families of the militia. The rest could go to the devil for all he cared."

Jean-Michel said, "There will be time to be angry later. We must all get to safety now. I don't know what to do about Nan. She will alert the entire forest the minute we touch her. If only we had your dog, Darcy. Stroking his fur was soothing to her."

Nan rocked back and forth on the ground, tapping her leg with a leaf. Jean-Michel took a rabbit's foot on a rawhide string out of his shirt and pulled it over his head. Very gently he ran the charm up and down the girl's arm, and like magic, she began to stroke the fur and make cooing sounds. He hung it down the back of his shirt, and when he turned around, Nan climbed onto his back without a struggle to play with the rabbit's foot.

The thunder continued to roll, and the wind picked up. Darcy carried a toddler on her back and guided one of the children. She almost fell several times in the mud, but she forged on. When they reached the clearing by the fort, they waited in the brush for instructions from Jean-Michel. He told them they must not all run to the gate at the same time. They would take turns, each adult escorting several children to the fort as discreetly as possible.

He turned to Darcy and said apologetically, "You will be the first to scale the hill. I'm sorry, but I must remain behind to protect the others."

"What's so terrible about going first?" she asked.

"You may draw friendly fire. Our soldiers will not recognize you in the dark, and they may believe that you are the enemy.

Darcy swallowed hard. It had never occurred to her that she may be killed by her own people.

Jean-Michel continued, "Once you gain entrance to the fort, go to the battery and scan the clearing for danger. When it is safe for us to proceed, wave a torch."

Darcy's heart was pounding furiously. She squatted down and looked at Adrianna's five-year-old boy and asked, "Are you a strong little man?"

When he nodded, she said, "I want you to hang onto me with all your might as I run up that hill. Don't worry. Momma will be coming later. I promise to keep you safe."

His eyes reflected complete faith in her. She squeezed the chubby hand of the little girl on her back and looked at Jean-Michel. He scanned the clearing and said, "Now!"

Darcy grabbed the boy to her breast and dashed into the clearing. It was extremely difficult to scale the hill carrying one child on her back and another in her arms, but she could not hesitate a moment.

Madly, she scrambled up the slippery grass, her lungs exploding, and her heart slamming against her chest. Suddenly, the toddler on her back fell to the ground with a cry. Before she could make another sound, Darcy had her tucked under her arm, and she began to run again. Breathless and terrified, she looked up at the sentries. No one had seen her in the darkness. She bolted toward the fort and arrived at the gate screaming, "It's Darcy McBride! Open the gate! I have children here!"

The surprised guard opened up, and after telling the soldiers to hold their fire, Darcy grabbed a torch, ran up to the south battery and leaned over the wall. She searched the clearing for danger and waved the torch from side to side. Adrianna burst into the clearing next, holding her infant, followed by two of the older children. They sprinted up the hill, across the clearing, and into the fort safely.

Darcy looked around once again for danger and waved her torch for Jean-Michel to proceed. He bolted up the hill with Nan and two others. Suddenly, there was the report of a rifle, and she looked for Jean-Michel in the darkness. She could hear him yelling to the other children to continue running to the fort, and finally, she saw him pull himself to his feet, tucking Nan under one arm.

More shots rang out as he stumbled toward the gate. Darcy dashed down to help pull in the first two children. They were shaken but unharmed, and Jean-Michel staggered in, dropping Nan into Adrianna's arms. She was sobbing from fear and joy as she covered her children with kisses.

Too weak to stand any longer, Jean-Michel dropped onto his hands and knees, and Darcy bent down holding his arm. His hair had come out of the leather thong and hung in loose strands around his face. Bright, red blood was soaking through the shoulder of his shirt, and he mumbled, "I'm dizzy."

He was taken to the surgery where several women tried to stop the bleeding. Darcy stood by the bed, watching Jean-Michel's expressionless face. He lay with his eyes closed and winced only once when they tried to find the bullet. "It looks like it went in one side and out the other," said a plump, gray-haired woman. "That's good. You'll heal quickly." She patted his hand and said, "I'll just finish with this bandage and let you rest."

When she was done, the nurse straightened up the area and moved on to another patient. Jean-Michel lay on the bed, motionless and white. Satisfied that he was asleep, Darcy turned to leave the surgery. The minute she stepped away from the bed he whispered, "Where are you going?" and he opened his eyes. "You know that you are responsible for this, don't you? You and your foolish notions."

Darcy blanched. She knew that he was right. It was an utterly impetuous, foolhardy undertaking to move children under fire, and Jean-Michel had paid the price. She hung her head.

"As punishment you must stay by my side," he murmured.

Darcy looked at him. "You don't hate me?"

"No, Miss McBride. Quite the contrary," and he closed his eyes.

Darcy stayed by his side well into the night. Jean-Michel did not wake up once as she dozed in a chair beside him. Sometime in the middle of the night, a guard woke her and said that Colonel Lawrence would like to speak with her.

Darcy dreaded seeing Nathan. She knew what he would say, and her anxiety increased the closer she got to his office. The parade ground was filled with people sleeping on packs or curled up on the ground as she walked into Nathan's office. The guard escorted her in and waited. Nathan did not look up right away, continuing to write. When he looked up, at last, his face hardened. He dismissed the guard and stood up.

Walking around his desk, he said, "Do you know what I do to subordinates when they act against my direct orders?"

Darcy said nothing, looking at the floor.

"I sentence them to hang. That's what I do. Now as I recall, you managed to avoid that sentence once already. You must lead a charmed life because you will avoid hanging again," he said.

"But you will not avoid this," and with the back of his hand, he struck Darcy.

Lawrence's jeweled ring cut her lip, and she was knocked back several steps. She put her hand to her face but said nothing, only looked at the floor. She remembered the horrors of the beating from Liam too well, and she was not about to encourage Nathan.

"You'll have one more," and he slapped her across the other cheek. "That is for being impudent in my office yesterday."

He pulled down his jacket and straightened his cuffs, as blood trickled down Darcy's lip. "Now leave me."

Darcy staggered from his office, wondering how she ever could have cared for this hard, ruthless man. The siege had brought out a savage side in him, which she had not previously encountered, and she would never trust him again.

She returned to the surgery and after cleaning her lip sank back down into the chair by Jean-Michel to fulfill his request that she stay by his side. In spite of all that had happened, Darcy was so exhausted that she fell into a deep sleep almost immediately.

The wound started giving Jean-Michel pain and

roused him. When he opened his eyes, Darcy was back, and he raised his head to look at her. The candlelight was dim in the surgery, but he could see that she had unpinned her hair, and her dark tresses tumbled down over her shoulders and breasts.

He felt as if he were a voyeur watching this beautiful woman while she slept, but he could not help drinking in every detail of her loveliness. She sighed and turned her head and Jean-Michel's eyes narrowed. He saw the gash across her lip and knew immediately that she had been to see Lawrence. His jaw tightened. He had never liked Nathan, and he detested him even more for adding to this woman's misery. As his affection for Darcy grew, his hatred for Lawrence deepened. It was too painful for Jean-Michel to watch Darcy anymore, and he turned his head to the other side of the bed to try to get some sleep.

When he awoke later that morning, a shy, young nurse with nervous hands was changing his blood-soaked bandage. Darcy sat on the corner of the bed and presented a bowl of broth to him.

"Now sit up. It's time you gain back your strength."

"I fear I cannot sit up," he teased.

"Don't push me," Darcy warned. "You are perfectly capable of sitting up."

"It's far too painful. You'll have to feed me."

She frowned. "You take advantage of me, Lupé,'" and she put a spoonful of soup into his mouth. Suddenly there was the crack of gunfire and Darcy jumped, spilling broth all over him. Jean-Michel winced.

Darcy dabbed his shirt with a towel apologizing profusely.

"No, I'm all right," he said chuckling.

There was cannon blast next, and it shook the

room. Everyone anticipated new casualties. The surgery became a busy place once more. Darcy helped Jean-Michel into a clean shirt. As she straightened it around him, he reached up suddenly and stroked her injured lip. She turned away to hide the pain on her face. It had been years since anyone had shown her compassion, and it seemed to cut her like a knife.

She left the surgery after that, vowing to stay away from him. Why did he affect her this way? His very presence unnerved her. She must not allow him to get close to her. She had lost too much already. She was not about to lose her heart.

The day dragged on endlessly, and the surgery filled with injured soldiers. Darcy cleaned and dressed countless wounds, her apron spattered with blood and mucus as she moved from patient to patient. She looked at Jean-Michel several times, and each time he appeared to be sleeping. At one point she grew concerned and sent a nurse to see if he needed help. The woman returned reporting he was resting peacefully.

The gunfire slowed but did not stop entirely that evening and when the last patient was settled in, Darcy went to find Shenanigan. Since the beginning of the attack, she had not seen the dog, and she was worried. Spattered with blood from head to toe, she went to her room to clean up, and the minute she entered the room, Shenanigan crawled out from under the bed, his tail wagging. She laughed and bent down to hug him. "There's my brave hero!" she cooed, as he licked her face.

After washing up and changing her dress, she decided to get some air in the parade ground. The assault had stopped, and the air was clear and quiet.

She glanced in the surgery, only a few candles were lit, one by Jean-Michel's bed. He spied her as she walked past and motioned to her. Reluctantly, Darcy went in to his bedside. She told herself she would not let her guard down this time. He ran his eyes over her face and hair as if he were memorizing everything and then said, "I want you to know that I was teasing you when I said you were responsible for my injury. There was nothing you could have done to stop those gunshots."

Darcy nodded and mumbled her thanks. She hoped this would be the extent of their conversation, but he continued, "Adrianna was here to see me today. I gave her the rabbit's foot for Nan. I hope it brings her luck."

There was a long pause as Jean-Michel searched her face, and then he asked, "It's been a long time since anyone's been kind to you, hasn't it?"

The conversation was taking a personal turn, and she stood up asking, "May I get anything else for you tonight?"

"Sit down, Darcy," he said softly.

She swallowed hard and sat down. Slowly he reached up and pulled a pin out of her hair, and a long tress tumbled down onto her shoulder.

She closed her eyes, fighting the desire. One by one he removed each pin until her hair fell softly around her face.

"I must go," she murmured.

His hand moved to her chin, and he urged her down to meet his lips, but she pulled back. "No, this cannot be. I don't know you. I don't want to know you."

Shaken, Darcy turned and left the surgery.

Chapter 22

The siege continued into the next day, but with fewer casualties. By late afternoon, the gunfire had stopped, and there were rumors of an outbreak of smallpox in the enemy camp. There was a widespread relief, but no celebration. The mention of smallpox struck terror into the hearts of settler, soldier and Indian on both sides.

Darcy did not return to Jean-Michel's bedside. She continued to work in the surgery but invited no contact with him. She made up her mind to return her complete attention to Nathan. She believed that he might be tiring of her, and the thought of being sold to someone else terrified her. This was reason enough not to become involved with Jean-Michel.

As the days passed and the enemy retreated north, life gradually returned to normal. Jean-Michel's strength returned, and he was released permanently from the surgery. He made little attempt to converse with Darcy. He believed now that she was in love with Nathan and that it had been nothing more than a foolish infatuation on his part.

He stole glances at her, though, chiding himself for being a silly schoolboy, yet he could not keep his eyes from following her. He was growing ever angrier and resentful of Darcy for stealing his peace of mind, and when the meetings resumed with Colonel Lawrence, it was difficult for him to be civil.

In keeping with the mood of victory, Nathan invited his officers and their wives to dine with him and toast the outcome of the siege. "I want you to wear your loveliest gown tonight, Darcy," said Nathan. "I believe the blue taffeta with the green stomacher would be suitable for the occasion. The few provincials in attendance will be impressed."

He looked in the mirror and straightened his cravat, and then adjusted a powdered wig carefully on his head. Darcy hated the dandified fashion and much-preferred men looking natural.

Nathan donned his finest dress uniform for tonight's festivities. His red coat was decorated with a rich gold braid running down each lapel and cuff. Under it, he wore a matching waistcoat with a crisp white shirt. His breeches were also red, and his tall black boots were polished to a high shine.

Darcy cut an equally elegant picture in her royal blue taffeta. Per Nathan's request, she had chosen the green stomacher decorated with tiny blue flowers, and around her neck she tied a green ribbon holding a little gold locket he had given her before they left Providence. The dress was cut very low, and Darcy suspected that was why Nathan had chosen it. She believed he wanted to flaunt his possession and make the officers envy him. She caught him looking at her, as she was applying some powdered sage to make her eyelids green, and she smiled.

He nodded his head. "You look perfect."

Darcy sensed that she was back in Nathan's good graces. She had worked hard at flattering him lately, and she had expended a lot of energy giving him pleasure. This had not been particularly difficult since she had been frustrated after the several encounters with Jean-Michel.

Darcy and Nathan greeted guests as they arrived, and everyone was offered a drink. Although she had little experience as a hostess, Nathan marveled at how adept Darcy was putting everyone at their ease. As if she was a woman of refinement and breeding, she moved around the drawing room making conversation and attending to the guests. She was determined to make Nathan proud of her and prove to him that she had abandoned her headstrong ways. With her rich taffeta gown rustling, Darcy moved over to Nathan's side and whispered, "Are all of the guests here, Nathan? Shall we move into supper?"

"I believe so," he said, looking around the room. Then he looked over her shoulder and said, "Oh, thank you for joining us."

Turning to greet their latest guest, Darcy saw Jean-Michel. Her smile dropped, and she said without thinking, "Nathan, I thought you were only inviting officers."

Lawrence chuckled uncomfortably and said, "Darcy, I'm surprised at you. Jean-Michel Lupé is the finest surveyor in the provinces. Please apologize."

"That won't be necessary," Jean-Michel said, coldly.

He did not like encountering Darcy any more than she liked encountering him. He too had dressed for the occasion but in somewhat simpler attire. His black hair was not powdered but tied back neatly in a pigtail. He wore an ink-bottle blue topcoat with tails which dropped to his knees and a matching waistcoat. The white linen shirt he had chosen was of the finest quality, and his breeches were dark brown. His boots too were polished to a high shine, and under his arm he carried a tricorne hat.

"Allow me to take your hat, Mr. Lupé," said Darcy trying to be civil. She couldn't help but notice that his coat color matched his icy-blue eyes. When she returned, she heard Nathan say, "I am in your debt, Mr. Lupé for protecting Miss McBride on her foolish expedition to rescue the McDermott family several nights back."

Jean-Michel said, "Miss McBride did a fine job of protecting herself. In fact, she doesn't need anyone's help."

Nathan's eyebrows shot up, and he looked from one to the other. The animosity was obvious. Determined to learn more he said, "Mr. Lupé, we have been working together all this time, and I am afraid that I know nothing of you personally. Please join Miss McBride and me at the head of the table this evening."

Darcy looked down and swallowed. As they walked into the dining room, Jean-Michel scrutinized her. He noticed the low-cut gown and heavy makeup. He believed that Nathan was parading her tonight as his courtesan. Although she looked elegant and seductive, he much preferred the woman in the cabin that stormy night during the siege--the elusive Irishwoman with the curious blend of femininity and fierce independence.

Tonight she was masquerading as a china doll for the benefit of Lawrence's pride. "She's a fool to love that lecherous old man," he thought as he stepped into the dining room.

The long table looked beautiful covered with a white linen table cloth and two shimmering candelabras. For practical purposes, no china had been brought to Fort Lawrence, but twenty pewter plates lined the table, each one topped with a white linen napkin. A lovely pyramid of apples, nuts and wild berries comprised the centerpiece, and once they were seated, each guest's wine glass was immediately filled.

Before dinner was served, Nathan stood up and

proposed a toast, "To our success putting down the French and the Abenaki, and to the health of His Majesty King George the Second."

Reluctantly, Darcy took a sip of her wine. She found the toast to be rather grandiose considering that smallpox had ended the siege, but she drank anyway.

Steaming leg of lamb and tongue were brought in and set on elevated dish crosses. There were fresh green beans and corn and a beautiful raspberry flummery topped with candied flowers. Nathan was determined to make the British officers feel at home and impress these provincials with the elegance of English entertaining.

The evening that had started out so enjoyable for Darcy dissolved into torture. She lost her spontaneity, and all she could think about was Jean-Michel sitting across from her. She thought falling back into Nathan's arms would cool her feelings toward this man, but the encounter tonight brought everything back in a rush.

Her heart pounded, and she ate very little of the meal she had so looked forward to tasting. Nathan and Jean-Michel were chatting cordially, when suddenly Lawrence turned to Darcy and said, "You are very quiet this evening, my dear. Are you well?"

Darcy nodded, and Colonel Lawrence decided it was time to explore the nature of the relationship between these two uncomfortable dinner guests.

"Tell me, Jean-Michel," Nathan said smiling, "Are you married?"

"I am not," Jean-Michel stated flatly, and he offered no further information.

Nathan continued, "Oh come now. Surely there must be someone close to your heart?"

"I assure you, Colonel Lawrence, there is no one,"

he returned, looking irritated.

"Why ever not?"

Jean-Michel looked directly at Darcy and said in a voice heavy with sarcasm. "Because men don't love women. They only need them. Don't you agree, Miss McBride?"

Darcy was furious, not only because Lupé was mocking her, but because Nathan would recognize those words. One of the women seated next to her interrupted her thoughts and complimented her necklace.

"Thank you, Mrs. Williams. I received this locket from my dearest Nathan during our time together in Providence." Darcy smiled at him, reached up and stroked his cheek.

"But there is nothing in it," she said, showing the empty locket to the woman. Darcy turned back to Nathan and said, "Would you consider sitting for a miniature so I may have *your* likeness with me always?"

"Of course, my dear," he said searching her eyes. She seemed so sincere. Nathan thought maybe he had imagined everything. He realized now that it was foolish to think that she might be smitten with that provincial of French blood, and he felt confident of her affection once more. Darcy leaned close to his ear, whispered something suggestive, and they chuckled.

Jean-Michel went white with rage. He saw Lawrence's eyes run over Darcy's shoulders and breasts, and he fought the urge to stand up and smash his face. With victory in her eyes, Darcy looked over at Jean-Michel. She was determined to end this infatuation here and now. She would show him that she was completely taken with Lawrence. The evening had taken a turn for the better, after all, she thought.

Nathan was feeling magnanimous now toward Jean-Michel and asked, "I do wish you would consider a commission in His Majesty's service. I know you prefer the militia, but your skills and quick mind would take you far. Forgive me for saying so, but it *is* your duty as a subject to serve the Crown."

Darcy stopped eating her dessert and looked at Jean-Michel, waiting for his reaction. She thought she detected a hint of anger in his eyes, but outwardly he appeared cool.

"Thank you, but as you know, I am not interested."

Nathan chuckled indignantly, "After everything we do for you provincials, your lack of gratitude amazes me."

Jean-Michel sat up straight and said hotly, "Gratitude, gratitude for what!"

"Well, for one thing," Nathan said haughtily. "We are over here defending your hearth and home."

"That certainly was not apparent when you invited only militia to the fort during the siege, leaving everyone else to fend for themselves." Jean-Michel slid his chair back and put his napkin on his plate. "We owe you nothing. In fact, we 'Provincials,' as you call us would be better off without King George and his meddlesome army!"

"Sir, I find your skills in the field above reproach, but your belligerent attitude smacks of rebellion!" said Nathan.

Nathan stood up abruptly inviting the guests into the main room for port. When the company had assembled in the other room, Darcy looked for Jean-Michel, but he was gone.

He had left in a rage grabbing his hat and crossing the parade ground to his room. Grabbing a bottle of whisky, he came back outside to a table in front of his quarters. He slammed the bottle down on the table and straddled a chair. Jean-Michel poured himself a stiff drink and tossed it back in one gulp. The whiskey burned, but he knew that it would dissolve his rage.

He looked across at Colonel Lawrence's quarters. From where he was sitting, he could just see inside the drawing room. He watched the guests move about, talking and laughing. It appeared as if the soiree was coming to a close. Jean-Michel poured himself another drink, ran his hands through his hair and stewed.

Tom English was the first to leave Lawrence's gathering. He approached Jean-Michel, sat down and said, "What the devil's wrong with you? You look like you could tear somebody to pieces."

"Nothing is wrong. Here have a drink," he said, pouring Tom a whisky. They watched the party break up, and Tom did most of the talking, relaying bits of gossip he learned at the supper.

When the last guest said good night, Jean Michel could see Nathan take off his coat and stretch in the sitting room as Darcy collected empty wine glasses. They seemed to be ignoring one another, when suddenly Nathan caught her by the hand, pulled her over and kissed her. Holding Darcy in one arm he reached over to unfasten the drapes, and the last thing Jean-Michel saw was Darcy reaching up and putting her arms around Nathan's neck.

"What's wrong with you tonight? You haven't heard a word I've said," complained Tom.

Jean-Michel was staring at the curtain, smothering his rage. "I'm leaving tomorrow," he announced. "The Abenaki and the French are gone, and we are done consulting with Lawrence. I have no further interest here."

He poured himself another drink and one for Tom.

"You're determined to start your journey with a headache, aren't you?" laughed Tom, pushing his drink away. "As for me, I am done for tonight." He stood up, bade Jean-Michel a safe journey and retired to his quarters leaving Jean-Michel alone to fume.

* * *

It was a cloudless night, and a full moon flooded the parade ground as Darcy stepped out to take some night air. She had tried to get some sleep, but it eluded her. There had been too much tension at the dinner, and she needed to clear her mind. After Nathan had fallen asleep, she rose from his large four-poster bed and put on one of her everyday gowns. She left Nathan sleeping peacefully. He had ended the night feeling satisfied with his celebration supper--his mistress and himself.

Darcy took a deep breath of night air. Except for the few guards on duty, the parade ground was empty, and she stretched deeply. Unaware that she was being observed, she adjusted the shoulder on her gown and started to the well for a drink of water.

As she crossed in front of the officers' quarters, Jean-Michel stepped out in front of her and said in an exaggerated Irish accent, "Well, bless me soul! If it isn't the Irish princess herself!" and he swept down into a low courtly bow, mocking her.

Darcy made a large circle around him and kept walking. With her chin in the air, she said with disdain, "Go to bed. You're drunk."

The next thing she heard was a long string of French exclamations which she guessed were curses, and startled, she swung around to look at him. Jean-

Michel changed to English and said, "You really think that you love that old man, don't you?"

"Yes, Colonel Lawrence gives me great pleasure," said Darcy.

"Pleasure, pleasure!" he laughed. "What would you know about pleasure when you take a wizened old Englishman to your bed? I know now for a fact that you are afraid of your own desire."

"Don't be absurd."

"Then try a man in the prime of his life with French blood coursing through his veins."

Darcy turned to go. She walked a short way when suddenly she felt him grab her wrist and swing her around. "I'm leaving the fort tomorrow, but carry this with you the rest of your life. Jean-Michel Lupé was the only man who could ever touch your soul." He turned into his quarters and slammed the door, leaving Darcy alone on the parade ground.

Chapter 23

Darcy spent the rest of the night in her quarters on the bed, staring at the ceiling. It was pointless to undress because sleep would not come. She could not understand why she was so affected by the news that Jean-Michel was leaving the fort. She should have rejoiced; instead, she brooded.

Darcy marveled at his arrogance saying that he touched her soul. *He certainly had a high opinion of himself.* Dawn broke, finding her still ruminating about Jean-Michel, and she sat up, looking out the window. Rays of sun began to lighten the sky. She stood up and opened the door. Tiptoeing past where Nathan slept, she crossed the sitting room and quietly stepped outside.

The parade ground was empty, and she looked over at the officers' quarters. Darcy did not want to be detected by anyone, most of all Jean-Michel, but she had to know if he was gone. As she approached, she noticed the door was ajar, and she listened. Hearing nothing, she took a breath and stepped over the threshold to look inside. Aside from rumpled bedding, there was no sign that Jean-Michel had ever been there.

She looked around the empty room, and a feeling of deep loneliness filled her from head to toe. It was as if this man had never existed. It seemed impossible that she would never see him again, but America was a vast continent, and it was possible that he was gone forever.

Suddenly, she had an idea. If she hurried, maybe she could catch one last glimpse of Jean-Michel leaving the river valley. She raced out of his room and ran madly up the ramp to the top of the wall, thoroughly startling the guard on duty. Stretched to her full height, Darcy stood by the gatehouse and strained to see him. She ran her eyes over the valley and down the river, looking for movement, but she was disappointed--there was nothing. She couldn't believe it; that was it. He was gone. She stood alone for a long time staring out into the vast ocean of trees until the guard approached her and said, "Are you all right, Miss?"

Darcy looked at him blankly and made no reply.

* * *

Summer turned to autumn at Fort Lawrence, and the winds grew cold and the leaves on the trees turned to crisp reds and yellows. Although the weather was more temperate in Ireland, Darcy found the change of seasons in the New World to be dramatically beautiful. She resumed her visits with Moses Tinker, who had emerged one day shortly after the end of the siege from his hiding place on the bluff.

Darcy also made regular visits to the McDermott homestead, and today she was traveling down the path to help Adrianna make soap. Fall was usually a busy time of year butchering, tanning hides and smoking meat for the winter, but the French and Indians had slaughtered all of their cattle and burned all the crops in the siege. There was still enough rendered fat for soap, but the food stores were getting alarmingly low.

Moses and Darcy had picked every apple they could find, pressing some into cider and leaving the rest to winter over in the root cellar. They had also smoked some venison but again the French and the Abenaki had hunted out the area leaving the settlers with little game.

On several occasions, Darcy had suggested to Nathan to send out a hunting party, but his faith in the

British army was blind. He was fully confident that supplies would arrive well before the snow.

"Good day, McDermotts!" shouted Darcy as she walked down the hill, waving to the little ones playing in the yard. Darcy was proud of the new cabin she had helped Adrianna build. Moses had come over every day to help them erect a new structure after the fire. It went quickly, especially because the chimney had remained intact.

During that time, Darcy and Adrianna had become best friends. They were good company for each other because they were bonded in their common love of Ireland. There were countless customs and idiosyncrasies which they shared because of their background and each made the other a little less homesick.

Darcy passed the large cast-iron pot hanging over the fire, and when she peeked into the crucible, she saw that it was filled with fat for making soap. Once this fat had been heated to the right consistency, the women would add lye, made from wood ashes, and stir it until saponification occurred. It amazed Darcy that two such unclean substances could render such an efficient cleansing agent.

"Is your mother inside?" she asked Mark, who was sitting in front of the cabin weaving an oak splint basket. He nodded, and she rumpled his hair as she passed. He was Adrianna's eight-year-old boy. He had light skin, sandy blonde hair, and a rough-and-tumble attitude. She guessed that he would much rather be climbing trees or flying a kite, but he begrudgingly obeyed his mother and worked on the basket.

Adrianna's children reminded Darcy of the Mullin family. She often thought about Teila, Keenan, and the children. She prayed that Teila still lived, but she had a dark intuition that she died shortly after Darcy had been transported.

She entered the cabin and looked immediately to the hearth where Adrianna spent most of her time. As Darcy suspected, she was there with her eleven-year-old daughter Deirdre, making a suet pudding and johnnycake. She resembled her mother; only her smooth hair was a chestnut brown.

"Good day, Darcy. We are all ready for you, but sit down first and have some johnnycake," said Adrianna with a smile. She is so pretty, thought Darcy, looking at Adrianna's rosy complexion and blonde hair. Several men had been showing interest in her, but Adrianna would not hear of it. Darcy knew that she still grieved deeply for John.

"Will we be doing a lesson today, Miss McBride?" asked Deirdre.

Darcy was teaching her to read. The girl had a wonderfully keen mind. Her enthusiasm reminded Darcy of herself several years back with Father Etienne, and she knew he would want her to pass the skill on to other eager minds.

"My little darlin', there won't be time today. Your mother and I must make soap," apologized Darcy, but when she saw the disappointment on the girl's face, she said, "Oh Deirdre! Don't look at me like that! Alright, we'll find some time."

"Oh, thank you, thank you! Do you know that I was able to read Matthew 19:19 to Mama last night? You know the one about loving thy neighbor as thyself?"

"Darcy knows that one well, Deirdre," said Adrianna as she checked the pudding. "She put it into practice the night she and Jean-Michel came to rescue us."

After a moment, Adrianna asked, "Did Jean-Michel ever say where he was going, Darcy?"

"No," she said. Adrianna was always mentioning his name, and it aggravated Darcy. She wanted to move on with her life and forget about him.

"The cabin looked wonderful when I walked into the clearing today," said Darcy changing the subject.

"We should all be proud," said Adrianna, biting her lip and looking down as if something was wrong. Darcy saw the look but said nothing.

Eating her johnnycake, she looked around the keeping room of the cabin. The fireplace was large and included an oven with a cast-iron door and above the mantel hung a flintlock musket. Adrianna had two pewter plates on the mantel along with the family Bible, a huge leather-bound edition, which she had brought from Ulster.

On one side of the fireplace was a spinning wheel which Adrianna had borrowed, and directly across from it was a settee made by Moses. Two neatly made beds with bright quilts were against the walls, and the windows with oiled paper panes shed a lovely golden light into the cabin. A ladder led up to the loft where several of the older children slept, and Darcy's eyes rested on the badly scorched brass bed warmer standing by the fireplace. Until she came to the Colonies, she had never seen such a tool, and she thought putting hot coals in it and running it between the covers before bedtime was a most ingenious way to make cold nights more palatable. Darcy was nervous about her first winter in the Northern Colonies. She had heard that they were brutal and long, and she had never experienced deep snow.

"I have something I want to discuss with you, Darcy," said Adrianna, wiping her hands on her apron." She turned to Deirdre and asked, "Would you go watch the fat to make sure it does not burn?"

"We will read later, Deirdre," Darcy assured her, and the girl smiled. Darcy liked her and did not want to see her spend her entire youth just trying to stay alive. This was the reason she taught this tall, gentle girl to read. Books could whisk her away from the endless struggle, and her imagination could set her free. It satisfied something deep within Darcy to be near a family again.

When Deirdre left the cabin, Adrianna sat down at the table with Darcy. "I don't know how to say this, but I'm going back to Ireland before the winter sets in, Darcy."

"What?" she cried, jumping up. "No! Don't do this, Adrianna!"

"I know. I know. I'm sorry," she apologized, her eyes filling with tears. "But I fear that I cannot survive alone out here with the children."

"I can't believe what I am hearing. You just rebuilt a cabin and furnished it, and now you make this impetuous decision to return home," said Darcy, still astonished.

"Without John, there is no reason to stay. This was his dream, not mine. I was so caught up in his death and then the flurry of rebuilding that it wasn't until I could sit down and think that it all became clear. I feel so dreadfully guilty abandoning you and Moses after all your hard work, but I cannot--"

"No," said Darcy softly as she walked to the fireplace, "You cannot let obligation make your decisions for you. You would resent us in the end."

Darcy felt discouraged and tired as she sat down heavily in the chair. There were few women on the frontier and to lose all the children as well felt unbearable. She wished that she could convince her friend to stay. With one last effort, she said, "What about remarrying? There are dozens of healthy, capable men out here and several have been showing interest in you, Adrianna."

"No," she said shaking her head. "I cannot marry out of desperation. I've seen too many women wither and die because they endure men that they don't love. Just like--" and she stopped.

Darcy sat up straight. "Like who, Adrianna? Like me? Go ahead. Say it."

"All right I'll say it, like you, Darcy," and taking her friend's hand, she continued. "You are a perfect example of a woman trapped and slowly dying of loneliness."

"How dare you say such a thing!" said Darcy jumping up. "May I point out that you are the one running back to Ireland?"

"You're right, Darcy. I *am* scared and lonely," she said as large tears rolled down her face. "I miss John so much. I shall never see him again."

Darcy forgot her anger and hugged, Adrianna. She was right. She shouldn't have to marry someone just to survive, yet out here on the frontier, it seemed to be the only way.

Adrianna dried her eyes on her apron and said, "Heed my words, Darcy. Don't be afraid. You still have a chance to be with the one you love. My chance is gone forever."

"What do you mean?"

"I mean find Jean-Michel," Adrianna said, and she

grabbed Darcy by the arms shaking her. "Find him! Leave, Nathan. Run away from him as far as you can. He has stolen your self-respect. He has stolen who you are."

"Adrianna, you know that I am a convict," she said, jumping up and pacing. "I cannot just run away, and you are wrong. I could never love him." Suddenly, she exclaimed, "Why is this conversation about me?"

"Because I must say it before I leave. What I've been thinking all along. Look at me, Darcy," Adrianna demanded.

Darcy pursed her lips and looked up.

"If you were set free today, tell me you wouldn't stay with, Colonel Lawrence. You would stay with him because he is safe. You can't be hurt by someone you don't love."

"I'll listen to no more of this insanity," snapped Darcy. She turned and left the cabin, slamming the door behind her.

Deirdre was just outside the door. The girl had heard too much. Darcy was sorry that she had promised a lesson. She took a deep breath and said, "I'll take the fat from the fire, and you get your hornbook. We'll have our lesson now."

They sat on the grass, and the crisp autumn wind blew their hair and ruffled their aprons as they worked together in the sunshine. Darcy felt herself unwind, and when the lesson was over, she went back into the cabin to speak with Adrianna. She was bending over the hearth and looked up at her with a red, tear-stained face.

"I thought that you had gone," she exclaimed.

"No, I was outside doing a reading lesson with Deirdre" Darcy took Adrianna's hand and led her to the table. "When are you leaving?"

"Before the month is up," she said quietly." I have spent four winters here and I know the snows come early. We must be in Boston before the end of November."

Darcy sighed and sat down at the table. A month was not very long. "Is there anyone who may want the homestead?" she asked.

"No one yet," replied Adrianna. "But this area will attract more settlers now that there is a fort."

"You'll see Ireland again, Adrianna," said Darcy smiling wistfully with her chin on her hand. "I miss it so much. Every night when I sleep, I dream that I am back at the abbey on the bluff.

"I want to leave knowing that you are happy."

"Oh, Adrianna, I am fine," she reassured. "I will be a free woman in a little more than six years. I will return to Ireland and stand once again on the abbey bluff, ready to start life anew."

* * *

The month flew by quickly, as Darcy helped Adrianna make final preparations. The air took on a sharp edge, and the skies turned an endless gray. The leaves abandoned the trees, leaving their naked branches stretching desperately into the sky.

The McDermotts were scheduled to travel to Boston on All Hallows Eve with a company from the fort which Colonel Lawrence had released for the winter. He was happy not to have to provide them with rations during the lean months, and since there was no threat of attack during the snow, they were not needed and could return in the spring.

Tears rolled down the cheeks of Adrianna and the children as they assembled on the parade ground, ready to make their departure. To the children, they were leaving the only home they'd ever known, and it was very difficult for Adrianna to leave the remains of her husband. She knew that she would never return to the Colonies, and he would sleep forever on the other side of the world.

Leaves swirled around the ankles of the women as they embraced. Adrianna urged, "Bare is the companionless shoulder, Darcy."

"Don't worry about me. Think of me on the abbey bluff at home again someday in *our* Ireland, Adrianna." She handed her a loaf of bread, with a sign of the cross cut into it, and said, "Here is some boxty for your journey. After all, it is All Hallows Eve."

"So it is, Darcy. I hope that traveling this day is not a bad omen."

"That is why you must eat the bread."

Darcy turned and presented Deirdre with a copy of *Don Quixote* that Nathan had bought for her before they came to the fort. She told the girl never to give up on her dreams. Darcy lived vicariously through Deirdre. She was innocent and eager, setting out with a thousand dreams yet to be fulfilled. She too had been optimistic once and filled with hopes and dreams.

The company was assembled and ready to depart. The smaller children rode on a cart while Adrianna and the others walked between two formations of regulars. Taking nothing but a few personal articles, they set off on their journey to Boston and to the green hills of Ireland beyond.

Darcy watched and waved to them as she stood on the south battery. They circled through the valley and were eventually swallowed up in the endless wilderness. As she watched them go a group of geese flew over her head, and she observed that they too were in formation. She could hear them honking their warning to leave the north land before it was too late.

Everyone seemed to be abandoning Darcy in this frontier outpost, and she felt trapped. She listened to the melancholy honking of the geese in the distance, and she was overcome with a deep sense of forboding.

Chapter 24

Darcy tried to keep busy throughout November. The food and supplies had not yet arrived, and she found herself constantly worrying about the upcoming winter. It brought back terrible memories.

She resumed her routine of visiting Moses after her work was completed each day, but she knew that she would be unable to get down to see him once the deep snows started. On several occasions she visited the McDermott homestead, wishing that she could live with Shenanigan in the cozy cabin. She knew that it was a pipe dream, though; Nathan continued to demand her attention every night in his quarters.

Lately his taste in pleasure had taken a more licentious turn, and Darcy was growing uncomfortable with these new avenues. He was never cruel to her, though, and she was grateful for his tolerant attitude regarding her daily outings.

Darcy found great comfort in her visits with Moses. She would sit by the fire and read to him from the Bible, or they would simply share the news of the day over a supper she had prepared. She enjoyed making him venison stews or chicken puddings, and on one occasion she surprised him with a small queen's cake tart.

Darcy inspected his food stores and assessed that he had enough for the winter, but she did not tell him that food was growing alarmingly low at the fort. She knew that Moses would insist on giving her meat, and he had just enough to keep himself alive.

Darcy worried about Moses getting lonely during the wintertime. For many, many months he would have no company, and one day she suggested, "Why don't you take Shenanigan for the winter?"

"Why? He's your dog. He should be with you."

"When it gets cold, I couldn't bear to have him sleep outside, and Nathan won't allow him in the commanding officers' quarters."

He reached out, and Shenanigan got up to meet his hand. "Well, I do like the old boy, and he would be company for me," Moses said, petting the dog affectionately.

"Oh, thank you, Moses," Darcy said, feeling relieved.

As Moses sat smoking his pipe in front of the fire, Darcy decided to ask a question which had been nagging her for some time. "Moses," she asked returning the Bible to the mantel and sitting down in a chair beside him, "What do you know of Jean-Michel Lupé?"

He let out a puff of sweet-smelling smoke and said, "Hmm, very little, but I knew his father well. We trapped for years together up north. Everyone called him 'The Wolf."

"Why?"

"Well, I guess *Lupé* means *wolf*. The Wolf married a pretty, little English girl and built her a fancy house just down south of here on the Piscataqua River. That's where she raised their two boys. He had a good-sized French trading post near Quebec so he wasn't around much."

"Where is The Wolf now?"

"Dead, his wife too," he said, tapping his pipe out.

"What about Jean-Michel's brother. Does he live at the family home?"

"No, I think I heard once that he was studying in France. Jean-Michel takes care of the place, but most of the time he's in the interior."

"The *interior?* Is that the woods?"

"Yep, the wild, the woods. He does land surveys."

"So this Jean-Michel, he is alone?" asked Darcy.

"No, I didn't say that. He's been with some woman down there for years. She lives somewhere on the Piscataqua too."

There was a long silence, as Darcy absorbed the news that Jean-Michel had a woman. She felt like she had been punched in the stomach. So all of the affection he had showered on her had been self-serving--merely an attempt to lure her into a liaison.

Darcy stood up and swung her cape over her shoulders, "Moses, I must go now. That sky looks full of snow. Just to be safe, may I leave Shenanigan now?"

"Yes, we could be snowed in early this year," he said looking outside.

She bent down and kissed his old cheek, hugged Shenanigan tightly and set out into the cold wind. Several flakes of snow fell on her cloak, as she walked back to the fort. By the time Darcy reached the gate, she was practically blinded by white.

It snowed all that evening and right through the following day. The flakes were large and heavily laden with moisture. The snow blanketed everything, and when Darcy looked out onto the parade ground, it was well up to the knees of the soldiers as they struggled to their posts. She had never experienced anything like it. The snow was infrequent in Ireland, even in the mountains, and it never accumulated in such huge amounts.

She dined with Nathan that evening, something which she had not done in weeks. He was usually too busy to sit down to supper, and she was frequently out of the fort at that time. They sat alone in the candlelight of the dining room and were served supper by Nathan's cook, Molly.

Darcy noticed that Nathan was quiet tonight, and she conducted most of the conversation while he ate his chop in silence. After giving her impressions of the snow, she asked, "How long before this melts?"

"What?" Nathan asked as if coming out of a dream.

"Certainly this snow won't last. It's only mid-November," she said.

"You don't realize do you?" he said looking at her, clearly astonished. "This is the northern part of Massachusetts Colony. We are snowed in here now until spring, my girl."

Darcy sat staring at him in disbelief. *It was too early; certainly, this snow was a fluke and would melt in a week.* Then she remembered with a jolt that the supplies had not made it through yet.

"But we can't be snowed in. The supplies are not here! There is not enough food to get us through the winter!"

"We will get by," he said and took another bite of his chop, looking down sullenly.

It was apparent now why Nathan had been so quiet through dinner. He was worried. If he hadn't been so smug about the arrival of the food, none of this would have happened, thought Darcy. Hot anger boiled up inside her, and she said, "If you would have just sent out a hunting party, we would have food enough for the winter. This is your fault, Nathan!"

Immediately she wished that she could retract her words. He slammed his fist down on the table sending the dishes up into the air and down again with a crash, "I'll not have your insolent attitude!"

Darcy stood up, throwing her napkin onto her plate and ran from the room. She could not breathe. She ran through the sitting room and out the door, gulping the cold night air. *This could not be happening. She survived starvation once; she could not endure it again.* It all passed before her eyes: the nagging pain, the grotesquely bloated bodies and the smell of burning flesh as a funeral pyre was lit. As horrible as these images were, Darcy feared the silence the most-- the silence which came from no energy to speak and the quiet resignation that life was no longer worth enduring.

Darcy gasped for air, and then she felt someone pulling her skirt frantically. She looked down and saw Molly's five-year-old boy gazing up at her, terrified.

"What's wrong? Are you sick? Should I get Mama?"

Darcy realized where she was and shook her head. She tousled his hair and said, "I am just fine. I just needed some fresh air." She turned him around, giving him a playful spank on his bottom, sending him back to his mother.

Feeling chilled and unsteady, she returned to the sitting room, shutting the door behind her and held her hands out to the fire. When she looked into the little boy's terrified eyes, she realized that she must not scare these people with the horrors of hunger. They must not know what was ahead.

Darcy reached up and took out her chain. That old pewter cross had pulled her through starvation once, and this time, she had Father Etienne's charm to give her hope. In Ireland, there had been no spring to live for, no end in sight. In the New World, there was rebirth and optimism. She would survive.

*   *   *

Initially, life changed little at Fort Lawrence. Food was rationed immediately and most people, although eating less, felt no nagging hunger. It was not until after Christmas when they were reduced to hard tack and salt pork a few times a week that everyone became alarmed. The first to sicken were the elderly. Although they were few in number; they all died within a month. Darcy knew that illness and disease always preceded starvation. It mercifully weeded out the weak but left the strong behind to battle the agony.

The snow continued to fall, and the cold grew in intensity. North winds blew in the faces of the soldiers as they walked along the shoveled paths around the fort. They kept their faces down and their shoulders up, but nothing seemed to help them escape the bitter wind on their cheeks.

Most days Darcy stayed inside by the sitting room fire, spinning or working on a quilt. There was plenty of dry wood to heat everyone's quarters, and she knew that they were all blessed that they did not have to struggle to stay warm too.

During the day, Nathan would work in his office, but in the evening, he would join her by the fire. They discussed the affairs of the day, and some nights they would sit side by side and read. They never mentioned the hunger.

Nathan noticed how thin Darcy had become. She took less food than the others, and he wondered if once a body experienced starvation, it can exist thereafter on less. Although she never mentioned the Irish famine to him, Nathan was aware that it had happened. The English had turned a blind eye to its existence, and some even saw it as divine retribution for being Catholic. He never thought he would experience hunger himself. He wondered what she was thinking or remembering during this time, and he wondered if she hated him.

Twelfth Night approached, and Darcy asked Nathan if she might go down and see Moses.

"You are so naive. You cannot walk through this deep snow, my darling."

"I thought that I might try using those wide Indian shoes. I just wanted to bring him a small gift for Twelfth Night."

The fire crackled and snapped as Darcy waited for a reply from Nathan. He reached over from his chair and squeezed her hand, "My dear, do you have the strength?"

"I may look thin, Nathan, but I am not weak."

Nathan agreed, and with the weather cooperating, she strapped on a pair of snowshoes and set out for Moses' cabin. She found it amazing how the shoes kept her on top of the snow, and although they were clumsy, they were efficient.

The sun was out and the air was crisp, but not bitter. It felt glorious to be away from the fort, and it was a pleasant diversion from the hunger. As she passed through the woods, she spied a red cardinal feeding on some pine nuts in the snow. The scarlet against the pristine snow was the first bit of beauty she had seen in months. She marveled at how the rugged frontier held beauty even in the depths of winter. As she approached Moses' clearing, she heard a dog barking, and she shouted, "Shenanigan, come here, boy!" He burst through the trees and practically jumped into her arms. Darcy didn't realize how much she had missed her old friend.

The door swung open and there stood Moses

giving Darcy a large toothless grin. "Well, well look who's here. Come in and warm your bones. I see you are using snowshoes."

Darcy stepped inside the cabin and practically fainted from the smell of dinner. The fire crackled under a big cast iron pot, and Moses swung open the oven door, pulling out a tray of biscuits.

"Here sit down. You are just in time to eat. There's plenty here. I always make enough for a couple of days.

Darcy removed her cloak and sat down by the fire. He poured her some cider and filled her plate, and then he filled his own. After giving thanks, Darcy put a spoonful of stew into her mouth. She must not look too anxious, Moses may grow suspicious. As she emptied her bowl and drank her cider, she felt the life-giving nourishment course through her body. Moses looked at her out of the corner of his eye and pushed the platter toward her. "Here, take some more. There's plenty."

Powerless to refuse, Darcy ate until she was satisfied, and sank back into her chair exhausted. The long walk through the snow and good food relaxed her completely.

"Why are you so thin, Darcy?" asked Moses, suspiciously.

"I've been sick for some time, but I am on the mend," she lied. Darcy knew that he would question her appearance, so she had answers prepared ahead of time.

Having another cider by the fire, they visited all afternoon contentedly, and when the shadows started to fall, Darcy said, "I've brought you a small gift in honor of *Nollaig na mBan*."

"Oh!" he laughed. "I haven't heard Twelfth Night called that since me pappy died."

She handed him a sampler she had been working on for the past two months. On the cloth was an Irish Blessing and sprinkled everywhere were tiny embroidered shamrocks. She had stretched it over a crude frame. "I know that you can't read it, Moses, but the spirit of the blessing will be upon your home."

"Tell me what it says, Darcy," he asked.

She picked up the sampler and read,

"Wishing you always-
Walls for the wind,
And a roof for the rain,
And tea beside the fire.
Laughter to cheer you,
And those you love near you,
And all that your heart might desire!"

Moses turned his head brushing a tear from his eye. He had missed Darcy this winter, and her kindness touched him. Admiring her workmanship, he thanked her and rested the sampler against the chimney in the center of the mantel. Then he reached into a box full of whittling tools and produced a small whistle for Darcy.

"You made that for me? There are many folk in Ireland that play the whistle well, and now I can learn too." She put it to her lips and blew a shrill note.

Moses jumped and Shenanigan slid under the bed. He laughed, "Please, don't learn here!"

Giggling, Darcy hugged Moses and pulled her cloak closely around herself. She said goodbye and stepped outside. It was dark, but a full moon lit her way home.

The winter moonlight cast long shadows across her path. When the wind picked up, it sent the trees into an eerie dance. Tales of the Banshee crept into her mind, and Darcy quickened her pace. The Irish told of a wailing woman who warned of death, and if it were true, the Banshee was indeed walking among those at Fort Lawrence tonight. When she arrived at the gate, she breathed a sigh of relief.

The month of February brought disease in earnest. Dysentery raged, and Darcy spent most of her time in the surgery, nursing the sick. On two occasions she was called in to act as midwife, and in both cases the babies were stillborn. Although the children at the fort were not yet starving, they were extremely thin, and their heads looked too big for their frail, little bodies.

Nathan developed a nagging cough, and many nights Darcy was kept awake listening to it wrack his body. She had been too busy and ill herself to be concerned about him, but one morning, when she was headed out to the surgery, she noticed that the door to his room was still shut from the night before.

She knocked, and when there was no response, she looked inside. What she saw frightened her. Nathan was in bed, on his back with his eyes closed and not moving. Fearing that he was dead, she moved closer and listened for breathing. It was shallow, but he was breathing. Darcy touched his forehead and found it burning with fever.

Quickly she ran to find the surgeon. When they returned, he examined Nathan and told Darcy that it was a severe congestion of the lungs.

"Will he be all right?"

The surgeon sighed and said, "It is unlikely, my girl. Given his age and the poor nourishment, he may live only one or two days."

Darcy was stunned. This had all happened so quickly, and she couldn't believe that this was the end for Nathan. Tirelessly she worked to keep him alive.

Although she had never loved Nathan, she was fond of him, and she never forgot certain freedoms he allowed her during her servitude.

She abandoned her work in the surgery and moved a bed into his room. Darcy fed him broth and sponged him with cool towels endlessly. His sleep was fitful, and he tossed restlessly in bed, coughing and straining for air. He lingered into the month of March, and one night Darcy heard him call her name. She sat up quickly, lighting a candle.

His eyes were open, and giving her a weak smile, he whispered, "My little colleen."

It took several more weeks, but Darcy pulled Nathan through the most dangerous time of his illness. When she finally had time to leave his quarters, she realized that the air had warmed, and the snow was melting. Spring had come to Fort Lawrence.

Chapter 25

The steady drip, drip of maple sap into buckets was music to Darcy's ears. As she struggled through the mud, she realized that this would probably be the last time she would need to empty the containers. The sap had slowed now to almost a stop, and it had gradually become thin and tasteless, signaling the end of the sap flow.

She learned that the settlers would boil the sap down until it was reduced to a thick syrup and use it as a delectable substitute for refined sugar. Many gallons could be lost if it was taken off the fire too soon, producing a thin syrup, or even worse, let the substance over-boil and caramelize. This whole process would be accompanied by a celebration called a Sugaring Off. There would be dancing, food and plenty of libations served throughout the day.

Much to everyone's relief and joy, the rations arrived and the residents of the fort were thriving again. It seemed the unit carrying the food had made it as far as Fort Pepperell on the Piscataqua River and been stopped by the November snowstorm. They wintered over at the fort, and the instant the roads became passable, resumed their journey.

Nathan had made a full recovery and returned to his post as commanding officer. He immediately prepared the fort for another attack. The French and Abenaki would return from their winter camps and possibly resume their attack soon. There had been great loss of life at the fort, and morale was extremely low, so Nathan allowed the Sugaring Off to be held for one day inside the walls.

Things returned to a more normal schedule and most of the patients were cared for and discharged. Looking back on her first winter at Fort Lawrence, Darcy could see that the hunger in no way approached the magnitude of suffering endured in Ireland. Most of the deaths at the fort had been from disease and no resident actually died of starvation.

Longing to wash the hardships and memories of the winter away and start anew, she soaked all evening in a tub of warm water. For the first time in months, she washed her hair and filed her nails into smooth ovals. To Nathan, she never looked lovelier. Although she was thin, her eyes seemed brighter, and he found respect in her fortitude which he had never appreciated before. He would never forget that she had saved his life, and for this, he would be forever grateful.

The night before the Sugaring Off, everyone bustled about the parade ground making preparations. The women were busy cooking, and the regulars were erecting a platform for fiddlers. Firewood had been assembled under three large crucibles, and the maple sap awaited its transition in several huge barrels.

Darcy had been baking pies all day in the kitchen when one of the women said there were some officers who requested pints of ale. She added that one of the men said he would take his drink only from the daughter of Brian Boru. Darcy was bending down by the hearth, and she stood up suddenly hitting her head on the bricks of the fireplace. Rubbing her head, she asked, "What does he look like?"

"He's very good-looking, but he has a cheeky attitude. See for yourself. He's the only one not in uniform."

As Darcy had suspected, there at the table was

Jean-Michel Lupé. When he looked up, she stepped back out of sight into the kitchen.

How dare he come into her life again and shatter her piece of mind. He was a face from the past, and any feelings she might have had for him were over. Yet her heart was pounding furiously, and her palms were soaked.

It was apparent to everyone in the kitchen that Darcy was agitated, and the women questioned her, but she ignored them. She was too busy looking for a way to escape. There was only one door, and crawling out a window was ludicrous, so she decided to face him head on. *I am no longer affected by this man, and I will prove it.*

Drawing a pint, she straightened her back, took a deep breath and walked out the door. She felt his eyes on her as she approached the table. Suddenly Moses' words echoed in her ears. "*He's been with some woman down there for years. She lives somewhere on the Piscataqua too.*" The jealousy she had buried all through the winter bubbled to the surface, and when Darcy reached the table, she slammed the pint of ale down so hard that the contents drenched Jean-Michel's face and shirt.

He jumped to his feet, spewing forth profanities in French, as his comrades burst into laughter. "What the hell!" he exclaimed.

Darcy made no reply, turned on her heel and left. After Jean-Michel had recovered from his anger and the ribbing from the two officers, he started to think about what Darcy had done. She was furious with him about something, and he was determined to know what it was. If he could elicit that kind of passion from her, undoubtedly she still cared for him.

Lupé was headed to do a survey in the north and had been called to Fort Lawrence for a final consultation with Lawrence. He was overwhelmed with relief when he saw Darcy. He knew of the starvation at the fort from the beginning. The unit trying to deliver the rations spent the winter at Fort Pepperell, near his home, and all winter long he was anxious about her. Jean-Michel had been less successful than Darcy dismissing the events of last summer. He believed that distance and Elizabeth Campbell's bed would quell his desire for the fiery Irishwoman, but he had been mistaken.

He reminded himself again and again that Darcy loved Nathan Lawrence. He told himself that he was here only to make final preparations for his field work, but seeing Darcy again he felt the desire build once more. He memorized every detail of her appearance and every mannerism. These memories he would take to the interior to banish his loneliness on dark nights.

The long-awaited Sugaring Off festivities began the following afternoon. The morning was spent in final preparations, and by noon the fires had been set and the large pots filled with sap. All day long the liquid would be watched as it bubbled and boiled, and more sap would be added until the crucial cook-down began. The end result of a successful sugaring off was a year-long supply of thick, rich maple syrup used on everything from johnnycakes to sweet potatoes.

While growing up, Jean-Michel had attended many of these festivities, and it surprised him that Darcy was not in attendance. He thought she would be interested in this New World tradition, and after a brief meeting with Colonel Lawrence, he went out onto the parade ground to look for her.

Jean-Michel was happy to be out of the stuffy office and in the fresh air. He did not like Nathan Lawrence, and after their less than cordial parting last summer, there was a strain between them. He found the entire fort brimming with excitement.

The tables were crammed with pumpkin and corn puddings, sweet potatoes, venison, rabbit, and veal. The sweets were just as diverse including, Indian pudding, apple pies, and gingerbread. He helped himself to a hearty plateful of food and joined several of the officers at a table.

The sky was gray, and the air was crisp as Jean-Michel and the others shared drinks and played draughts. Over the course of the afternoon and well into the evening, he had been watching the crowds, but still had not seen Darcy. As he was having a good-natured discussion with Captain Trevor regarding who was a keener shot, she came through the gate accompanied by an old man.

Jean-Michel instantly took in every detail of her appearance. She wore a dark, green skirt with a green-and-white striped bodice, laced tightly over her white chemise, and although her hair was pinned up, the wind had freed several strands, which softly framed her face. She was flushed from the cool wind, and her eyes sparkled.

As they wound their way through the crowd, Jean-Michel noticed something familiar about the old man. He jumped to his feet, and with his hand extended, he exclaimed, "Why, Moses Tinker! It's been years."

They shook hands warmly, and Jean-Michel invited him to join them at their table for a drink. Darcy walked on, not caring to encounter Jean-Michel. She planned to avoid him until he set off for the interior in a few days.

Moses and Jean-Michel reminisced about old times and family until the sun went down and torches were lit for the music and dancing.

Jean-Michel watched Darcy, as she stood outside the door of the commanding officer's quarters. Finally, he asked Moses, "What do you know of this McBride woman?"

"Ha! She asked the same thing about you," said Moses, taking a pull on his beer.

"Really? What did she want to know?" asked Jean-Michel, leaning forward.

"Oh, nothing much," he said, scratching his gray head. "Where you lived, who your family was--that sort of thing, but the conversation ended on the spot when I told her you had a woman. She stood up and left the cabin and never mentioned your name again."

Moses looked at Jean-Michel out of his good eye and said, "I find that odd, don't you?"

Jean-Michel did not answer. He was looking at Darcy. It was clear now why she had been so angry with him. She was jealous and that pleased him immensely. He sat back in his chair, crossing his arms over his chest and said with a smirk, "Damn!"

The fiddlers struck up a tune, and Darcy watched the dancing closely. The dancers joined hands or held each other at the waist. Most of the steps were foreign to her and looked very difficult.

"I'll never get used to their crude style of dancing," said Nathan, as he joined Darcy in the doorway.

"What style of dance do you do, Nathan?"

"Certainly something more dignified and refined," he said with a sniff, "but I must be tolerant. They are peasant stock and know nothing else."

Darcy detested Nathan when he spoke of class

distinctions, reminding her of his high-born breeding. She looked at him and gave him an insincere smile, as he leaned against the door frame smoking his pipe.

Almost as if he had heard Nathan, Jean-Michel said to Moses sarcastically, "There's Colonel Lawrence, benevolent father to us crude provincials."

Next, he saw Captain Trevor approach Lawrence. Lawrence nodded his head, and Trevor swept Darcy out for a dance.

Darcy was grateful to Captain Trevor for his patience while she learned the different dances. It took several songs before she could master the steps, but soon she kept up with him. He was a big handsome curly-haired man with a broad smile, and Darcy found him amusing.

She accepted several more dances from other men then stepped to the side to catch her breath. As she was finishing a glass of cider, she felt someone take her hand and realized that it was Jean-Michel. He had removed his jacket and rolled up his shirt sleeves revealing the well-defined muscles in his forearms. He said nothing to her, and she followed him reluctantly out to the dance area. They danced one time, Darcy refusing to look him in the eye. She stepped away immediately when the song was over. She was tense and uncomfortable in his arms, and she turned to look for Captain Trevor again.

As the evening progressed, spirits soared. Everyone was consuming more food than they had eaten the entire winter. Toward midnight, Darcy was starting to feel fatigued. The drinking and the dancing had taken its toll on her, and before another dance-starved soldier could grab her, she stepped into the shadows of the store room to hide and catch her breath. Pushing the hair off her wet forehead, she leaned against the wall of the building and sighed. She was warm, and her bodice was far too tight.

Darcy reached down and began to loosen the strings of her garment. Suddenly, someone said, "I should make my presence known before you go any further."

Darcy jumped. It was Jean-Michel. He had followed her to the shadows. "How long have you been there?"

He made no reply. When she tried to leave, he stepped in front of her and demanded, "Why did you slam my drink down on the table this afternoon? Are you angry with me?"

"It was merely an accident, nothing more" and she stepped around him to go back to the dance.

"That was no accident," he said taking her shoulders and pinned her against the storeroom wall.

"Why were you asking Moses questions about me?" he murmured, looking at her lips. He was pressing his body so hard against her own that she could not breathe.

"Let me go," she demanded, trying to wiggle away from him.

Never had she felt such intensity from a man, and it confused and startled her. His passion was so extreme that she didn't know if he was going to strike her or kiss her.

"You were angry when you heard of Elizabeth, weren't you?"

He moved his lips close to her ear, and she could feel his warm breath as he whispered, "Tell me that you are jealous, Darcy. Say it," he demanded. "I want to hear you say it."

He brushed his lips along her ear, and Darcy closed

her eyes, putting her head back. The pressure of his body, the masculine smell of sweat, and the sound of his breathing were too much to bear. She could not fight him. Her blood began to warm. His hands slid over her body, and she arched her back, pushing her breasts against him.

Just as he was about to kiss her neck, she remembered how Elizabeth's name sounded on his lips. She pushed him back and said, "You know that I love Nathan. Now let me go."

"Miss McBride!" a man barked. It was one of Nathan's officers. "Colonel Lawrence would like you to retire for the night."

Darcy jumped back, panting. She straightened her hair and smoothed her gown, as the soldier watched with a smirk. Without looking back, Darcy retreated once more to the safe haven of Nathan Lawrence.

Chapter 26

Jean-Michel lay on his bed and stared at the ceiling. *How could I have been so foolish? How could I have given that woman the opportunity to refuse me again?* He had allowed his passion to dictate his actions, and he vowed to curb his desire permanently with this McBride woman.

He rolled over and tried to sleep, but the minute he closed his eyes his mind would take him to the shadows with Darcy, and he could smell her scent once more. Although she wore lavender, another scent haunted him more--a deeper, more sensuous perfume which he knew was her own.

Jean-Michel tossed in bed trying to forget her, but the memory of her body next to his, and her soft breasts as they pushed against his thin shirt bothered him. He wished that he could bed Elizabeth tonight and cool his desire for that arrogant Irish tease. Elizabeth never aggravated him. She was always a serene compliant companion never arguing, always generous and kind.

He knew that Elizabeth Campbell was the woman he should marry, but for all of her loveliness and grace, she did not have the fire he longed for in a woman. Even before her husband had died, he knew that Elizabeth secretly loved him. Several months after Edward's drowning, she came to Jean-Michel and told him of her true feelings, and for the following nine years, they had been companions. During that time she had made no demands of him, never complained and always welcomed him with open arms.

Everyone described Elizabeth as beautiful, with soft blonde hair and large brown eyes, and although Jean-Michel found her to be a satisfactory lover, she failed to inflame him. Her docile, submissive attitude bored him, and in the nine years of their relationship, there had never been a cross word between the two. The more Jean-Michel thought of the serenely beautiful Elizabeth, the calmer he felt. He could see her soft brown eyes, hear her quiet voice, and he felt himself growing drowsy until finally he dropped off to sleep.

Jean-Michel avoided Darcy over the next month, spending much of his time preparing for his field work. He was waiting for the ground to dry out and the air to warm enough to make an extended journey. By mid-May the days were long, the nights were warm, and Jean-Michel was ready to set out.

The morning before he was scheduled to depart, Jean-Michel met with Colonel Lawrence one last time. They spent the entire morning examining specifications, and finally, Jean-Michel asked, "Now, who have you commissioned to be my assistant?"

There was a long pause, and Nathan said, "I hate to tell you this Lupé, but I can spare no man."

"What? It's impossible for me to do field work without an assistant especially an engineering survey of this magnitude," exclaimed Jean-Michel.

"My company has not yet arrived from the south, and even with reinforcements it may be difficult to defend this fort. I expect a raid any day now," said Nathan, shaking his head. "I am sorry to inconvenience you."

"Inconvenience me? The job won't get done. It's obvious, Colonel, that you know nothing of surveying.

An assistant is essential for accurate calculations. If you cannot provide me with someone, then you are going to have to find yourself a different surveyor."

Jean-Michel gathered up his things. As he put his hand on the door to leave, Lawrence said, "Please wait."

Heaving a sigh, Nathan opened a drawer of his desk and took out a letter. Showing it to Jean-Michel, he said, "I received this correspondence today. In a little over a week, my wife will be visiting me at Fort Lawrence. She has no idea of the danger here, and I am allowing her to stay only a short time before I send her back to Boston."

Jean-Michel crossed to the desk and read the letter. He tossed it down and asked, "What does that have to do with me?"

"Surely you can see the precarious position this puts me in. I cannot continue to share my bed with Miss McBride, but I do not want to sell her indentured service."

"I still don't understand what you're driving at," said Jean-Michel, clearly annoyed.

"I'm offering you the assistance of Miss McBride during your field work."

Jean-Michel's blue eyes grew wide with astonishment. "Have you lost your mind, Lawrence? I cannot cart a woman with me to the interior!"

"You underestimate the strength of this woman, Lupé. You know nothing of her. She has survived famine, escaped hanging and without so much as a complaint, endured the starvation this winter. I have every faith that she will be an able-bodied assistant for you."

Jean-Michel shook his head. Lawrence must be truly desperate to ask him to take Darcy to the interior for weeks. Anything could happen there.

Almost as if Lawrence had read his mind, Nathan warned, "Don't take me for a fool, Lupé. I realize that she is a highly desirable woman, and I expect her to be returned to me unsullied. She is your assistant only, and I remind you Miss McBride is my property."

Jean-Michel turned and walked to the window. From where he stood, he could see Darcy building a fire under a crucible. He had vowed never to touch her again, and now he would be alone with her for weeks. Celibacy would be torturous, but the opportunity to be next to her day and night stirred him.

* * *

Unaware of how her life was about to change, Darcy added more wood to the fire, trying to get a large pot of water to boil. She was about to dump a basket of goldenrod into the water to dye some wool when a soldier approached her. "Colonel Lawrence requests your presence in his office immediately, Miss McBride."

Wiping her hands on her apron, she walked to the Colonel's office, and the guard swung the door open for her. Nathan was seated at his desk, and Darcy's eyes narrowed when she saw Jean-Michel standing behind him. When the guard shut the door, she sat down.

Nathan cleared his throat. "Darcy, I have some news for you that I know you will not like," and standing up, he continued. "For the next several weeks, you are to serve as assistant to Mr. Lupé when he surveys for the new fort on the Kensington River."

Darcy was stunned. She looked at Jean-Michel and then back at Nathan. Her mouth dropped open, and she laughed with disbelief. "Surely you jest!"

"I assure you, Darcy, I am quite serious," returned

Nathan.

Darcy looked from Nathan to Jean-Michel and back again trying to make some sense of this turn of events. Jean-Michel stood in the back of the room, remaining quiet.

"You are sending me into the wilderness alone with another man? Why?"

"Because Lupé is in dire need of an assistant, and I can spare no man when we are under threat of an attack."

Sensing that Nathan was withholding information, she asked, "Nathan, I want to know the entire story. Did he have something to do with this?"

"No, this was entirely my doing. In fact, Jean-Michel was against it initially."

"Then why?" she asked, standing up, beginning to feel angry. "Tell me, Nathan! Why?"

"All right, if you insist," said Nathan, shrugging his shoulders. "I wanted to spare you the hurt and embarrassment in front of Mr. Lupé, but if you must know, I am sending you to the interior because my wife joins me here in a week's time."

Darcy had forgotten that Nathan had a wife, and it took a minute for her to absorb it. Then she stood up and began to pace. "So this was your solution. I can see that suddenly I am a liability, so you allow this man to take me to the interior to use me any way he sees fit."

"He has given me his word that you will not be touched," assured Nathan.

Darcy laughed and said, "This is all very convenient for you men, isn't it?"

Struggling with fear and anger, she said nothing for a long time. Once again her destiny was dictated by another, and her independence was assaulted. "There must be another way."

Nathan stood up and rubbed his brow. He was tired of arguing with her, and he decided to end the conversation. He knew Darcy feared being sold to another, so he said bluntly, "I can sell you to another man. Would you prefer that?"

At this suggestion, Darcy blanched, and Jean-Michel looked down at the floor. He did not feel right watching her squirm under the domination of Nathan Lawrence. He assumed that she was fighting to stay with Lawrence because she loved him.

Darcy swallowed hard. She was terrified of the prospect of a new owner, but it was not in her character to be submissive. The fury of betrayal burned inside her. "Nathan Lawrence, I have endured your depraved, carnal ineptitude for over a year now, and the moment I grow inconvenient, you abandon me."

Nathan's face turned scarlet at this scathing commentary on his sexual prowess, and he stepped around the desk raising his hand to strike her.

Jean-Michel jumped and caught his arm. He looked into Nathan's eyes and said, "I'd rather you didn't do that."

Panting with rage, Nathan stared at Jean-Michel. He had been emasculated twice within a minute, and his pride was severely injured. Lawrence knew he would regret turning his anger on Jean-Michel, so he lowered his arm and burned a look into him, thinking, *I detest this half-breed bastard, and I hope he rapes the hell out of that bitch! The minute she returns from the field, I will sell her.* Nathan heard the door slam and knew that Darcy had left the room. Jean-Michel gathered his things and left as well.

Darcy headed out to the parade ground where she

had been dyeing yarn. She picked up the wool and jammed it furiously into the pot with a stick. Hearing footsteps behind her, she turned around and faced Jean-Michel. "We will leave at dawn," he instructed. "Bring nothing more than a few personal belongings. Prepare yourself for long days walking in every kind of weather. I don't use a tent. We will sleep under the stars."

"You touch me once, Lupé and I'll kill you when you sleep," she said, coldly.

The pity that Jean-Michel had been feeling for Darcy dissolved, and he said in a voice heavy with sarcasm, "I am aware of your high moral character, Miss McBride, and I wouldn't dream of staining your pristine reputation." As he walked away, he called, "I'm no longer interested in your kind."

Darcy watched his back, clenching her fists. She was boiling more fiercely than the water in the pot next to her.

* * *

Darcy refused to go to Nathan's room that night, and try as she might to sleep, she could only toss and turn. She had struggled for over a month to avoid Jean-Michel, and now Nathan had thrown her into an expedition where she would be alone with the man for weeks.

His comments about her virtue had stung yesterday, and she upbraided herself for caring about his opinion. Darcy had to admit she had used her appeal to obtain a decent position of service, but Jean-Michel had no right to classify her as wanton.

Just before dawn she dressed in her most comfortable gown and collected a few things which she rolled into a bundle to be carried on her back. She strapped her shot pouch and powder horn over her chest and bent down to hug Shenanigan good-bye. Last night she had asked one of the boys at the fort to feed and watch him while she was gone, and the child seemed overjoyed.

Before closing the door to her room, she grabbed her musket and crossed into the sitting room. She did not pause outside Nathan's door. She did not care to say goodbye to him. As far as Darcy was concerned, he had abandoned her, and any respect she had for him was gone forever.

Jean-Michel waited for her at the gate, and when they set out, the sun was beginning to light the morning sky. He was dressed in a soft buckskin shirt belted at the waist along with breeches and leggings tied upon his legs. His dress was suitable for a long journey in the wild.

Laden with packs heavy with food and supplies, they ventured deep into the vast interior following an ancient path traveled only by Indians and deer for centuries. Darcy followed silently in Jean-Michel's footsteps, looking only at his back or the ground beneath her. They stopped to rest only occasionally. Their mid-day meal consisted of jerky, or *pemmican,* as Jean-Michel called it.

They did not converse, and the further they ventured from the fort, the more vulnerable Darcy felt. She realized that Nathan and the four walls of the fort had kept her body and heart protected, and now with every step she took, she was more and more defenseless.

Jean-Michel found himself in a similar situation. He had a deep love of the wilderness, and to be alone with

Darcy in a place of such primal beauty weakened his resolve to resist her.

As sunset approached, he left the path and began to ascend a steep hill. Darcy followed him, struggling through the brush grumbling, as the branches grabbed at her skirts. He looked back and smiled. "Don't fret. It's worth the hike up here."

When they finally reached the summit, they stood on the rocks of a high cliff overlooking the valley through which they had traveled most of the day. The broad expanse of deep green spread out before them and the setting sun cast long golden rays across the treetops.

Jean-Michel looked at Darcy, as the breeze gently moved her skirts. He watched her stare at the panorama as if she were hypnotized. *She too has a love of the land.*

"It was worth the climb, wasn't it?"

"Tis grand up here," she said, looking at the Windsor River winding in the distance. "This is what we in Ireland call, a *thin place*."

"A thin place, what's that?" he asked.

"They are places on Earth where the ancient Celts believe the boundaries between the natural world and the supernatural worlds are thin. This is one of those places."

Jean-Michel nodded his head. Darcy's life had been so different from his own, but her spirit was the same. If only she would allow him to step inside. "I thought you would like the view," he said.

"Your homeland never fails to inspire me," she replied.

"But it is your home too."

"No," she said shaking her head. "When my term is

over, I will return to my own cliff tops in Kerry."

It had never occurred to Jean-Michel that she might want to return to Ireland someday. He slid the cumbersome pack off his back and said, "This is where we will sleep tonight. The breeze will keep the bugs away, so drop your pack and help me build a fire."

"A fire? You can't build a fire here. The Abenaki will see it."

"I have no fear of the Abenaki," stated Jean-Michel, in a matter-of-fact tone as he pulled his tinderbox out of his pack. "They know and respect my father's name, so they will not harm me. In fact, I spent several summers among them when I was a boy. They are a people much maligned by the British."

"Sweet Mary, that's fine for you, but what about me?"

Jean-Michel shrugged and said, "Sweet Mary! Now that's another matter."

A spark jumped from the flint, and he blew gently on the dry leaves to ignite the fire. When he had finished feeding it with some twigs and birch bark, he stood up and said with a twinkle in his eye, "Don't worry, I'll tell them that you are my woman, and they'll not harm you."

Darcy pursed her lips and began to gather kindling for the fire. As darkness closed in around them, the fire offered warmth and protection from predators, and it bathed them both in a golden glow. Darcy tore up some dried meat and started to prepare a stew.

"There are some leather breeches in my pack you can add too," Jean-Michel said.

She straightened up and looked at him.

He laughed. "Oh, I suppose you don't know. Leather breeches are dried beans."

Darcy laughed too and shook her head. They ate their supper in silence by the fire with the black wilderness surrounding them.

Finally, Darcy asked, "Tell me about your father. I am very curious about The Wolf."

"How do you know that they called my father, 'The Wolf'?"

Darcy stammered something about Moses and then fell quiet. Jean-Michel grinned and said, "That's all right, I've teased you enough for one day. I will gladly tell you about 'The Wolf.'"

Jean-Michel leaned back on one elbow and said, "He was a big, booming, good-hearted fur trader who loved my mother with all his heart. He treated her as if she were a priceless work of art, and I believe that secretly he did not feel worthy of her."

"And your mother, what of her?"

"My mother," he said thoughtfully. "She was very gentle, a highly educated woman, much more reserved than my father. She had the way of a great lady about her, yet she was incredibly strong. My parents loved each other dearly even if they didn't always understand one another."

Jean-Michel stared into the flames for a long time, thinking about his parents. When the fire popped, he blinked as if waking up and asked, "What of your family? Tell me about them."

"I have no family left. My father disappeared when I was a wee babe, and except for my brother Liam, the others died in The Hunger."

Jean-Michel could have kicked himself for asking. He watched Darcy bite her lip. She seemed reluctant to talk.

After a few moments she said, "When my mother

died, Liam, Bran and I went down to the ocean and lived in the caves, eating kelp and bits of snail to survive."

"Are these your brothers?"

"Liam was my brother, Bran was not. He was my betrothed. I waited many years for him, and he turned out to be a sniveling traitor running off with his pockets full of money."

So there had been someone back in Ireland. He wondered if this Bran had something to do with her arrest.

"What happened to your brother?" he asked.

"He was hanged."

Jean-Michel frowned.

Darcy stood up and gathered the supper dishes. It was clear to Jean-Michel that this topic was over. He did not want to fall back into the painful silence, so he asked, "When you came up to Fort Lawrence, did you walk?"

"No, I rode a horse."

"A harse!" he said, laughing about her accent.

Darcy put her chin up and said with a smile, "Well, at least, we don't call beans *leather breeches*."

"All right!" admitted Jean-Michel, putting his palms up.

Darcy sat back down and watched the fire.

"You mentioned thin places earlier today," he said. "I believe in these places. I have seen them. I have felt them."

"They have a way of transforming you," agreed Darcy, remembering the abbey.

Jean-Michel looked at Darcy. She could feel his eyes on her, and she felt herself grow uneasy.

"So if you and I were together in a thin place, Darcy, would I be able to read what is in your heart?"

"If you see anything in my heart, please let me know." She stood up abruptly, realizing that she said too much. She wanted to get as far away from him as she could, but there was nowhere to go.

Jean-Michel watched her look around frantically, and he felt pity for her. "Darcy, we have a long day ahead of us tomorrow. You'd better get some sleep."

She nodded her head. Having a task made her feel better. She stepped away from the fire into the darkness to slip out of her gown, as Jean-Michel untied his leggings and took his boots off.

He pulled his buckskin shirt over his head and stretched out on his bedroll. He was beyond tired tonight and his legs were sore. He knew that he would be better tomorrow. The first day was always the hardest.

Darcy was on a bedroll not far from him. How could he endure weeks alone with this woman? He was asking the impossible of himself, and he cursed Nathan Lawrence for putting him in this position. Swallowing hard, Jean-Michel rolled over with his back to Darcy. He would find a way. He would simply have to find a way.

The morning sun woke them both, and after breaking camp they left the cliff top and resumed their journey. The day was warm and by mid-afternoon oppressively hot.

Jean-Michel stopped in the shade of some spruce trees and said, "Do you hear that? It's a waterfall. We can get fresh water, and I can bathe. It's been too many days and the heat is stifling.

Darcy was surprised. Jean-Michel saw her expression and said, "Does it surprise you? I know you like to bathe too. I smelled the freshness all over you the night we danced."

Jean-Michel gave her a crooked smile and gathered his things, disappearing into the woods. Darcy reached into her pack, looking for her drinking gourd. She sat down heavily on a log and watched a tiny bird hop about eating seeds. She rubbed her forehead and thought about her outburst last night. Why did she say that she didn't know what was in her heart? She knew that it was empty. It was hard and cold and incapable of love.

She stood up and started to pace. This heat was suffocating, and she wished Jean-Michel would hurry back so she could cool her body and her feelings in the rushing waters. Why did he continue to try to seduce her? She must never let him know that her resistance was wearing thin. She wondered if he knew that her eyes were continually on him.

When Jean-Michel returned, he pulled his damp hair back with a leather thong and rubbed his skin with pennyroyal to repel the bugs. Darcy grabbed her pack and headed for the waterfall, eager to wash the heat away. It was only a short distance through the trees, and she saw the little waterfall cascading down into the river below.

Slipping her clothes off, she stepped onto the rocks and got under the crashing water. The pummeling of it helped clear her head, and after giving her hair and body a hearty scrubbing she dried off, dressed and returned to Jean-Michel. He stood up when she came through the trees as if he had something to say to her, but stopped. When she started to pin up her hair he caught her wrist saying, "No, don't put your hair up. Please leave it down."

Darcy pulled her arm away from him and said, "Don't be absurd." Darcy was uncomfortable, knowing that a woman should keep her hair up unless she was behind closed doors.

"We are alone. I am the only one who will see it."

Darcy bit her lip, knowing that Jean-Michel's request was very intimate. Hesitantly she dropped her arms. He sighed as if he had been holding his breath and then picked up his pack to go.

They walked all afternoon, stopping only occasionally for water or a bit of food. Jean-Michel told Darcy to eat steadily throughout the day, in small amounts, to keep her energy up and to save her appetite for a hot meal at night.

When the sun began to set, he traversed a steep hill, and Darcy followed, grateful to be going up to where the mosquitoes and flies would plague her no longer. The site was atop another cliff, and the beauty of the landscape was as lovely as the night before.

"We are very lucky that we have not had to journey in the rain," said Jean-Michel, as he built a fire.

"And if it rains?" asked Darcy.

"We find a cave to sleep in."

Darcy did not like the sound of that, but she decided she would not worry about it until the time came. After dinner, Jean-Michel opened his pack and took out a book. The entire day he had struggled within himself as Darcy walked in front him on the trails. As he watched her dark tresses spill down her back, he wanted to pull her close a thousand times, but he would not risk rejection again. He needed no more reminders that she did not want him. He had revealed too much by asking her to leave her hair down earlier in the day.

Darcy watched Jean-Michel as he stretched out on his side to read a book, wondering why he had suddenly turned so cold and indifferent. She was angry with herself for wanting his attention, but she had looked forward to talking with him by the fire. It was also disappointing that she had left her hair down for him all day, and he never even acknowledged the gesture.

She walked over by him and took a peek at what he was reading. "Oh, you're reading *Othello*, Are you sympathetic to him or do you believe he was a fool?"

Jean-Michel looked up from his book and said, "Hmmm? Oh, definitely sympathetic. He was a victim of Iago's treachery."

Suddenly he blinked, "You have read *Othello*?'

"I have," said Darcy matter-of-factly, as she poked the fire. He did not see the smirk on her face, as she stirred the ashes. She relished the amazement on Jean-Michel's face. She knew now that she had his attention for the rest of the night.

He demanded, "How is it that you can read?"

"Oh, does it surprise you that an Irish convict has a mind?"

"No, but--well, what else have you read?"

"Many things," she said, shrugging her shoulders. "The Bible, of course, but my first work of fiction was *The Arabian Nights*. I've read most of Shakespeare's works and Milton, Dante--"

"Who taught you to read?"

"A priest."

Jean-Michel was sitting up now cross-legged, staring at Darcy, trying to comprehend what he was hearing. He was simply astounded. He had met few women in his life who could read, but what was even more amazing was that she was well-educated. All his life he had longed to have a woman who could meet him on his own intellectual ground, and it had been this mysterious Irish woman all along.

They talked late into the night. Jean-Michel marveled at Darcy's ability to debate his opinions and offer her own impressions. He realized she had endured not only physical hunger but intellectual starvation.

Darcy was delighted as well. She had always found Nathan's impressions of literature to be flat and uninteresting. They always reflected his narrow, elitist views, and when he did ask her opinion, which was seldom, he dismissed her ideas as pedestrian. She hadn't realized how much she had missed talking with someone who treated her as an intellectual equal.

Jean-Michel watched Darcy's face as she talked about Odysseus and Penelope, and suddenly he interrupted saying, "It is a cruel twist of fate that you are bound to another, Darcy."

Their eyes locked a moment, and then Darcy looked down. "I don't want to go back to Nathan, Jean-Michel."

She knew she had revealed too much, so she stood up abruptly and announced, "It's late."

As they took out their bedrolls for the night, Jean-Michel asked, "You said that you were educated by a priest. I thought that they were not allowed in Ireland?"

"You're right. They are not, but we smuggled a Jesuit into our town. He befriended me shortly after he arrived and taught me how to read."

"What did you say the name of the town was in Ireland?"

"Kilkerry, it's in County Kerry on the west coast."

Jean-Michel frowned. He stayed in front of the fire for a long time, staring at the flames until he was certain that Darcy was asleep. He stood up and went to his pack, pulling everything out and throwing it onto the ground. When he reached the bottom of his bag, he yanked out a long leather pouch holding letters. His hands shook as he stood by the fire, reading the words. When he finished, he looked up and gasped, "It can't be!"

Jean-Michel sat down heavily onto the ground, shaking his head. *It was impossible. She couldn't be the same woman. Ireland was too large, and there must be hundreds of women like her living there.* But he knew in his heart that there was only one woman who could be described as Pandora. It was Darcy McBride.

Gradually and with complete astonishment, Jean-Michel admitted to himself that the Jesuit, who had educated Darcy was his own brother, Etienne Lupé.

Chapter 27

Jean-Michel kept the news from Darcy at least for the time being. It was too soon after making his own discovery, and he was still recovering from the shock of it himself. As the morning wore on, he found himself eager for news of Etienne, so he decided to tell her when they stopped to rest on the Kensington River. As they approached the broad expanse of water, Jean-Michel told Darcy that they would be headed north from here to an abandoned settlement, and it was there that he would begin the survey.

After climbing a large flat ledge overlooking the river, Jean-Michel swung his pack onto the ground. He sat down on the edge of the rock letting his legs dangle freely over the water, and Darcy sat down beside him. They ate some biscuits and watched the water tumble across the rocks beneath their feet. "This spot reminds me of a place where I sat with a friend a long time ago. In fact, it was the man who taught me to read," said Darcy. She looked up at the sky, squinting in the sunlight, and took a deep breath. "Only it smells different. The last time was by the ocean. We sat on a ledge like this and ate strawberries in the sunshine."

Jean-Michel saw his opportunity. "Etienne liked strawberries, didn't he?" asked Jean-Michel.

"Yes, he--" As if a lightning bolt hit her, Darcy jumped to her feet and cried, "How do you know his name?"

He took her hand and said, "Sit down, Darcy. We must talk." Mechanically she sat down, her eyes on him. "Darcy, your friend Father Etienne is my brother."

She stared at him, struggling to comprehend the

news when suddenly she cried out, "What! This is impossible. You shall not use my fondest memories for your sport! How did you find out about him?"

Jean-Michel reached inside his shirt and pulled out Etienne's letters for her to read. "He referred to you as his little Pandora, but I knew it was you."

Darcy yanked the letters out of his hand and opened them. There before her eyes was the lovely penmanship of Father Etienne. When she read the words *my little Pandora,* she gulped back tears. She had no idea that he had given her that name, and it broke her heart to read it. She read and reread the letters describing her life, as Jean-Michel watched her. She shook her head and asked, "How can this be?"

She looked up into Jean-Michel's eyes and saw the evidence she needed. There was the same look. "How could I have not known?" she blurted out. "So much makes sense now! Your brother being educated in France, your love of books, and both of you insisting on bathing!"

"He was the one to convince you to bathe regularly, wasn't he?" said Jean-Michel.

She nodded her head. "That was so like him. He was on a personal mission to clean up Europe!"

Darcy couldn't take her eyes off Jean-Michel. She studied him as if she had never seen him before. There was little physical resemblance, but he had the same dignity and sense of humor.

"We don't look alike, do we?" he said.

"Not really. You are younger for one thing."

"Yes, he is eight years my senior."

"If only I had known from the start who you were. It all could have been different."

"Didn't the name Lupé give you a clue?"

"I never knew your brother's surname. To me, he was always Father Etienne."

This connection with home was the best news Darcy had received since her arrival in the Colonies. She hadn't realized how homesick she had been. She shook her head and said, "Looking at you, Jean-Michel is like having him alive again."

The smile dropped from his face. "What?"

Darcy did not move.

"What did you say?" said Jean-Michel, and he grabbed Darcy and shook her. "Tell me!"

Darcy's eyes grew wide with horror, and she swallowed hard saying, "You--you didn't know? Your brother slipped and fell on the cliffs of Kerry over a year ago. I thought you knew."

Jean-Michel blinked and then stood up abruptly, looking out over the river. Darcy was horrified. What had been a celebration a moment ago now turned to agony. They stood in silence for a long time. Darcy expected to see tears in Jean-Michel's eyes, but his face was hard and cold. He reached down for his pack and mumbled, "We must move on now."

They resumed their journey following the Kensington River northward. He walked in front of her in silence, inviting no conversation and asking no questions.

Mid-afternoon they stopped on the shore to rest. When Darcy reached out to touch him, he jerked away and barked, "Don't!"

Gone was the engaging companion from last night and left in his place was a cold shadow. Darcy wound her long, dark tresses back up into a knot and pinned them tightly. The intimacy had vanished between them.

As the day wore on, Darcy became angry. It all

seemed like a terrible twist of fate. She believed that Jean-Michel blamed her for the death. After all, if Father Etienne had not come to Ireland to help her people, he might still be alive.

By late afternoon, the warm sunshine gave way to dark thunderclouds, and rain. Drenched and tired, they followed the Kensington River northward until evening. When the rain continued, Jean-Michel chose a cave in which to spend the night. The cavern was high above the river, and it was difficult traversing the slippery rocks with their packs. When they reached the cave, Darcy felt short of breath, and her heart started to pound. The palms of her hands began to perspire, and a sense of panic washed over her. She bolted to the mouth of the cave to gasp for air. *I must not allow him to see that something is wrong. He does not need to be comforting me tonight.* She squared her shoulders and built a fire near the opening.

She walked over to the pile of firewood to gather some kindling, but when she straightened up, Jean-Michel was gone. Instead, two boys squatted near the fire. She rubbed her eyes and stared. *Who are these boys?* She walked around the fire to see their faces, and her mouth dropped open in horror. Sitting on the floor of the cave, warming themselves by the fire were Liam and Bran. They were no more than fourteen or fifteen years old. Their bodies were thin and emaciated, and they were bald. They were oblivious to Darcy, and when she opened her mouth to speak, she was mute. The boys were busy cracking shells with bony shaky hands putting slimy bits of seafood into their mouths. Darcy noticed green stains on their fingers and lips from the kelp. They were dirty, and their clothing hung on them like scarecrows. Overwhelmed by her memories and by her grief, she reached out to touch Liam. He crumbled instantly into a pile of rags. The bile rose in her throat, and she rushed to the mouth of the cave to retch. She stood up, pushed the hair from her face and looked back into the cave. Jean-Michel stood in the firelight looking at her. "You're ill?"

Darcy wiped her mouth and straightened her gown. Swallowing hard, she took a deep breath and reentered the cave. He offered her some food, but she refused.

Realizing that her dress was wet and filthy, she stepped to the back of the cave to change clothes. It was a difficult task pulling the sodden material over her head, and as she stood in her white shift gathering up her wet gown, she heard someone call her name. Thinking it was Jean-Michel, she looked out to the fire, but he was gone again. In his place was a little girl. The child walked over to the mouth of the cave and looked over the ledge expectantly as if someone had just called her name. When she turned around, Darcy recognized herself as a child.

She too was dressed in rags and what little hair she had was dirty and matted to the scalp. Her eyes seemed too large for her body, and her skin hung in loose folds over her small skeleton.

Darcy closed her eyes, trying to shut out the image. She thought that she had locked these memories away forever. Hot tears rolled down her face as she choked back sobs. Years of anguish surfaced, and she stood alone at the back of the cave drowning in despair.

Suddenly, she felt someone hug her and stroke her hair. Jean-Michel whispered, "I have been very selfish. I was so absorbed in my own pain that I didn't realize the agony you must be going through being in a cave again.

I'm very sorry. I'm very sorry."

The warmth of his embrace and the kind words calmed her fears. At long last she had been able to cry, and some of the horrors of the famine could now be left behind. Darcy stepped away from him, wiping her eyes. "How could I ask you for help, Jean-Michel? You had your own grief to bear."

He led her to the ledge, and the cool breeze following the storm helped revive her. "You have many ghosts haunting you," said Jean-Michel. "I see you drift off and go places I will never understand. Who visited you tonight?"

Darcy took a deep breath and rubbed her forehead. "I saw my brother and Bran during The Hunger, and I saw myself. It was nothing more than my foolish imagination."

Darcy took a deep breath and said. "Please forgive me for the death of your brother."

Jean-Michel frowned and he said, "What?"

"It's my fault that he is dead. If we hadn't been on the coast that foggy night, he would still be alive."

He put his hands up. "Wait a minute. Slow down. What are you talking about?"

"After telling the British of our smuggling ring, Bran needed to clear his conscience, so he went to your brother to confess his treachery. Realizing that we would all be killed if he didn't warn us, Father Etienne set out that night in the dense fog. He lost his footing and fell to his death off the cliffs of Kerry trying to save our lives."

Jean-Michel sighed. "There is nothing to forgive, Darcy. He died doing his life's work, and you are testimony that it did not go in vain."

She looked down and said, "Thank you." Then she

loosened the clasp of her necklace and placed the cross and charm into the palm of his hand.

"I want you to have this. The cross was given to me by my mother. It saw me safely through the famine. The charm of hope belonged to your brother, and it has seen me to you."

Jean-Michel searched Darcy's eyes. He knew with this gesture she admitted there was a bond between them. As his fingers closed around the necklace, he murmured, "You have forever changed the lives of the Lupé men, Darcy McBride."

* * *

The following morning they arrived at the abandoned settlement for the survey. It consisted of a trading post and the remains of five log cabins all in decay, most with roofs open to the sky. Nature was reclaiming the site, and every structure was covered with vines and moss.

Darcy thought the cabins looked lush and cool, and her romantic imagination had her speculating about what human dramas might have unfolded here. When she asked Jean-Michel about the settlement, he told her that he had been here as a boy. At that time, the settlement had shown promise, but two severe winters and an outbreak of smallpox had driven the residents back to Acadia. "The settlers were French. I was here with my father. He was trying to buy the trading post."

He shrugged and said with a sly smile, "I paid little attention. I was more interested in the little girl with the big, brown eyes. It was over there by that oak tree where I received my first kiss." He smirked and said, "She was completely taken with me."

"Arrogant," said Darcy, rolling her eyes.

She was pleased to see that Jean-Michel was in

better spirits today. She noticed that he was wearing her chain under his shirt.

"It may have been here that Etienne met Father Rale," he said. "He was a Jesuit missionary in these parts. Some thought him fanatical, but he guided Etienne to his calling."

Jean-Michel was lost in thought for a moment and then said, "Come. We must get started."

He opened his pack and pulled out all kinds of technical-looking equipment for the survey. Darcy picked up a small brass instrument and examined it. It appeared to be a circle within a circle, and she carefully turned it over in her hands.

"What's this?"

"A ring dial, it's a timepiece similar to a sundial but very accurate."

Next, he pulled out a mahogany box and opened it. Inside was another round brass object, with a glass face. Jean-Michel told Darcy it was a Vernier, also called a surveyor's compass. He showed her the tripod on which it rested, and after assembling a long pole, he handed it to her and said, "Here's a perch pole. Take that and those chains and follow me."

All day long he scribbled notes into a book about the land, the water, and the vegetation, bending down to inspect rocks and trees as if he were looking for treasure. Occasionally he would have Darcy take notes for him or hold the perch pole. Earlier in the day, Jean-Michel had set some snares for rabbits and when he needed her assistance no longer, she checked the traps. When she found them empty, she prepared another dried meat stew which by now was growing tedious.

Large white clouds sailed across the sky, and they were thankful the rain had passed. They sat on the grass and ate their meal outside one of the abandoned cabins.

Jean-Michel said, "Tell me about my brother. He left home many years ago, and I imagine his appearance had changed."

Darcy put down her plate of food and sat back. "Well, he had some gray hair, but not much. He usually wore a long black cassock, but he never looked severe."

"Was he well-liked in Kilkerry?"

"Aye, he was worshiped. Your brother answered a need in each of us. He instinctively knew what spoke to our souls."

"You knew him well, didn't you?"

"I believe I was closer to him than anyone in Kilkerry," Darcy said, sighing. "We would talk for hours sitting on the cliffs or in the ruins of the abbey."

"Just as we did several nights ago," said Jean-Michel.

"Oh no," said Darcy. "It was more than that. Your brother was the only person on Earth who ever really knew me."

Jean-Michel clenched his teeth and looked away. Darcy had shared the most intimate details of herself, he thought, the most private core of her being with his *own* brother. Etienne had won the prize, years before him. He was furious with jealousy. He stood up abruptly and threw his plate of food into the fire.

Darcy watched in shock as he walked up the hill to resume his work. She stood up to follow him. "Did I say something wrong?"

Jean-Michel met her with cold silence. Why should he offer her any explanations? All she ever offered him was a locked door. From now on he would meet her in kind.

Darcy waited for an answer and then picked up the perch pole. The remainder of the day they worked in strained silence. She could feel the fury emanating from him, and she knew that she should keep her distance. She went over their conversation, and all she could conclude was that Jean-Michel resented her for sharing Etienne's final moments on earth. That evening as the silence continued, Darcy considered approaching him, but noticing the dark rings under his eyes and menacing attitude, she reconsidered.

Jean-Michel went up river to bathe, in hopes that the water would cool his jealousy, but he returned still moody and sullen. He continued to brood throughout the evening, and when they finally laid out their bedrolls, he was so exhausted he fell into a deep sleep.

The sun woke them early, and Darcy hoped that she would be met with a better attitude, but when no eye contact was made over breakfast, she started to become frustrated. By afternoon the heat was oppressive. The air was thick, and Darcy's drenched gown clung heavily to her skin. She stood in the hot sun, holding chains and poles while Jean-Michel took measurements and made calculations.

Even though her hair was pinned up off her skin, the perspiration rolled down her neck and between her breasts, soaking her gown. Jean-Michel fared no better, and as the afternoon warmed, so did his temper. At last, the sun began to set, and he told Darcy that they would camp on the cliff top tonight to escape the heat and bugs.

She hated the thought of building a fire on such a hot night, but it was inevitable for cooking. As soon as supper was finished, she left the flames and the boiling temper of Jean-Michel to look at the stars. It was a relief to step into the cool darkness as she walked over to the edge of the cliff to look out over the river valley in the moonlight. The view took her breath away. Lighting the darkness were thousands of fireflies glowing and winking. They sailed across the night air magically animating the panorama. She heard Jean-Michel step up behind her.

"Why did you try to seduce my brother?" he said.

Darcy's jaw dropped, and she looked at him with horror in her eyes. She raised her hand and slapped him across the face with so much momentum, it knocked him back several steps. "How dare you make our friendship base!" she cried.

Before she could say anything else, he yanked her to his chest and jerked her chin up, "I know my brother too well. He took his vow of chastity seriously, and that was very convenient for you, wasn't it? He could satisfy your heart, but never take your body. Then along came Nathan Lawrence. He could win your body but never win your heart. Jean-Michel is here now. He will have both," and he kissed her.

All the jealousy and repressed desire he had been harboring bubbled to the surface, and he said hotly, "You had no right to share yourself with my brother. Understand this, Darcy McBride. You were mine then, and you are mine now."

Jean-Michel kissed her again, running his lips over her neck and her hair. "I love you. From the moment I saw you, something moved in me. No woman has ever clouded my judgment and stolen my peace of mind so completely."

He had taken Darcy's breath away. She felt the ache of desire pound within her, yet she said, pushing him away, "I don't want you in my life."

Jean-Michel stepped back panting, perspiration soaking his shirt. "What is it? I know you desire me. I can feel it." He pulled her back to him and said, "Tell me why!"

Before Darcy could stop, she said, "Because I have been afraid to admit it to you—to myself. I am in love with you."

Their eyes locked, and Jean-Michel swallowed hard. Then scooping her into his arms, he carried her down the path into the valley. He smothered her face and neck with kisses, running his lips down to where her gown met her breasts. He took her to a small lake bathed in moonlight and carried her fully clothed into the cool waters.

"I want to hear you say it," he demanded.

"I love you, Jean-Michel. You are the *only* one I have ever loved."

Chapter 28

Progress was slowed greatly on the survey because of the distracted lovers. Try as he might, Jean-Michel could not concentrate. Darcy would brush past him or look at him a certain way, and he was upon her, pressing his body next to her, drowning in her scent, exploding with desire.

Jean-Michel had known many women, but Darcy brought intensity to the act which he hadn't thought possible. He had guessed from the start, that the anger she bore from the years of repression made her blood boil, but he had no idea until now how deep her passion ran. He was beside himself with a hunger for her, and he knew that she felt the same way. She had denied his advances for so long that now he felt himself losing control, taking her repeatedly throughout the day. Yet above all, the single element which inflamed him the most was the fact that he was madly in love with her.

Never in his life had he felt a bond so great and a feeling so all-consuming. Jean-Michel found himself losing sight of his boundaries, and it was no longer clear to him where Darcy left off and where he began. She could be completely out of his sight, and he could still feel her inside of him.

Darcy was equally affected. For the first time in her life, she had someone to love--he did not own her, he did not feed his pride at her expense, and when he took her body, he touched her soul. The walls she had carefully erected, Jean-Michel eroded and Darcy felt her heart opening to him. She told him things that she had told no one and the more she unburdened herself, the more she loved him. At last, she had found one person she could call her own, and he could banish her loneliness forever.

Darcy would watch Jean-Michel and marvel at the soft glow in which he was bathed, and she knew that it had nothing to do with the light and everything to do with her feelings for him. Never had she made love so intensely, and she sought his attentions continually. Darcy was well aware of the power she had over Jean-Michel, and she actively seduced him away from his work and into her arms. She could at last put to rest her fears of being incapable of love.

In spite of being completely taken with Darcy, Jean-Michel was not happy. He worried continually for her safety because of the French and Abenaki practice of ransoming prisoners. If they found out that Darcy was Colonel Lawrence's mistress, they would immediately take her hostage, and Jean-Michel knew that his influence was limited in this regard. He did not share his anxiety with Darcy, feeling driven to finish the survey as soon as possible.

He decided to return by way of the coast, and even though it was a less direct route, it was safer. If their tracks had been discovered on the way up, there was a good chance there would be an ambush when they returned. He told Darcy he wanted to show her the coastline, and she did not question him further.

Darcy too was anxious on several counts. She could not forget that she had six years left of her indentured service and that tomorrow they would start their journey back to Fort Lawrence. One night as they lay side by side staring at the stars, she pulled herself up on one elbow and said, "Jean-Michel, I can bear it no longer. How can I ever return to Nathan Lawrence?"

"Don't you think that was my first thought? He

shall never have you again, Darcy. The moment we return to the fort, I shall purchase your service and set you free."

"And are you indeed free yourself, Jean-Michel?" she asked.

Jean-Michel knew exactly what Darcy meant. He would have to return to his home and tell Elizabeth that he loved another, and the thought of hurting her was grueling to him. "I must see Elizabeth one last time Darcy and break with her."

"You will be down there alone with her again? She will recapture your heart." Darcy said, sitting up. "I know that she is beautiful, and you have had ten years together. She is practically your wife."

Jean-Michel pulled Darcy back down into his arms and said, "You are the only one. How can you doubt that? In ten years, Elizabeth never moved me the way you did that first night when I saw you crossing the parade ground at the fort."

He kissed her, and Darcy felt the warmth of security wash back over her. The great losses she had experienced made it necessary for Jean-Michel to tell her over and over again that he would never leave her. He pointed up at the stars and said, "See up there, Darcy? That cluster of stars is Sagittarius, the great archer, and he is taking aim at Scorpio. He is successful in killing the demon, and so too shall I kill the demons that haunt you. If ever you are away from me, look up at those constellations and know that I am still your protector."

"How could I ever find them again?" she asked.

"That's not important," he said. "Just know that they are somewhere in the night sky just as I am somewhere loving you."

There was something in his tone which made her feel uneasy. Her intuition told her that he was apprehensive about something. She said nothing and put her head down on his chest.

They left the next day and followed the Kensington River east toward the coast. Per Jean-Michel's request, Darcy left her hair down. He loved watching the dark tresses dance in the wind as he walked behind her. By late afternoon, she began to smell the ocean, and she noticed the river drop below them as they followed the rocky riverbanks to the sea. Everything started to change. The winds picked up, and Darcy noticed that many of the trees looked gnarled, as if they could not grow upright in the incessant wind.

When they finally broke out of the woods onto the cliffs, the view took Darcy's breath away. She stared out at the ocean as the wind snapped her skirts. Turning to Jean-Michel, she shouted over the crashing of the waves, "This is it, Jean-Michel! This is the landscape of my home." She stood with her palms outstretched and drank in the energy and vitality of the sea once more.

* * *

They turned south and walked the coast until midday, and finding themselves at a point high above the crash of the surf, they sat down for something to eat. Jean-Michel could tell Darcy had mixed feelings about being here. "You are homesick, aren't you?"

She nodded, looking down at her hands in her lap. "Being here again has made me miss home and people that are long gone. I remember the night your brother received the letter from you about your mother's death. We walked all night along cliffs like these."

Darcy looked at Jean-Michel. "We never speak of your brother. We must do it sometime. He is the reason that we are together. If he hadn't helped me understand myself, I would be with Bran Moynahan right now and thoroughly miserable. I loved your brother as a friend--nothing more. Please believe me."

He looked out at the sea for a moment and then back at Darcy and said, "I'm trying to believe it, but when you speak of him your voice, your face, everything changes."

She slid over, put her lips near his own and whispered, "Perhaps it is the allure of the Lupé men."

Jean-Michel leaned in to kiss her and then stopped himself. He stood up abruptly pulling her to her feet. "There will be none of that now. You tempt me too much. We must move on, my little witch."

When they resumed their journey, he doubled their pace. This was the time of year the Abenaki saturated the area. By late afternoon large, black clouds began to form in the sky. The winds picked up, tossing the trees and churning the ocean. Jean-Michel stopped and looked up at the clouds. They were filled with electricity.

"Darcy, this does not look good. We must seek shelter right away."

Suddenly, there was a flash of blinding white light followed by a deafening bang. Jean-Michel pulled Darcy madly across the cliffs, searching for shelter. It was too dangerous to go under the trees, and on the cliffs they were targets for lightning, so he searched frantically for a cave.

The wind blew Darcy's hair in her face and tangled her gown around her legs. They heard trees cracking and uprooting and debris tumbling around them.

Just as the rain began, Jean-Michel found a spot along the edge of the cliff to lower himself to some caves. He climbed down the rock face with great care and then jumped into the cave. He leaned out ready to catch Darcy's hand to pull her inside too. She lowered herself down the rock face but froze when it was time to go into the cave.

The approach down the steep incline, the ledge over the ocean, even the size of the cave was identical to that of her previous home. The last cave had been large and over a river. This one was too similar to her famine sanctuary, and there was no question about it-- she would not enter it.

"Darcy, now!" shouted Jean-Michel.

She shook her head and tried to say something, but no words would come. The rain pelted her in the face and soaked her gown, making it heavy and cumbersome. The wind and thunder were deafening, and Jean-Michel knew that the rocks were becoming slippery.

"Come to me now!" he roared with his hand stretched out.

"I will not. They are all in there!"

Darcy tried to climb back up, but she lost her grip and started to fall. Jean-Michel lunged for her and caught her by one wrist and the bodice of her gown. She tumbled off the rock face, and as she fell the front of her gown ripped which left Jean-Michel holding onto only one slippery wrist as she dangled from the ledge. She dared not look down, but she knew that she would be smashed on the jagged rocks below if he were to lose hold of her.

Jean-Michel ground his teeth and dug his fingers into her slippery skin. Down below was the wild surf striking the sharp rocks.

Remembering his brother's death, Jean-Michel

gave one hearty pull and stepped back, putting Darcy on to the ledge of the cave. He grabbed her and rocked her back and forth whispering words in French and English.

Darcy murmured, "I'm sorry. I'm sorry. I thought if I came in here, they would all haunt me again."

Jean-Michel pushed her wet hair back and sighed. "They won't be back because I am here now.

* * *

Darcy and Jean-Michel followed the coast for days. Sometimes the vegetation was so thick they were driven inland, but always they were near the sea. It was heaven for Darcy to breathe the salt air and hear the surf pounding again. She was falling in love with this new land, and although she longed to return to Ireland, she believed that here with Jean-Michel is where she belonged.

One night by the fire, Darcy said, "I love my homeland, but I don't know if the British will ever leave Ireland."

"Maybe not, but someday we will drive the British from *this* land," Jean-Michel replied. "And the Nathan Lawrences will be banished forever."

"You speak treason so easily. I heard you at the dinner. You must be careful," Darcy said.

"I speak the truth."

"Maybe, but I remember the look on Nathan's face that night. He has not forgotten that comment."

"There are many who feel the way I do. The British will be gone in our lifetime, Darcy."

"I wish I could feel that optimistic about Ireland," she sighed, shaking her head.

"Here is where the Irish Catholics will find their freedom. They must call this home." Jean-Michel paused and then said, "Are you calling this home,

Darcy? Will I lose you someday to Ireland?"

Darcy could not answer easily. She did not leave Ireland of her own volition and to say goodbye to it forever was too painful. She looked down while Jean-Michel watched her anxiously.

"You are my home, Jean-Michel. Let there be no question about that, but to say that I am banished forever from Ireland is like cutting my heart out. I will never be at peace if I don't return one more time. I had told Adrianna before she left that one day I would stand on the abbey bluff, a free woman."

"And so you shall," he said taking her face in his hands. "You shall return to your home and together we shall stand on the cliffs of Kerry."

The route along the coast was more time-consuming, but Jean-Michel was grateful that he had chosen it. They traveled without incident.

They were a short distance inland when they stopped by a stream to replenish their water and rest for a while. The day was warm. Darcy dipped a cloth in the stream, and Jean-Michel watched her as she trickled water over her arms and neck.

The sun had given her skin a rosy glow, but her light complexion never acquired the deep tan of Jean-Michel. He loved the dramatic difference between her pale skin and dark hair. As he watched her stretch, a longing come over him to see her with child, and he called her over. She sat down beside him on the bank of the stream and hugged her knees, smiling at him. Jean-Michel looked into her green eyes and said, "I want to see you carry our child."

The smile dropped from Darcy's face, and she swallowed hard. "I believe that the famine came during the years when I should have been developing a suitable womb." Darcy bit her lip and said, "Because of this, one day you will leave me."

Whatever loss Jean-Michel felt, he did not share with Darcy. He did remember the day they had received word that Etienne had been ordained, and his mother had made him promise to carry on the family name. Pushing it from his thoughts, he stroked Darcy's cheek and said, "I found the one I love, and I ask for nothing more." He reached over and put his arm around her, easing her back onto the bank. He picked a blade of grass and ran it down her neck and across the tops of her breasts, and leaning down, kissed her gently.

After they had made love in the warm afternoon sun, Jean-Michel slept, and Darcy gathered up some clothes, heading upstream to find a suitable place to do laundry. She squatted down in the shade, soaking one of her gowns in the water, and just as she was about to put soap on it, she was yanked off her feet and grabbed tightly around her waist. Before she could scream, a hand was clapped over her mouth and a large Indian held a knife to her throat. Her heart was racing furiously, and she believed that before Jean-Michel ever awakened, she would be scalped mercilessly.

Darcy gasped for air, but the Indian was holding her so tightly that she could not breathe. Several more Abenaki stepped out from the bushes. One Indian started to search her pack. He was dressed in nothing more than a breechclout, and his head was completely shaved except for one tuft of hair tied with rawhide. He was pulling out clothes, cooking utensils and tools, and when he reached the bottom, he pulled out a rosary. He stood up and said something to the others, and they ran their fingers over the wooden beads.

The Indian, who had been holding a knife to

Darcy's throat, stepped away from her, held up the rosary and asked her something in French, but all she could do was look back helplessly. Suddenly, she heard Jean-Michel shout, "*Qu'y a-t-il!*" and the party whirled around as he approached with a rifle in hand. He was frowning and addressing the Indians in French. She could tell by his demeanor that he demanded her release immediately. A tense moment passed as the group sized him up.

Darcy had never seen Jean-Michel like this before. He showed absolutely no fear, acting offended that they had touched his woman. He looked challengingly from one to the other. Although he carried a rifle, she knew that it was his manner, not the firearm, which would win her release. Darcy felt the grip loosen around her waist, and she could now breathe.

The Indian, who had the knife to her neck, seemed to be the leader, and he spoke with Jean-Michel rapidly in French. Because of her limited abilities in the language, Darcy only caught a few words, but when Jean-Michel said the name *Lupé*, the Indians looked at each other. They motioned for him to lift his shirt. He obliged showing them a large jagged scar that ran down his ribs. They looked from the scar to his face, and like magic all hostility dissolved, and they let her go.

The leader returned Darcy's rosary, but Jean-Michel insisted that the Indian take it as a sign of friendship. The brave put the rosary around his neck, and as quickly as they had arrived, the Abenaki party was gone.

With wobbly legs, Darcy sank onto the grass as Jean-Michel scanned the woods for any further threat. There was so much that she did not know or understand about him. He had told her that the Abenaki admired his father's name, but the fear and respect she read on the faces today was for Jean-Michel.

Satisfied that there was no further threat, he held out his hand and pulled Darcy up, clamping his arm around her waist possessively. "Are you all right?" he asked. When she nodded, he let her go and said, "We must move quickly, Darcy. Anything can happen now."

After the encounter with the Abenaki, they moved at a feverish pace. Darcy had hoped to have another day alone with Jean-Michel before returning to Fort Lawrence, but he would not hear of it.

Gone was the passionate lover who could not keep his hands off her, and in his place was a man dragging her through the wilderness with the ferocity of an animal. Not wishing any more encounters with the Indians, they slept without a fire on a high bluff overlooking the ocean that night.

Jean-Michel told her that the fort was only a half day journey up the Windsor River and that they would sleep for only a few hours before setting off again.

When they stretched out on the bedrolls that night, she hugged his arm and asked, "That scar you showed them today. Why did they want to see it?"

"To prove my identity. I received that scar when I was a boy visiting my father's post. I was a bit scrappy in those days, and I got into an argument with one of the young Abenaki braves. As you can see, the outcome was not in my favor."

Shortly after that, Darcy dropped off to sleep. After a few hours, Jean-Michel was shaking her and telling her that it was time to go again. They set out at the same swift pace, and Darcy was exhausted. Judging from the dark circles under Jean-Michel's eyes, he too was weary, but what drained his energy was his anxiety about Darcy's safety. If the Abenaki knew she was Colonel Lawrence's mistress, a rosary would not buy her freedom. He could not rest until he reached the fort and bought her indentured service.

At last, Fort Lawrence came into view, and Darcy was surprised at how happy she was to see the timbered walls again. She desperately needed to rest, and she was worried about Jean-Michel. Ever since the encounter with the Abenaki he had lost his peace of mind, and his face looked drawn and tired.

Darcy had no doubts that Nathan would sell Jean-Michel her papers. It was apparent after their last meeting that he had washed his hands of her completely, and after Jean-Michel bought her freedom, they could be married.

They arrived at the fort mid-morning, and Shenanigan practically knocked Darcy over with affection. Jean-Michel went straight to his quarters to finish the results of his survey. He would be meeting with Lawrence most of the afternoon presenting his findings, so Darcy decided to rest and take a bath.

It did not feel right being back in Nathan's quarters, but she knew that she would be leaving before the night was over. She collected what few possessions she had and put them on the bed. With the exception of the gown on her back, she elected to return everything else to Nathan.

Darcy made several trips back and forth for bath water, and by the middle of the afternoon, she eased herself down into a deliciously soothing bath. She put her head back and let herself daydream about her new life with Jean-Michel when suddenly the door opened, and Nathan Lawrence walked into the room.

Darcy sat up, grabbed a towel and pulled it over

the top of the tub. The gesture was not lost on Lawrence, who entered the room, lighting a pipe. Darcy looked very inviting to him and finding her in this compromising position was very erotic. "I have been meeting most of the afternoon with Lupé going over his findings. As usual, his work is above reproach, and he said you were a very good assistant." He let out a puff of smoke while Darcy watched him apprehensively. "I trust you were chaste on your journey, my little colleen?"

Darcy hated it when Nathan called her that name. From his lips, it sounded condescending. She said nothing and tried to calm herself. This encounter was not what she had expected and neither was Nathan's behavior.

"I've sent my wife back to Boston. We had a nice visit, but I found myself preoccupied with thoughts of the private moments you and I have had."

Darcy swallowed hard, fearing what she was about to hear.

Nathan's eyes traveled down her neck and shoulders, and he stated, "I'm going to forgive you for the insults you had lavished upon me before you left, and I will attribute it to fears that I did not love you. At the time, I was angry and ready to sell your papers, but I have since reconsidered."

Darcy's heart began to pound furiously. *How could this be? Surely Jean-Michel would convince him otherwise. She could never return to this man's bed.*

Nathan saw the look of dread on Darcy's face and rankled. *So she had no desire to bed him again. What had gone on during the expedition? Well, no matter. She was back now.*

Nathan was looking forward to the evening. It

seemed to him as if Darcy had been gone for an eternity, and after seeing the heavy, sagging breasts of his wife, he longed to explore her youth again. He walked over and snapped the towel off the top of the tub.

"Don't you ever forget; you belong to me."

Nathan returned to his office where he and Jean-Michel worked into the evening. As the room began to darken, there was a knock at the door. Molly entered to light some candles. Nathan looked up and said, "Don't bother with that, Molly. We are just finishing up. Please set another place for dinner. Certainly you will dine with me this evening, Jean-Michel?"

Jean-Michel accepted his offer. Nathan held up one of his maps and looked at it carefully. Along the borders, Jean-Michel had sketched intricate pictures of the plants and flowers indigenous to the survey site, and Nathan said with admiration, "I see you are an artist as well, Lupé."

Jean-Michel shrugged and said simply, "It adds another dimension to the work, nothing more."

Before adjourning to dinner, Nathan unlocked a drawer and pulled out a leather bag. He tossed it on the desk and said, "You will find all of it in there, and an additional bonus as well. I will send the results of the survey to Governor Shirley immediately, and I believe he too will show you some form of gratitude."

Jean-Michel picked it up and followed Nathan into dinner. The dining room table was set for two, and Jean-Michel was relieved. He did not want Darcy to suffer the humiliation of being discussed as property when he made his proposal to Lawrence tonight.

Molly served them ham smothered in gravy and fresh vegetables, and it tasted delectable to Jean-

Michel. He had not consumed fresh food in weeks, and he ate heartily. As always, Nathan Lawrence was a good host and the wine flowed freely. Their dinner conversation was cordial, and Nathan shared odds and ends of news from Fort Lawrence with Jean-Michel. Jean-Michel listened politely and then said, "I think you should know, Colonel, that we encountered an Abenaki party near the mouth of the Windsor River."

Nathan nodded and wiped his mouth. "I believe that they are gathering for a large-scale assault."

After pouring Jean-Michel another glass of wine, Nathan sat back in his chair and folded his arms over his chest. "So will you return home now? It is rumored that you have a woman down on the Piscataqua."

"That is not what I would like to discuss right now," said Jean-Michel. "But there is a matter of business regarding Miss McBride."

Nathan stopped chewing and his eyes narrowed. "Whatever could that be?"

"I would like to purchase her papers," said Jean-Michel brusquely.

Nathan cleared his throat trying to curb the wrath that was building inside him. It was apparent now that they had done more than simply survey, and although it angered him it did not surprise him. He had acted impulsively sending Darcy away with this attractive man. He had taken her for granted, and now, after weeks of being celibate, Lawrence needed to be satisfied again. During her absence, he had found himself preoccupied with thoughts of her. He had been looking forward to tonight immensely, but this news stung him. "She is not for sale."

Jean-Michel frowned. Before the expedition Lawrence seemed to have lost interest in Darcy, and now this flat refusal shocked him. "Name your price, Lawrence. You know I can pay it."

"I repeat the woman's indentured service is not for sale."

Jean-Michel's nostrils flared as his breathing quickened. Struggling to maintain control, he clamped his jaw and looked out the window at the torches flickering on the parade ground. Turning back, he said, "Why? Why will you not part with her? She means nothing to you."

"On the contrary, I care deeply for her."

Jean-Michel slammed his hands on the table and said, "If you cared anything about her, you would set her free!"

"The woman has committed a crime," said Lawrence hotly. "You knowingly misused my property!"

"Your property!" Jean-Michel snapped. "Don't talk to me about property and law. You are a thousand miles from the drawing rooms of London now, Lawrence. You are in the wilderness of the New World, and it's time you had a taste of frontier law. We write our own destinies here, and no British dandy is going to tell me what I can or cannot do!"

Jean-Michel stormed out of Lawrence's quarters, slamming the door behind him. He walked briskly across the parade ground, looking for Darcy. He found her waiting for him in front of the officers' quarters. "Darcy, we leave the fort immediately."

Without asking for an explanation, she followed Jean-Michel to his room. Slinging his firearm and powder horn over his back, he grabbed her by the wrist and walked in long strides across the parade ground. He wore a dangerous look on his face, and when they approached the gate, the guard was so intimidated, he opened up immediately.

The black wilderness yawned before them, as they stepped out of the fort into the night. Darcy felt the thrill of freedom wash over her. For the first time in her life, she answered to no one. From here on she would be with a man from choice, not obligation.

Jean-Michel took her hand, and they started for the trees when someone shouted, "Stop in the name of the King!"

The gate of the fort opened, and a flood of soldiers was upon them. They were dragged back inside the fort, across the parade ground to headquarters where Nathan stood with his arms folded on his chest. He looked at Jean-Michel and said, "You dare defy me? You have been a party to helping a convict escape, Lupé, and that is a crime punishable by death. You shall be removed to Boston in the morning where you will stand trial. Take him to the stockade."

Darcy was stunned. She began to struggle. "Why are you doing this!" she screamed. The soldiers tightened their grip.

"You will see this is all for the best when you settle down," Nathan said calmly. Turning to the soldiers, he commanded, "Take her to her room and guard her door."

Moments later, they tossed Darcy into her room and slammed the door. She clutched her forehead. *Why had Nathan changed his mind?* She paced back and forth terrified for Jean-Michel. What could she do? How could she free him?

Gradually, the evening shadows grew long, and Darcy grew hopeless. She wished that the expedition had never happened. By loving her, Jean-Michel had inherited all her problems, and she may be the cause his death. She would be responsible for the demise of two Lupé men.

Prior to the survey, the arrangement with Nathan had been tolerable, but now, after experiencing love, she could never go back to the degradation with Nathan. She sat down and buried her face in her hands. At that moment, the door opened, and Nathan stepped into the room. She refused to look at him. Without saying a word, he took her hand and led her to the sitting room. He walked over to the cupboard and poured them each a glass of claret. Handing her a glass, he said, "My dear, that man is far too impetuous. He would only hurt you. Believe me, you were only a toy to make the long expedition more tolerable."

Darcy would hear none of it. Nathan rested his elbow on the mantel and rubbed his forehead as if he was weary, "I didn't want to tell you this, but I know that you are ignorant of this fact. Lupé is engaged to be married to a woman by the name of Elizabeth Campbell of the Piscataqua Valley. I hear she is a woman of breeding and beauty, suitable for a man of wealth and social standing."

Darcy looked up at Nathan, her eyes wide and said, "I know of this Elizabeth Campbell, but Jean-Michel never told me he had money."

"Oh yes, my little colleen," said Nathan nodding his head. "He is one of the richest men in northern Massachusetts, and I imagine he will buy his way out of this altercation with me. My point is that a man of his station will never marry an Irish convict."

Darcy shook her head slowly, not wanting to believe it. "No, that's not true."

"My darling Darcy, this infatuation of yours has clouded your judgment. You and I both know that you can bear him no children, and he is obliged to carry on the family name." Nathan walked over and stroked her hair. "My darling, at best you would be his mistress."

As if someone had punched her in the stomach, Darcy felt breathless and weak. "But he loves me," she murmured.

Nathan looked at her with pity in his eyes. Darcy became confused and began to doubt Jean-Michel. In the heat of passion maybe he told her what she wanted to hear, to gain a liaison. Perhaps for two weeks she had been immersed in a dream. She had forgotten who she was. In a mad rush, it came back to her; she was nothing more than an Irish peasant who had learned to read, and he was an aristocrat from the Massachusetts Colony.

Nathan took her by the hands, drawing her up into his arms. He brushed his lips across her neck and said, "Oh, how I've missed you. You've always belonged with me, Darcy. You know that." He sat down on the chair and pulled her onto his lap. As he slid his lips over her skin, Darcy swallowed hard. Everything was happening so fast, and she was feeling so confused. *No, she could not endure this again.* As Nathan dictated what happened to her body, Darcy's spirit stood up and walked to the door. With great relief she realized that she felt nothing as Nathan took her--there was no fear, no hurt, and no pain. Darcy's spirit passed out the door to walk on the cliffs of Kerry.

.

Chapter 29

Jean-Michel sat on the floor of the stockade with his head in his hands trying to think. He had promised Darcy that he would never leave her, but his hot temper had clouded his judgment. He had delivered her right back into bondage.

He had never suspected that life would reveal to him such boundless love, yet they had been together for such a short time, and it had all been too good to be true. If Nathan Lawrence had his way, Jean-Michel would be wiped from the face of the earth, but that was not going to happen. He would think of a way out of this but try as he might, there were too many obstacles. When he became frustrated, he remembered what Etienne had told him years ago that God always reveals the way, simply wait for it to unfold.

The door of the stockade opened suddenly, and Jean-Michel was pulled roughly to his feet by two of the regulars. They bound his hands in front of him with a leather thong and took him across the parade ground. Jean-Michel was stunned. Daylight had come, and he still had no plan to free himself and Darcy. He looked frantically for her among the faces gaping at him, but she was nowhere to be found.

The door of Lawrence's office opened, and Jean-Michel was pushed roughly inside. Nathan looked up from his chair, leaned back and said, "I think it's a pity that I must deliver you to Governor Shirley under these circumstances, but it is out of my hands, Lupé. You broke the King's law."

Jean-Michel said nothing, only stared straight ahead. He was not going to be goaded into another confrontation.

Nathan handed Jean-Michel's notes and maps to one of the escorts and said, "Sergeant Adams, I want you to deliver him to the authorities as soon as you arrive in Boston and take his work to the Governor immediately thereafter. I know he anxiously awaits the results of the survey."

Lawrence turned back to Jean-Michel and said, "I asked Miss McBride if she cared to see you one final time, and she expressed no interest. I believe I have enlightened her as to your motives, Lupé."

Jean-Michel remained expressionless. The guards marched him toward the gate. He could tolerate Sergeant Adams, but he despised the two regulars who accompanied him. They were filthy, toothless fools with brutish attitudes. He knew that they would take this opportunity to bolster their manhood and mistreat him.

Jean-Michel continued to search the faces of the fort, looking for Darcy. His heart began to race and his palms sweat. What if he were to hang and never see her again? He must look into her eyes one last time. He stopped abruptly and looked back at Lawrence's quarters. One of the guards, a big soldier with curly black hair and a low forehead named Ives, gave Jean-Michel a swift kick, growling, "Get going, you high and mighty bastard."

The four passed through the gate and approached the trail which led to the lower Massachusetts Colony. Ives and Scroggins elbowed and kicked him as they walked through the clearing, but he continued to strain to get one last look at Darcy.

Sergeant Adams ignored the behavior of the two regulars as walked ahead of the group, his eyes straight ahead. He resented having to deliver this prisoner and these maps so many miles to the south. He preferred to pass away the hours at the fort doing nothing. They had all grown complacent during the summer months. There had been no sign of the French or the Abenaki, and they believed that they had thoroughly intimidated them in the siege the year before.

The party was just about to enter the woods when Jean-Michel decided to turn back one last time to look for Darcy, but Scroggins hit him with the butt end of his musket doubling him over in pain. They dragged Jean-Michel roughly into the woods, hurling insults at him and spitting on him. Sergeant Adams remained unconcerned.

Jean-Michel was exhausted, the rapidity with which he had delivered Darcy to the fort, the sleepless night in the stockade and the abuses he was enduring took its toll on him. At midday, the party stopped in a small clearing to rest and eat. Jean-Michel sat wearily leaning against a tree, rubbing his wrists where the leather thong was cutting into his skin. He saw Ives and Scroggins passing a bottle back and forth while Sergeant Adams was tearing sullenly at his jerky.

After relieving themselves, the two sat down in front of Jean-Michel and nudged one another. Scroggins, an overweight, greasy soldier with bad breath, leaned toward Jean-Michel and said thickly, "You remember me? I was the one who caught you trying to give it to Lawrence's whore the night of the dance. I watched the two of you for a long time before I said anything."

He stuffed some hardtack into his mouth and said, spewing crumbs all over, "I can't blame you. I'm going to set a charge of gunpowder off inside her myself."

The two threw their heads back and roared. Ives

wiped his nose with his sleeve and said, "Say, I got an idea. We could follow her some afternoon when she goes down to see that crazy old man and give it to her good. Lawrence won't believe her if she told; he don't trust her anyhow."

Jean-Michel knew Scroggins was right. Lawrence would no longer believe anything Darcy told him. He also knew the lascivious nature of these men, and rape was the sort of sport which amused them.

"It's time!" they heard Adams bark, and they rose and resumed their journey.

By late afternoon, the drinking had sapped the energy of the two reprobates, and finally, they left Jean-Michel alone. The heat and the flies were becoming insufferable, and he could hear Scroggins behind him swearing continuously. Adams and Ives were ahead of Jean-Michel as they entered a dense thicket where the trail narrowed. When they rounded a curve, the two were momentarily out of Jean-Michel's sight.

Suddenly, he heard one of the men in the front scream, and Ives burst around the corner slamming abruptly into him. He had terror in his eyes, and before Jean-Michel could step back, someone snapped the guard's head back, slitting his throat. Jean-Michel was spattered with blood. It was an Abenaki who killed Ives, and he tossed the body to the ground. Jean-Michel saw Darcy's rosary around the Indian's neck.

Seizing the moment, Jean-Michel turned around and kicked Scoggins in the groin. When the man doubled over he drove his knee up into his face. Within seconds, another Abenaki warrior was upon the regular, slitting his throat too.

Panting, Jean-Michel faced the brave wearing Darcy's rosary. The Indian took three large strides up to him and cut the leather thong which bound his hands, and then he tossed Sergeant Adam's musket and shot pouch to him.

Searching for some token of gratitude Jean-Michel reached for his most precious possession; the cross and charm from Darcy. He pulled it over his head and held it out to the brave. The Indian looked at the gift and then looked into the eyes of Jean-Michel. He turned away and began searching the dead bodies instead.

Jean-Michel put the chain back around his neck. The Indians were beginning to scalp and he preferred not to watch. Turning to the south, Jean-Michel set off toward his home on the Piscataqua. There he would regain his strength and devise a plan to bring Darcy back to him forever. Etienne was right. God was indeed revealing the way.

* * *

The warm weeks of summer dragged on for Darcy at the fort. She attempted to return to her former life, but the memories were too vivid and the pain was too great to forget. It had all been an illusion, she could see that now. She had fallen in love with a man that did not exist. Darcy had seen in Jean-Michel exactly what she had wanted to see. She hated herself and her poor judgment, yet continually his words haunted her, "Trust me, you are home now, Darcy."

His voice came to her without warning at any time of the day, during any activity, but mostly at night. It would wake her up, and her eyes would fill with tears. Nathan sensed this preoccupation with Jean-Michel, and he lavished affection on her more than ever. He took her to his bed often, in hopes of capturing her attention once more, but she always seemed aloof and disconnected.

Darcy resumed her afternoon visits to Moses Tinker, and he welcomed her back with enthusiasm. Shenanigan would race joyfully by her side as she made her way to his cabin. Although it was dangerous, Darcy felt safer outside the fort. She would walk the trails and daydream of returning to Ireland, or sit for hours listening to him tell of adventures from his past.

Moses knew that there was something wrong with her, but he never said a word. He had lost the love of his life too, and he found that the pain and loneliness never lessened. That was something he would never share with Darcy. He made small talk instead. "Have you met the new family farming the McDermott homestead?"

"Yes, the Wyndom family, and they have four children. They aren't as friendly as the McDermott's though. They are very religious people, and I believe they think I'm a harlot. I shall try to befriend them one last time, but if they snub me again, I won't return."

"Why do you go back?"

"Oh, I don't know, Moses. I guess that I get lonely for the company of a woman.

The next day Darcy worked at the fort for hours, scraping a deer hide. Her arms grew tired trying to remove the bits of fat from the skin. It was tedious work, and she had to be careful not to slice through to the hide, rendering it useless or at the very least, unattractive.

After completing several other chores, she put some corn pudding into a crock and set off for Moses' cabin. Darcy whistled for Shenanigan, and they started down the trail.

The woods seemed unusually quiet this evening, and when Darcy looked up in the trees, the birds were not chattering and hopping about. Shenanigan ran off ahead of her, but when she caught up to him, he was standing still and sniffing the air. Darcy's hands began to perspire. Her musket ready, she walked down the trail and through the crops Moses had planted, scanning for danger.

"Darcy, quickly!" barked Moses, when he caught sight of her from the cabin door.

When she stepped inside, Darcy saw a girl of about sixteen years sitting by the hearth holding a child. The little girl was covered with black soot, and she stared at Darcy while she sucked her thumb.

"Who are these children, Moses?"

"They are two of the Wyndom girls. A war party raided their cabin today and killed their father. They don't know what happened to their mother and two brothers."

Darcy looked over at the two petrified youngsters on the bed and then back at Moses.

"How is it they are here?"

"A few minutes ago Faith here came here with the little one under her arm. Seems she was out picking berries, and when she went back to the house, she found her father's body and her sister hiding in the beehive oven."

Darcy looked at the little girl. That would explain the ashes and soot covering her skin and clothing. "But no mother or brothers to be found?"

"That's right."

Faith Wyndom stood up and cried, "They may be at the fort! I've got to know. Please take me up there."

Darcy shook her head. "Oh no, it's too dangerous. I can't take you up there. They could be overrunning the fort right now. You're better off with Moses. He'll take you into the hills to a cave where you will be safe."

The girl had a wild look in her eyes. She grabbed Darcy's gown and screamed, "Please, I've got to find them!"

Darcy looked over at Moses helplessly. All he could do was shake his head and say, "Gawd Almighty."

They knew that it was unlikely Faith would find her mother and siblings at the fort. The French and the Abenaki frequently took prisoners and assimilated them into the tribe or sold them as servants in Quebec.

Understanding though how frantic the girl must feel, Darcy sighed and said, "All right. I'll take you up with me, but not the child." Looking at Moses, she asked, "Are you leaving right away?"

He nodded. Faith dashed to her sister and wrapped her arms around her. "When this is over, I will come and get you. Pray hard, little Catherine, and we will be safe."

Darcy looked at Moses. Something told her it would be a long time before she would see him again, and she asked, "Will you take Shenanigan? I don't have a good feeling--" She caught herself, not wanting to alarm the girls. "I love you, Moses Tinker," Darcy said.

"Damnation! Don't talk like that. I'll see you again soon. Now go!"

Darcy grabbed Faith's wrist and said, "You must run faster than you have ever run before."

The girl nodded, and after peeking out the door, they bolted into the clearing. Never letting go of Faith's wrist, Darcy dragged her down the trail at top speed to the fort. The guard on sentry duty was surprised to see Darcy return so quickly, and he swung the door open immediately.

"Where is Colonel Lawrence?" she asked.

"In the commissary," he replied.

"Have any settlers come through in the past hour?"

"No, ma'am."

Faith looked at Darcy, tears filling her eyes, "Maybe they are hiding in the woods. They could still come to the fort."

Darcy took her to the women's quarters knowing that they would watch over her. Wasting no time, she headed to the commissary to find Nathan.

He was going over the books with the clerk. When she walked in, he looked up and said impatiently, "What is it, Darcy?"

"I must see you alone."

He handed the books to Stuart and walked over to the door and said, "This better be important."

"There has been a raid on the Wyndom homestead. They have killed the father and taken the mother and two children as prisoners. Two of the girls escaped to Moses' homestead."

Lawrence nodded his head as if he had anticipated this. "So the French have finally arrived with their savages. I must be frank, Darcy. There is about to be another siege, and I am not confident of the outcome. I asked for reinforcements, but they were not convinced that a large-scale assault would occur, so if we fall, do what you have to do to save yourself and meet me at Fort Pepperell. I shall regroup there and take the fort back at a later date."

"How can you say such a thing? We have repelled them before. How can you have so little faith in your own garrison, Nathan?"

"I am only being realistic, Darcy. I fear that their numbers will be too large. They want this river badly. It is a strategic point near Quebec, and I believe they know of our plans to build yet another fort on the

Kensington River. They will try to expel us from this area now before we become too strong."

Darcy stared at Nathan and was speechless. He had very dispassionately informed her that there was a good chance she and others were about to die.

She returned to the women's quarters and found Faith staring straight ahead into the fire. Her brown hair hung in tangles around her face, and her dark eyes looked vacant. Darcy squatted down in front of the girl's chair. "Faith, there may be an attack here at the fort any time now. Do what you have to do to stay alive. It is the only way."

Slowly Faith turned and looked at her, a dazed look in her eyes.

"She is so young," thought Darcy. "She is too young to be all alone."

Darcy remembered that they were people of strong faith, and she reached up to the mantel for the Bible. She handed the book to the girl and said quietly, "Remember your name."

"We'll take good care of her. Don't fret," assured Mrs. Stafford, the nurse who had taken care of Jean-Michel during the last siege.

Darcy returned to Nathan's quarters and went straight to the cupboard, pouring herself a glass of rum. She was determined that she would not go sleepless tonight. Her nerves were raw, and she sat down, feeling the spirits warm her.

It reminded her of the first night she had met Father Etienne. They had shared brandy in front of the peat fire on that wild windy night so long ago. Little did she know how their lives would intertwine and how his younger brother, living an ocean away, would fill her heart.

After another drink, Darcy's limbs began to feel heavy, and she rose and went to Nathan's bedroom. Before the expedition with Jean-Michel, Nathan would call Darcy to his room when he wanted her company, and she would return to her own quarters to sleep, but now he insisted that she share his bed the entire night.

His bedroom was much more luxurious than Darcy's quarters. He had a large bed lined with crisp white sheets and topped with a multicolored quilt made by one of the officer's wives. In one corner was a cupboard holding liquor and his private library and next to his bed was an oak commode fitted with shiny brass hardware.

Wearing only her shift, Darcy slid under the covers. She loved the soft feeling of Nathan's feather mattress, and feeling very tired, she drifted off. She was only vaguely aware of Nathan's presence when he joined her several hours later. He had been making preparations to defend the fort well into the night, and even though there was still work to be done, he knew that he needed sleep to keep his head clear.

He slid under the duvet next to Darcy, but before he could pull her close, his hand dropped, and he fell asleep. A few hours later, there was a loud bang and light flooded across the bed.

Someone, standing in the doorway, shouted, "Colonel Lawrence, wake up! They are coming over the walls!"

Nathan jumped out of bed, pulling on his breeches and boots. Still buttoning his shirt, he bolted from the room leaving Darcy alone and stunned.

She threw the covers back and pulled her gown over her head. The last thing she did before leaving the room was to belt her skirts up so she could be ready to run. She rushed through the dark sitting room and out the front door. What she saw paralyzed her. The commissary and the barracks were ablaze, casting a hellish light on the carnage which unfolded before her eyes. Everywhere soldiers and civilians were running and shouting. Some lay before her bleeding; others were already dead. Shots were being fired, as well as cannons. Screams of agony filled her ears. Men in buckskin and blue uniforms poured over the walls in a steady stream along with hordes of Abenaki Indians, dashing madly across the parade ground.

Suddenly, Darcy saw men pointing at her. She heard someone shout something in French. She had made a fatal mistake; she had lingered too long in Nathan's doorway, and they had guessed her identity. Bolting across the parade ground, Darcy searched frantically for a hiding place. She was knocked off her feet by two men struggling but was up again in a heartbeat, running for her life.

Then it came to her. As foolhardy as it might seem, she would hide in the powder magazine. The flames were alarmingly close, and the whole fort could blow at any time, but no one would be foolish enough to pursue her there. She ran inside and hid behind several barrels of black powder. Straining her ears she heard no one follow her. She reached for the cross around her neck, but it was gone. Remembering that Jean-Michel had it, she closed her eyes and swallowed hard. She realized that if she were to die now, no one would grieve for her.

Darcy darted to the door of the magazine to watch for her moment to escape. She scanned the parade ground. In the firelight, not far from the powder magazine, she saw a large man dressed in buckskin struggling with a young girl. Grabbing her shoulders, he bent her over the top of a barrel. Darcy realized, with a jolt, it was Faith Wyndom.

As the Frenchman began to pull up her skirts and unbutton his pants, Darcy felt a surge of rage. This creature would not steal Faith's peace of mind the way hers had been stolen. Darcy bolted out of the powder magazine back into the mayhem. Searching frantically for a weapon, she dodged soldiers fighting, jumped over corpses and flaming debris. At last, she saw an ax standing by the wood pile, and she picked it up bolting back toward Faith and her attacker.

Darcy stopped abruptly in back of the man. She swung the ax over her shoulder, and with all her might drove the weapon deep into his back. The man straightened up and roared. He staggered, reaching in vain for the ax deep in his back and crumbled to his knees.

Instantly, Darcy grabbed Faith's wrist, and without a backward glance, raced across the parade ground. She heard someone shout, "That's her!" and dropping the girl's wrist, she screamed, "It's me they want, run!"

Darcy fled up the ramp to the top of the fort wall, and pulling her skirts up as high as they would go, she swung herself over the sharp timbers of the fortification. The roughly hewn wood tore at her skin and ripped her dress, as she slid down the timbers. She landed heavily on the unyielding earth below. Every ounce of air knocked from her lungs. She was stunned. After a few moments, Darcy gathered herself and struggled to her feet.

Suddenly, an Abenaki warrior dashed toward her. She started to run, but he was too fast. He caught her, threw her down and lashed a rawhide thong around her wrists tightly. Terrified and exhausted, Darcy knew that she was too late. She was now a captive to be ransomed as Colonel Lawrence's mistress.

Chapter 30

Jean-Michel woke up in a cold sweat. Something was horribly wrong. But as he cleared away the cobwebs of sleep, nothing revealed itself to him. He had returned to his home on the Piscataqua River safely, and his injuries had healed well, but for days now he had a nagging feeling that Darcy was in trouble.

He sat up and touched the cross from her as it rested on his bare chest. It had stayed safely next to his heart since the day she had given it to him, but he wondered if she may be in need of it now. Impatiently, he threw the covers off and walked to the window.

Jean-Michel was bathed in bright moonlight, as he looked outside. Ever since he had arrived home, Lawrence's words haunted him. "I believe I have enlightened her as to your motives, Lupé.

It was indeed common knowledge that he and Elizabeth had an understanding, but he must get to Darcy somehow and reassure her that he had broken his engagement. He could feel in his heart that she had lost faith in him and that her fire for him did not burn as brightly.

Jean-Michel's hair was loose, and it lay in tangles around his face and shoulders. He ran his hands through it impatiently as he paced the floor of his bedroom. He was growing frantic without her. How he wished that she were by his side to calm his fears and rest her beautiful green eyes on him.

He looked around his bedroom at the curtained, four-poster bed, the mahogany writing desk, and the lush draperies. He knew she would feel out of place here just as he did. At first, it would be amusing to pamper and bathe her in luxury, but he knew Darcy too well. Soon she would grow bored and need to strike out, throwing herself into an adventure.

He longed to steal her from Lawrence and take her deep into the interior forever--just the two of them wandering under the stars away from laws and wars and ruthless governments. Etienne had seen something wonderful in that woman long before he even knew she existed, and he came to believe that his older brother had sent Darcy to him as a farewell gift.

Before she arrived, Jean-Michel had given up all hope of finding someone to love. Women of dignity and education didn't venture onto the frontier. Then, like a miracle, there she was standing next to him, shooting a musket on the wall of the fort with that fiery blend of frontier independence and patrician gentility. He could wait no longer. He had to get back to her, and he must leave immediately.

Suddenly he remembered Elizabeth. He had been home for days recuperating and attending to business, and never once made an effort to call on her. Of all of the reasons to return home, the most pressing and the most painful was breaking his ties with her. Before he could return to Darcy and give himself heart and soul, he must complete this final errand.

It took another day for Jean-Michel to put his affairs in order, and he worked at a feverish pace meeting with his tenants and caretakers, answering questions and attending to details. It seemed like an eternity before he could begin the journey back to Fort Lawrence.

Upkeep of the sprawling timber frame home was not the only responsibility which prevented Jean-Michel from leaving immediately. The vast landholdings of the family needed constant attention. From the very beginning, these affairs dominated a huge amount of his time, and he accepted surveys not for the money but as an excuse to escape the tedious nature of business and venture into the vast wilderness which he loved.

The home had been built by his parents many years ago when the sawmill had opened. It was a large multi-gabled structure which loomed over the Piscataqua River. The dark lap siding had been exposed to the harsh northern elements for years now, but with Jean-Michel's meticulous care, it had survived. Several chimneys reached up from the steep roof, and they warmed the many rooms of the home, but the element which revealed the vast wealth of the Lupé family was the large number of windows gracing every gable. Light flooded every room and illuminated the richly decorated interior. Jean-Michel's mother had insisted that the furnishings be of the finest quality but never ostentatious.

Even with all this luxury, Jean-Michel did not feel at home. He was happiest when he roamed the vast interior and slept atop a cliff under the stars. Deep in the heart of Etienne had been that same wanderlust, and when he coupled it with his great love for God, the Jesuits became his true calling.

This wanderlust had been passed down to them by their father who could never be bounded by four walls. It had caused great pain to Jean-Michel's mother, and this was one of the reasons Jean-Michel would never marry Elizabeth Campbell. She would be just like his mother, living her life all alone in an empty house.

He finally sent a note requesting permission to call on Elizabeth one warm summer evening, and when he rode up to her home, he saw her standing by the door waiting for him. Jean-Michel was sincerely happy to see Elizabeth, and he dismounted, kissing her gently on the lips. She was indeed lovely, he thought. She was tall with a slim body curving gently under the rich blue taffeta dress, smelling of sweet lavender. Her straight blonde hair was pulled up behind her head, and her blue eyes gazed at him serenely. What Jean-Michel had always found the most attractive about Elizabeth was her full sensuous mouth. He used to love to kiss her lips, but this time, they seemed cold and lifeless.

Over dinner, he was preoccupied with thoughts of Darcy. He found himself comparing the two women. The more he indulged in this pastime, the more restless he became. Sitting at the dining room table with Elizabeth, he felt like a fraud, yet he could not seem to find the right time to tell her the truth. He knew Elizabeth was willing to do anything for him. She would never dream of contradicting his wishes, but Jean-Michel wanted a woman with her own mind and her own soul.

Elizabeth took a sip of wine and asked, "Why did you take so long before coming to see me, Jean-Michel? In the past, you always rushed into my arms the minute you returned home."

He knew he should tell her of his love for Darcy, but he choked on the words. So he steered the conversation to lighter subjects.

After supper, they walked arm in arm along the river as twilight fell. For nine years they had walked here in the evening together.

Jean-Michel had always found it peaceful and relaxing, but tonight he was anxious. When he looked down at Elizabeth, she would smile back serenely, every hair in place.

He could never imagine her racing through the woods with a child on her back or dancing lustily in the torchlight. True, she was capable of bearing him many healthy children, but she was too fragile and vulnerable to live life by his side. She had never left this valley, never tasted life and never suffered a day in her life.

Suddenly, she put her arms up around his neck, pressing against him. "Why haven't you kissed me yet, Jean-Michel? You are acting very mysterious this evening." She kissed him, and Jean-Michel pushed her away gently saying, "I cannot."

"Why? What's wrong with you this evening?" she asked. "There should be no secrets between us. We have been lovers for years.

Shaking his head, Jean-Michel sighed and said, "That is precisely the problem. We have never been lovers--rather I have not loved--," and he broke off.

Elizabeth stood motionless waiting for him to finish. A light breeze off the river blew her hair gently. She bit her lip a moment and then said, "I am no fool, Jean-Michel. I know you have never loved me."

"Oh, Elizabeth," he said, at last, taking her hands, "dear, devoted Elizabeth. I would probably be better off with you, but I love another, and if she still lives, I must spend my life with her."

Her eyes filled with tears, and she said, "I thought," and she stifled a sob, "I thought we had an understanding, Jean-Michel?"

"I can honor it no longer. I am truly sorry, Elizabeth."

He walked slowly up toward the house and mounted his horse. He looked back at her as she stood by the river. Jean-Michel knew that Elizabeth would always be waiting for him, and he knew in his heart that he would never return.

*   *   *

Jean-Michel was scheduled to depart for Fort Lawrence the following morning, and as he was cleaning his musket on the front steps, he noticed a rider approaching. It was John Bartholomew, his caretaker.

"Good day, John! Come to see me off?" he called.

John did not smile as he rode up, and before his horse had stopped completely, he dismounted and ran up to Jean-Michel.

"Fort Lawrence has fallen!" he said, panting. "You cannot go up north, Jean-Michel. The French and Abenaki are everywhere."

Jean-Michel felt sick. "How many dead? What do you know?

"I know very little. Colonel Lawrence and some of the others are at Fort Pepperell."

"Is there a woman with Lawrence?" asked Jean-Michel anxiously.

"No, why?'

Without answering, Jean-Michel jumped onto his horse and tore down the road headed for Fort Pepperell. He sped along the path, splashing along the muddy riverbank, and when he arrived at the fort several officers greeting him.

"Where's Colonel Lawrence?" he asked, as one of the regulars took his horse.

"He's in there, in a meeting with his officers, but I wouldn't--"

Jean-Michel swept past them and threw the door open with a bang. Nathan Lawrence was sitting at a desk, examining some maps with his officers, and in three large strides, Jean-Michel was upon him, grabbing him by the lapels and lifting him out of his chair.

"Where is she?"

Lawrence stared at him with his mouth open, stunned. Instantly, the officers jumped on Jean-Michel, tearing him away from the Colonel and restraining him. Lawrence barked, "What in God's name is this man doing here? He's under arrest!"

"My escorts met up with some friends," sneered Jean-Michel. "Now tell me where she is!"

Nathan studied Jean-Michel for a moment and said to his men, "Let him go."

The soldiers dropped his arms and stepped back.

"I want to be done with you once and for all, Lupé," growled Lawrence. "The woman's gone. She's been ransomed by the French. They wish an exorbitant price; one which I shall not pay. If you can pay it, she's yours. She's far too much trouble."

"Was she harmed?"

"I wouldn't think so. Not if they were planning on selling her back to me."

Jean-Michel said, "I need to speak with you in private, Lawrence.

Nathan's eyes narrowed, he thought a moment, and then he gestured for his men to leave.

Jean-Michel came right to the point, "I must ask a favor of you."

Nathan looked surprised and then laughed disdainfully. "You are hardly in a position to be asking anything of me, Lupé."

"I will pay the French their ransom, and I will pay you for her indentured service. After that, I shall give Darcy her freedom, but I wish to do this in your name only. I do not want Miss McBride to know that I ransomed her. She must not feel that she owes me anything. I want her to come to me of her own free will."

Nathan stared in disbelief at Jean-Michel and then said, "My god, man! You're really in love with her," and he threw his head back starting to laugh. Lawrence had always assumed that Jean-Michel's motives were similar to his own. He had no idea it went beyond lust.

He shook his head and said good-naturedly, "I can't say that I blame you, Lupé. She is a fascinating woman."

He sat down at his desk and nodded. "You may use my name, but it may be too late. I have already sent my refusal. She could be anywhere now." He scrawled a few words on a note, signed his name and handed it to Jean-Michel, "That says you are representing my interests. I wish you luck. You will need it."

Jean-Michel returned home immediately. All his money was tied up in banks in Boston and London, and frantically he tried to think of a way that he could obtain money for Darcy's ransom without wasting precious time on a trip to the south. If he did go to Boston, Darcy might slip through his hands forever.

He returned home and walked immediately to the cupboard, pouring himself a stiff drink. The news of Darcy's capture had unnerved him, and it now was clear why he had been uneasy. He stared out the window, knowing that it was likely he might never see her again. They could take her anywhere, from Quebec to the deep interior, and she could be swallowed up in the wilderness forever.

Nevertheless, he must find her even if he had to search for the rest of his life. Suddenly it occurred to Jean-Michel how he could buy Darcy's release and never have to travel to Boston.

He dashed up the stairs two at a time and bolted

into his mother's room. Opening her delicate writing desk, he began running his hands over the smooth, highly polished wood, looking for a catch. He stopped, pushed a small lever, and a door previously invisible opened in the back of the desk. He pulled out a drawer, and there lying in a velvet-lined box, was an exquisite emerald necklace which had belonged to his mother. After her death, he had taken her jewels to Boston, but he had overlooked this piece, and now his mistake had served him well.

He thanked his mother with a silent prayer, as he slipped the necklace into a drawstring bag. He placed it around his neck and under his linen shirt. Strapping on his pack and grabbing his rifle, Jean-Michel left the house and headed toward Fort Lawrence in search of Darcy, determined to return home with her before the summer was over.

He traveled swiftly, stopping to sleep only a few hours at a time. He had not a moment to lose, and his heart pounded in anticipation and fear. As Jean-Michel drew near the fort, he climbed a promontory to scan the horizon. As he had hoped, he spied smoke circling upward, and he knew an Abenaki party was nearby. He headed in the direction of the camp, taking care not to startle them into an attack.

Stopping by an oak, he stuffed the drawstring bag holding the necklace into a hole of the tree. Turning in the direction of the Abenaki party, he shouted some words in French and announced his name. Slinging his rifle over his back, Jean-Michel thrust his hands into the air and approached the camp. Suddenly two warriors jumped into his path, pointing muskets in his face.

A third Abenaki approached Jean-Michel and asked him what his business was in the area. He asked about

Darcy, and the Indian said that she had been taken up to Quebec several days back. Jean-Michel's heart sank. He had hoped she was still detained at Fort Lawrence, and after showing his gratitude, he started back toward the tree for the necklace. Once he was certain he was not being watched, he withdrew the bag and placed it around his neck again.

Jean-Michel knew the journey to Quebec would be an arduous one, and he suffered for the sake of Darcy. He did not know what abuses she might be enduring, and it was painful to think that yet again she was being treated like a piece of property. With a deep sigh, he turned to the north, heading for Quebec and Darcy.

.

Chapter 31

LaRoche marveled at the stamina of the woman from Ireland. She had carried a small child on her back for days now and never once uttered a complaint or showed any sign of fatigue. He watched her, as she walked a few paces ahead of him, part of the long train of Abenaki and their prisoners headed over the mountains into the territories of New France.

He had never seen hair that dark against skin that light and he couldn't help but notice how the bright sun had reddened her cheeks. Most of his life, Raoul LaRoche had encountered native women, and although many of them were beautiful, no one had ever captured his attention in such a way.

His entire life had been spent on the frontier, and from the moment he was born, everyone knew that he would be a voyageur. As soon as Raoul could walk, he was groomed to follow in his father's footsteps. He was proud of the many years he had served as a bowsman, transporting hundreds of tons of furs from the wilds of the interior to the bustling community of Quebec, but now those days were over. He had grown too weak to paddle from twelve to eighteen hours a day and a persistent dry cough nagged him, sapping his energy.

This was his first summer in retirement, and Raoul jumped at the chance to join in the fight against the English. He was afraid he would become useless and bored, drowning in self-pity and brandy, so when the call to arms was sounded, he answered. Little did he know he would encounter this woman from a land alien to him and be swept away by her loveliness.

All day long Raoul followed behind Darcy and

watched her back. He loved the way she moved and the graceful way she held her head. He had not gathered enough courage to speak with her as of yet, but he found himself daydreaming about what he would say. The squat voyageur would then chastise himself for being foolish, remembering that a lady of her caliber would never find him attractive.

He knew that he was short and that he had an overdeveloped torso, but these characteristics were considered admirable qualities in a successful voyageur. Unfortunately, the fairer sex did not agree with this view, and when he was around Darcy, he was painfully aware that he was only remotely attractive. She never looked twice at him, and he asked only that she acknowledge his presence.

On their break to eat that day, Raoul positioned himself so he could see Darcy while he smoked his pipe. Maybe tonight he would approach her by the campfire. His English was not perfect, but he spoke enough to give her a kind word, and perhaps he could learn a little bit about her.

Raoul pushed his dark curls away from his bearded face. Part of the mystique of the profession was the voyageur's obsession with hair and dress, and Raoul was no exception. He took great pride in his long, curly hair, and he always kept it neatly combed and impeccably clean.

He looked around at the party and estimated that there were about twenty Indians and three prisoners making the trek northward. Of the prisoners there was the Irish woman, the little boy she carried on her back and an older girl, Raoul judged to be about fifteen or sixteen. He gathered that they were not related, but he could not be sure. They did not often speak, and they kept to themselves. He guessed that they did not wish to provoke the Abenaki with idle chatter or bring unwanted attention to themselves.

On the third evening before retiring, Raoul gathered his courage and approached Darcy. She was sitting in front of the fire humming a tune to the boy in her lap. LaRoche squatted down by her, removed his red, woolen cap and said in a voice thick with a French accent, "*Pardon, mademoiselle.* My name is Raoul LaRoche. May I carry the child for you tomorrow?"

As if awakening from a dream, Darcy looked over at him. She blinked her eyes and said, "I did not know anyone in this party could speak English."

The moment she looked at him, Raoul's reserve crumbled. Never in his life had he seen eyes that color, and he was so distracted he completely forgot what he was going to say. He looked down at his cap and mumbled, "My English is not good."

"Please sit down," offered Darcy.

Raoul's heart leaped. At last, she had noticed him. Darcy turned and looked into his face, and he felt himself blush. Raoul cursed himself for revealing his feelings, and he looked down at the ground. Darcy did not miss this humble gesture, and she felt immediate affection for this unassuming Frenchman. Although he had a thick square build, he had a nice face and sweet smile. His skin was swarthy and weather-beaten, and she supposed it was a result of years spent laboring in the sun. She noticed that his nose was broad and flat, most likely the result of a break years ago, but by far the most outstanding characteristic was the gentle expression of his eyes.

"My name is Darcy McBride. This child is Isaiah Warren and my companion seated over there is Faith

Wyndom. Would you tell us please, where are we going?"

The realization hit Raoul that no one had bothered to tell these prisoners what to expect. For days now the party had been crossing the mountains headed north to the Chaudière River, but these English were completely ignorant of their destination. Raoul carefully organized his words and explained, "At first they were taking you to Quebec to be a servant woman, but the Abenaki have changed their minds. They will present you to Father Cesaire as a gift. You may become nuns or workers in his mission. It is likely the boy will be adopted into the tribe."

"I thought that I was to be ransomed by Colonel Lawrence," said Darcy, beginning to feel confused and afraid.

Raoul hesitated a moment before saying anything. He was unsure how she felt about the English officer who refused to rescue her, and he did not want to cause her pain, but there was no way to avoid it. He cleared his throat and said, "The Colonel refused to pay the note. I am very sorry."

Darcy gasped as if she had been slapped. So Nathan had finally abandoned her. He had threatened to sell her papers on many occasions because of her willful ways, but in the end, it came down to money. Gold had been more precious to him than her safety, and once again she was nothing more than a commodity.

Raoul could see the anger build on her face, and he said, "He is a very foolish man to leave you."

Darcy's face softened into a smile, as she replied, "You are a very nice man, Monsieur LaRoche."

A long silence passed as the embarrassed LaRoche

struggled to find something to say. He stared into the fire mute and helpless, wishing that pleasantries would bubble more easily to his lips, but he was not an articulate man, and conversation did not come naturally in any language.

"Where is this mission?" Darcy asked, finally.

"On the Chaudière River," said Raoul, greatly relieved that she had given him something to say. "It is very near my home, which is a settlement of mostly retired voyageurs."

"You are a voyageur?"

"I once was but not any longer. As you can see, I am not a young man. It is very difficult work to be a voyageur, and the days are very long."

Suddenly, a dry cough wracked his body, and for some moments, he was rendered helpless. When Raoul recovered, he apologized.

Darcy had heard stories about the voyageurs, but she had never met one. She examined her new acquaintance and found his dress to be most unusual. He wore a long red shirt with a brightly colored sash around his waist and a breechcloth with deerskin leggings. On his feet were soft moccasins, and she could see him turn a little red woolen cap, over and over nervously in his hands. Darcy had been only vaguely aware of his presence until now, and she wished that he had introduced himself earlier. It had been torture knowing nothing of her fate.

She had been so preoccupied with keeping Molly's son safe and calming her own anxieties that she had not examined any of her captors until tonight. Taking care to avoid eye contact with anyone on the journey, she had always looked down at the ground. She was terrified of rape, but so far no one had attempted to touch her or Faith.

The presence of Raoul by her side gave Darcy the courage to look around the campsite for the first time. She noticed that several of the Indians had gathered by the fire: some were cooking salmon, others were mending moccasins, and several were listening to a story. They were all dressed in breechcloths and leggings, and many wore shirts of woven fabric or buckskin. During the heat of the day, they frequently removed their shirts and were naked to the waist, and many wore beaded belts around their waists or across their chests. Several wore crosses and Darcy remembered Jean-Michel telling her many of the Abenaki had been converted to Catholicism by the Jesuits.

The Abenaki spoke to each other predominantly in their native tongue, and only occasionally did Darcy hear them speak French. They paid little attention to their prisoners, and so far they had not been unkind to any of them.

Although the pace of the journey had been grueling, Darcy knew that she should keep up with the others, and she encouraged Faith to do the same. They had no patience for weak women, and it was essential that she and Faith move along with the party. Faith was growing alarmingly thin, and Darcy noticed that she herself had lost a lot of weight. She was unbearably tired every evening, and she turned to Raoul and said, "I would be very grateful to you if you would carry the child tomorrow. Thank you for the offer."

"I am sorry that I did not offer before, but they would not allow it. Tomorrow is our last full day, so I shall risk it. You must rest now. It will be another long day tomorrow."

Raoul stood up and with a slight bow left her for the night. Few prisoners had been taken from Fort Lawrence. Many of them had escaped, but most of them had been killed during the siege including Nathan's cook Molly. It was extremely painful for Darcy to share the news with the little six-year-old boy that he would never see his mother again. Life on the frontier was indeed cruel.

The next day proved to be grueling, but knowing that it was the last one made all the difference in the world to the prisoners. Raoul carried the child the entire day, and Darcy noticed how he tossed the boy around lightly. Isaiah liked the retired voyageur, and Darcy believed the child's intuition told him that Raoul could be trusted.

Darcy turned and looked over her shoulder. The dark, densely forested mountains separated Jean-Michel from her, perhaps forever. He would never know what happened to her, and by now she was probably nothing more to him than a distant memory. She must turn and look to the future, realizing that she must forget him and do what she had to do to stay alive. For as long as she could remember, Darcy had to struggle to survive, and she believed in her heart that it would never change. She had never known anything else.

The following day the party approached the shores of a large river Raoul told her was the Chaudière. The Indians pulled several large canoes out of hiding and loaded the prisoners and packs into them. Raoul climbed in the bow of her canoe and picked up a paddle. Several of the Abenaki joined them, and Darcy sat directly behind the voyageur with Isaiah.

She noticed the ease with which he maneuvered the canoe, and it was impressive to see the strength of his arms and back as he propelled the craft swiftly through the water. This was second nature to him, and he turned and explained, "This canoe is called a *batard*. It only seats ten men. The *Canot du Maitre* or *Canut du Nord*--those are the true crafts of the voyageur. They can carry more furs than you can ever imagine and fourteen strong men besides. They are a beautiful sight cutting across a lake, still as glass."

Darcy looked across the water at Faith riding in one of the other canoes. She looked relieved to be off her feet and to have a fresh breeze in her face. Fragrant pines bordered the river as it ran its course northward, and it reminded Darcy how very far from Ireland she had journeyed. There was very little in this new land to remind her of home, and she wondered if she would ever see Ireland again.

They paddled along for a time, and suddenly Raoul burst into song. Darcy looked around for a reaction from the Indians, but they didn't seem to notice anything unusual. He finished and said, "On our long voyages to the outposts, we sing to keep a rhythm to our paddling, and it also passes the time." He continued to hum for a while and then asked, "What of your people? Do they not sing?"

"Oh yes. Many of our songs are stories, some are poems and others praise God."

"But you cannot sing in church, *oui*?"

"Yes, the Catholic Church allows song."

"What? You are a Catholic? This I did not know."

"Most of Ireland is Catholic, Mr. LaRoche."

"Then Father Cesaire will not have to convert you."

"No, but he will have to convert Faith. She is not Catholic."

They paddled most of the morning, and Raoul had

the opportunity to find out how Darcy had been transported to the English Colonies and how her papers had been sold to Nathan Lawrence. The more he spoke with Darcy, the more infatuated he became with her. Raoul LaRoche had never been in love, and these feelings were alarming to him. He loved everything about Darcy, and the more he learned about her, the more he wanted to know. He held no illusions about her loving him in return, but that didn't matter--he only wanted to be near her. As he paddled along deep in thought, he looked up and saw a tall, dark figure standing on shore and he announced, "Look! There's Father Cesaire."

Darcy looked up and saw a man dressed in the dark robes of a Jesuit standing motionless on the shore. As the canoes rounded a bend in the river, a stretch of buildings became visible to her. Lining the shore were five or six oblong structures with frames made of heavy branches lashed together and covered with bark from the trees. Indian women and children began to pour out of the homes to welcome their men home from battle.

There was a mood of celebration in the air, but before the canoes were unloaded, the Indians dropped to their knees to give thanks to God for a safe journey.

As she knelt with the group, Darcy stole a look at the Jesuit missionary. He was a tall, bony man of middle age with volumes of long, black hair and tiny blue eyes. He was tight-lipped and exceedingly stern, and Darcy guessed that he expected perfection from himself and everyone around him.

Father Cesaire said a few words in Algonquian and then in French blessing them all. As Darcy rose from her knees, she felt his cold eyes rest upon her, and he turned away to speak with one of the Abenaki leaders who explained that the prisoners were a gift to their Jesuit father.

The priest looked at Faith and little Isaiah, smiled at them and looked back at Darcy with a look of distaste. She turned her back and looked around at the mission. On a hill behind the longhouses was a European-looking structure she believed to be a church. It resembled a log cabin but was larger, and in front of it stood a tall wooden cross.

Suddenly, she heard a smooth voice say in English, "I understand that you are a gift to the mission."

Darcy turned around, faced the Jesuit missionary and nodded her head. She turned away, not encouraging conversation with the man. Father Cesaire was everything Father Etienne was not, cool, detached and judgmental. It was obvious that he ran this mission with an iron fist, and Darcy was not welcome here. When she looked over at Faith, she could see the girl was thoroughly intimidated by Cesaire.

Raoul stood behind Darcy and listened quietly as the Jesuit addressed Faith. "You, my child, and the little one are welcome," and turning to Darcy, he said, "But you are not. They have told me who you are, and your sins are too great. We do not need your kind here corrupting our innocents."

Darcy's jaw dropped. Never had anyone passed judgment on her so quickly and so harshly. Words of anger and indignation bubbled to her lips, but Raoul jumped in and defended her. "Father Cesaire, you have only just met Mademoiselle McBride. She is not what you think."

"I don't need to know more. This woman would be a distraction and divert too many from the paths of righteousness. I must pray now," said the priest, and he walked up the hill with Faith and Isaiah.

LaRoche said to Darcy, "Is it a sin to dislike a priest, Mademoiselle McBride?"

Darcy took a deep breath and said, "If it is, then I sin too, Mr. LaRoche. Why does he dislike me?"

"I don't think he likes women, especially attractive ones. They are too painful a reminder that he has taken a vow of celibacy."

Suddenly, it occurred to Darcy that she had nowhere to go. The Abenaki had brought her deep into the wilderness, over the mountains and now Father Cesaire had refused her a home. Darcy looked around at the tall pines surrounding her and the endless wilderness which divided her from the English Colonies. How would she get back? She could not travel alone, and no one was offering to take her home. Where could she sleep? The realization swept over her that she was a woman completely alone and vulnerable in the middle of the frontier without food or shelter.

Raoul saw the terrified look on her face, and his heart began to pound. She had no place to go, no one to turn to for help, and like himself was all alone. Perhaps, just perhaps, for the first time in his life, love would smile upon him. Gathering every ounce of courage, he swallowed hard and said, "I know that you have no one, and it would be my honor, Mademoiselle McBride," he stammered, twisting his cap in his hands, "if you would marry me and share my simple life."

Darcy said nothing and stared at Raoul as if she didn't understand a word he said. A fine mist started to fall out of the gray sky, and she looked up, letting the soft waterfall upon her face. She had always hoped to marry for love, but that was just a dream. She was standing in the middle of a vast wilderness and a gentle man was offering her love and protection.

Without reservation, Darcy turned to him and said, "I accept, Mr. LaRoche, and thank you for your generosity."

Raoul, who had been waiting anxiously for her reply, was completely astonished. This glorious woman consented to be his wife, and she would carry his name and maybe even his children. Just moments ago he was miserable, thinking he had to say good-bye to her, and now he would be near her forever. *Life is indeed wonderful!*

He reached down, took her hand and kissed it tenderly saying, "We shall ask Father Cesaire to marry us immediately."

They walked up the hill, and Darcy paused for a moment before entering the church, realizing that this was the first time she had been in an actual church. She found it ironic that on her first visit, she was not here to pray or to receive Holy Communion but to sin most grievously, callously taking vows that she didn't believe and marrying a man that she didn't love. Darcy stepped inside, ready to embark on living a lie. She knew she was not the first woman to do it, and she knew with certainty she would not be the last.

.

Chapter 32

The settlement to which Raoul brought his new bride was very small and very insular. They were suspicious of strangers especially those who came from the English Colonies, so Darcy spent most of her time alone. There were no more than twenty families residing in the community, and they all had some connection to the voyageurs. Most of the women were Abenaki or at the very least, part Abenaki, and they kept exclusively to themselves.

The few men that were around this time of year were of middle age or older and all were retired voyageurs. They smoked together and reminisced, speculating on how far to the interior their sons and brothers may be going this season and when they would return.

The home of Raoul LaRoche was part of the cluster of hewed timber cabins by the Chaudière River, north of the mission. Darcy found their cabin to be of adequate size, neat and clean. They had a plot of potatoes along with a garden of other root vegetables, and their diet consisted mainly of fish and game.

Raoul enjoyed the way Darcy prepared food and kept house. Although the customs and traditions of the Irish were somewhat different from the French, he liked the novel ways she prepared meals, and only on occasion did he find something distasteful.

Months had passed now since their wedding, and Darcy had developed a sincere affection for Raoul. His kindness never changed nor his moods and she found him to be a sweet and devoted husband. His sexual demands were few, and he was always gentle, never cruel.

Their lives had taken a set routine beginning in the morning with chores, a large midday meal, and then in the afternoon, Raoul would leave the cabin to visit with the men while Darcy attended to her sewing or baking. Evening was the time reserved for the two of them, and they would visit by the fire while Darcy worked the loom, making fabric for herself and Faith. They had journeyed to New France with only the clothes on their backs, and Darcy worked night after night on clothing for them both.

Raoul was delighted that Darcy could read, and she read to him from the Bible every night before bed. Up to this point Darcy had been able to use Nathan's small library but now, for the first time since she had learned to read, she was completely without books. She found comfort in the Bible, but Darcy hungered for more and without friends or even the camaraderie of Shenanigan, Darcy began to feel terribly lonely.

She would stand on the banks of the river and look across it as if she were waiting for something. Since it was a thoroughfare to Quebec, there was canoe activity and travelers on foot to watch, but most of the time the river was empty, and she searched the waterway for no reason at all.

Darcy chided herself for being ungrateful to Raoul. Many women had been happier with less, and they would give anything to have a kind husband who loved them, but try as she might, she could not convince herself that she was lucky. Darcy would look at her life stretching out before her and fight the urge to take a canoe and run, but she knew that she would be enslaved in Quebec or die in the wilderness trying to return to the English Colonies. How could she be buried here the rest of her life and devote herself to a man she did not love? With certainty, Darcy knew that it was only a matter of time before she would die of loneliness.

Every morning the entire community would walk up to the mission for Mass with Father Cesaire, and although he remained aloof, he allowed Darcy to receive the sacrament of Holy Communion. On Sundays, she would visit with Faith when church was over, and they would sit together on the grass and exchange news.

"How have your lessons in the Catholic faith been going with Father Cesaire?" asked Darcy one sunny day as they sat on the bank of the Chaudière.

"Quite well," the young woman said, as she brushed back a lock of her chestnut hair. "But many things are different in your church, Darcy, and to be honest, I don't always agree."

"That's all right, Faith. If you believed everything *he* said, then you would think I'm a harlot."

"Never!" gasped Faith. "But I fear for our visits. I don't think he will allow me to see you much longer. The only reason Father lets me speak with you now is to help me with my homesickness."

"Are you terribly homesick, Faith?"

"Yes," and large tears began to roll down her cheeks. She brushed them off and said, "I miss my family so much, and I pray every night that Catherine is safe and happy living somewhere with Mr. Tinker."

Darcy took her hand. "He will take good care of Catherine. Moses is a good man and needs someone. In a way, this has been a blessing for him. What of Isaiah? How does he fare?"

"I believe he adjusts better than us. He is truly

loved by his new Abenaki family, and one day he will forget that he was born in the English Colonies."

Raoul approached the women, signaling that it was time to go home. Faith caught Darcy by the wrist and said, "Does your husband know that you love another?"

Darcy frowned. "What are you talking about?"

"It is written all over you. Any woman could see it."

Darcy felt a lump in her throat and said nothing.

It was a beautiful autumn day, and when they reached their cabin, Raoul said, "Come, Darcy, pack a basket, and I will take you in the canoe to enjoy this beautiful afternoon."

Darcy was thrilled. She ran into the house, gathered up some food and rushed back out to the canoe. They spent the entire day lazily exploring the river and walking in the woods. At one point, they paddled down some rapids and then passed a wooden cross driven into the ground. When the water calmed, Raoul removed his cap, saying a prayer to St. Anne, the patron saint of voyageurs.

"Why is the cross there?" Darcy asked.

"That is where a voyageur lost his life. We always mark the spot so all that pass will pray for his soul."

Shortly after that, they chose a spot on the riverbank to stop and eat their lunch. Darcy gazed up at the clear cloudless sky, relishing the aroma of the pines. Raoul kissed her and said, "You have made me the happiest man alive. I cannot believe that you are my wife."

They returned home late in the day, and even though Darcy was grateful for the outing, the loneliness continued. She would stare up at the night sky, trying to find the constellations Jean-Michel had told her about, but Sagittarius and Scorpio were lost in the vast multitude of the heavens. It mattered little. Jean-Michel was lost to her as well.

The wind began to turn cold on All Hallows Eve, and Darcy decided to warm the cabin doing her baking for the week. Early in the morning, she lit a fire in the oven, allowing it to burn until the stones became hot. After sweeping out the coals, she put her bare arm inside to test the temperature. Picking up her peel, Darcy slid a crock of baked beans to the back of the oven, knowing that they would take all day and then added her bread and rolls. Raoul had taught her many new ways to bake bread in the French fashion, and she found the experimentation amusing. Today she was trying baguettes.

After she had completed her baking, Darcy walked outside and sat down by a sapling to make cornmeal. A large rock hung from a rope which was tied to a young tree, and with this rock she pounded the corn down to a coarse meal, using the flexible sapling to do the work for her on the upswing. Many of these chores had been new to Darcy when she first came to the New World, but now they had become second nature to her. Her days were full from beginning to end, but her heart remained empty. Nothing seemed to matter anymore, and she felt herself sliding into despondency.

To amuse herself and observe All Hallows Eve, she lit a bonfire to ward off ghosts and wandering souls. It was twilight. The wind sighed sadly as it passed through the pines, and the sky was a steely gray. Darcy shivered as she looked up at the ceiling of clouds. It was indeed an eerie evening, and back in Ireland, they would have spoken of the Banshee walking. Raoul was late tonight, and Darcy knew that the conversation and tobacco must be entertaining.

The bonfire crackled and popped on the banks of the Chaudière, sending sparks flying high into the night sky. She gazed into the flames, thinking of the ghost stories she heard as a child and smiled to herself. A movement caught her eye, and she saw a figure coming toward her along the banks of the river. Many travelers came down from Quebec, following the river, and Darcy looked back at the fire, unconcerned. As the traveler came closer, she looked once more, and she could see in the twilight that it was a white man, but he was not in the dress of a voyageur. His clothing appeared to be that of a settler. Something was familiar about the figure, and it gave Darcy pause. She stood motionless and stared at him. The closer the man came, the more anxious Darcy felt, and fear began to wash over her. She thought perhaps it was a ghost. Suddenly, the specter dropped his pack and began to run. In an instant he was upon her, kissing her face and her hair. It was Jean-Michel.

"My god, you're alive! You're alive!" he kept repeating as he held her face and kissed her lips and her cheeks over and over again.

Darcy was stunned. With her arms at her side, she stared at him as if he were not real. *This cannot be happening. Jean-Michel would never be standing on the banks of the Chaudière, holding me. This is a cruel trick played on me by fairies.*

The brilliant light of the bonfire flooded them as Jean-Michel brushed the hair away from her face. "I have come to take you back. You are safe now."

At last, she put her arms around him, feeling the warmth of his body, realizing that he was indeed flesh and blood. "How did you find me?" she asked, breathlessly.

"The Abenaki told me that you had been taken to Quebec, and after searching there for months, I gave up and was returning to the English Colonies. It is purely by the grace of God that I find you now."

He pulled her close to him and held her so tightly that she could barely breathe. "Tell me that you still love me, Darcy."

She felt his strong legs against her. He bent her head back and kissed her deeply. Instantly she was drowning in desire. It had been so long since she had felt passion, and now, as he lavished his affection on her, she lost her head. His lips moved down her neck as his fingers pressed into her back, and they embraced in the firelight until Darcy pushed him away and gasped, "No, you must not, Jean-Michel!"

"Why?" he said as he stepped back.

"Because I am a married woman."

He looked incredulous and searched her eyes for answers. Just as she was about to explain, a voice shouted, "*Bonsoir!*" They turned and saw Raoul walking down the hill with a smile on his face.

"Welcome, wayfarer!" he said to Jean-Michel in French. "I am Raoul LaRoche, and this is my wife, Madame LaRoche. May we help you?"

Jean-Michel turned and looked at Darcy with hurt in his eyes. She looked down at the ground. He swallowed hard and then said politely, "Thank you, Monsieur LaRoche. I am an acquaintance of your wife. We had just been reminiscing when you arrived."

Darcy was unsure how much Raoul had seen, but judging from his solicitous attitude, he had witnessed nothing. Her heart was thumping against her chest, and she knew that she appeared agitated. Her French had improved greatly since coming to New France, and she heard Raoul exclaim, "You know each other? What a surprise. Are you too from Ireland, Monsieur?"

"No, I am from the Colony of Massachusetts."

"You are very brave to be up here during wartime."

"My business here was of great importance," Jean-Michel said, looking at Darcy.

"As you can imagine, we are not fond of the British here, but since you are a friend of my wife, I will make an allowance. Please, will you join us for supper?"

"No, thank you, I must be on my way," returned Jean-Michel, feeling his stomach tie up in knots.

"Please, Monsieur."

Reluctantly Jean-Michel walked up to the cabin. Fighting back tears of outrage and sorrow, Darcy made supper while the men smoked at the table. Just a few months ago, she had been dreaming of keeping house for Jean-Michel, and here she was the wife of a retired French voyageur, cooking for her lover as if he were a stranger.

Darcy watched Jean-Michel closely, committing to memory every detail of his appearance. He was dressed in a white linen shirt of the highest quality, and he had on dark breeches with expensive leather boots. She realized what a fool she had been not to have guessed that he was a man of wealth and breeding. Nathan Lawrence was right. She would never fit into his life.

Darcy looked away, but inevitably her eyes went back to him unable to resist drinking in every detail. She had never forgotten how appealing he was with his dark skin and long black hair tied back with a leather thong. There was only a shadow of a beard on his face. She watched his icy blue eyes appraise Raoul. Suddenly, as if he knew she had been watching him, he turned in his chair and looked directly at her. Darcy jumped and moved back to the hearth, saying nothing.

The men continued to make small talk. They found common ground in the Lupé trading post of the past. Darcy knew Raoul could go on forever once the voyageur stories started, and she was relieved that she did not have to contribute anything to the conversation.

Jean-Michel pretended to be listening, but he was distracted by Darcy. How could she have married this squat, little man? How dare this old voyageur call Darcy his wife and take her to his bed. She was not his wife. She could never be his wife. From the moment she was born, she had been meant for him and him alone.

Jean-Michel decided at that moment to tell them his reason for coming. "It is no coincidence I have found your wife, Monsieur LaRoche. I have been in fact searching for her."

Darcy stood up from the hearth, holding her breath. Her eyes were on Jean-Michel.

"The man who held Madame LaRoche's servitude has changed his mind. I was to pay the ransom and take her back to New England, but I see that I am too late."

Darcy was aghast. He was merely running an errand for Nathan Lawrence. She remained motionless trying to absorb the blow.

After a few moments, she bent down to stir the bubbling stew, choking back hurt and rage.

"Oh, Mon Dieu!" declared Raoul. "I am glad that I found her first. She would have been lost to me forever."

Raoul asked Jean-Michel if he had a wife and children. "No. There is no one," he replied.

Darcy stood up from the hearth and said, "Oh come now, Monsieur Lupé. It is common knowledge that you will marry the refined and elegant Elizabeth

Campbell of Piscataqua then take a woman on the side."

Jean-Michel stopped smoking and stared at Darcy. He was stunned by her words.

Ignoring Jean-Michel, she turned to Raoul and explained, "In England, gentlemen marry ladies and keep lower class women as their whores. This is the convention."

Raoul chuckled and added, "Well, it is the way in France too."

Jean-Michel was livid. He looked at her and said, "What you say is often the case in Europe, but this is not England or France. It is the Colonies and we have our own minds. Love is my only criteria for matrimony. Too many people marry out of need. Wouldn't you agree with that observation, Madame LaRoche?"

Jean-Michel saw Darcy's jaw tighten, and she looked away. Raoul brought the talk back to fur-trading stories, and Darcy fell back into agonizing silence. The whole night reminded her of Nathan Lawrence's dinner party over a year ago when she and Jean-Michel shot barbs at one another all night.

Jean-Michel stood up and thanked them both for supper. Raoul looked surprised and said, "Surely you will sleep here tonight. The weather is growing cold."

"No, thank you, Monsieur LaRoche, I prefer to sleep under the stars. You can certainly appreciate that choice being a voyageur."

"That I can," he acknowledged, nodding his head.

The truth was Jean-Michel could not bear the thought of Darcy sleeping next to that man. He would put as much distance as he could tonight between the LaRoches and himself and return as soon as possible to apologize and marry Elizabeth Campbell.

As he unlatched the door to leave, he turned to Darcy one last time and said, "I don't believe you have to search for Sagittarius in the night sky any longer, Madame LaRoche. There is a new constellation now."

Darcy said nothing and kept her eyes on the floor. She could not bear to watch him walk out that door and leave her forever. The door shut, and she turned to clear the supper dishes. She knew that if she didn't stay busy, she might lose control and run out the door after him.

"What was that about the stars?" asked Raoul, as he lit his pipe.

"Oh, nothing much. He is a surveyor, and they know about constellations." Darcy looked at Raoul for signs of suspicion, but he seemed unconcerned as he sat in front of the fire. She could rest. He had not seen them embracing in front of the bonfire.

Darcy started to clean up from the meal. She was on edge and welcomed work to help burn off her pain and anxiety. When she picked up Jean-Michel's supper dishes, she froze. There, concealed under the napkin, was the chain with the cross and charm. Hot tears blurred her vision as she stared at the symbol of their commitment to one another. She could not bring herself to put it around her neck again, so she placed it in her apron. Closing her eyes, she tried to fight back the tears, knowing that with this gesture, Jean-Michel had severed his ties to her forever.

Chapter 33

Darcy never put the chain on again. It had rested on Jean-Michel's chest for months, and if she were to wear it now, she might feel close to him again--something which she did not want. Slowly she was losing her faith in God and her hope. She felt tired and empty. In the past, she had taken comfort in the knowledge that God was with her, but now her prayers seemed futile and useless. She became cold and apathetic again, and the familiar cynicism returned. The walls which Jean-Michel had eroded were now back up and firmly in place. So as her tears dried up, so did her emotions. Darcy could no longer feel anything but emptiness, and she merely existed, going through the motions of a life devoid of joy.

Raoul had his own difficulties which were causing him great anxiety. His cough had worsened, and he found that even crossing the room now caused him to feel as if he were suffocating. He spent most of his time by the fire wrapped in a blanket, and the only things that pleased him were smoking his pipe and watching his lovely wife move about the room.

Darcy was busy from sunrise to sunset, burdened with Raoul's chores and her own. He felt guilty and wanted to help, but every time he would rise from his chair he would end up slumping down again, completely exhausted.

He noticed how quiet Darcy had been lately. Life was difficult up here, and she never quite seemed to fit in with the others. He tried to fill her void of loneliness by asking her about her life in Ireland, but she seemed disinterested and even secretive about her past. As much as Raoul wanted to be everything to Darcy, he knew that it was impossible.

Winter came early in New France, and the river hardened quickly. Darcy had never seen so much snow, and when the temperatures dropped, she found herself trapped in the small cabin listening to the relentless coughing of Raoul. Many nights he kept her awake as the spasms racked his body, but she never left his side. She knew that he took great pleasure in the intimacy of sleeping next to her, and she did not have the heart to refuse him. The lack of sleep took its toll on Darcy, and she too fell ill for weeks with a fever. Raoul was too sick himself to help her, so it was up to Darcy to continue to cook and keep house for them both. Slowly she recovered, and by Christmas, she was back to full health.

She made a feeble attempt to celebrate the holiday by decorating the mantel and windows with evergreen boughs while Raoul made a birch-bark crèche and placed corn-husk dolls inside. She had no idea that he was such an artist, and she marveled at the small replicas of the Holy Family and the other meticulously crafted figures of the Nativity. Raoul explained that the French had the custom of observing Christmas with a *Reveillon*, which was an all-night celebration following Mass on Christmas Eve. Darcy dreaded this affair. She knew that once again she would be snubbed as the English outsider, but when she heard that Faith would be there her attitude changed.

She bustled around the keeping room, making puddings and tarts to contribute to Monsieur and Madame Brunette, the hosts of the *Reveillon* at the settlement. Raoul would join them later at the party.

The journey up to the mission for Christmas Eve Mass would be far too taxing for him.

Darcy strapped on her snowshoes before midnight and made the trek alone to Mass. After church, a long parade of settlers walked through the snow-muffled woods on their way back to the settlement and the *Reveillon*. Darcy and Faith joined the procession as well. Everyone carried a torch as a symbol of Christ bringing light into the world. The forest looked black and foreboding surrounding the small group, but everyone found comfort in the brilliant light and warmth from the dancing flames.

The home of the Brunettes was the largest in the settlement, and they had dressed it gaily in evergreens and dried red berries found in the woods. The food was delicious and abundant, and although much of it was new to Darcy and Faith, they enjoyed sampling everything. A particular favorite of Darcy's was the *Buche de Noel*, a rich cake decorated to look like a Yule log.

Everyone was dressed in their finest clothes. The men were in their best shirts with brightly colored sashes tied around their waists, and the women were either in their Sunday finery or dressed in beautifully beaded Abenaki clothing. Zigzag or triangle designs decorated their long shirts, and more often than not, the bead work was in the shape of a cross to celebrate the acceptance of Christ into their lives.

Several men carried Raoul to the *Reveillon* later, and he stayed with the retired voyageurs, leaving Darcy and Faith alone in the corner. The two women were happy to be on their own, anxious to share news and tidbits of gossip.

Darcy was startled when she saw Faith's

appearance. The young woman appeared frail, and there were heavy, black rings under her eyes. "Faith, you look ill. Seeing you so thin and drawn scares me," said Darcy.

"I'm very tired. That's all, Darcy," protested Faith. She picked at her food and gave her friend a weak smile and said, "If I could just get a good night's sleep, I would feel better, but once I go to bed, everything starts to bother me."

"What bothers you? Is Father Cesaire cruel to you?"

Faith jumped at the sound of his name and looked down at her plate of food, hesitating before she answered, "No, not cruel."

"I don't believe it. What is he doing to you, Faith? I don't care what anybody says. I think the man is wicked," snapped Darcy.

"No, you mustn't say such a thing, Darcy, especially on Christmas Eve. Please let's speak of something else. I want to have fun tonight."

Reluctantly, Darcy dropped the subject and Faith asked, "How is Raoul? You should be worried about your husband instead of me. His cough is not getting any better," said Faith.

"I *am* worried, Faith. It is so hard for him to breathe, and now he can't even get out of a chair without assistance. I know he feels guilty, but I can't convince him that I don't mind helping him. He gave me a home and love when I needed it, and I can never repay him enough.

"He is a good man, but he is not the husband you hoped for, Darcy," said Faith, shaking her head. "You too look ill. Your heart seems to have died."

Darcy looked at the floor, ashamed. "Don't say

such things. Life has taught me that I must do my best to survive and wish for nothing more." She jumped up to attend to Raoul during a bad fit of coughing. A few moments later, they gave their thanks to Monsieur and Madame Brunette and returned home, cutting short their all-night celebration.

*   *   *

Winter seemed endless for Darcy with the days dragging on and on, but when she complained, Raoul would tell her to not wish for spring because the melting snow would bring renewed battles with the English and the Indians.

At least, there is plenty of food to eat this season. Darcy remembered last winter at Fort Lawrence and the severe privations endured by them all. She couldn't imagine the French occupying the fort now, and she wondered if Nathan would try to recapture it when the snow melted.

One February afternoon, there came a sharp knock on the door, and Darcy and Raoul jumped with surprise. In the deep snow and cold of winter, it was unusual to have a visitor. Darcy opened the door, and there stood Claude Gauthier, a close friend of Raoul's, holding his red cap in his hands. He stepped inside the keeping room, and Raoul said to him, "Come and warm yourself by the fire, Claude. It is so good of you to come."

The retired voyageur sat down in a chair next to his lifelong friend and looked around the room uncomfortably. He kept darting glances at Darcy until finally he said, "I'm sorry, Raoul, but I have come with bad news today, especially for Madame LaRoche."

Darcy looked up from the spinning wheel and stopped peddling. She did not like the look on his face.

He continued. "Father Cesaire has sent me to tell

you that he found the body of your young friend Faith in the mission this morning."

Darcy gasped and stood up, clutching her bodice. Reluctantly, Claude went on, "That is not all, Madame LaRoche. The young woman hanged herself."

"No!" cried Darcy.

Raoul dropped his blanket and stumbled over to Darcy to hold her in his weak arms. With every ounce of strength he had, he rocked her back and forth gently offering her comfort. Claude put his cap on and quietly left the cabin.

At last, Darcy raised her head and looked out the window at the sun as it cast long shadows on the snow. Raoul was surprised to see that as grief-stricken as she was, she had not shed a tear. She patted Raoul on the hand, helped him to his chair and sat down to resume her spinning. Darcy never said another word about Faith's death, and when Raoul encouraged her to talk about it, she refused.

* * *

The air was bitterly cold when Darcy walked up to the mission to see Faith one last time. It was there her body awaited burial, and after Darcy had paid her respects, Faith's remains would be wrapped in bark and put on a high stand until the spring thaw. Since she had taken her own life, no Mass would be offered. Darcy knelt down in front of Faith reminding herself that the girl was better off dead.

As she was leaving, Father Cesaire emerged from his rooms behind the altar. The somber figure approached her, and she turned her back on him not wishing any communication.

As she placed her hand on the door to leave, he said coldly, "You have been here for six months, and you have never given me your confession, Madame LaRoche. Your sins are many. I think that it is time you make peace with God."

At these words, Darcy whirled around and exclaimed, "*My* sins are many? How dare you judge me. I have no proof, but I have an idea of what you did to that innocent child in there, and you better attend to your own conscience, not mine!"

Darcy walked out of the church and slammed the door behind her. From that day forward, she never set foot in the mission church again.

* * *

Slowly the woods came back to life, as the snow melted, and the river opened up. At first, large chunks of ice sailed down the blue waters of the Chaudière and then gradually the ice melted and canoe traffic resumed again. Migrating birds returned, and the trees and floor of the forest were alive with chipmunks and squirrels scurrying about gathering food. Darcy loved the way they chattered and scolded her as she walked out to gather saplings to weave baskets. This skill was new to Darcy, and she knew that her work paled in comparison to the beautifully crafted baskets of the Abenaki women, but she made the attempt out of necessity and after a while she came to enjoy the weaving.

Raoul continued to suffer from his cough, and then one day he took a turn for the worse. He could no longer get out of bed, and he was wheezing and gasping for air. He coughed up large quantities of blood, and Darcy was scared. He no longer asked for his pipe, and his diet consisted only of liquids.

She constantly worried about him and never

strayed far from his bedside. Her days were filled with loads of bedding and soiled clothing from Raoul, and her hands grew red and chapped from continual washing.

Friends of Raoul came by to visit, and Darcy knew that they were really there to say good-bye. They never stayed long, and although they were cordial to her, they never extended themselves with words of comfort or any small talk. She knew that they hated her because she had come from the English Colonies.

Raoul asked Darcy to read to him from the Bible every evening. If he hadn't asked, she would never have opened the book again. She had turned her back on God. She believed the Creator had abandoned her, and she decided to meet Him in kind.

One afternoon, when she was working in the garden, she saw the dark figure of Father Cesaire sweep into the cabin. She knew that he was there to give Raoul his Last Rites. The priest did not come looking for Darcy, and that was fine with her.

Gradually the weather warmed and one a spring evening before the mosquitoes hatched, Darcy threw open the windows of the cabin to allow Raoul some fresh air. A breeze on his face seemed to help him breathe easier. She sat on the corner of his bed and began to comb his hair away from his face. He opened his eyes and said to her weakly, "You have been very good to me, Darcy. You are too young and full of life to be buried here in this settlement taking care of a dying man."

"I have done nothing out of the ordinary," she replied.

"I must ask your forgiveness for something, my dear wife."

"Raoul, you have always been so kind to me. How can there be anything to forgive?"

He searched her face and then said, "I know that you have always loved another," he said breathlessly. "And I deliberately kept you here because I was too selfish to live without you."

"What nonsense you talk of, Raoul," she exclaimed, starting to feel her body tense.

"I saw you on All Hallows Eve, Darcy, that night by the bonfire, kissing the man from Massachusetts. It is he you love." He paused to catch his breath. "I should have released you then, but I was too selfish, and I held you prisoner here. I knew that I was going to die soon, and I wanted your face to be the last thing that I gazed upon before I went to God."

Darcy pressed her eyes shut. *So Raoul had suffered in silence all this time. Never a cross word, never an accusation.* She looked down at him again. "There is nothing to forgive, Raoul. I should be asking *you* for forgiveness."

Raoul smiled weakly, closed his eyes and drifted to sleep. Late that night, he had a fit of coughing which was too much for his weak body. Blood gushed from his nose and mouth, and with Darcy holding him in her arms, he died. Raoul LaRoche was granted his final wish. The last thing he saw before he departed was the face of his wife, Madame LaRoche.

All by herself, Darcy cleaned and prepared the body for burial. At sunrise she sat in a chair, staring straight ahead. She dreaded going to the mission to inform Father Cesaire of Raoul's death. The cheerful spring day didn't lure her outside, and well into the afternoon, Darcy continued to sit in the chair, not moving.

She was so tired--tired of fighting to survive, tired of uncertainties and tired of loving someone that she could never have. Darcy examined all her options, but more and more the escape which Faith had chosen seemed the most appealing choice. She stood up and opened the door of the cabin gazing out at the cold rushing waters of the Chaudière River. The current was swift and likely to sweep her away quickly, and the icy waters would numb any pain that might occur once she submerged herself. Yes, this was the best avenue to oblivion.

She took a step forward, and suddenly she heard a voice from the past whispering in her ear. At first, Darcy couldn't identify it. Then the words became clearer, and she could hear Teila say, "How dare you speak indifferently of your life, especially when we risk our lives for you. Father Etienne gave his life trying to save you and the others, and now you repay him with this blasphemy!"

Darcy reached up and touched her cheek. She could almost feel the slap Teila had given her so long ago. She closed her eyes and said, "But I'm so tired. I'm so very tired."

Again she heard Teila say angrily, "And now you repay him with this blasphemy!" Over and over she listened to the words. Finally, she walked over to the small cracked mirror on the wall, pinned her hair up and started for the mission to inform Father Cesaire of her husband's death.

No matter how arduous the task, no matter how much suffering she had to endure, Darcy knew that she must continue living. Taking her life would never be an option again. Across the vast expanses, the spirit of Teila had pulled her from the pit of desperation once more, and Darcy found the strength to go on.

Chapter 34

The entire community attended the funeral of Raoul LaRoche. They were all polite to Darcy, but she knew that they would not welcome her permanently into their community. She had been endured for Raoul's sake only, and she knew now she would have to go.

After the burial, Father Cesaire approached Darcy. She watched with apprehension, as his dark figure approached. He was a peculiar-looking man with his wild shock of jet-black hair falling down in tangles around his face. Darcy thought that he had a maniacal look to him. He approached with his thin lips pursed, and then said, "You must realize, Madame that you are not welcome here, and I am in agreement with the community. I sent a courier this morning to inform your English Colonel Lawrence that you are once again available for ransom if he is interested. I will allow you to await his reply in Monsieur LaRoche's cabin. If he does not respond, you will be sold in Quebec in the autumn."

Darcy had the feeling that Cesaire was expecting her to be grateful, but she simply turned and walked away. The cabin was empty and quiet when she returned that afternoon, and Darcy realized how much she missed Raoul. Over the months, she had grown to love him in her own way. She picked up his pipe and held it in her hand, turning it over and over and thinking of him. Darcy hoped sincerely that she had brought him a bit of happiness in his final days.

The loneliness lessened as the days went on, and when the sun grew warmer, Darcy would sit by the river and watch the eagles circling in the sky. She wondered if Jean-Michel was married yet, and she speculated that Elizabeth Campbell may be already carrying their first child.

Weeks turned to months, and the possibility of Nathan sending someone grew more and more remote. She knew that any day the priest would send her to Quebec to be sold as a servant. For all of the uncertainties, Darcy made the most of every day. Since she was leaving before winter, there was no need to fuss over crops or the garden, and with Raoul being gone, there was no reason to cook or clean, so every day she took long leisurely walks, bathed or sat on the porch.

One sultry evening as Darcy was preparing supper, large thunderheads gathered in the sky. The winds picked up and brought a hard, driving rain upon the settlement. She had just finished her meal when there was a knock on the door, and her heart jumped into her throat. Darcy knew that the time had come for her to go to Quebec.

She opened the door encountering a small Abenaki boy who told her in French that Father Cesaire would like to see her immediately. Taking a deep breath, Darcy squared her shoulders and started out the door. Suddenly, she remembered something and stopped. She re-entered the cabin and put the cross and charm necklace around her neck. As angry as she had been with God, he had granted her these few months of peace, and she was grateful.

The pouring rain soaked Darcy to the bone as she followed the silent child through the woods to the mission. The wind ceased, and they walked in a downpour, punctuated only occasionally by claps of thunder. Her gown felt heavy and sodden, and her dark hair hung in wet strands about her face.

As she started up the hill toward the mission church, she could see the outline of Father Cesaire, standing next to someone. She could tell they were watching her. The rain blurred her vision, and when she reached up to wipe the water from her eyes, she realized that the figure standing with the priest was Jean-Michel.

Her heart jumped. Darcy tried to calm herself, remembering that by now he was probably a married man and maybe even a father. Nevertheless, she took long strides up the hill, stopping so close in front of Jean-Michel that their garments touched. The rain rolled down their faces, as they looked into each other's eyes.

Father Cesaire watched them with disdain and demanded, "I will take the Colonel's donation to our mission now, Monsieur."

Jean-Michel dragged his eyes from Darcy, stepped back and reached inside his shirt, producing a small leather pouch. When Father Cesaire reached out for it, Jean-Michel pulled it away. He warned, "Not so fast, I have instructions to interview the prisoner alone before I make the payment."

The Jesuit's eyes narrowed, but he bowed politely and said, "As you wish, Monsieur." Father Cesaire retreated to the shelter of his church to await payment.

Jean-Michel looked down at Darcy and asked, "Are you well?"

"They have not harmed me. Why was Nathan so slow in responding?"

"He has been very busy with other matters, and only now had time to contact me regarding your ransom."

Jean-Michel looked furtively at the heavily wooded area surrounding them, and taking Darcy by the shoulders, he said with urgency, "You must listen to me carefully, Darcy. We are in grave danger. General Wolfe has taken Point Levi just north of here. He has given instructions to saturate this area with British regulars and Iroquois. They will not care who we are. Once they have the taste of blood, all reason will be washed from their minds. You must be prepared to run for your life."

Darcy heard what he said, but she did not feel afraid.

"Next, there is the business of your ransom. Colonel Lawrence has asked me to tell you that he cannot overturn the Crown's punishment, but as far as he is concerned from this day forward you are a free woman."

Darcy stared at Jean-Michel, her eyes wide with astonishment. *Had she heard him correctly? Did he say that she was free?* The words echoed in her ears, and she blinked.

Father Cesaire approached and Jean-Michel handed him the pouch containing the emerald necklace. The priest bowed and with the shadow of a smile said, "Watch yourselves, my fine New Englanders. You are in French territory during wartime. Anything can happen."

Jean-Michel watched him, as he disappeared into his church, and then he turned to Darcy and said, "From this moment forward, you are free to do as you choose, Darcy. Where will you go?"

She didn't answer right away. Her thoughts raced as well as her heart. For the first time in years, she was free. Even in Ireland, she had not been free, so for the first time ever, she was free.

Jean-Michel searched her eyes and asked, "Will

you go back to Massachusetts to live?"

"Oh, no," said Darcy shaking her head. "There is nothing there for me. I shall return to the coast of Kerry. This land has never been my home."

Jean-Michel stared at her a moment and then stepped back, mumbling, "I understand."

Darcy was confused and searched his face. "But you are married--" Before she could finish her sentence, there was the report of a firearm, and Jean-Michel gasped, clutching his side. He looked down at his waist, and when he removed his hand, a bright spot of blood began to soak his shirt.

Jean-Michel said breathlessly, "Run!"

Before Darcy could move, an Abenaki warrior began running towards them with his tomahawk raised. Jean-Michel pulled the rifle from his shoulder, and with all his might slammed the butt of the gun into the stomach of the Indian, who doubled up.

Darcy bolted for the woods assuming that Jean-Michel was behind her, but when she looked back, he had fallen to his knees. "No!" she screamed, dashing back to him.

Another Abenaki bolted from the woods toward them. Her heart pounding, Darcy raised Jean-Michel's rifle, set her sights on the Indian and pulled the trigger. There was a loud blast, and when the smoke cleared, he had fallen. But the warrior struggled to his feet and began running again. He raised his tomahawk ready to smash Darcy's skull when suddenly he dropped his weapon and staggered forward, slamming into her, an arrow protruding from his neck. Clinging to her, he slid down her body.

All at once, there was the cracking of muskets and war cries as Iroquois and English descended on the

French and Abenaki village. Darcy bent down and put Jean-Michel's arm around her neck.

He roared, "Damn it! I told you to run!"

Ignoring him, Darcy straightened up bearing his weight on her shoulders. Jean-Michel showered her with oaths in French, as she pulled him to the cover of the trees. When they reached the brush, she fell to the ground exhausted.

Panting, Darcy pulled Jean-Michel's blood-soaked shirt up to examine his injury. A letter tumbled to the ground, and she picked it up stuffing it in her bodice. The bullet had gone into his side and exited the back cleanly, but the blood was running out of him in a steady stream. She could tell that he was growing weak quickly.

"Please, listen to me, Darcy," he said with great effort. "Governor Shirley has offered a bounty of twenty pounds for scalps. Get to safety at Point Levi."

Ignoring him Darcy gave the hem of her dress a yank tearing the material into long strips. She wound them tightly around his torso and then tied them off. Jean-Michel grabbed her wrist and said, "Are you listening to me!"

Darcy's snapped, "All my life some man has been telling me where I can and cannot go. I am a free woman now, Jean-Michel Lupé, and I'm staying here with you!"

Jean-Michel dropped back and closed his eyes. A few moments ago he would have given anything to hear those words, but now all wanted was for her to get away.

It was twilight, and blasts of light from gunfire lit the mission and the village around it. Most of the Abenaki warriors were conducting raids in the south, so the community was left defenseless against the Iroquois and English.

An Iroquois warrior and an aged Abenaki were fighting, close to where Darcy and Jean-Michel were hiding in the brush. The younger Iroquois slammed his tomahawk into the old man's skull and then threw him face down onto the ground. After straddling him, he ran the blade of his hunting knife around the scalp. He placed his foot on the Abenaki's shoulder and yanked the scalp from back to front.

Darcy watched, paralyzed with fear as another scene unfolded before her eyes, this time involving a British regular. He was struggling roughly with a young Indian woman, and after knocking her unconscious with the butt of his gun, he scalped her as well.

Jean-Michel grabbed Darcy's arm and whispered, "We've got to get away from here!"

Slinging his arm over her neck, she whispered, "There is a cave near here on the river where we can hide, but first I must stop at the cabin."

They drove deep into the forest, stumbling blindly over brush and undergrowth in a frenzied hurry to safety. Several times the burden was too much for Darcy, and she lost her footing sending them both to the ground. Try as he might, each time they fell, Jean-Michel could not suppress crying out in pain, and Darcy would crumble into a thousand apologies.

She was relieved when the cabin was finally in sight, and they approached it from the back cautiously. She guided him to Raoul's bed, but when he protested, she put him on a chair by the table instead.

Quickly Darcy lit a candle, covered the window and grabbed some fresh bandages and several blankets. Rolling them all into a bundle, she tied it onto her back.

Next she picked up Raoul's musket, loaded it and strapped on his shot pouch.

"Is there brandy?" asked Jean-Michel. He lay slumped onto the table, dark rings under his eyes. His lips were white and his complexion gray. Darcy pulled down a bottle from the mantel, sat down and quickly poured them a drink.

Jean-Michel looked at Darcy. "You're trembling,"

"No, I'm not," she argued. Darcy could not admit fear tonight. What she had witnessed at the mission struck terror into her heart, and if she were to admit her true feelings she may not find the courage to continue.

Jean-Michel looked around the home of Monsieur and Madame LaRoche. He could picture Darcy making supper by the hearth or spinning at the wheel, but when his eyes rested on the bed, he felt the jealousy burn.

"Did you ever think of me when you made love to your husband?"

Darcy stopped with her drink in mid-air, and then slowly put it down. She paused and said, "I gave my body to him Jean-Michel, but never my heart. You are the only man I have ever made love to." They listened to the rain on the roof, and Darcy stood up, looking out the window. "When I needed to remember how good life can be, that is when I brought your memory up from my heart."

Suddenly, violent screams came from the settlement, and Darcy jumped back from the window crying, "They're here! We must hurry."

Jean-Michel blew out the candle, and after slinging the musket over her shoulder, Darcy slid herself gently under his arm again. They stole quietly into the night, struggling together through the black wilderness. With the added burden of a musket, Darcy's shoulders were breaking, but she was determined to get them to safety.

They followed the Chaudière River north, searching for a cave. Darcy was petrified they might meet someone on the well-traveled path to Quebec, so she urged Jean-Michel to move even faster. He gave every ounce of strength he had left to double the pace. He could see that the blood had drenched his shirt and was starting to soak Darcy's gown too.

They found a cave, but it required that they climb up several large boulders to gain entrance, and Darcy feared that Jean-Michel could not traverse the slippery rocks. They stood panting below the cave. Darcy shouted over the roar of the river, "Can you get up there?"

He nodded weakly, and Darcy scrambled upon the first rock. She dropped her pack and her musket and sat down. With her legs apart and her hands outstretched, she grabbed Jean-Michel by the wrists and pulled him with all her might. He managed to get a foothold and pushed himself up, falling heavily on top of her. They collapsed there, sapped of strength. They repeated this step one more time until they were inside the shelter of the cave.

Ignoring her fear of caves, Darcy started to make a bed for Jean-Michel. She lit a candle, put blankets down and pulled out a dry shirt that had belonged to Raoul. After easing him onto the blankets, Darcy tore the filthy, mud-soaked shirt off of Jean-Michel, and then cleaned and dressed his wound. She paused for moment to look at him. His dark hair was untied, and it fell loosely about the pillow. She remembered that the only time he wore it down was during sleep or their most private moments together. It was very painful to remember that these moments were now reserved for Elizabeth, and without thinking Darcy reached out and ran her fingers across his chest.

Instantly, Jean-Michel opened his eyes and looked up at her. She leaned forward and murmured, "I must go to Point Levi and bring help for you. Promise me that you will live, Jean-Michel."

So softly that she could barely hear him, he whispered, "Give me a reason to live, Darcy."

"I can give you many reasons," said Darcy, as she clutched his arm. "Live for your wife, Jean-Michel. Live for your unborn children."

"Wife?"

Darcy's eyes grew wide. "You did not marry Elizabeth?'

"How could I when I loved another?" said Jean-Michel.

As difficult as it was to speak, Jean-Michel was afraid he might die and never tell her. He swallowed hard and said, "Don't go back to Ireland. If you do, I will die of loneliness. Stay with me and be my wife."

Tears welled up in Darcy's eyes, and she pulled the necklace over her head, putting it around Jean-Michel's neck once more. "You must fight. Fight and when I return, I will be your wife."

A smile flickered on his lips, and he closed his eyes. With no time to lose, Darcy covered him with a blanket, bent over and kissed his lips. They seemed so cool and his face so lifeless. Panic flooded over her, and she bit her lip so hard that it began to bleed. What a cruel joke it would be if Jean-Michel were given to her and then taken, all in the same night. How could she live, knowing that he was waiting on the other side of the thin veil?

Reluctantly, Darcy slipped out of the cave and down the rocks. Tonight she would be fighting for Jean-Michel's life *and* her own.

Chapter 35

Every fiber of Darcy's being was on alert. The forest seemed charged with energy, and adding to the night's dangers was the fact that the sky had partially cleared. Clouds rolled swiftly across the moon, and without warning the forest could be flooded with light. She moved along the river, stopping to listen for danger, her ears and eyes straining.

Darcy knew that the English and French were clumsy in the woods, and there was a good chance that she would hear them before they were upon her, but the silent stealth of the Indian was what she feared. The encampment at Point Levi was not far, yet she was not sure how she could approach the English without surprising them into gunfire, and General Wolfe's marauders now saturated the area.

Darcy's mind returned to Jean-Michel alone and possibly dying in the cave on the river. She wondered if the candle had burned out, and if he was there in the dark, watching the stars of the night sky as the lifeblood drained out of him.

The ground was wet and slippery beneath her feet. She headed up a hill along the river and smelled something burning. The path led to a clearing where she observed a settlement reduced to ashes. All that remained were the burned-out shells of cabins and barns. Even though it had been destroyed earlier in the day, the smoke still curled up from the black skeletons as if it was a funeral pyre. It smelled thick and sweet. Darcy moved cautiously into the clearing, looking tentatively into the woods with her musket poised. She tried to steady herself. Suddenly the clouds moved off the moon, illuminating several charred corpses in a cabin. Startled and repulsed, Darcy continued on.

Suddenly, someone stepped into her path, a large, heavy-set man dressed in greasy buckskin. He had only one arm. His wild eyes and filthy beard told her he was a vagrant backwoodsman. He lunged at her. Darcy jumped, misfiring her musket. Terrified, she raced toward the woods. Before she could reach the safety of the brush, she felt a sharp pain in her thigh and the report of a firearm.

Clutching her leg, Darcy ran, but in an instant, the backwoodsman was upon her, grabbing her. Her heart was pounding furiously, and she could hear him muttering in French. She struggled furiously, sickened from fear and the foul smell of urine.

Suddenly, Darcy remembered what Dominique did on the ship long ago and with all of her might she sank her teeth savagely into the man's shoulder, right through his skin. When he let out a roar of pain, she broke free.

The assault seemed to unleash the madman's fury, and before Darcy could escape, he grabbed her long hair and yanked her to the ground. Straddling her chest, he delivered several painful blows to her head, and when he drove his fist deep into her face, she slid into a daze. He rolled her over onto her stomach, and Darcy thought she was about to be raped. Instead she felt intense burning on her scalp along the hairline at the back of her neck. The pain was excruciating, and she struggled wildly under his weight, yet no pain was greater than the horrifying realization that this backwoodsman was beginning to scalp her.

She screamed, and then heard a sharp crack. The air was driven abruptly from her lungs as the man slumped onto her back with a thud. The pain had stopped, and as if in a dream, she heard someone say in English, "Get that son of a bitch off her and take her to Point Levi."

Darcy felt someone pick her up, and she whispered, "Please."

"Don't speak," said the soldier, "You are safe."

"No," insisted Darcy gasping. "Go to the caves by the mission. There you will find another."

"Yes, yes," he said, putting her off.

Darcy struggled to get free herself and said, "Jean-Michel will die."

"Jean-Michel. Jean-Michel Lupé?" asked another soldier.

Darcy murmured, "Yes."

"I knew him when I was posted at Fort Pepperell. Where did you say he is?"

"In a cave at the bend in the river near Cesaire's mission," she said breathlessly. "Hurry--dying."

With that final word, Darcy slid into oblivion only to awaken moments later in great pain. The man who carried her tried to be gentle, but because of the bleeding, he found it necessary to hurry. The jostling was excruciating. She was losing blood quickly from the lacerations on her head and from the bullet wound in her thigh. The blood ran down her neck, soaking her gown and her strength.

Gradually the pain decreased and everything went black. At last, she could put down her struggle to survive. Detached and unemotional, she watched her life as a child, moving from the carefree early days of her youth to the horrors of the famine on through her indentured service in the New World. When she reviewed her time with Jean-Michel, she became confused and unsettled.

Gradually, as if the pastels of a watercolor were being painted on a canvas, a scene came into focus. Darcy smelled the cool, salt air of the ocean and felt the wind on her face. She heard a seagull screech and realized that once again she was standing on the cliffs of Kerry. It was a warm cloudless day, and she was in the abbey. As she had always known, it would wait for her keeping vigil over the valley as if it was a benevolent landlord.

She gazed across the sweeping landscape, drinking in the blue of the sea and the green of the mountains. Only she could not remember how she had returned. It seemed as if only moments ago she had been struggling for her life in the woods, and now she was standing on the cliffs of Kerry, fully recovered.

Elated at being home, Darcy stepped out of the abbey and started down the bluff to find the villagers. Suddenly, a familiar voice said, "They won't be able to hear you or see you, Darcy."

Whirling around, Darcy encountered Father Etienne. He was dressed in his black cassock, and his hands were clasped in front of him as if he had been waiting patiently for her. He looked healthy and full of life, and Darcy threw herself upon him, embracing him.

"What are you doing here? I thought you were dead!"

"I did not die, Darcy, but I am of this earth no longer."

"How can this be? I just hugged you. You are not a specter. I can see you clearly, and I can touch you."

"That is because you are not of the earth either," he replied simply.

Darcy opened her eyes wide in astonishment and

asked, "What do you mean? I am dead too?"

He nodded and said, "You are of the earth no longer. You have been granted your last wish, and that is to see Ireland once more."

Darcy searched Father Etienne's eyes and then walked over to the cliffs. She felt the breeze blow her hair and looked down at the waves breaking on the rocks. Her struggle was over at last, and she was glad. She could rest now and no longer feel the relentless pounding in her chest and hunger in her stomach. At last she could sleep peacefully.

He stood beside her and said gently, "It's time to go home now. All the way home, Darcy," and he held out his hand.

With the trust of a child, Darcy placed her hand in his and said with confidence, "I'm ready."

"It is that easy for you?"

"Yes," she said shrugging her shoulders. "Everyone I have ever loved is dead, my mother, my brothers and sisters, Teila, you and now Jean-Michel."

She looked into his eyes, and suddenly a rush of fear overtook her. Darcy had seen Jean-Michel in his face and she drew back.

"What is it?' Father Etienne asked.

"Where is your brother? Is he with you?"

"That, I cannot say."

"I won't go until I know, Father."

"You must make the choice," he insisted.

Darcy looked out across the broad ocean toward the Colonies and struggled within herself. The thought of returning to life on Earth without Jean-Michel was unthinkable, but if she chose death and he lived, she could only whisper to him through a thin veil and wait until he joined her.

"You must tell me what to do!" she pleaded.

Father Etienne shook his head, "It is yours to decide, Darcy. It is your finest test of faith."

Her eyes filled with tears, and as if it were raining on the watercolor canvas of Kerry, her homeland and Father Etienne melted away. Everything went black again, and she heard wailing and moaning as if many people were in great pain. Darcy could no longer feel the cool breeze on her face, and the air suddenly smelled thick and stale. Suddenly, she flew upward at breakneck speed. Up and up she raced and then as if hitting a great obstacle, Darcy stopped with a jolt, her spirit rejoining her battered body.

She began to retch uncontrollably, and her head throbbed with excruciating pain. Gone were the tranquil mountains of Kerry and the reassuring hand of Father Etienne. They were replaced instead by a large makeshift surgery in a tent crammed with war-torn soldiers writhing in pain and misery. On every side of Darcy were men with legs ripped off by cannon balls or dead soldiers with holes in their chests from musket fire. Everywhere she looked she saw pain and suffering. She sank back into oblivion not ready to witness life's agonies again.

The next time Darcy opened her eyes, the scene had changed again. She was lying on crisp muslin sheets under a light-blue duvet. Sunshine streamed across the bed, and she could smell lavender sachet. The bedroom was impeccably clean and cheerful. She had not slept in this much luxury since she had been at Nathan's quarters in Providence, and she rubbed her eyes in disbelief. The intense pain was gone, replaced by a dull throbbing. She tried to move but was stiff and very sore. She saw a crystal water decanter on her nightstand, and she wished she were strong enough to pour herself a glass of water.

Thirst nagged her, and with great effort she pulled herself up and reached for the decanter. Her hands shook as she poured a glass of water, but when she lifted the glass, it slipped out of her hand and crashed to the floor, shattering to pieces.

The door opened and a plump little woman came in, smiling. "Well, well. You are awake and thirsty. I'm glad. I'm Mrs. Plunkett. Now I'll just clean this up and get you some tea and a scone."

Darcy cleared her throat and licked her dry lips.

"Where am I?"

As she brushed the glass into a dustpan, the nurse replied, "You are in the quarters of Major Quentin Randolph. He is serving under General Wolfe here at Point Levi, and this home has been requisitioned for him."

The woman left the room before Darcy could ask any more questions, so she slid back down into the warm recesses of the bed and fell back to sleep, too exhausted to think of anything.

It took over a week before Darcy felt strong enough to walk, and although still sore, she could bear weight on the injured leg at last. The nurse removed the bandages from her head, and Darcy was relieved when the woman told her there had been little scarring. The majority of the lacerations had been behind her ear and at the back of her neck, so her appearance remained unchanged. Darcy had never been so grateful to have her long, dark tresses.

She wanted to thank the soldiers for saving her life and hopefully Jean-Michel's life too. The minute she could speak, Darcy asked Mrs. Plunkett to check the surgery roster for Jean-Michel, but he had not been found. Darcy began to grow restless and anxious. She wanted to ask Major Randolph about him, but the officer never came in to meet her. He remained a generous but aloof host.

Mrs. Plunkett said that he was seldom in residence. "He is a very busy man and spends most of his time at the front."

"Why am I here?" asked Darcy.

"Major Randolph is a very kind man and does not believe women should be housed in the surgery with the regulars."

One day Mrs. Plunkett came into the bedroom and gave Darcy a clean shift and dark red gown to wear. "It is time you dress and get some fresh air, my lovely girl." The nurse dragged in a tub and filled it generously with warm water. Darcy eased her wounded body down into the bath and groaned. It eased all her pain and relaxed her aching muscles. Gingerly she scrubbed her scalp, soaping the hair matted with blood and washed the filth from the rest of her body.

After soaking, she stood up and toweled herself off, feeling fresh and free of infection at last. As she laced her bodice over the shift, she noticed how tightly she could pull the strings. She had grown very thin.

Breathless after dressing, Darcy sat down on the edge of the bed and noticed a letter on the nightstand. Picking it up she recognized the letter she had placed in her bodice the night Jean-Michel had been injured. She was surprised to see that it was addressed to her. She broke the seal and read the words of Nathan Lawrence.

My Dearest Colleen,
You are by now aware that you are a free woman. I

had no intention of paying the exorbitant sum to the French for your ransom, and it was Jean-Michel Lupé who traveled to New France on both occasions to pay for your release.

He asked me to take credit for his actions, and I reluctantly agreed. Lupé believed that you would feel beholden to him if you knew the truth, and he wanted you to exercise your free will in matters of the heart. My knowledge of this affair goes no further, and I wash my hands of the charade completely. I wish you happiness and good health,

Nathan Lawrence

Darcy sat down heavily on the bed. The news that Jean-Michel had given her the gift of freedom touched her more deeply than any words of love or tender caresses. He had given her unconditional freedom, and the only thing that had been important to him was that she came to him of her own free will.

There was a knock on the door, and Mrs. Plunkett looked in saying, "Are you ready?"

Darcy nodded and started down the stairs with the woman's assistance. By the time she reached the last few steps she was able to walk by herself, and Mrs. Plunkett opened the front door, flooding the hallway with bright sunshine.

"Now don't go far, dear," she said. "There are some lovely spots over there by the little brook where you might want to sit for a while."

It felt wonderful to stretch her legs again, and Darcy walked around the garden enjoying the warm sun on her skin and the smell of the wildflowers. She wandered away from the house along the banks of the stream. There was an opening in the pines bordered by wild roses, which led back to a small pond made private by lush vegetation and hundreds of red columbines. Darcy stepped into the bower and sat down at the edge of the pond. She stayed there for a long time sitting in a patch of sunshine which glimmered through the trees. The secluded spot breathed energy and strength back into her body.

She returned there every day until she was fully recovered. Knowing that she should not take advantage of Major Randolph's hospitality any longer, Darcy composed a letter of sincere thanks, and after saying good-bye to Mrs. Plunkett, she headed one last time to her secluded spot.

Darcy believed that she might find the guidance she needed there and that it would become clear what path she must take. Loneliness flooded her when she thought about her future, but she reminded herself that now she was a free woman and could choose her own destiny.

Sitting down in the warm sunshine on the banks of the pond, Darcy felt herself relax. She drew up her knees and hugged them, watching the woods come to life. A tiny wren hopped about on the ground not far from her and cocked his head looking at her. The squirrels and chipmunks chattered, as they darted around the floor of the forest, racing up and down the trees. Darcy did not move when she spied a deer approaching the pond for a drink. It bent down and drank, occasionally raising its head to watch her. Suddenly the deer's head shot up, startled by something behind Darcy. It turned and bolted into the safety of the woods.

Before she could turn around, she heard the words, "Someone told me once about a place like this.

It's called a thin place."

Darcy did not move. She held her breath and closed her eyes afraid to break the spell. At last she turned around. It was Jean-Michel. In two steps he was upon her, pulling her up into his arms and kissing her.

"You're alive! They found you, Jean-Michel!" she gasped.

He said nothing, but continued to cover her with kisses. He was overcome with joy at finally being able to hold her again, and he said at last, "You have no idea how long I have been waiting to do this."

"Where have you been?" she asked, running her hands over his hair and face, reassuring herself that he was not a ghost.

"Working with Major Randolph."

Darcy said with surprise, "I have been staying at Major Randolph's home."

He nodded. "I know, Darcy. When I found you in the surgery weeks ago, I approached Major Randolph and had you transported to his quarters. When I was called away, his housekeeper, Mrs. Plunkett had instructions to nurse you back to a full recovery and keep you there until I returned. She has been sending word daily on your recovery."

Darcy gasped with astonishment. "Then you knew all along!"

"Yes."

Jean-Michel vowed never to let Darcy out of his sight again, and he pulled her close, running his lips across her neck and shoulders impatiently.

Darcy pushed him back and said, "Let me look at you."

She ran her hands over his linen shirt, touching his broad shoulders. With her fingers, she lightly caressed his face and stroked his dark hair. He too had made a full recovery. His color had returned, and the familiar intensity was back in his blue eyes.

Gently, Darcy touched his side where the wound had been, and Jean-Michel nodded. "It healed quickly. The men you sent that rainy night lost no time taking me to the surgery at Point Levi. It took me a while to mend, but the minute I was able to walk I searched and found you in a bed not far from my own."

"Jean-Michel, there is something you must know," said Darcy, with a sigh. "I read the farewell letter from Nathan Lawrence several days ago. In it he explained everything to me, and I know that you are the one who paid the ransom."

The smile dropped from Jean-Michel's face, and he dropped his arms, stepping back from her. "I never wanted you to know. I wanted you to have your complete freedom and come to me by choice."

"You speak of choice, freedom?" Darcy laughed. "From the moment I found you, my choices were over, my freedom was gone. That night when you sat in front of the officers' quarters and stared at me so boldly, I felt something. I didn't know what it was, but from that moment, you owned my heart."

Jean-Michel sighed deeply. He realized now that Darcy felt no obligation to him or owed him no debt. She had given herself to him freely.

* * *

Quebec was a major victory for the English, and although the war continued, the fate of the continent had been determined.

Darcy and Jean-Michel found a priest to marry them, and in a year they journeyed to Ireland to visit the land where Etienne Lupé had been laid to rest.

Darcy had at long last fulfilled her dreams, and with Jean-Michel by her side, she stood on her beloved cliffs of Kerry once more.

ABOUT THE AUTHOR

All her life Amanda Hughes has been a "Walter Mitty", spending more time in heroic daydreams than the real world. At last, she found an outlet writing adventures about audacious women in the 18th and 19th Centuries. Her debut novel *Beyond the Cliffs of Kerry* was published in 2002, followed by *The Pride of the King, The Sword of the Banshee, The Grand Masquerade* and *Vagabond Wind*. Amanda is a graduate of the University of Minnesota, and when she isn't off tilting windmills she lives and writes in St. Paul, Minnesota.

Please visit her at
http://www.amandahughesauthor.com

Made in the USA
Columbia, SC
25 February 2019